BRIGHT LIKE
MIDNIGHT
SAVAGE U

Special Edition

J. Wolf

C000161130

Editing: Monica Black, Word Nerd Editing

Proofreading: My Brother's Editor

Cover Design: Kate Farlow, Y'All That Design

Cover Photo: Wander Aguiar

To Todd and Claire: You're no Zadie and Amir, but at least you tried.

Prologue

Zadie

Four Months Ago

THIS WAS MY FIRST hostage situation, and by and large, it wasn't as terrifying as I would have expected. Not that I had ever put a lot of thought into being held hostage. If movies were anything to go by, it seemed there should have been a lot more rope, duct tape, zip ties, and sobbing—on my part. And not that I wasn't afraid—I was—but I wasn't falling apart from terror, and I didn't believe my death was imminent.

That may have been incredibly naive since there was a gun. Any time my captor stood up, I saw it tucked haphazardly in the back of his jeans. The gun scared me. I kept my eye on it when I could, and when he sat down, I watched his hands carefully.

He had nice hands. It was a strange thing to notice about the man holding me as collateral for the money my roommate

Helen owed his boss slash brother, but we were an hour into this thing, and I was bored.

Still too afraid to really move or speak, but bored, and as a pianist, hands were something I always noticed.

My captor flopped down on the armchair diagonal from my love seat and propped his booted feet on the coffee table. Normally that would bother me, but since this furniture belonged to Savage University, and oh yeah, he had a gun, I kept my lips pressed tight.

With a sigh, his dark, wary gaze swept over me in a slow pass. My hands were clutched tight in my lap to stop from fidgeting under his assessment.

Bringing his hand up to his mouth, he muttered, "Damn." No explanation, but his straight, black eyebrows were furrowed into an angry line.

"What's your name, little mama?" He sounded like he'd eaten gravel then lined his throat with lacquer. Rough and smooth all at once.

"Um, I think Helen told you. It's Zadie."

His head cocked. "Zadie what?"

I licked my lips, but my tongue had gone desert dry. I wasn't great at talking to guys on a good day. The gun tucked in this man's pants and the fact that I wasn't sure if he'd shoot me meant this clearly wasn't a good day.

"Zadie Night."

His lips were dusky pink and seemed to be positioned in a perpetual scowl. When I said my full name, they quirked, tipping up in the corners. It didn't qualify as a smile by a mile, but it was something.

"That's a real name?"

"Um, yes?" Should I have given him a false name? He already knew where my dorm was. Since he was sitting in my suite, it wasn't like he couldn't find me again after this...if I lived through it.

"Sounds fake." He flattened his palms on his legs, smoothing down to his knees. "Amir Vasquez."

My stomach lurched. I barely eked out a whisper. "I wish you hadn't given me your last name."

"That's a strange thing to wish. Good thing there are no genies here or you would have wasted it."

"But..."

His hands flipped over, palms up, a show of impatience. The way he spoke belied that gesture. Each word was drawn out, sitting on his tongue until he was ready to release it. Lazy disinterest laced every syllable, but his sharp gaze said he was anything but.

"But what, little mama? Speak."

"It's just that, I've seen your face, I know your name. So..."

His forehead crinkled with his raised eyebrows. "Finish your sentence, Zadie Night."

I swallowed hard then blurted, "Won't you have to kill me now?"

There was a long pause where Amir only stared at me, his dusky lips parting slightly. His movement was too sudden for me to protect myself. My face was in his hand, and I hadn't even had the chance to gasp a breath.

"Are you going to tell someone I was here tonight, Zadie Night? Will you run to your phone as soon as my back's turned and dial nine one one? What will you tell them? That I sat in a room with you? You're not tied up. No one is barring the door. You could walk away at any time."

"You have a gun," I pointed out.

"Do I?" His fingertips stroked my cheek. "I've never seen it before. This must be your roommate's gun. You wouldn't want Helen getting in trouble for holding an unlicensed hand-gun, would you?"

"I'm not calling the police, not if you don't hurt me or Helen."

Narrowed slits stared back at me for a long moment before he dropped my face and reclaimed his original position in his chair, lounging like a lazy prince.

"If Helen brings me the money she owes Reno, no one's get-ting hurt tonight." There was nothing lazy about his vigilant gaze.

That was a big "if," so his reassurance did nothing to set-tle me. Helen owed Amir's brother, Reno, a lot of money. It wasn't her fault, but she had to pay it anyway. Me being trapped here with Amir was supposed to be her incentive to bring back the cash as quickly as she could.

But what if she couldn't?

"Will you hurt me if she doesn't?"

He hadn't stopped watching me, but my question sent him forward, his elbows on his knees, black eyes drilling into mine.

"If it comes to that, I won't take any pleasure in what I have to do." He steepled his hands beneath his chin. "Let's hope Helen pulls through and neither of us have to experience that."

I nodded, wishing I could rewind time back to when I was bored. There was nothing comforting in knowing the man holding me hostage was a legit bad guy, not just a regular person who'd gotten mixed up with the wrong crowd. Tears welled in my eyes before I could stop them. I turned away so he wouldn't see them trail down my cheeks, but I couldn't hold in one quiet sniffle.

In my periphery, Amir sprung from his seat. He stood over me for so long, I was forced to look up at him. When I did, he swiped his thumb over my wet cheek, then sucked my tears off like drops of nectar. I shuddered, and he walked away, pacing the confines of the small living area I shared with my two suitemates.

He paced and used his phone while I sat, sinking into the stifling silence.

A while later, there was a knock on the door. Amir opened it, spoke in murmurs to whoever was on the other side, then closed it again. He stopped in front of me and placed a white paper bag on the coffee table. The scent of oregano, garlic, and tomatoes drifted from it.

"Eat, little mama," Amir gruffed, then walked away again.

I didn't want to, but the hours were ticking by, and despite the churning in my stomach, I was hungry. Still, I wasn't sure I'd be able to keep anything down. Gingerly, I opened the bag to find two take-out containers, one holding half-dollar-sized raviolis and sauce, the other filled with garlic knots. From over my shoulder, Amir handed me a plate and fork before he circled around to sit beside me. He dished food onto his plate like it was nothing—like he hadn't told me this situation could end with me being beaten or killed.

When I didn't move, he set his plate down, grabbed mine, and filled it. Then he wrapped my fingers around my fork, took my chin in his hand, turned my face toward his, and gave me a hard, commanding look.

"*Eat*, Zadie."

I sucked in a ragged breath and tore my face from his hold. "I will. It's just...you're making me nervous right now."

He growled but didn't reply. I shifted as far from him as possible—which wasn't far—and tried to eat. I was anxious on way too many levels. The food sat like sawdust on my tongue, nearly impossible to swallow. I managed to get down one ravioli and half a garlic knot before I called it quits. Amir was shoving his food into his mouth like his conscience was clear and he wasn't holding a girl hostage. He also had his long legs spread so wide, his thigh was practically on top of mine.

I started to get up to take my plate to the sink and dump out the food I wasn't eating, but Amir snagged the loop of my jeans and yanked me back down.

"You didn't eat."

"I'm not hungry."

He leaned over me, bracing his hand on the arm of the love seat, scanning my body. My mom called me curvy. At the very least, I was chubby. Had been my whole life. By Savage U standards—where the girls were disproportionately thin, tan, and blonde—I was a whale, and some of the girls here liked to remind me of that.

"You don't skip meals." He stated this as fact. No malice behind it, but it hit me right in my rounded stomach and dug deep.

"I ate."

"Barely."

"I'm sorry I'm not able to eat when I'm not sure if I'll be alive by the end of this," I said meekly.

He barked a laugh that sounded so menacing, I squirmed in my seat. "I'm not going to *kill* you. Now, eat the dinner I bought you before I get offended."

I bit my tongue before I could tell him that wasn't much better. Knowing I could be beaten bloody instead of murdered didn't really ease my mind. But I tried eating since it seemed I didn't have a choice. I wouldn't want to offend my captor.

A-hole.

God, I couldn't even curse him out in my head for fear of repercussions.

I ate one more ravioli and the rest of my garlic knot before I held my plate out to Amir. "Is this enough?"

He scowled at my filled plate like it was a direct insult to him. "More."

Using his fork, he cut a piece of ravioli off and held it to my mouth. I opened automatically, and he placed it with surprising gentleness on my tongue. He fed me two more ravioli like this before I covered my mouth with both hands. Amir grunted and scowled at me like I'd killed his firstborn, but he relented.

Another hour or so passed of Amir pacing and using his phone, and me cleaning up the dishes, followed by falling back into boredom. When I couldn't take it anymore, I slipped my phone from my pocket to scroll through my emails or read the dictionary. *Something*. As soon as it was in my hand, though, it was snatched away.

"Password, little mama."

"Password?"

He glanced up. "To your phone. Give me the password."

"Why?"

He leaned over me, one hand on the back of the couch, the other cupping my throat.

"Give it to me."

I gave it to him, and he didn't release me, even after he entered it. His thumb kept stroking my fluttering pulse, and he let out a low humming sound that sounded strangely like he was trying to comfort me—even though *he* was the one violating me.

Tipping my head back gave me room to breathe and allowed me to study my captor up close while his attention was on my phone. Under different circumstances, I would have found him intimidatingly attractive. With bronze skin that spoke of possibly Middle Eastern or Latino roots—maybe both, given his name—thick, short, black hair, long, sooty eyelashes, and a mouth that looked so soft, only sweet words should've ever passed it, the phrase "tall, dark, and handsome" might have been coined to describe him.

He released a long sigh, pocketed my phone, and took a seat in the armchair, once again studying me.

"You don't have a boyfriend."

Again, he said this as a statement, and if he'd looked through my meager texts, he knew it as fact.

"No, I don't."

"Do you want one?"

"I don't know. Maybe. I'm busy, though, so—" I stopped myself from explaining. It wasn't his business, and by now, I was pretty sure he wouldn't shoot me if I didn't answer.

He canted his head, studying me from under thick lashes. His eyes were dark, so dark, it was hard to tell where exactly he was focused.

"Do you fuck?"

I flinched. "What?" Oh, I heard, I just couldn't process what he was asking. This was definitely none of his business.

"Do. You. Fuck, Zadie? Do you like cock?"

"Why in the world would you ask me that?" The second the question was out of my mouth, something else dawned on me. He'd said he wouldn't murder me, but he'd also promised violence. "Are you—? You wouldn't—"

Amir's gaze grew impossibly darker. "I'm talking about fucking. Rape isn't fucking. And no, I'm not going to force you. I want to know why a girl who looks like you isn't fucking anyone."

A coil of spikes unfurled in my chest, but only partway. We were still having an uncomfortable conversation Amir seemed insistent on having.

So, I shut it down. "No. I don't like it. We're not going to have a *Go* moment, so can we drop the subject? I preferred silence."

He only showed more interest, taking another long look at me. "*Go?*"

"It's a nineties movie I watched with my mom. These friends leave their other friend with a drug dealer as collateral and they wind up in bed." I shook my head. "That's not going to happen."

He flicked his fingers out. "It would make the time go faster." Then he let his hand fall. "But I'm more curious than anything. Why don't you like cock, little mama?"

Every time he called me that, I got feverish. It was a ridiculous pet name, but something about the way he gritted it out of his plush mouth spiked my temperature and sent shivers down my spine.

"The drug dealer in *Go* had a better personality."

Amir smirked and made a clucking sound with his tongue. "Maybe. Then again, you don't really look like Katie Holmes. I don't care either way."

My first thought was, *oh, so he did know the movie,* followed quickly by, *wow, the truth in that statement kind of burns.*

"Did someone hurt you?" he inquired.

"Did someone drop you on your head?" As soon as the words were out, my hands flew to my mouth, and I stared at Amir with wide eyes. He didn't look pissed, though. He very nearly smiled, and something like a chuckle rattled in his chest.

"You're funny," he stated dryly.

"Thanks," I squeezed out of my clamped throat.

He slid down in his chair, stretching his long legs in front of him. The whole time, he never took his eyes off me. Sometimes they rested on my face, others, they danced around my chest and middle.

"Answer the question, little mama."

"People have hurt me, but not in that way," I replied. "Have you hurt people?"

"Oh yeah I have," Amir blinked, letting his eyelids stay at half-mast, "but not in that way."

"That's good to know."

"So," he licked his bottom lip, "tell me why a girl like you doesn't have men blowing up her phone to link up? No dick pics, no one begging for your nudes, not even one simp. Are you uptight, Zadie? Do you think you're too good to take cock?"

"What do you mean, a girl like me? What am I like?"

"You know how you sound." His sultry lips tipped into a smirk. "You know what you look like."

My hand rose to my cheek of its own volition. "I'm just...I look like me."

"Oh, shit." His chuckle was without humor. "You really don't know?"

"Are you making fun of me?" I hated how meek I sounded. Why did I care what he thought of me?

But I knew why. As perverse as it was, I had been instantly attracted to this man, even through my terror. After having a gun pointed in my face, the last thing I needed was for my captor to tell me he thought I was a hideous beast.

Amir instantly sobered. "No, Zadie, I'm not. You asking me that question pisses me off, though."

"I didn't mean to."

"Yeah, I know you didn't. I bet you've been sweet since the day you were born."

I pursed my lips. "I did tell you you weren't charming."

"And my feelings were really hurt." His eyes were intense, but his expression remained impassive. "Tell me why you don't have a man."

His voice...god, it settled like coal in my belly, heating me from head to toe. He had no idea what he was asking pressed on a patch of raw nerves. Why wasn't I with someone? Why did I turn away from every guy's attention? I had my reasons, very real ones, I wasn't going to share with my captor.

At the same time he pressed on those nerves, he also hit something else: my anger. So much had been taken from me, and this was only one more thing. I *should've* had a phone filled with texts, at least one simp, a few unwanted dick pics, guys asking to see my boobs. But I was locked down tight, keeping to myself, missing out on those annoying, ubiquitous-to-almost-everyone college experiences.

"I don't think I'm too good to fuck." I clasped my hands in my lap and whispered, "I *do* like it."

Amir stilled. "What did you say?"

I leveled him with an unwavering stare. "I said I do like...fucking. I miss it, it's been a long while, but I like it."

He scooted to the edge of his seat and took his gun from the back of his pants. For one split second, I thought he was going to shoot me. But then, with his gaze on me, he placed the gun on the coffee table and held his hand out to me.

"Come here." His gravel had turned to dust, coating his command in something soft and muted. "Come here, little mama. Talk to me."

I wondered what I was doing, why I'd said that, and how I could be considering slipping my hand into his. His beautiful hand with long, tapered fingers and calloused palms.

My eyes met his. Black like midnight, and just as dangerous. I sucked in a deep breath and made a decision.

It was either going to be the best or worst I'd ever made.

But for once, it was mine.

I slipped my hand into his.

CHAPTER ONE

Zadie

I HAD NO TIME. I never ran late, but I was tonight. It was nerves, most likely. They'd been slowing me down. My hands were trembling a little. My feet felt like they weighed a thousand pounds. But I'd managed to put on a little mascara without stabbing myself in the eye, so I was calling it a win.

I checked my phone as I walked out of my room into the living area. Two minutes. Jeez, I never cut it this close.

"I don't like your boyfriend."

Stopping in my tracks, I stared at my suitemate, Elena. Blonde, tan, thin, and so beautiful I could weep. *She* fit in at Savage U. The day she showed up to claim the third room in our suite, I'd been braced for the worst—my roommates freshman year *had* been the worst. Elena Sanderson was sharp tongued, sarcastic, somewhat narcissistic, and a little unhinged, but she'd aimed all that outward. To me, she'd never been anything but funny, and I would even say kind.

"What?" I shoved my phone in my purse. I didn't have time for a conversation, but I was frozen on my spot.

Elena was spread out on a love seat, books, papers, and laptop around her. She nodded and flicked her fingers in my direction. "Your boyfriend. He's absolutely wretched. You're so pretty, and you're rushing around, frantic not to be late for a date with him. It makes me sad. One, because a man should always wait on his woman, and two, because he's not good enough for you."

"That's...I don't know what to say."

She shrugged. "Helen thinks it too. She won't say it because she doesn't want to hurt your feelings."

My eyes widened. "You've been talking about me?"

"No. I don't have to. It's extremely obvious."

"It is?"

Helen Ortega was one of the most honest, up-front, real girls I'd ever met, but not in the brutal way Elena was. She was a stunningly beautiful, skateboarding badass who had always had a soft spot for me, but especially since her troubles spilled over onto me a few months ago. After my hostage crisis, she'd been a little extra careful with me.

So, if she didn't like the guy I was sort of seeing, it wouldn't surprise me she hadn't said anything. Leave it to Elena to bring the truth.

"What are you *doing*, Zadie?" Elena pushed aside her laptop to stand in front of me, her hands on her hips. I was miniature, and she was tall and lithe, so I had to tilt my head back to look at her.

"I'm just...he's not really my boyfriend."

She rolled her eyes. "Thank Prada for small miracles. But I mean, why are you spending time with him? You can do so much better, girl."

I wasn't so sure about that, but if I said that out loud, she'd get angry with me.

"He's funny, and...I don't know, it's nice to go out and do things. I spent all last semester in this suite. It's time to shake things up."

Her hands squeezed my shoulders. "I'll take you out. There's really no need for you to go out with *him*. If it's about getting laid, I'm sorry I'm not available for that service, but I'm certain I can find you someone who is."

I would have laughed if my phone hadn't vibrated in my purse. "I'm sorry, I have to go. He's waiting." She didn't remove her hands, so I was stuck. "I need to go, El."

She stared at me for a long beat before releasing me. "Go. But if he lays an unwelcome finger on you, do not hesitate to kick him in the dick and call me to finish the job."

The lead finally lightening in my feet, I raced to the elevator and then through the lobby, bursting out of my dorm. Nerves still writhed like worms in my stomach, and only worsened as I approached the car. The passenger door swung open. As soon as I slipped inside and closed it, the car pulled away from the curb.

"Hi," I said softly.

Elliott, the guy I'd been seeing for the last couple weeks, drummed impatient fingers on the steering wheel. A muscle in his square jaw ticced before he relaxed.

"You owe me an apology."

I sucked in a breath. "Okay. Um...I'm sorry I was running late. My roommate started talking to me and—"

"I'd appreciate it if next time you send me a text if you're not going to be where you promised you would be." He glanced over at me, sweeping his sharp brown eyes over me from head to toe. "You look nice."

"Thank you, Elliott. You do too."

He reached across the console to place his hand on my leg. He didn't go too high, but he curled his fingers around my inner thigh in a way that said he had every right to do so. And I guessed since I'd never stopped him, he probably thought he did.

Elliott Schiffer wasn't a very nice guy, but he was persistent in his interest in me. We'd shared a class last semester, and since then, he'd doggedly tried to catch my eye. I didn't quite understand it, but since I also didn't date, I had always politely, but firmly, turned down his invitations to join him for a meal or to attend a party.

Things changed recently, and when Elliott once again asked me to have lunch with him in the dining hall, I'd relented. Over the past two weeks, we'd done that four or five times. We'd gone to a movie, studied together in my suite, watched Netflix in his. It hadn't all been unpleasant, but under normal circumstances, I wouldn't have gone on more than one or two dates with Elliott before—again, politely but firmly—extracting myself from the situation.

My circumstances were anything but normal lately. I was a boat without sails, floating around to find *anything* that would lead me to safe harbor.

Elliott wasn't really a safe harbor, but I was hoping he would be that *something* that took me there.

"I was surprised you wanted to go to this party." He squeezed my thigh. "It doesn't seem like your scene. Things can get...out of hand. You still have time to change your mind."

I smiled at him, which he caught in his periphery. "No, I want to go. I feel like all I do is study. I haven't been to even one big college party." I placed my hand over his. "Besides, I'll be with you, so I know I'll be fine."

"You know I'll take care of you, Zadie." His hand slipped an inch up my thigh. "You need someone to take care of you. You're too sweet to be out in the world on your own. I knew that from the first time I saw you."

I hated what he was saying, but it wasn't exactly untrue. Not that I was too sweet, but that I needed someone.

I laughed. "The first time you saw me, I was almost in tears from being yelled at by Dr. Marino. God, that guy..."

Elliott didn't laugh. "He's a fucking prick. I should have reported him for how he treated you."

On the first day of class last semester, our sociology professor had been running late. He'd burst into the classroom and knocked me splat on the ground. His coffee had spilled everywhere—thankfully not on me—and he had been *pissed*. Somehow, his ire had been directed at me, even though I was the injured party. I'd held in my tears, but, man, it had been a close one.

"Fortunately, I survived and will never have to take a class taught by him again."

"Fuck him," Elliott muttered under his breath.

"Yeah." Pressing my legs together, I shifted to the side, ensuring my skirt didn't ride up too high. "Let's not talk about that. I'd love to forget it. Tell me about the party. What should I expect?"

Elliott liked to feel important, and this was just the thing to give him that. He spent the rest of the drive rubbing my thigh and telling me about the past parties he'd been to. This one was at a warehouse on the opposite side of Savage River to Savage U. As we got closer, driving down the quaint main street and past the massive Savage River High School, light seemed to be sucked from the atmosphere. The roads became less smooth, the buildings dirty and some dilapidated, and then we were in a more industrial area on the very outskirts I'd never had cause to go to.

Elliott parked in a *no-parking* zone along a crumbling curb. Since this wasn't my first time in his car, I knew to wait for him to round to my side and open the door for me. He got insulted if I let myself out.

He held my hand as we walked to the entrance of the warehouse, keeping me close to his side. My knees were shaking, so I was grateful to have his support, even though I didn't love how proprietary he was with me.

I became even more grateful when we entered the warehouse. It wasn't packed, but there were people scattered all over in the vast, dimly lit space. From the scattered furniture, it looked like someone—or a few someones—lived here.

Elliott leaned down and pressed his mouth to my hair. "Don't worry, Zadie. I won't let anything happen to you."

"You won't leave me?"

He peered at me. His gaze wasn't warm, but it was possessive. "I'll have to for a little bit, but I'll find someone for you to stay with. Let's get drinks and not think about things like that."

The bar was actually just a folding table covered in myriad liquor bottles and stacks of red Solo cups with a keg standing beside it. Since the last thing I wanted to do was get wasted, this was more than enough for me. Elliott studied his choices while I grabbed a cup and went to the keg, determined to figure out how it worked.

I stood there, fingering the hose, tracing my nail over the valve, fairly certain I would be able to fill my cup with beer, especially considering these things were used by drunken frat bros. If they could do it, so could I.

Except the hose was swiped out of my hand, followed by my cup. "I'll do that for you, Zadie." Elliott pressed a kiss to the side of my head. "You know I would never allow you to pour your own drink."

When he handed me the halfway-filled red cup, my lips curved in what I hoped was a gracious smile. "Thank you so much, Elliott. What a gentleman." Then I pushed out a giggle for good measure.

That seemed to please him. He cupped the back of my head and dragged me into his chest. His half-mast erection dug into my hip, and he made no effort to pull away.

"I'm not always a gentleman, baby," he cooed.

"Oh." So far, Elliott had been gentlemanly to an extreme. His chivalry almost felt like a weapon, forcing me into a box marked 'my little woman.' This move, this heavy flirtation, was unprecedented. I didn't know what to say.

He tucked my curls behind my ear. "You're so sweet when you blush." Then he tapped my cup. "Drink, but don't get sloppy, okay? I don't like when girls get plastered. It's not a good look."

I didn't know how to respond to that, but he didn't need it. He saw someone he knew and tugged me along with him.

As Elliott spoke to his friends, I scanned the warehouse. Music vibrated the air, filling the massive space. Groups and couples were scattered around, but the center seemed to be reserved for dancing. There was a pool table and a foosball table. Both were being used. Most held cups, many were passing joints. The scene wasn't as debaucherous as I'd imagined, but the night was young.

Elliott squeezed my hip. "I need to go take care of a couple things. Are you good for me to leave you here with Shawn and Robbie?" He nodded to his suitemates, who I'd met once before.

"I'm fine. Take your time. I'm enjoying people watching," I replied.

He touched his lips to my temple. "Stay here, Zadie. Don't talk to anyone. I'll be back as soon as I can."

He waited until I nodded in agreement, then he disappeared through the throngs of people. Shawn and Robbie didn't seem to be interested in me, so I sipped my lukewarm beer and wandered away from them a little. I didn't go far, because I didn't want to deal with Elliott being angry that I hadn't listened.

My heart stopped then thrashed when I spotted him. My pulse fluttered madly in my throat. Even from half a football field away and all these months since we'd been in close proximity, Amir made me nervous.

This was his brother's party. Of course he was here. I'd known he probably would be when I overheard Elliott mention it, but nothing could have prepared me for my reaction to him and the probability he would see me too. If there had been a chair close, I would have fallen into it. My knees were so wobbly, and my stomach lurched like a boat in a storm.

Amir wasn't drinking. He wasn't smoking. Leaning against a steel support beam, his arms folded over his chest, he gave the appearance of being relaxed, but I didn't think he was. He made slow sweeps of the space, turning his head from one side to the other, even as a girl draped herself on his shoulder. He pulled her closer, his hand on her plump backside. She spoke to him, and he replied, but he remained watchful. Vigilant.

Goose bumps puckered my skin at the memory of his eyes on me. The feel of him taking me in, peering at me so intently, as if he could see all the way to my core. No one had ever looked at me that way before. Or since. I wasn't sure I had even liked it, but I would never forget it.

I hoped he hadn't forgotten either, because he was the reason I was at this party tonight. My plan had worked perfectly up until this point.

I didn't know how I was going to do it, but before the party faded, I was going to have Amir Vasquez's attention.

CHAPTER TWO

Amir

MY HANDS TWITCHED. My skin itched, too tight on my body. I needed to relax. Find a release. Let go. But these fucking parties my brother threw weren't the place for that.

I was working. Watching the crowd. Monitoring Reno's people. Ensuring everyone knew whose territory they were being given the privilege of occupying.

The fact that I was working for Reno, my big brother who'd barely gotten himself through high school, only made my skin tighter. If our uncle hadn't had a heart attack, a come to Jesus moment, retired, and passed the baton to Reno, he'd still be pissing away his time, selling weed to his friends.

Giving Reno even a modicum of power had been a mistake. He had no idea how to run a business, legal or otherwise. The only reason he was able to maintain his power was through my near-constant intercession and his own brutality.

Not that I wasn't brutal in my own right. I just used my brains a hell of a lot more than Reno ever had.

I have stat homework due Monday I would much rather be using my brains to finish.

Vanessa fell into me, wobbling on her heels from too many shots of tequila mixed with a few lines of blow. She should've been an expert at walking while out of her mind since she was rarely sober.

"Hey, baby," she cooed. "You're so grumpy. Why don't you smile?"

I took a handful of her ass, holding her upright. At least she felt good pressed against me. That was something.

"Why don't you go to bed?" I countered.

"Are you coming with me?"

I let myself look at her for a beat. Bronze skin, fat ass, big, natural tits, plump lips—Vanessa had all the ingredients I needed to get me hard and get me off. And she had, more times than I would bother trying to count.

Getting off was a necessity, but my hand was more interesting than Vanessa at this point. She relied on her attributes to entice, then she lay there with her legs open or her lips parted, acting like a human receptacle.

A dead lay was a dead lay, no matter how hot she was.

"Not tonight. I'm working."

"Awww," she whispered against my neck. "That's too bad. I miss you, baby."

My hackles rose at those words. I'd had enough of this.

"You were in Marco's bed last night, Van. I think you're doing just fine." Gripping her waist, I unlatched her from me and shoved her a foot away. "You need to walk away. I'm not interested. There's plenty of willing dick for you to ride, it's just not gonna be mine."

She gasped like she was surprised I'd speak to her that way, but this was the only way I'd ever spoken to her. She wasn't my woman. Van spread her legs for any of my brother's crew. She was easy in every way, but telling me she missed me? No. That wasn't me. It never would be.

In the dim warehouse light, Vanessa's angry flush glowed red, but she kept her puffy lips shut. This girl had been around men like me long enough to know how to behave. She could go be pissy with her friends, but not to me. Her opinions and feelings weren't welcome here.

"Fine. Be a dick. But don't come begging for me when I'm gone, Amir. 'Cause you *will* miss me, and the only way I'll come back is if you beg." She swiveled, almost falling on her ass, and marched away in a crooked line, staggering into a few people before the crowd swallowed her up and she disappeared.

Beg. Jesus, that was a joke. There was no woman alive I'd beg to have.

· • • ●• • • • ·

A smack on the back of my head brought me out of my stupor. Before I had the chance to react, Julien plopped down on the beat-up coffee table in front of me, cackling.

"Yo, dude, are you in la-la land or some shit?" He covered his mouth, but there was no disguising the fucker was laughing at me.

"Something like that." I raised a brow at the one friend I'd maintained since childhood, Julien Umbra. "It's peaceful in la-la land. Must be because you're not there."

He flipped me off, but his wide grin didn't dim even a fraction. A long time ago, his mom said he left the womb smiling, and I believed it. He didn't have the kind of life that brooked his sunny disposition, but he held tight to his innate goodness, and in this world, that was saying something. I'd kept him out of Reno's crew and would die before I let him join. Being on the periphery was bad enough.

"Unfortunately, I'm gonna be the bearer of bad news. That little fuck Schiffer's here and he's unloading product."

I sat up straight, scanning the crowd.

"Molly?" I asked.

Julien shook his head. "Nah. Marco bought from him to check his inventory. It looks like he's got all scripts. Percs, Oxy, some Addies. From what Marco saw, Schiffer's cleaning up. The crowd is liking what he's supplying."

I rubbed my chin, attempting to maintain a level head even as my blood boiled. This kid knew better. He really did. That was why he'd been staying out of my eyesight. You didn't walk into Reno's party and sell your own product. That wasn't how it worked. Schiffer was small time, no real competition for Reno, but it was the principle and the fact that we'd caught him at this game more than once. Obviously, the lesson hadn't been drilled into his head hard enough.

"Bring him to the back." I nodded toward the courtyard behind the warehouse. Surrounded on three sides by brick walls with barbed wire on top, it would give us solid privacy. We didn't have any neighbors, so it was ideal for the kind of talk we'd be having.

"He came with a girl," Julien said.

I rotated my head on my neck, stretching it out, getting the blood flowing. "Bring them both."

· · · • · • • · · ·

I was already outside, waiting for them, when Marco and Julien shoved Elliott Schiffer into the courtyard so hard, he went down on his knees. They followed him out, a short girl walking calmly between them.

If she'd been struggling, yelling, cussing, spitting, I wouldn't have given her a glance until I'd dealt with Schiffer or needed to use her to deal with Schiffer. It was the lack of dramatics that brought my attention to her. Something sharp plunged into my gut when I met big blue eyes under the midnight sky.

Zadie Night.

"What the fuck're you doing here, little mama?" My fists went to my hips as I helped myself to a slow, up-close perusal of her for the first time in months. I couldn't find any pleasure at the sight of her, not with how we left things and her appearance here with Elliott Schiffer.

"Don't touch her!" Schiffer climbed to his feet, whipping his attention back and forth between me and Zadie. Marco and Julien barely had their hands on her shoulders. They weren't hurting her. She was standing like a docile little doll between them, her gaze burning into me.

"Did I tell you you could stand?" I walked forward, fisted the top of Schiffer's hair, and swept his feet from under him. He landed on his knees with a crack, gritting his teeth to keep from crying out.

He glared at me, eyes wild and face flushed. "What do you want from me? I didn't do anything."

I kept my hand in his hair and yanked his head back. "Do you know who I am?"

His mouth ticced. "Everyone knows you're Reno's brother."

"Amir," I spit out. "I'm Amir. That's Marco and Julien. I have to tell you, we take personal offense on behalf of Reno that you thought it was okay to come into his territory and spit in his face. The disrespect, Schiffer. The audacity to sell your product right under his nose. Do you think Reno's a little bitch?"

Zadie gasped, and the pure sweetness in the sound was almost enough to distract me. Almost. If I hadn't been on the very edge of losing my mind and ripping her apart at her pretty little seams, it would have.

"No, of course not. Reno doesn't sell what I do, and I'm small. My supply is minuscule compared to Reno—"

I jerked his head hard, bending so we were almost nose to nose. "What the fuck do you know about Reno's supply?"

Schiffer's shit-brown eyes bulged. "Nothing, nothing. I'm sorry. I'm really sorry. I was being stupid. I'm so stupid. This won't happen again. It won't."

"No, it won't." Taking my hand from his hair, I shoved his chest. He skidded on his ass across the brick ground. "Convince me it won't happen again. I need you to assure me."

His face had gone purple. Sweat dripped down his temples. His shaking hands reached into his pockets, yanking out folded bills and two baggies filled with pills. Knowing how small time he was, they were most likely stolen from his rich friends' mommies' medicine cabinets.

"Keep it." His tone had gone from threatening to placating in the span of a minute. The little shit must've realized the kind of trouble he was in. "Take it all. Please, I want you to have it."

I knocked the bills and pills from his hands. The wind whipped it all around in a whirling dervish of depravity.

"You think you have to *give* it to me? I own your shit. I own you right now. If I take you to see Reno, tell him what you've been doing, what do you think will happen?"

His swallow was audible, and I swore to all that was holy his bloodshot eyes filled with tears. This big man, who showed up at a Savage party intent on horning in on Reno's business, was crumbling before my very eyes. I would have been laughing if he hadn't brought little Zadie Night along for the ride. That, I didn't find amusing in any way.

He raised his hands in supplication. "I screwed up. I know it. Please, I'll do anything. I have more money at home. I'll pay you. Just please, please don't tell Reno. It'll never happen again."

His patheticness disgusted me, further serving to piss me off. My foot shot out, striking him in the gut, and he immediately folded to his side. That had felt good, but it wasn't enough, so I unleashed on him, hitting his legs and back over and over until Julien shoved me back a step.

"He got it, man. He got the message." He spoke low, calm, the way he always did to get me back in my head. The thing of it was, this time, I hadn't left. I knew exactly what I was doing. I wasn't going to kill this little shit, but I wanted him to limp out of this courtyard and *feel* the message I imparted a long time after.

"Please, Amir." Her whisper was watercolors on canvas. Too delicate for a place like this.

"Please, what?" I folded my arms over my chest as I stood over her groaning boyfriend.

"Please let him go." Her soft little chin trembled, but she held it high.

I cocked my head. I had every intention of letting him go, but I still wanted to see how this would play out with her. "Why should I? Do you have any idea what your boyfriend was doing?"

She shook her head. "He's not—"

"Zadie, baby,"—Schiffer crawled onto his knees—"don't talk to him."

Julien gripped my arm, holding me back from taking Schiffer down again. He didn't get to tell Zadie what to do—not when it came to talking or not talking to me.

"Please, Amir. He won't do it again." She took a step toward me. The outside spotlights glinted off her silky, light-brown curls. "Just let him go and—"

"What will you give me, Zadie?"

She blinked. "Give you?"

I nodded slowly, shrugging Julien's hold off my arm. "I told your boyfriend I need assurance this won't happen again. Since I don't believe him and you've thrown yourself in front of him, what will *you* give me to assure me this shit is done?"

Her pink tongue darted out to lick her lips. "Um...well, I don't have much, but—"

I slid my piece from the back of my jeans, aiming it at Schiffer's head. Zadie squealed. Schiffer whimpered and most likely pissed his pants. Julien threw his arms out. I didn't look at him to see his expression, but I knew he thought I'd lost my mind. I knew exactly what I was doing.

"What. Will. You. Give. Me. Zadie?" I gritted out.

Schiffer attempted to block his head with his arms. "You can have her! She'll work for you or suck your cock. You can take her. Please, Amir. *Please.* She'll do anything you want her to do."

That...surprised me. If I had less control, I would have blown his head off for making the suggestion. For giving Zadie away instead of sacrificing himself.

"Too fucking far," Julien ground out. "Way too fucking far."

Zadie mewled like she'd been physically injured. But she didn't cry, nor did she drop to her knees. Her eyes grew rounder, never leaving me, not even to glance at her boyfriend who'd just unnecessarily sacrificed her to save his own ass.

"I'll do it," she rasped.

My nostrils flared. "You'll suck my cock, little Zadie?"

She wrapped her arms around her middle. "If that's what it takes for Elliott to walk out of here alive."

My chin lowered. I blinked at her, wrapping my head around what she was saying. It was almost impossible to understand. No, I *didn't* understand. It enraged me that she cared about this piece of shit so much, she would give me her body to protect him.

And he would let her.

"All right." Safety on, I tucked my piece in my pants and held my hand out to her. "Come here, Zadie."

She came without hesitation, slipping her small hand in mine. "Please, Amir," she whispered. "I think he gets it. He won't do it again."

Little Zadie Night was a trembling flower in a storm, but she'd put on her brave face for her man. Then again, she'd shown the same annoying courage the first time we met. At least then it hadn't been as misplaced.

I shifted my attention to the blubbering waste of flesh on the ground. "Get up, Schiffer."

He lifted his head first, wincing at Zadie by my side, but his mouth stayed shut. Then he staggered to his feet, swaying slightly, his shoulders rolling forward. All that false bravado he'd had minutes ago had fled as quickly as his loyalty to his girl.

"Are we clear here?" I asked.

His head bobbed on his neck. "Yeah, we're clear. It won't happen again."

Releasing Zadie's hand, I wrapped my arm around her shoulders and jerked her against me. "And this little treasure is mine now. Do you understand?"

The color drained from his face. His mouth gaped. I waited for his protest, but it didn't come. He pressed his mouth into a firm line, then nodded. "I understand."

Zadie made a low, strangled sound. I wondered if her precious heart was breaking.

"If you see this girl on campus, who is she?" I pressed.

"Uh..." Schiffer rubbed his chest, stole a glance at Zadie, then aimed his eyes toward the ground, "I don't know her. She's a stranger."

"Wrong," I barked, making the girl beside me jump. "You don't see her. She doesn't exist to you. Your eyes stray to her even once, I'll consider this peace treaty broken and be forced to tell Reno you were spitting in his face tonight. You feel me?"

"I feel you," Schiffer choked out.

I tipped my chin at Julien and Marco. "Take care of him. I need to have a conversation with Zadie Night about what it means to be my property."

No doubt Julien strongly disapproved of what I was doing, but he knew the score. His mouth stayed on silent as I steered Zadie through the warehouse. Her short legs scampered to keep up with my swift pace, but I wanted her out of here as quickly as possible. She didn't belong here. Not in this place, not with these people. Hell, she *definitely* didn't belong with me. But I'd paid in full, and now, she was mine.

My SUV was parked across the street. I opened Zadie's door for her and watched her climb into the passenger seat without any protest, then I locked her in and rounded to the other side. I jumped in, turned over the ignition, and pulled away from the curb, driving us back to Savage U.

After unlocking my phone, I tossed it to her. "Put your number in there. Then call yourself so you have mine."

"Okay," she said quietly.

"What do you think is happening right now?"

She looked up from my phone, the screen lighting up her face. "I think you're going to explain what it means to be your property."

I hit the steering wheel. "No, Zadie. Don't repeat what I said. Tell me what *you* think is happening. What do *you* think it means to be my property?"

Her exhale was delicate. "I haven't really thought about it. You mentioned sucking your—"

"We're not doing that tonight." My lip curled with disgust, though I wasn't half as disgusted as I should have been. "Not when that asshole's scent is on you. I don't want his sloppy seconds, no matter how pretty you look when you're afraid."

I expected her to make a quiet protest, like she had that night in her dorm, but she remained silent. Her shallow, panting breaths were the only sounds between us.

"I'm taking you back to your dorm. You'll go upstairs and text me a picture of you secure in your room. You have tomorrow free, but when I contact you, I expect an immediate reply. On Monday, after your classes, you'll come to my house and we'll go over what it really means to be owned by me."

She said nothing, but there was no question she heard me. Even though I didn't want to give her a break, I did. Zadie might've had poor taste in who she gave it up to, but a girl like her wasn't in situations like what went down in that courtyard very often. Or ever.

She needed a minute, and quite fucking frankly, so did I. If I started making more demands now, I'd overstep into a realm even I wasn't into. Taking Zadie as my property was walking the line, but I wasn't pulling back from *that*. No, I planned to enjoy every second of having Zadie Night under my control.

CHAPTER THREE

Zadie

AMIR PULLED INTO A parking spot in front of my dorm. Adrenaline had me rooted to my seat, but he didn't seem in any hurry for me to leave his SUV. Silence covered us like a suffocating blanket.

He tapped his thigh and commanded, "Come here, Zadie."

My stomach bottomed out, but I didn't let it stop me from crawling over the console to do as I was told. I'd only ever sat in Amir's lap, and I found doing it again was as easy as riding a bike. He positioned me sideways, my legs draping over his rangy thighs. Then his hands were in my hair, tangling in the sides, tipping my head back.

For a long, drawn-out moment, he only stared, but it felt penetrative, like he was invading me. If he hadn't been holding me the way he was, I would have looked away.

"What are you going to do now?" he asked.

I rubbed my lips together. "Whatever you want me to."

The air vibrated around us. Amir's shudder was subtle, but he held me so close, I couldn't miss it.

"That's right. Because I own you, Zadie Night." He dragged a finger down my cheek. There was no affection in the move. It was solely proprietary. "You're my own, personal little good girl. Right now, you're going to run inside, lock up behind you, and text me just like I told you to."

My head was in his vise grip so I couldn't nod. My smile was tremulous, but I managed. "Okay. I'll do that."

He dragged his fingers out of my hair, only to claim my cheeks. "Don't worry, Zadie. Your boyfriend is safe as long as you cooperate."

"He's not my boyfriend."

His midnight eyes turned to stone. "That's right, he's not. Glad you feel me on that, little mama." He gave my butt a smack then opened the door. "Get out."

My escape wasn't graceful, but as soon as I found my feet, I ran from my captor and didn't look back. When I shut myself in my bedroom, I fell down on my bed, sucking in air as deeply as my constricted chest would allow, then I pulled out my phone and snapped a picture of my room to send to Amir.

Less than a minute later, he replied.

MyCaptor: *That isn't what I told you to do, Zadie. Try again.*

Me: *This is my room.*

MyCaptor: *Do I need to come back and explain myself to you more clearly?*

I knew what he wanted, I just didn't want to give it to him. I also didn't want him knocking on my door, so I held the phone out again, this time snapping a picture of my unsmiling face, wrinkling my nose so he could see how annoying I thought he was.

Five minutes ticked by without a response. I held my breath, waiting for him to bust into my room and throttle me for making a face at him. When my phone chimed with a text, I yelped.

MyCaptor: *Being cute won't get you out of this. You know that, right?*

Me: *I wasn't trying to be cute. I'm sorry.*

MyCaptor: *Go to sleep. Remember to answer immediately when I text.*

Me: *Okay, I'll remember.*

MyCaptor: *Say good night to me, Zadie.*

Me: *Good night, Amir.*

Of course there was no reply.

It didn't matter anyway. I'd gotten his attention like I had wanted. My mistake was underestimating the depth of Amir's depravity. Well, one of my mistakes. I hadn't really planned what I'd do with his attention once I had it, but this...this hadn't been a possibility in my wildest dreams.

· · · ● · ● · ● · · ·

After two sleepless nights, I was drained walking into my last class on Monday. Fortunately, it was a large lecture, so if I zoned out, my professor probably wouldn't notice.

I trudged up the steps of the lecture hall, heading to my usual seat halfway up.

"Hey," someone in the row ahead of me called out.

I kept going, assuming they were speaking to someone else since I didn't really know anyone in this class.

"Hey."

Stopping on the step before my row, I scanned to the right, finding four frat bros grinning my way. My stomach twisted in knots.

"Hi," I whispered in response.

The guy closest to me chuckled, drawing my attention. Deacon Forrester. I'd met him twice while with Helen, and both times, he'd been obnoxious and had called me her *fat friend*. We were a month into this semester, and he'd said hi to me once before. It had been disconcerting then, and it was still disconcerting now.

"Hey, Zadie. Are you having a nice day?" He leveled me with a somewhat friendly look, but his bros were snickering beside him, so I didn't return it. Instead, I rushed past, mumbling something vague that probably didn't make any sense. I didn't believe he was sincerely asking me anyway, not with his buddies laughing at his side.

I sat in the very back, well away from laughing boys. I'd known guys like that in high school, and I'd learned to avoid them like the plague. College hadn't magically transformed them into men with souls. They were still little boys who got their kicks through humiliation.

If I were Helen or Elena, I'd walk back down there and say, "No thanks. I already have a homicidal drug dealer on my hands, I don't really have room on my plate for an arrogant frat boy."

But since I was just me—pathologically shy—I quietly took out my laptop and crossed my fingers Deacon and his friends would forget I existed.

Amir lived off campus, in a neighborhood of houses that were pretty much all rented by college students. His was a tidy bungalow with a front porch that ran the width of the house. There were two nice wooden rocking chairs and two less-nice folding chairs occupying the space. The welcome mat in front of the door said, "Cum Inside." I had a hard time believing Amir had picked that out.

I barely knocked before the door swung open. The smiling face greeting me wasn't Amir's, but one of the guys who'd handled me with surprising gentleness on Saturday night.

"Hi." I held up my hand in a little wave.

"Hey." He leaned against the jamb, giving me a long once-over. "What's up, buttercup?"

My fingers twisted in the hem of my long cardigan. "I'm reporting for duty. Is my owner home?"

His smile grew wide. A bark of a laugh burst out of him. "Oh, my boy's in trouble with you, isn't he? He thought he was getting a meek little thing, but you've got some sass behind that sweet. I'm into it." He reached out, grabbing me by my nape, and yanked me inside the house.

"I think I'm the one in trouble," I uttered.

He squeezed my neck. "Nah. I was worried about you, you know? You've got this fragile chick kind of vibe going. But I'm thinking maybe you've got a little fire in you."

I shook my head. "I don't think I do."

"We'll see." He winked, then pushed me deeper into the house, still holding the back of my neck. "I'm Julien, by the way."

"Zadie."

His laugh was softer this time. "I know. I've heard it around here enough, I won't forget it."

I would have asked what exactly he'd heard, but Amir emerged from upstairs, scowling with such malice, I braced for him to reach for his gun and shoot Julien and me to the ground.

"Take your fucking hand off my property." Each word was low and menacing. If there was a friendship between Amir and Julien, it had disappeared in that moment, leaving behind icy disdain.

Julien's grip on my neck instantly disappeared. He held both hands up to show they were empty and he was innocent.

"My mistake," he soothed. "It won't happen again." But under his placating tone, I heard an edge of amusement. I didn't think he was afraid of Amir, not really.

"Fuck off, Julien," Amir spat.

Julien chuckled, proving my theory, and slid away from me. "All right, all right. I'm fucking off. Just, you know, try not to damage your *property* irreparably. That would be a damn shame."

Amir's eyes narrowed to obsidian slits. "It would be a damn shame to find yourself without a roof over your head, asshole."

Julien winked at me again. "That *would* suck. I bet Zadie would take pity on me and let me crash on her couch, though."

Amir glared at him, but he gave him no further reaction. Still, I wanted to laugh at the impossibility of these two men having any kind of relationship, let alone the friendship that was obvious beneath their old, violently inclined, married couple bickering.

"It's only a love seat," I answered. "You'd have to really curl up."

Julien and Amir both swung their attention to me. I had no idea why I spoke. It had just slipped out without meaning to. Julien shook his head, grinning. Amir was less amused.

"He'll never set foot in your dorm."

Julien groaned. "I think that's my cue to exit. Don't worry, I'll look for your sense of humor while I'm out." He saluted

Amir, gnashed his teeth at me, then saw himself out the front door. Once he was gone, the house was chillingly silent.

That was, until the floorboards creaked as Amir advanced on me. "Do you think, as my property, you're allowed to flirt with my friends?" He took my chin in his hand, tilting my face back.

"No." I didn't deny his ludicrous accusation. It seemed the less I said, the better.

His eyes flared at my clipped response. His hold on me tightened to the edge of pain. "No, what?"

"No, I'm not allowed to flirt with your friends."

His chin lowered, and he gave me an assessing glare. "You look tired. Why haven't you been sleeping?"

I shifted my messenger bag on my shoulder. "I'm a little bit stressed. When I have a lot on my mind, I can't sleep."

Amir stepped forward, slipping the bag from my shoulder and dropping it to the floor. I winced when my laptop clunked on the hardwood but kept my protests to myself.

"What's there to think about? I own you. Your thoughts are the ones I give you." He rubbed the thick stubble on his chin. "I can't imagine what you'd have to worry about."

My nose crinkled, but I dug my teeth into my bottom lip to stop myself from speaking. My silence didn't seem to please Amir, based on his sharp intake of breath and hands balling into white-knuckled fists.

"Don't be cute," he uttered lowly. "It won't make me soft on you."

"I'm not being cute." My hands fluttered to my chest. "I promise."

With a groan, he walked away, hands braced on top of his head. Then he turned back, jerking his head toward the massive leather sectional. I followed him and took a seat two cushions away. Tucking my crossed ankles to the side, I smoothed my skirt along my thighs, making sure it draped over my knees. Amir watched every single one of my movements with a hardened jaw.

When the silence stretched on, I glanced around the room from beneath my lashes, and barely suppressed my gasp. Between two windows sat a beautiful upright piano. My fingers twitched, longing to play. I hadn't had time in my schedule for a music class this semester, so the only time I could get my fix in was if I snuck into an empty class in the music building—I'd done it once and had been so nervous I almost puked—or went home to visit my parents. Needless to say, I was jonesing.

"Tell me you haven't spoken to Elliott Schiffer." It was a demand, not a question.

"I haven't." I plucked at a flower on my skirt. "He hasn't tried to contact me either. We don't have any classes together, and his dorm is on the opposite side of campus."

He shook his head. "I'd be disappointed in you for giving it up to that piece of shit if I cared what you did."

I almost rolled my eyes since it was really freaking obvious he cared what I did. I didn't think it was because he cared about *me*. More like saw me as someone he should be able to control. I didn't roll my eyes, though. Amir had power and I didn't. He could crush me if he wanted to. I was banking on him not wanting to choose that path, but the odds weren't great.

When I didn't speak, he went on. "Here's how this is going to go, little mama. You're going to send me your schedule. The hours you're not in class, you're on call for me. Anything I need, you will jump to do it. You feel me so far?"

I nodded. I felt him way too much.

"You cook?"

I nodded again. "Yes."

"Any good?"

"I can't cook every type of food, but I think I'm pretty decent."

His hand went to his chin, scrubbing as he stared at me with a pinched brow. "You're making me dinner every night. If Julien and Marco are here, you'll cook for them too, but you're mine, not theirs. Clear?"

"I'm clear, except—" I pressed my lips together, not knowing if I was allowed to object.

"Speak, Zadie."

I flipped my hands over in my lap. "Well, I don't have a car, so I can't buy groceries for your dinners. Unless...do you want me to ride the bus?"

He sucked in a great deal of breath then exhaled slowly. "No. I do not want you on the bus. Text me a list. I'll have someone pick up what you need."

"Okay," I squeaked out. "My roommates might wonder where I'm disappearing to every night, but—"

His brows rose. "But you'll figure that shit out because it's not my problem?"

"Right."

I would be here, in this house every night, with Amir. Amir and his guns. I shuddered, goose bumps sprouting up and down my arms.

"I want you to start tomorrow. You'll be here after your last class."

"My last class ends at one. I normally go to the library and—"

Before I could finish my sentence, Amir was on his feet, bent over me, his arms bracketing my head, challenging me with his eyes to finish my objection.

"Day one, Zadie. Day one, and you're already attempting to defy me. I let that motherfucker go because you made me a promise. You gave yourself to me. I'm being nice to you, little mama. If I wanted, I could whip my cock out, stuff it down your sweet little throat, and coat your insides with my seed. So, please, tell me about the library. Tell me why you can't be here when I tell you to be here."

He was too close, too heated, too powerful. His warm, spicy scent invaded my space just like he did. I averted my gaze to a place over his shoulder, keeping some part of me to myself. An inkling of control. Amir shattered it, moving his face into my eyeline. Our gazes clashed, and he held me in his unblinking stare.

"I have to study. But if you need me here at one, I'll rearrange my study times." I sucked in a breath. "I'll make it work."

He picked up a piece of my hair and slipped his finger into the center of my curl. Then he pulled it taut. "You'll be here at four tomorrow."

"Okay."

He tapped my lips with his fingertip. "Every day, Zadie. I need you here every day unless I tell you not to come. Do you feel me?"

"Yes."

His finger slipped between my lips when I spoke. He dragged it along the edge of my bottom teeth, then dipped in farther to touch my tongue. His withdrawal was as sudden as his invasion, trailing a line of my saliva across my lower lip and chin until he was no longer touching me. My heart didn't get the memo, though. It thrashed wildly in my chest, attempting to climb out of my throat.

"It's too bad you didn't fight me."

His meaning didn't dawn on me until he had straightened and stalked across the room to stand in front of the windows facing the porch. With bated breath, I watched as he adjusted the front of his pants. He made no effort to hide it, but he didn't shove it in my face either, despite his threats. I didn't know what I would have done if he had.

"You can go, Zadie." Amir glanced at me over his shoulder. "Get out."

Surprised, but not one to look a gift horse in the mouth, I jumped to my feet and rushed toward the front door, grabbing my discarded bag along the way. Just as I opened the door, Amir's voice directly behind me glued my feet to the floor.

"Do you have more skirts?" he asked.

I whirled around, my lips parting. "Skirts?"

"Like you're wearing. Do you have more of them?"

Pinching the flowy blue material between my fingers, I struggled to catch up to the change in subject. Skirts? He wanted to know about my wardrobe? It wasn't like it was exciting or anything. Certainly not sexy like the girl who'd been draped on him at the party.

"Zadie," he gritted out.

"I have a few," I answered quickly.

He folded his arms over his chest. "I want you in a skirt while you're cooking, unless I tell you something different."

His demand struck me as funny, so I quipped, "Should I wear my frilly apron too?"

Amir didn't laugh. I hoped Julien had luck finding his sense of humor because boy was he devoid of one. Jeez.

"If you have one, bring it. I'll let you know if I like it." He tipped his chin toward the door. "Go now."

"I'm going." This time, nothing stopped me from breaking free into the fresh air, away from Amir's oppressive stare and cranky demeanor. It wasn't until I was completely out of his view that a weight lifted off my shoulders.

I could do this. Amir still terrified me at times, but four months ago, he'd let me see beneath his steely facade once, so there was no going back to the time before I knew he could be something other than dark and glowering.

I settled in his lap. He pulled me closer, my shoulder wedged beneath his arm, my breasts pressed to his chest. His warm, spicy scent assaulted my senses. God, he smelled so good, I wanted to shove my nose in his throat and inhale his flesh.

He stroked my cheek with his knuckles and held my hip with his other hand. "Tell me, little mama, why haven't you been fucked in so long?"

Why had I said that? I hadn't been fucked ever. I was a sophomore in college and kind of embarrassed by that, but I shouldn't have cared what this particular man thought of me. I should have been the one judging him, for Christ's sake. He was the drug-dealing sociopath holding me hostage, and like Helen had said, I didn't need to have had a man's dick in me to validate my existence as a complete woman.

But I wasn't a badass like Helen, and I did want to be fucked. I wanted that experience, especially since I'd been robbed of a normal life for years.

"I've been busy," I said.

He cupped my cheek. "No. That isn't the reason."

"I'm shy."

His thumb fitted in the dip between my bottom lip and chin. "I believe that, but that's not it. Tell me the truth."

I tried to shift on his lap, worried I'd crush him. Amir's legs were long and lean, and beneath my plump ass, they felt like steel bars. When I moved, his hold on me tightened.

"The truth is, I haven't felt comfortable with anyone in a long time." Or ever, but he didn't need to know that.

He turned my head so we were almost nose to nose. "Why not?"

"I don't know." I shook my head, wishing I'd stayed on my love seat. This was too much.

"You know, you didn't have to tell me you miss fucking."

My heart stopped. I tried to avert my gaze, but Amir tipped my head until my eyes were on him again.

"What's that about?" He used that voice again, like gritty lacquer, smooth and gruff. When he spoke to me that way, with his arms around me, his scent burned into my memory, it didn't matter that he was my captor and I was his hostage. Heat pooled low in my belly. My thighs involuntarily rubbed together. Amir stopped breathing, no doubt noticing. "Zadie..."

"I really don't know why I told you," I whispered.

"Are you comfortable with me?"

"Not really."

"Because you're afraid of me?" His hand splayed on my belly, and two fingers found their way beneath the hem of my shirt, trailing along my tender, untouched skin.

"I don't think I'm as afraid of you as I should be."

His head dipped, his nose grazing mine. "Make no mistake, Zadie Night, I am the bad guy here. You feel me?" His midnight stare went hazy as I nodded. Then he pushed his hand up my shirt, flattening over my ribs. "But if you want to show me this body, know this: I will appreciate every inch of you."

The gun on my coffee table wouldn't let me forget he was the bad guy, but the way his hands felt on me made me want to.

"Okay."

His exhale ghosted over my lips. "Okay?"

"Yes."

Amir's mouth quirked into something like a smile that was only halfway menacing. Forever passed while I held my breath for so long I was in danger of passing out from both lack of oxygen and nerves. And then finally, finally, *he lowered his mouth to meet mine.*

CHAPTER FOUR

Amir

PRESSING THE HEEL OF my hand into my eye, I willed the throbbing ache in my skull to disappear. I had too much shit to do to be dealing with one of my headaches.

Julien walked up the steps of the porch, throwing his backpack down on the ground, and flopped down in the chair beside mine. "S'up?"

I nodded to the computer in my lap. "Writing."

He leaned over me, scanning the paper I'd been trying to write for the last two hours. "Oh shit. Is that for commerce? You have Krasinski, right?"

"Yeah. He's as big of a hard-ass as you said."

Julien and I were both juniors in the business school. He was majoring in marketing. I was in operations management. Savage U had one of the best business schools in the country, and the professors were at the top of their field. Dr. Krasinski had a reputation that went beyond the hallowed walls of Savage U. Internships and employers looked highly on applicants with recommendations from him. So I was busting more ass in his class than I ever had.

Julien gave my arm a slug. "See? The torture you're going through right now is karma for making fun of my misery last semester. Krasinski is no joke. You'll walk out of his class a hundred times smarter than you walked in—after he whips your brain around a blender all semester."

I tried to laugh, but the sharp pain behind my right eye sobered me instantly. "Fuck."

Julien cocked his head. "Did you take something?"

"No."

"Jesus, don't be a martyr. Go get a pill."

"No."

He turned toward the slightly cracked front door. "She's in there, isn't she?"

With a heavy exhale, I opened my eyes. "Yeah. She's dusting."

Julien sputtered a laugh. "Oh, shit. You're taking this ownership thing so seriously, you have that girl *dusting*?"

"I do. I could have her doing a lot worse. She made the choice to take on Schiffer's punishment. I'm not letting that slide. He disrespected Reno, and by extension, me. In my eyes, she showed the same disrespect by being there with him."

He sobered, studying me intently. "So, Schiffer gets off completely free while that girl has to dust our raggedy house?"

Setting my laptop on the small table beside my chair, I leaned back and clasped my hands on my stomach. "His punishment is losing the girl and having to wake up every day with the knowledge that she's mine and will do whatever I want her to. He never gets to touch her, look at her, or even think about her."

"You're cool with being an asshole. Got it. That doesn't explain why you won't go inside to grab a Tylenol when you're obviously in pain."

Climbing to my feet, I grabbed my laptop. Julien knew exactly what he was doing, and I was rising to his bait, but fuck, my head was splitting in two. "Look at me going inside."

With a snicker, the asshole followed me into the empty kitchen. The house was quiet except for the barely there squeak of the floorboards in the living room where Zadie must have been.

She'd shown up at four sharp, wearing another one of her ultra-feminine skirts. This one came down past her knees with a slit going up to midthigh. There'd been nothing inherently sexy about her skirt, plain white tee, Chucks, and jean jacket, but she filled out every spare inch of fabric with her tits, ass, hips, and cute little soft belly. I had to walk out the door when she started dusting or I would have made good on my threats and stuffed my cock between her pretty lips. I wouldn't have felt bad about doing it either—she was mine and had agreed to all that entailed—but I preferred an enthusiastic partner. So my ass was outside while *her* plump ass was inside. That was the only way it would work.

I swallowed a couple painkillers and chugged a large glass of water. Julien handed me a Coke from the fridge, and I first pressed it to my eyelid, then popped it open and took a long swig. He'd been around me while I had a headache enough times to know my routine.

Julien was making himself a sandwich, and I had a hip propped on the counter when Zadie came in, faltering at the sight of the two of us in the kitchen.

"Oh." Her gaze swung to his loaded sandwich. "I was coming to start dinner."

Grinning, he brought his sandwich to his mouth. "Have at it."

The way she crinkled her nose at him made me want to bend her over my lap and spank the annoying habit out of her. It bothered me enough when she made that face at me. Seeing her do it toward Julien drove a railroad spike through my head.

"Are you even going to be hungry?" she asked.

He nodded enthusiastically while he chewed. "Hell yeah."

"He's a garbage disposal." I folded my arms over my chest. "He consumes enough for three men."

Her gaze slid past me back to Julien. "Is there anything you don't like to eat?"

"Nope. Food and me get along. What are you making us tonight, Chef Zadie?"

She giggled softly, gravitating to his side of the kitchen. Her casual conversation with Julien while she'd barely acknowledged me heightened my fury, making the pain in my head sharpen like a fucking knife.

"I was planning on pasta primavera with grilled chicken. I usually omit the chicken when I'm cooking for myself, but I thought a houseful of men would want protein. So—"

"Whose property are you, Zadie?" I growled, taking a prowling step toward her. "Do you belong to Julien? To Marco? To all three of us?"

She backed up until her ass hit the island and she could go no farther. My hands came down on either side of her, trapping her in place. "Who, Zadie?"

"You." Her shoulders curled inward, like a flower retreating into itself when the sun set. "You own me."

"That's right. I do. So why are you asking Julien what he likes to eat? Why are you telling him what's for dinner tonight?"

"I'm sorry," she rasped.

Dipping down, I got in her face. "Answer me." When she refused to look at me, I lifted her chin with my knuckle. "Answer me, Zadie."

Her eyes were round and blue like robins' eggs. Her nose twitched, but it didn't crinkle.

"Julien's easier to talk to." Her response was barely above a whisper, but I heard every syllable.

"He's not your friend." I held on to her jaw and speared Julien with a hard look over her head. He continued eating his sandwich, making no move to interfere. He wouldn't, unless I completely lost my mind, which never happened. But there was something about Zadie that tested me. "Do you not remember who brought you to me at the party? Julien is loyal to me, not you. He knows you're mine. Don't go to him for protection from me. You won't find it."

"Okay." Her chin trembled, but she held tight to her tears. "I won't do it again."

"I know you won't, because you're a good girl." Releasing her jaw, I trailed my fingers over the velvety skin of her cheek and down the side of her neck. "You want to be good for me."

"I do."

I touched my nose to hers. "Make me dinner, little mama. I hope you brought your frilly apron. I'm going to sit here to watch the show, and I'll be disappointed if you don't have it."

"I have it."

"Good." I straightened. "Get going."

With a smirk, Julien stuffed the last of his sandwich in his mouth and strode past me to exit the kitchen. I circled the island, grabbed a seat on one of the stools, and opened my laptop back up to the paper I'd been working on before Julien came home. My head was still throbbing, but some of it had been dulled from the meds, so at least I didn't want to claw my brain out anymore.

I typed one word before my eyes were pulled from the screen to Zadie tying a neat, fluffy bow at the small of her back. She turned around, heading for the fridge wearing an apron that looked like it came from the fifties. Why the fuck did that make my dick feel like it was going to punch a hole through my pants? Probably because I was picturing her in the apron and nothing else. Maybe I'd clear Marco and Julien from the house for the night and order her to do just that. That show would be for my eyes only.

While she chopped vegetables and boiled water, I wrote another paragraph, but it was like pulling teeth to get my thoughts from my brain to the screen. And when I did, they were such utter garbage, I slammed my fist down on the back-space button, deleting it all.

The chopping had stopped. Zadie was watching me beat up my computer from beside the stove.

"Is everything okay?" she asked.

"Just trying to write a paper on the plastics industry in China."

"Krasinski?"

"Yeah." I cocked my head. "How'd you know?"

"I took that class last semester."

"With Julien?"

Her shoulders lifted slightly. "Yes, I think so. I recognized him at the party, but we never spoke during class. I didn't even know his name." She started to come closer but stopped herself. "Do you need help? I know it's a really difficult course. I had to study all night sometimes, but I got an *A*, so if you have questions..."

If I wanted to, I could tell her to write the paper for me, and she would. We were both well aware of the power dynamic here. I had it all, and she did as she was told. It fucking infuriated me that she would bow even lower, asking me if I needed help without me first demanding it. I'd thought Zadie had bigger balls than that, even under her soft and meek exterior. Yes, I took pleasure in her giving in to me, but this? No. Her offering kindness when it wasn't deserved was weakness personified.

A vise tightened around my aching head. My angry heart thrashed wildly in the cage of my chest. Agitation drove me to need to do *something*.

"Why would I want that from you?" Clicking my laptop shut, I picked it up and crossed the kitchen to peer into the pots on the stove. Water was close to boiling. Meticulously chopped veggies were waiting to be sautéed. Spices lined the counter, carefully measured out. It looked good, great even, but fuck it. "Look up the number for Savage Pizza. Order two larges—one mushroom and onions, one pepperoni."

"But—" Her lips parted. "Should I put this away for tomorrow or—?"

I kicked open the stainless steel trash can we kept tucked under the end of the counter, picked up the chopping block, and dumped all the vegetables into it. Zadie's whimper barely registered. Once I'd started, I was on a mission. With one violent sweep of my arm, the spices landed in the sink and scattered on the countertop. Boiling water went down the drain. Satisfaction filled my chest to see it all gone, out of my sight, done for good.

Zadie clutched her hands under her chin, watching my actions with horror written all over her pretty face.

Slamming the trash can shut, I peered at her from beneath tightly furrowed brows. "We're not friends, Zadie. You don't come to my house, flirt with my friend, and act like we have something in common just because I'm taking the same class you took—along with the rest of the business school. If I need help, I'll ask Julien. Not you. Never you. You get what I'm saying, girl?"

Her apple cheeks were flushed red. Her teeth dug so hard into her lip, I would have been surprised if there wasn't blood when she let go. Little Zadie wasn't happy with me. Now, we were even. I hadn't been happy with her since the night we met, and the pit of disdain between us was only growing deeper by the day.

"Okay," she rasped. "I get it, Amir. Should I...should I make dinner for you tomorrow night? Is there something you would prefer more?"

"What did I tell you yesterday?"

She closed her eyes for a long moment, exhaling a shaky breath. "You told me to come here every day unless you said not to."

"That still stands. I don't want you in my house anymore tonight. Let's both hope you do better tomorrow so I don't have to waste a shit ton of food again." I snapped my fingers. "Call in the order and leave."

Zadie flinched like I'd struck her, and for a second, I regretted being harsh on her, but only for a second. She had a place here, and it wasn't going to be a comfortable one. I'd been nice to her once. That had been a mistake, but I hadn't recognized it until her dainty claws had already sunk beneath my skin four months ago.

Her lips were sweet. Pure and shy, following my lead. When I moved, she chased, nipping at me for more.

"I like that." My thumb pressed into her puffy bottom lip. "Your mouth is really sexy, like it was made for a cock, but I don't think you've ever taken one here, have you?"

"No," she breathed.

"Yeah," I drawled. "I knew that."

"Was I that bad at kissing?"

I chuckled at her question. "No, little mama. Nothing that sweet could be bad. You let me taste how thirsty you are. How many guys have had their mouths on you?"

"I'm thirsty?" She snorted. "You kissed me!"

I grunted. "You were sniffing after my mouth like a hound dog. Answer the question."

She crinkled her nose, and fuck me, it was adorable in a way that made me want to tear her little skirt to tatters and suck and lick her pussy to see if I could get her to do it again.

"Two. They were both high school boyfriends." Her demeanor changed in an instant, telling me she didn't have warm feelings about one or both of those guys.

"Which one fucked you over?"

Her body went stiff, and for a second, I was gratified at being right, but only for a second. Then I needed to know what had been done to her to cause that reaction. She tried to turn her head, but I held her steady. "Tell me, Zadie."

She sighed. "The second one. Drew. When I broke up with him after a few weeks, he didn't accept it. He got...intense."

"What's that mean?"

In an absent move, she dragged her fingers down my chest to rest on my belly. "He was in college but kept showing up at my school. And then it escalated. It got scary."

I curled my fingers around her wrist. "What did he do?"

"He left me poems. Sometimes they were obscene, sometimes scarily sweet. Flowers too. That was okay, I could deal, but then *he started taking pictures of me through cracks in my curtains. Then...then he broke into my bedroom while I was sleeping."*

Her tremble was subtle, but there was no mistaking it. This kid had scared the shit out of her. Soft, shy Zadie Night had been terrorized, and all I saw was red.

"What's his last name, Zadie?"

"Why? Are you going to slay my dragons?"

"If that means hunting this motherfucker down and feeding him his balls before I put a bullet in his dick, then yeah, I'm going to slay your dragons."

Snickering, she pressed her face to my throat. Her hot laughter on my raging pulse was like a balm over a blistering burn. It didn't go away, but she made it feel like it wasn't on fire anymore.

"He's been slayed with a restraining order. Plus, he lives in Oregon, where I grew up. He won't be sneaking into my bedroom ever again, not when he doesn't even know where I am." She brought her fingers up to my tautly held jaw, stroking with a featherlight touch. "I appreciate the offer though, Captor."

A low growl rattled the back of my throat. "Captor?"

"Isn't that what you are? I'm your hostage, and you're my captor."

Shoving her away enough for me to grab her face and jerk it toward me, I fixed her with a hard glare. "Whatever we are to each other when I walk out of your door, you'll tell me if this guy comes back. Agree."

She sucked in a breath. "I agree."

"Good, since it wasn't a question."

The way she crinkled her nose at me set off a chain reaction inside me. Fisting the back of her hair, I crashed my mouth into hers, claiming what was mine, even if it was only for the time we had left in this room.

Chapter Five

Zadie

The relief I felt when I trudged up to my dorm room and didn't find a note or flowers waiting for me had me sagging against the wall. The sting of Amir's harsh treatment was far too fresh for me to deal with one more thing.

Elena, Helen, and her boyfriend, Theo, were hanging out in our shared living area. El was in the armchair with her laptop and headphones on. Helen and Theo were snuggled on the love seat. Both had books opened in their laps, but they seemed to be ignoring them and paying attention to each other.

That was, until I walked in. Helen straightened, giving me a quick wave. "Hey, Z. Check the table, girlie. You got a treat."

"Oooh, a treat? What did I do to deserve that?"

She shot me a red-lipped grin. Helen's superpower, besides, of course, being a badass, was her red lipstick never faded. I'd walked in on her and Theo making out enough times to know kissing didn't destroy it. She'd painted it on my lips once, and it had immediately smeared all over my teeth, confirming I wasn't a red-lip girl—not like her. But who was?

"Hey, Zadie," Theo greeted.

My cheeks warmed. "Hi, Theo." I used to think Helen's boyfriend was a laughing frat bro like Deacon Forrestor. He had that look, and he'd once been friends with Deacon too, but he wasn't like that at all. I still blushed when making direct eye contact with him, because...well, he was Theo, and he was just as beautiful and badass as Helen.

I kicked off my Chucks, dropped my messenger bag carefully by the door, and headed to the small table in the kitchen nook we never used for eating. My heart stopped.

Two daisies, tied together with twine, lay there with a folded piece of paper beside them. This wasn't a treat. This was a nightmare.

Unfolding the paper, I held my breath as I read the words that had been typed there.

Daisies are white
Your eyes are blue
I think about you at night
I think of you in the morning too
    • *D*

Picking up the flowers and note, I swiveled around. "Where was this?"

Helen's perfectly arched brows flattened. "Someone left it propped against the door. Why? What does it say?"

"Nothing. It's just..." I shook my head. "It's nothing."

Elena hopped up from her chair, her headphones around her neck and hand held out. "Let me see this 'nothing.' Do you have a secret admirer, Zadie?"

"No." I gripped the paper at my side. "It's really nothing."

She snatched it out of my hand before I could move to stop her and read the note out loud. Then, with a bemused expression, she handed it back.

"Who's D?" she asked.

"I don't know," I whispered.

I was almost certain I knew exactly who D was, and though it had been three weeks since I received my first note from him, I still couldn't believe it. I couldn't believe Drew had tracked me down after a blissfully long period of silence.

She shrugged. "Well, he writes terrible poetry, so I can already tell he's not good enough for you. That's not even mentioning the fact that he's obviously a pussy if he can't tell you to your face that he's into you."

I forced out a laugh. "Yeah. It's kind of creepy too, don't you think?"

"Total creep city," she agreed. "If some kid left me weirdo poetry, I would laugh in his face if he ever got the guts to approach me. Then I'd hand him the origami middle finger I made out of it."

This laugh, I didn't have to force. Leave it to Elena to knock me out of my head and doomsday mood.

"Oh my god," Helen groaned. "If some dude is dumb enough to be into you, let's hope he's still smart enough to know you aren't a terrible poetry and flowers girl. I do not want to have to bear witness to his ruthless murder."

El tipped her chin. "What kind of girl am I?"

"What's the word I'm looking for?" Hells clicked her fingers. "Oh yeah. Fire and brimstone. That's more your speed."

Elena feigned trying to snatch the poem back. "Give me that, Z. I suddenly feel the need to start on my origami middle finger."

Spinning out of her reach, I escaped into my bedroom while Hells and El bickered back and forth. It was lucky they only bickered and didn't have hair-pulling, knock-down, drag-out fights. They'd gone to high school together, and to say they hadn't gotten along would have been an understatement. But, like in romance novels, forced proximity had gotten to them, and I was pretty certain they both held a grudging respect for each other. Unless, of course, Elena was biding her time before sucking our souls out, like Helen had accused her of last week.

Opening the drawer of my bedside table, I took out the other three poems and added the latest to the stack. When the first one came, it had sent an icy chill down my spine and a wave of panic so suffocating, I'd nearly fainted. I'd called my lawyer in Oregon to ensure my order of protection was still good. It was, but it didn't make me feel any safer.

My phone rang while I stared at the thin stack of papers like a deadly weapon, and my heart leaped into my throat.

Mom calling...

I answered.

"Hey, sweet thing," she greeted.

"Hi! What's shakin', Mama?" I replied.

"Nada. I had a minute of downtime, so I'm calling my sweet girl."

Flopping back on my bed, I smiled with tears in my eyes. "Did you know I needed to hear your voice?"

"I had an inkling, like the universe was pushing me to my phone. What's up, honey?"

This would be the perfect time to dump my stress on my mother. Actually, three weeks ago, when the first note arrived, would have been even better. She'd lived through the turmoil of Drew the first time around and hadn't once faltered in her support, no matter how hard I'd leaned on her. And I'd leaned *hard*.

But circumstances had changed over the last two years. Mom and Dad had gotten divorced after the year Drew relentlessly stalked and harassed me and my family. The stress we went through had been a big part of the straw that broke their marriage's back.

Mom remarried her college boyfriend and moved to California. Dad was still in Oregon, smoking a lot of weed and wallowing in his heartbreak. My stepdad, Max, was a nice man, and Mom was mad about him, but three months ago, he had been diagnosed with leukemia, and their newlywed life had been flipped upside down. She had become his caregiver, and I really wanted to be the person she leaned on.

So I couldn't give her this. Not one more thing. My dad either. If it escalated beyond notes and flowers, I might have to, but for now, I was handling it.

"I'm okay. I think it's your basic homesickness, slash being worried about Max, slash Dad, slash studying my brains out."

Mom sighed. "I can't do anything about your father except tell you he's a grown man and wouldn't want you fretting over him, but I know that doesn't help. I *do* have a cure for your homesickness, though. Why don't you come home for the weekend?"

I wish. Assuming Amir expected me at his house on the weekends, going home, even though it was only an hour away, wasn't a possibility.

"I can't, Mom. Not right now. I'm sorry."

She tsked. "No, don't be sorry. What if I bring Eli up next weekend and we have lunch with you? I don't think Max is up for the ride, but I think I can pry Eli from his video games long enough to get him to come along."

"Yes." My response was instant. Seeing my mom would buoy me, and Max's sixteen-year-old son, Eli, was more delightful than a teenage boy had any right to be. When our parents married, we'd bonded easily, even though we'd both grown up as only children. Or maybe that was *why* we'd bonded so easily, since we had each admitted to always wanting a sibling. "Please come to visit. Eli will probably just want to drool over my suitemates, but I don't even care as long as I get to smoosh his face."

Mom let out a soft laugh. "He's under the impression he played it cool in front of them. Let's let him believe that, okay?"

When Eli visited last semester, he'd laid eyes on Helen and Elena and tripped over his oversized feet. Cool, he was not. Charming and adorable? For sure. But I didn't think teenage boys were into being called adorable.

I giggled. "No problem."

"As for Max..." Her sigh was so heavy, I nearly felt the weight of it on my shoulders. "He's hanging in there, baby. His body is working hard right now, and he's so tired, but he was in good shape before his diagnosis, so he has that going for him. I'm staying optimistic, and so is he. We're just in the thick of things right now, and it feels...well, it's scary."

My chin quivered, but I pushed the worry out of my voice. She had enough of her own. She didn't need mine added to it. "Tell me if you need me, Mama, okay? I can put aside my studying to help you."

"Oh, Zadie, baby, I love you. We have an excellent support system around us. You can help me most by kicking butt in school and being my very cool daughter. Anytime you need *me*, I'm here. Always, always, no matter what's going on with Max or Eli. Understand?"

"Yes, I understand." That didn't mean I'd lay my worries on her. I just couldn't do that to her again. Not after Drew tore us apart the first time.

· · · · ● · ● · · ·

I had finally gotten my mind focused on studying when my phone chimed with a text. I ignored it, then it chimed again a minute later, so I picked it up to check it.

And wished I hadn't.

MyCaptor: *Send me a picture to show me where you are.*

MyCaptor: *What did I say about replying when I text you?*

With a sigh, I snapped a picture of my legs and feet. My laptop and notebook were covering most of me, so it was pretty obvious what I was up to.

Me: *Is this good enough?*

MyCaptor: *Face, Zadie.*

I sent him a picture of me snarling. I wished I could flip him off, but he'd probably break down my door to punish me if I did. After the way he treated me earlier, he was the last person I wanted to see.

MyCaptor: *Don't be cute with me.*

Me: *I wasn't trying to be. That was my disgruntled face.*

MyCaptor: *Why would you have any reason to be disgruntled?*

Me: *Do you really not remember what went down in your kitchen this afternoon?*

MyCaptor: *I do. But I don't understand why you're disgruntled.*

Me: *No reason. How was the pizza?*

MyCaptor: *Fucking delicious. Best I ever had.*

Me: *Good. I'm glad you don't regret trashing the dinner I was making.*

MyCaptor: *Not for a second.*

Me: *Okay, well, good. I love that for you.*

MyCaptor: *Sarcasm?*

Me: *Never.*

MyCaptor: *Sarcasm. You're brave over text, little mama.*

Me: *I'm just tired and need to study.*

MyCaptor: *Go. Study. Be here tomorrow.*

Me: *K. Goodnight, Amir.*

MyCaptor: *Be good, Zadie.*

I flung my phone across my bed. I had the fleeting fantasy of just not showing up tomorrow or ever again. What would he do? It was pretty obvious he could barely stand to be in my presence.

But I already had one obsessive, dangerous man hunting me down. I didn't think I could bear another. Besides, running from Amir would defeat my entire purpose for seeking him out in the first place.

As much as he couldn't stand the sight of me, I was hoping if push came to shove, he'd remember his unspoken promise.

"Whatever we are to each other when I walk out of your door, you'll tell me if this guy comes back."

When he said that, I'd been in his lap, the taste of him on my lips. He hadn't hated me, and I'd thought I might be able to really like him, despite, you know, the gun, captivity, and whole drug dealer thing. Things had quickly changed, though. The bubble we'd created that night had burst in a gory, bloody fashion.

Amir didn't have to like me to protect me, though. If I was his property, he wouldn't allow anyone else to touch me. At least...I hoped that was true.

If it wasn't, then I was on my own. There was no one else I'd be willing to bring into Drew's chaotic obsession. Not my mom, my dad, or my suitemates. My high school friends and my family had gone through hell during Drew's reign of terror. I'd limped away with divorced parents and friends who'd distanced themselves so much, we hadn't ever found our way back to each other.

Never again.

Amir...well, he could handle himself. He had the arsenal to prove it. His presence in my life was like a big stop sign. If Drew had two brain cells, he'd heed the directive. And then, when he left me alone again and Amir freed me from his ownership, I could walk away. I'd belong to no one but myself. I'd be free.

CHAPTER SIX

Zadie

THE ENTIRE TIME I was preparing the veggie lasagna for the boys, I held my breath, waiting for Amir to trash it. But, aside from letting me in the house and barking at me to change the sheets on his bed and vacuum the living room, he'd left me alone. From time to time, I caught a glance of him on the porch through the window, but he never came inside. I'd been so tempted to play his piano, but all I could bring myself to do was run my fingers over the keys.

Now, dinner was baking, and I wasn't sure if I was allowed to leave, so I set up my laptop on the kitchen island and started writing a paper that was due next week. The house was surprisingly quiet. If I hadn't been on edge, I would have found it comfortable. It didn't feel like how I imagined a typical college rental. The floors weren't sticky, the furniture didn't have tears, there weren't any Solo cups strewn about.

I'd changed Amir's sheets as quickly as possible, pausing only to gawk over the fine quality and obviously high thread count. And, god, his warm spice smell was everywhere in his bedroom. It was like walking through a cloud of his essence. His scent was the very best part of him. Being in that room, completely immersed in it, staggered me so much, I had to breathe out of my mouth so I could finish the job.

"Yo, yo, it smells *good* in here."

"Yeah it does."

Marco and Julien strode into the kitchen. Marco opened the oven to peek at what was cooking. Julien stopped at the island, popping a couple green grapes into his mouth.

I'd only met Marco once, last weekend when he'd helped Julien escort Elliott and me to Amir. His presence was darker than Julien's, more like Amir's, but not as scary. No one was as scary as Amir.

Like Julien, Marco was tall and lanky, built like a basketball player. Like Julien and Amir, he was unreasonably, intimidatingly attractive. Marco had a rich, dark-brown complexion, tightly cropped curls, and lips worthy of really good poetry. And when he came to stand by Julien, swinging his arm around his friend, he grinned at me, and I was sunk. There was no way I'd be able to have a normal conversation with this beautiful man, so I really hoped he didn't try.

"I can't believe you came back after the bullshit Amir pulled on you last night," Julien said. "You should've seen my tears when I had to eat pizza instead of your pasta." He dragged a finger down his cheek.

"I don't think I really had a choice." I shrugged, giving him a wobbly smile. "It wasn't a big deal. I can always poison his food next time." I covered my mouth in disbelief I'd let that slip. Being around two very attractive men apparently wasn't good for my brain.

Julien chuckled, and Marco almost smiled. "I like it, Princess Z. And I do think it was a big deal. A big, shitty deal."

Marco turned serious, giving Julien a nudge. "You need to stop talking. What Amir does with this girl is up to him. You don't question that—especially not in front of her."

Julien shrugged him off. "That's you. I call him out on his bullshit always. The day I have to hold my tongue is the day I walk away."

"Who's walking away?" Amir strode into the kitchen, his heavy, dark brow pinched into a straight line.

Marco clucked his tongue. "No one, man. I was just reminding this kid to keep his opinions to himself."

Amir braced his hands on the island, pointedly ignoring me even though he was standing so close, I caught a whiff of his spice and had to stop myself from leaning in closer for more.

"What opinion?"

Julien rolled his eyes. "I already expressed to you how un-called for it was for you to trash Zadie's food yesterday. Marco disapproves of sharing my displeasure with the girl herself."

"Property." Amir stroked my hair like I was his pet. "This girl is my property. She doesn't need to know your feelings. They don't concern her. If I want to throw away every dinner she makes, I will, and she'll come back for more. That's how this works." His fingers tangled in my hair and made a fist, tugging my head back so my face was pointed up at his. "Right, Zadie? You'll keep coming back."

"Yes," I whispered.

"See?" Amir gestured to his friends. "Zadie's on board. She doesn't have any problem with our arrangement. Why the fuck should you?"

Julien's nose twitched. "Because it's not cool, man. Another girl, I wouldn't say shit. But not her. She's not part of this. It was all on her idiot boyfriend. She's a nice girl, and you're—"

In a flash, Amir had my head cradled in the crook of his arm and his thumb hooked on my bottom teeth, keeping my mouth open.

"This nice girl would get down on her knees and blow me if I told her to. You know who she won't blow? You. Get the fuck out of here with your high horse. It's not gonna happen for you."

Julien's face flushed. His eyes darted from me to Amir. "Nice, man. I've had your back since we were kids, but I guess none of that matters, huh?"

Amir shook my head gently and stroked the side of my face. "Not when you're standing in *my* kitchen, openly disrespecting me in front of *my* girl."

He unhooked his thumb from my teeth, pushed my jaw closed, and wiped the saliva from my bottom lip. Then he ran his hand over my hair like a lover instead of a captor.

Julien's nostrils flared as he glared at Amir. Marco folded his arms and gritted his jaw, frowning furiously at me, like this was somehow my doing. And Amir continued treating me like he was the villain, plotting the end of the world, and I was the fuzzy little cat in his lap.

The oven timer beeped, interrupting the showdown. "I need to get that," I murmured.

Amir bent over me, bringing his face close to mine. "What did you say?"

"The oven beeped. I have to take the lasagna from the oven."

His eyes narrowed on me. "I don't know if I want lasagna for dinner. Maybe you should start over."

With a shake of his head, Julien spun around, grabbed a towel, and took the lasagna out himself. He placed it on top of the stove, gave me a chin jerk, then walked out of the kitchen. Marco let out a long groan and followed, leaving me with Amir, who released me and stalked to the oven.

I held my breath, expecting him to dump the lasagna in the trash. My heart might have broken a little if he did. This recipe was my mom's, and I knew just how delicious it was. He didn't throw it away. Instead, he dipped his head, inhaling the steam coming from the melted cheese and bubbling sauce, then turned around to face me again.

"You can skip cooking tomorrow. I need you somewhere else."

"Where?"

"A lecture at Brady Hall. I want you to go take notes for me."

My lips parted in surprise. That was unexpected. "Um...well, okay. I can do that."

"They have to be thorough, Zadie. I need to be able to write a report on the lecture like I was there."

Swallowing hard, I nodded. "That's no problem."

He looked like he wanted to say more, but he closed his mouth and rocked back on his heels. "You can go."

I didn't need to be told twice. Scrambling, I stuffed my laptop in my messenger back and hopped down from the stool, smoothing my skirt in the process. At the arch between the kitchen and front hall, I paused, bracing a hand on the molding.

"Amir?"

His eyes were already on me. "Speak."

My tongue darted out to wet my lips. "I can take a lot. I'll come here every day and clean and cook for you without complaint. But if you ever touch me that way in front of your friends again, I won't come back. I'd rather face Reno than be touched in that way." I nodded, my message conveyed, even if it was barely above a whisper. Spinning on my toes, I marched out of the house, my head held high.

Amir may have thought of me as his personal pet. And maybe I was. But the thing about pets? When even the shyest ones were mistreated, they bit back. My bark was quiet, but my bite could be wicked.

• • • •• •••• ••

MyCaptor: *Text me a pic of you at Brady Hall.*

I'd only just sat down. The chairs around me in the auditorium were quickly filling. Everyone was in pairs or groups, but I was all by myself. That was fine. Since my notes needed to be meticulous, I wouldn't have time to talk to anyone anyway.

I took a picture and sent it to Amir.

Me: *I'm here. Since I'll be taking the best notes you've ever seen, I might not be able to text back immediately, so you should leave me alone.*

MyCaptor: *Wow, you're incredibly mean, Zadie.*

Me: *Is this you leaving me alone?*

Someone slid past me and dropped into the only chair left in my row—the one right next to me. I stuffed my phone in my bag and opened my laptop, preparing a new document for my notes. The person leaned into me, his biceps pressing against mine.

"Hey."

I turned my head, frowning at Deacon Forrester. He was invading my personal space. And smelled faintly of alcohol. Fortunately, he seemed to be alone, no laughing frat bros at his back. That made me wonder *why* he was bothering to speak to me, since he didn't have an audience, but I couldn't exactly ignore him since he was right beside me.

"Hi."

His grin was wide, and seemed genuine, which only made my stomach lurch. Why would this guy be genuinely smiling at me?

"Are you in business analytics? I know you're not in my class."

I shook my head. "No."

He chuckled. "Then what the hell are you doing here?"

When I got home from Amir's last night, I'd looked up the topic of the lecture. The speaker was an expert in data mining and predictive analytics. I was an accounting major, so this wasn't my field, but I was a stone-cold nerd, so I was interested. Not that I would be spending my free time here if I had a choice, it was just that I didn't think it would be torture. I would never tell Amir that, though. He could go on thinking this was the worst punishment ever, and maybe he'd send me to more nerdy things instead of making me change his delicious-smelling sheets.

"I'm taking notes for a friend who couldn't make it tonight," I explained, even though it was none of his business and I did not like him.

He hummed and shifted in his seat, his leg pressing against mine. "You don't like me, do you?"

I scoffed and tried to subtly tuck my legs to the side to get away from him. "Why would you think that? Was it the horrible things you said and did to Helen? Or maybe when you proclaimed either of us would do to get you off? Or what about the way you and your friends laugh at me when I walk into class?"

"Hey..." He reached for my arm, but I yanked it away. "I'm guilty of all you said, but my friends don't laugh at you. They're very much laughing at me."

I shook my head, not believing him even for a second. "I don't want to talk anymore. I have to pay attention."

He waggled a pen in my periphery. "I do too. Maybe we can talk after?"

I faced forward instead of replying. Guys who didn't understand "no" were making me really tired. And why were they all coming out of the woodwork? It was like they could smell the chum in the water.

For the next hour, I listened intently, tapping away on my keyboard. At times, I felt like I was being watched, but when I glanced at Deacon, he always had his eyes on the speaker. Still, awareness prickled the back of my neck, and it took all my willpower not to rush out of the lecture hall.

When Drew had watched me before, I hadn't noticed. At least, not at first. He'd hidden in plain sight, following me on my day-to-day activities. And when I went places, he'd pop up, like we were randomly running into each other. In the beginning, I'd believed his excuses, but when it kept happening, I knew it wasn't right.

Someone else could've been watching me. Besides, why would Drew be here tonight, with so many people around? Maybe I was paranoid. Maybe Deacon had made me more uneasy than I'd thought and this was all due to that.

My heart fluttered like mad as the speaker wound down and people around me started packing up their things. I closed my laptop and grabbed my messenger bag, trapped from escaping by the people beside me who were also waiting to leave.

Deacon bumped me with his shoulder. "Can I walk you back to your dorm?"

I stared at him, not really registering what he'd just asked. It didn't really make sense. Not coming from him. Especially since I'd told him I didn't like him. Why in the world would I allow him to walk me home?

Just as I shook my head, the people beside me started making their way down the aisle, and I followed, clutching my messenger bag in front of me. If Deacon insisted on following me, I could whack him in the head with it. It wouldn't be as badass as the time Helen had gotten him with her skateboard, but it would do.

He stayed on my heels out of the auditorium and into the hallway, curling his fingers around my forearm. "I just want to talk, get to know each other. Don't be such a snob. Let me walk you home."

Suddenly, I was shoved back, and there was a body between Deacon and me.

"Not happening. You can walk your own ass home. I've got Zadie covered." Amir towered over Deacon. Even from the back, I could see his simmering fury in the clenched muscles along his spine and shoulders.

Deacon turned tomato red, puffing up his chest as if he stood any chance against a crazy man like Amir. "Excuse me, I was talking to her. As far as I've seen, Zadie doesn't have a keeper, so I think she should be the one to decide who gets to talk to her and walk her home."

It occurred to me while these two wagged their dicks at each other, I could just...leave. With the way they were facing, the exit was clear, and they were too busy getting out the measuring sticks to really notice.

So I did. I turned around and walked away, taking a deep breath of cool night air when it hit my face. Proud of myself for being brave and not letting myself be controlled, I hitched my bag higher on my shoulder and started the long walk back to my dorm.

I made it three steps before my bag was slipped right off my shoulder and a band of iron wrapped around my waist.

Spice filled my nose when Amir leaned down to whisper in my ear. "I can't even be mad, can I? My property needs clear instructions, and I didn't say to wait. You wandered off like a lost little kitty, but don't worry, I'm here. I won't let that happen again."

Anger knotted in my throat as my core flooded with heat. It was such a confusing dichotomy of feelings, I had no clue how to parse it out and wrap my head around it.

"Why are you here?" I asked.

"Why wouldn't I be?"

"Because you told me to come in your place. I took notes for you. Really good notes."

He sniffed. "Email them to me. I'll let you know if they're really good."

"But...why did you tell me to come if you were going to show up anyway?"

Amir's shadowed eyes danced over my face with something like amusement. "I don't think I have to explain myself to you, Zadie. Do I?"

"You don't have to do anything. We both know that." I folded my arms over my chest. "I can make it back to my dorm on my own, you know."

"Of course you can, but since you're my property, I'm going to protect you. Little girls like you shouldn't be out after dark on your own. You should know better."

Oh yeah, anger was definitely taking over the heat between my legs. Amir being a condescending asshat cooled me right off.

Facing forward, I clamped my mouth shut. Something told me Amir wanted me to react, but I wouldn't give it to him. I'd done what he'd told me to do, so I wasn't giving him another drop of me.

He controlled our pace across campus, digging his fingers into the soft flesh of my hip. His silence was as loud as a shout. I wondered if mine sounded the same. There were a million words on the tip of my tongue, but I swallowed them down each time they came close to spilling over.

When my dorm was in sight, Amir was the one to break the silence. "Why were you sitting beside that kid?"

"He sat beside me. It wasn't my choice."

"I get you have a type, Zadie, but you need to move on. He's not going to be your new boyfriend."

I cringed at the thought of Deacon as my boyfriend. "That's good. I don't like anything about him." My lip curled. "And he's *not* my type. I don't tend to have a thing for idiotic frat boys who say nasty things to me and my friend and laugh at me every time I walk by them. No thank you."

Amir rounded on me, coming to a stop in the middle of the path. His hand shot up to grip my jaw, tipping my head back to peer down at my face in the dark.

"Tell me what he said." He got close enough for me to smell his warm spice. "Right now, Zadie. Don't fuck with me. What did that kid say?"

I swallowed hard, barely breathing. "It happened before you owned me. I don't owe you that."

"Says who?" His thumb stroked the skin beneath my chin. His eyes pounded into me with a hard stare. "Everything, Zadie. All of you is mine."

"For how long?" I whispered.

He blinked, and his mouth parted, but no sound came out. I'd stumped him, taking him by surprise with a question that really shouldn't have been surprising.

"Hmmm...I don't know. I think I might like owning you." He dragged his nose along mine. "Then again, you might annoy me sooner than later."

My stomach sank. This couldn't go on forever, I knew that, but he was already ready to be rid of me? Or thinking about being ready? I should have been relieved, not twitching like a wounded bug with a broken wing.

"The rest of the semester."

"What?" I breathed.

"I own you. You're all mine until the end of the semester. Then I let you go."

A perfect end date to *us*. If my stalker hadn't crawled back into his hole by then, I probably wouldn't be coming back to Savage U next semester anyway. Amir didn't need to know that. He didn't need to know any of it, so long as he kept me and watched over me.

"Does anything change from how it is now? I just cook and clean and do your bidding?"

His mouth curled in the corners, but it was too devious to be called a smile. "My bidding? I like that." He lifted a shoulder. "I don't know yet. What do you think should change? Do you want to add some duties to your list?"

"That's up to you, isn't it?"

"Yeah. It is. I've got you, don't I?" The pad of his thumb traced the stubborn bump of my chin. "I'll think about it. For now, I want you to tell me all about the kid you were sitting beside tonight."

He wasn't going to let this go. My dorm was so close, but Amir's iron grasp on me was unrelenting. I knew this was more about a point of pride for him and not because he actually cared for me. Someone had been toying with *his* toy, and that wouldn't stand.

I sucked in a breath. "Deacon. He's in a frat, the same one as Theo, Helen's boyfriend. We have one class together, and lately, he says hi to me when I walk in. All his frat brothers laugh. I guess they think it's funny for him to even acknowledge the presence of a girl like me, so—"

Amir jerked me so hard, my forehead hit his chest. "What the fuck does that mean?" he growled.

Cupping my forehead, I blinked away the sudden tears stinging my eyes. "I'm not—I don't look like the girls here. I'm not the right type. I know that, and it's okay. Those idiots think I'm a joke. But I just...well, I think they're jokes too, so I guess we're even."

"You'd never laugh at anyone."

I swiped at my eyes with the heel of my hand. "Of course I wouldn't."

Shaking his head, Amir took a step back from me. "It kills me."

"What?"

"You." The sneer he shot me was so ugly, it made me want to curl up on the sidewalk. "You fucking kill me. You have no idea."

I rubbed the spot on my jaw he had been gripping. "I don't know..." And I really didn't want him to enlighten me. "Can I go inside now? I'll email you the notes as soon as I'm in my room."

"No." Amir's arm shot out, gripping my nape and pulling me into his side. "I said I'd walk you home. That's what I'm going to do."

So, he did. He held on to me like a possession, steering me all the way to the steps in front of my dorm. Then he backed me into the stone baluster at the base of the stairs and pinned me in with both arms on either side of me.

"If you want the truth, I wasn't coming tonight. I was going to let you send me the notes and be done with it."

I tipped my chin. "So, why didn't you? You didn't trust me to do a good job?"

"No. I knew you would. I don't think there's anything you'd willingly do half-assed, even if it's something for me. I know that because I ate your lasagna for dinner last night, breakfast this morning, and dinner again tonight. And when Marco saw the empty pan in the sink, he came close to taking a swing at me."

"What?" I pushed out a little giggle.

Amir's somber expression didn't budge. "You made that for me, no doubt hating me for making you do it, and it still tasted like heaven. I knew you'd take the most perfect notes anyone's ever taken because that's who you are. I don't think you're even capable of being less than your best."

I refused to let his compliment coat me in warmth. Honestly, I wasn't even positive it *was* a compliment, but it felt like it.

"So, why did you come?" I asked softly.

"Because I don't *trust* you, Zadie." He fingered one of my curls. "If I'm not watching you, how do I know you won't be meeting up with Schiffer? How do I know you're not gonna be fucking him the second the lecture's over? My little pet needs supervision."

I jerked my head away, banging my skull against the stone behind me. His baseless accusation hurt far worse, though. It was like we hadn't spent hours talking in my dorm. Like he didn't remember a single minute of it. It had only been four months ago.

Tsking, Amir tugged me into his chest and rubbed the back of my head.

"Need you back at my house tomorrow. Saturday night, we're going out, so don't make plans." He shoved his fingers in my hair. I braced for him to yank hard, but he didn't. He just stayed there like that, his hand buried in my hair, my head against his chest, holding me to him. "Go inside, mama."

My bag was back on my shoulder, and Amir was gone, backing away from me while watching every breath I took with narrowed eyes. I watched him back for a few flurried heartbeats, then I turned on my heel and ran inside.

Safe.

For now at least.

Amir might not have trusted me, and the feeling was mutual. After what we shared and the way he'd turned off his emotions like a light switch, there was no going back to that stolen moment from four months ago.

Amir kissed me like no one ever had. We weren't captor and hostage anymore. Something had shifted. Our desire had stirred up the air, our reality, the entire world, and resettled it in an entirely different way.

His hands were under my clothes, inside my bra. I shoved up his shirt. His skin was hot and smooth under my palms. I soaked him in, touching him freely, without a second thought. It felt like I wasn't me anymore. I was Amir's now.

And when he stood with me held flush to his body, I didn't stop him. My feet moved with his, taking us to my bedroom. And then I was on the bed, shirt rucked up under my chin, bra cups down, his mouth latched to my nipple, as he worked on the button of my jeans.

He reared back to his knees, and in the dim light of my bedroom, his wild eyes peered down at me. Fingers hooking into the waistband of my jeans, he pulled them off in one swoop. My legs tried to press together, but Amir caught my knees, putting pressure on them to keep them apart.

"Let me see you, little mama. Show me your whole universe," he growled like a wolf to his mate. My legs fell open, showing him. I wished I could close my eyes, but they were glued to his face. I didn't know how to read his expression. His parted lips and deeply furrowed brow. Then he touched me with the very tip of his finger, so featherlight, I barely felt it, and still, I nearly vaulted from the bed.

His exhale had jagged edges all around. "Like silk." His finger dragged down the center of me, pausing at my entrance. "Pretty, Zadie. So fucking pretty. Like a little flower, showing me your bloom. Wonder what you taste like."

"You can try me," I breathed.

His eyes flicked to mine. "No fucking way I won't. You're mine now."

For now, for now, for now. We were Zadie and Amir, not captor and hostage.

For now.

Chapter Seven

Amir

The notes were good. So good, I didn't even look at my own as I wrote my report. This girl had been meticulous, with her bullet points and highlights. She went above and beyond, and it pissed me off. I couldn't even explain why. It wasn't guilt. I didn't feel guilty over having this hold on Zadie. Not in the least. Hopefully she'd walk away at the end of the semester having learned to be more selective in who she let inside her. No more Elliott fucking Schiffers in her life or her bed.

Heels clicking upstairs turned my attention from the screen to the ceiling. She was up there now, getting ready to go out with us. That was after she'd cooked us dinner and folded my laundry. After she'd laughed with Julien, spoken softly to Marco, and barely looked at me. She'd barely looked at me since all this began, so that wasn't new.

Every time she was in my house, ants crawled under my skin. She was too *good*. Too sweet. Too pretty. Too smart. Being in the same room with her made me want to tear shit apart.

My mind needed to be elsewhere, focusing on the fight I was facing in a couple hours, or, at the very fucking least, on the paper I was attempting to pound out, but every time those heels clicked, I was back to Zadie and all the ways she was *too.*

A cabinet slamming, followed by a grunt and clattering on the granite counter had me shutting off my laptop and striding into the kitchen.

Julien shoved Marco hard, knocking him back a couple steps. "Fuck off. That bitch is *mine.*"

"We both know you snuck down here last night and ate half a dozen," Marco gritted out.

Julien thumped his chest. "I didn't sneak. I marched my happy ass down here and ate all the crumbs. The crumbs *you* left on the counter after *you* snuck your ass down here."

Marco clicked his tongue. "That's only because I knew you'd be a sneaky little shit and keep all that lemony goodness to yourself. And I was *right.*"

I slammed a hand down on the granite. "Enough. Do I live with toddlers? Look at you." Shouldering them out of the way, I grabbed the plate holding the last lemon bar and stalked to the other side of the island. "If anyone's eating this lemon bar, it's me. Pretty sure my pet baked it for *me.*"

I shoved the entire bar into my mouth, using my middle fingers.

Marco and Julien turned on me, looking prepared to murder me. It was Saturday night, we all had more important shit to be fighting over than baked goods, but none of us were backing down. Between the two of them, they'd packed away twenty lemon bars since Zadie had left them here last night.

"I hope you get nailed in the gut and spew lemon all over the place," Julien sneered, but there was no real heat behind it.

No doubt he'd enjoy the hell out of seeing me take a gut shot tonight, though.

Marco shook his head. "You never eat before a fight."

I scrubbed my hand over my mouth. "Never had anything good to eat."

Julien patted his stomach. "Gonna get fat and happy with that girl coming around every night, and I'm gonna love every minute of it. Maybe I'll get her to make me my own dessert next time so I don't have to share with you two assholes."

"Never happening." I slowly shook my head. "She's here for me. You're lucky I share what I do. That's all you'll ever get from her."

Rubbing the top of his head, Marco exchanged a glance with Julien. "What about when you're done with her?" he asked.

My fingers dug into my palms. "If that happens, we'll talk about it then."

Julien raised his eyebrows. "*If*? Are you thinking you're going to have a human pet forever?"

"That's not your concern." The thing that sucked about knowing him since we were kids was he wasn't intimidated by me. I could hold a gun to his head, tell him to get fucked, and he knew with one-hundred-percent certainty I'd never pull the trigger. Therefore, the glare I shot him only served to amuse him when anyone else would have been pissing their pants.

"You're keeping that girl indefinitely?" Julien pressed.

"I'll do whatever the hell I want with her. You don't question me when I throw away an old pair of sneakers, don't give me shit about her."

Marco hissed. Julien glowered. "What the fuck? You're equating Zadie to raggedy-ass sneakers?"

I folded my arms. "Zadie is my property, nothing more. What don't you understand?"

Movement in the door had all three of us whipping our heads in that direction. Zadie was there, her cheeks flushed crimson, winding the hem of her shirt around her fingers. She looked all pretty and sad, and it churned a frothing ball of fire in my gut.

"Hey, I just wanted to let you know I'm ready to go when you are." Teeth clamped on her bottom lip. "I'll wait outside so you can finish up your conversation."

She wasted no time darting toward the front door, and Marco groaned. "If she cries, I'm gonna be mad uncomfortable, man."

"She knows where she stands in this situation." I refused to be apologetic for anything I said. It wasn't like I hadn't said the exact same thing to Zadie's face. "If she cries, it won't be from anything I said."

"Mad uncomfortable," Marco muttered.

Julien shook his head. "You definitely didn't deserve that lemon bar."

My fists tightened. This was finished. It was time to spill some blood.

· · ● ● ● ● ● ● · · ·

Reno ran fights in his warehouses. They were big, hyped up, and mostly illegal. Like the rest of his businesses, he'd inherited the fights from our uncle, along with the cops he paid to look the other way. That wasn't to say he hadn't been raided—he absolutely had—but evidence managed to get lost, and charges were always dropped. Illegal fight rings were the least of Reno's crimes, and they weren't a high priority for Savage River's law enforcement.

The first time I stepped in a ring had been by force. When I was sixteen, Reno had been pissed at me for something trivial, and my punishment was going head to head with a thirty-year-old wall of solid muscle. I'd gotten my ass handed to me. My nose still didn't sit right, and my jaw creaked when I opened my mouth too wide, but I fucking loved the rush of it. I'd gotten addicted, even having the shit pounded out of me. Since that first fight, I'd trained, and had gotten stronger and faster. Now, I chose my opponents and when I fought. Tonight was my first in a month.

I needed it.

Cold fury had settled in my belly, and nothing I did would dissipate it. My limbs were jittery, needing action. My muscles were primed for exertion. Walking inside the warehouse, which was now an arena, and smelling the familiar scents of bodies, dirt, and old, coppery blood got my head swimming.

Julien and Marco were slightly in front of me with Zadie tucked between them. Julien had his hand on her shoulder. Touching my pet. Maybe it was in a friendly way, but friendly was unacceptable, especially after the way he'd been bucking against my ownership of Zadie over the course of the week.

"Zadie," I barked, and her shoulders jumped. "Come here."

She tipped her head up to Julien, as if asking his permission, and that was not acceptable. He very much fucking knew that, which was why he pushed her toward me without sparing her a glance. I took her hand in mine, the softness of it making a crack in my anger. Once I had her and Julien didn't, I held her gently and slowed my pace so she didn't have to scamper in her heels.

"I'm fighting tonight. Your job is to help get me ready, show me your pretty face while I'm fighting, and be there after I win to cool me down." We trailed around the ring, which was nothing more than a roped off diamond in the center of the room. When a fighter went down, he ate concrete. It'd been a while since I'd tasted it, but it wasn't easy to forget.

It was early, so the stands hadn't filled, but there were already people around. Some stopped to greet me and my boys, others nodded with respect. Marco went off to talk to someone he knew, and Julien stayed on the other side of Zadie. I wasn't happy with him, but at least I could be certain he'd keep her safe while I was in the ring.

"I have to watch the fight?" she asked.

"Yes." I peered down at her. She'd put on makeup for this. Lipstick a shade or two darker than her natural color. Something gray swept across her eyes, making them unnaturally big and bright. Something shiny above her cheekbones, pink on her cheeks. It was pretty, sexy, classy, and I had to fight the unexplainable urge to grab a towel and wash it all off. "That's part of why I brought you here. I want to hear you cheering for me while I fight. I want that sweet voice to get as loud as I know it can."

Her hand stiffened in mine. I only held her tighter. "Shut up, Amir."

I chuckled. "That wasn't so sweet, little mama."

"I'm not always sweet," she replied.

"Good. That's mine."

On the other side of the arena, behind a set of bleachers, was an entrance to what had once been offices but were now makeshift dressing rooms. Mine was empty, with only a couple chairs, a table, a stack of clean towels, and a few bottles of water.

A couple of the other fighters took my appearance as an invitation to come inside and socialize. It was normal for me. I never had a problem with it. But Zadie was with me tonight.

I wanted her to have space from the hardened men who took part in Reno's fights. Men like me. I let her move away from me to take a seat in the corner of the room when I got into it with a pair of guys I'd fought and defeated multiple times. They were decent fighters and always presented a challenge. Got me just the right amount of bloody, but not enough to win.

"Yo, my boy." Reno sauntered into the room, his two guards at his back.

I moved forward, clasped his hand, and patted him on the back. "S'up, man. How's it looking out there?"

He nodded, the ice in his ears glinting in the light. Reno had taken to wearing custom-made suits and oversized diamond stud earrings. He looked good, but incredibly douchey at the same time. Probably because he was all of twenty-four with snakeskin loafers he wore without socks. It was a look...or something, but I wasn't a fan. The Reno I grew up with, the soccer playing, grubby punk kid, would have taken one look at grown-up Reno and laughed his ass off.

"All good, man. How're you feeling, brother?" He raised his brows, and I heard the real question. Was I going to win him a shitload of money tonight?

"Feeling loose and ready." I rolled my shoulders and flexed my fingers. I had some time, but yeah, I'd be ready.

"Good, good. Just don't take him down too early. Let him get in there. Give them a show."

He was asking me to take some hits so the fight wasn't over too soon. It was an easy request for him to make when it wasn't his body taking the blows. But I'd never minded a little bit of pain, not in the ring or out of it.

"I can make that happen."

With a sharp nod, Reno's focus shifted to a spot in the room behind me. From the glimmer in his eyes, I knew exactly what he was seeing.

"Who's that sweet little thing you're hiding in the corner, Amir?" he asked.

I turned, holding my hand out. "Zadie. Come."

She pushed forward and rose from her seat. My back was turned to him, but Reno's groan couldn't be mistaken. I saw what he saw. Zadie had ditched her girly little skirts for a pair of black skinny jeans that hugged her thick thighs, round hips, and ass, and cinched high on her waist. When she walked on her high heels, those round hips swayed. I could say with certainty she wasn't even doing it on purpose, but she was fucking doing it.

She wore a pale-blue T-shirt on top, with a low *V*, and two long necklaces that kept dipping between her tits—full, plush tits that were another taste I'd never, *ever* forget. And with her soft, chestnut hair cascading down her shoulders and back in loose waves, Zadie had the modern pinup thing going with her own achingly sweet spin.

Reno liked flash, girls like Vanessa. Zadie wasn't anything like Vanessa. She was stunningly beautiful, though. Her beauty was quiet, but it was unmissable. The thing that drove me most crazy about her was she had no fucking idea what she looked like. She didn't see the heads she turned or men she left on their asses. She'd wrapped up Julien and Marco within days, and my boys weren't the kind to get wrapped up.

So, yeah, I saw what Reno saw and knew my brother well enough not to like him seeing what was mine. Even if Zadie was only my pet, she was still mine, not open for the taking.

Zadie came to me, and I wrapped my arm around her shoulders, tucking her to my side.

Reno's lids went half-mast, and his nostrils flared like he was trying to inhale her from three feet away.

"Zadie, this is my brother, Reno. Reno, my girl." She went still, and her little gasp was audible.

Reno gave Zadie a long, slow once-over. "She's yours?"

I inclined my chin. "She's mine. My girl." Zadie's arm circled my waist, and she pressed in deeper to my side. Yeah, she was smart, choosing me as the lesser of two evils. Reno would tear her apart like tissue paper. It was just who he was.

That was why I'd claimed her, right here, right now. If Zadie hadn't been mine, Reno would have sunk his teeth into her so fast, she wouldn't have known it had happened until he'd ripped a chunk out of her. He would have seen her as ripe for the picking—and he would have picked. A little power in him, and Reno had become insatiable. But beneath it all, he was still my brother, and he respected me enough to leave those who were mine be. That had only been Marco and Julien. Until now. I'd added Zadie to that list, whether either of us wanted it.

"All right, all right. Nice." The corners of his mouth tipped. "Vanessa's going to shit herself when she sees you with her."

I scoffed. "Vanessa was *never* my girl."

Reno chuckled. "I fucking hope not, since I had my dick in her last weekend. That would have been awkward." His eyes slid to Zadie. "Nice to meet you, *mami chula*. Take care of my brother, all right? I'm watching."

"It's nice to meet you," Zadie replied softly.

Reno grinned lasciviously at me. "Oh shit, you landed a shy girl?" He clapped his hands. "I fucking love it. Bet you she gets wild when you get her alone. I'm proud of you, baby brother."

He wagged a finger at Zadie. "Let's hope you're Amir's good luck charm so he can make bank for me tonight. I'm counting on you to do his body good, shorty."

A few more words, and Reno was out, probably to make his way around to all the rooms to hold court like the king he saw himself as.

As soon as he left the room, I turned on Zadie, holding both her shoulders. "When I'm fighting, you don't go anywhere by yourself. You need to stay with Marco and Julien. I can't worry about you when I'm up there."

Her head tilted, sending a mass of curls over her shoulder. "Why would you worry about me?" Her nose crinkled. "*Don't* worry. I don't plan on wandering around out there on my own. I'm smarter than that."

Nodding, I let her go. "Remember that. Now, I have to get prepped for my bout. Take a seat. When I need you, I'll let you know."

Marco handed me a bottle of water and three painkillers. No matter if I won or lost, I was going to hurt later. Better to have some meds loaded into my system before I needed them.

Zadie watched the whole time I went through my rituals. The pills, pushups, oiling my skin, more pushups. I didn't need her there, but her presence stoked the fire that always burned in my belly when she was around. That, I could use.

I'd take that fire to the man who thought it was wise to step in the ring with me and burn that motherfucker to the ground.

CHAPTER EIGHT

Zadie

JULIEN AND MARCO WERE my bodyguards for the evening. They didn't have to worry about me running away. First, I couldn't get very far in heels. Second, and more important- ly, the crowd was downright scary. Ninety-percent men, they leaked testosterone like a dripping faucet. The few women I saw were perched on the lap of one of the leaky men, boobs out, legs long, hair blonde, makeup sultry. I was thinking this was just another place I didn't fit in, then Julien pushed me into a chair in the front row before taking his seat beside mine.

"Can I keep my eyes closed the whole time?" I asked.

Marco leaned into my other side. "Nah. Amir wants you watching."

"Why?"

Marco's dark-brown eyes beat into mine. Every time I thought I'd worn him down, his guard went back up, and it was like we were complete strangers all over again. Granted, I barely knew anything about him other than he was an English major and really liked my lemon bars, but sometimes he cracked and grinned at me, and I wondered if we could be something like friends. His steely walls never stayed down for long, though. And they were high as ever tonight.

"Do pets get to ask questions? Your owner wants you to watch, so you watch," he intoned, then flicked his attention to his cell.

Properly put in my place, I took in my surroundings from beneath my lashes, careful not to make eye contact with anyone. I landed on Reno on the other side of the ring, one girl in his lap, another hanging off his shoulder. Two very large men in black suits flanked him, and from their somber expressions, I wondered if they'd ever smiled a day in their lives.

Reno glanced my way just as I was studying him. When he caught me, his mouth lifted into a smarmy little smile, then he licked his bottom lip and winked. I held in my shudder, tucked my hair behind my ear, and attempted to play it off like I hadn't noticed him. Instinct told me I *really* didn't want Reno's attention.

From my other side, Julien grazed my arm, drawing my gaze back to his. "He's not going to get hurt. Not anything major, at least."

My lips pursed. "And his opponent?"

His mouth twitched. "Not the same story for him. Never is. Are you actually worried about a stranger?"

"I'm not sure if worried is the right word. I just don't think I'll enjoy watching two men brutalize each other." I tapped my foot on the concrete floor. "And from the front row, no less."

Julien clicked his tongue against his teeth. "Yeah, I get that, baby girl. But Amir wanted you here, and since you're his, this is where you're going to be."

I released a long exhale, accepting this was my fate. "I won't like it, but I'll be fine." And I would. I'd faced worse than watching the man who'd held me hostage get pummeled—hopefully—or pummel someone else—less hopefully.

Amir's fight was second on the docket. I closed my eyes through the first one, which didn't last as long as I'd feared it would. But by the time one man was declared the winner, my stomach was in knots and I had to swallow again and again to stop myself from retching. The *sounds* of violence made me ill. Flesh slapping flesh. Moans of pain, grunts of breath being forced out by angry fists. And at the end, the chilling snap of a bone breaking followed by an animalistic squeal I would never, ever unhear.

Julien had taken my trembling hand in his at some point during the fight. I clung hard to him, attempting to get my heartbeat under control. I abhorred violence. I always had. It came from my dad. My mom was the one who'd killed bugs for us while we hid.

Julien was still holding it when Amir came jogging out from between the stands, his arms raised above his head as the crowd stomped and cheered. There had to be a few hundred people here, but Amir's gaze landed on me, and his midnight eyes hardened to steel when he saw where my hand was.

"Shit," Julien muttered, quickly taking his hand off mine.

I wanted to tell Julien not to worry. I would explain to Amir about the bone breaking and my shaking hands, but Amir's blatant fury had me in a choke hold. My throat closed in on itself, and not one sound would come out.

His opponent emerged next. He was similar in size to Amir, but older and more grizzled, with a flattened nose and tattoos that looked like they'd been done with a safety pin and ink from a ballpoint pen. For the first time, I was actually worried for Amir.

A girl with silky black hair, a tight pink minidress, and platform heels strutted up to Amir, leaned over the rope, and gave him a kiss on the cheek. He glared at me while she touched him, rubbing his shoulders like she was his personal trainer warming him up for the fight. Then he whispered something in her ear, making her press her boobs to his back and smile bright.

Beside me, Marco shook his head. "Vanessa doesn't give up."

"It doesn't look like he wants her to give up," I blurted.

Marco turned to me, giving me a slow, amused grin. "Kitty's got claws. Like that, Z."

"I don't have claws," I murmured, doubting he heard me over the roar of the crowd. The referee had stepped in the middle of the ring, calling for Amir and his opponent to meet in the middle. Amir gave me a long, sharp look before turning his back and walking to bump taped-up fists with the other fighter.

My insides were in achy knots. I'd rather Amir throw away a thousand of my dinners than sit through this. I hated every second of it, and it was only going to get worse.

After the referee spoke to both men, he stepped back, and the fight began. I kept my eyes open but unfocused on the action until both Marco and Julien hissed. My eyes shot up to the ring. Amir was on his toes, dancing back from Grizzled, a trickle of blood coming from his eyebrow.

Oh no. I did not like that.

Marco leaned into me. "He's going to want to hear you cheering, Z. I know you hate it, but you gotta let him hear that voice."

"I don't think I can," I rasped.

He reached around me, gripping my nape hard. Walls up, Marco's voice was even harder than his hold. "Yeah you can. Pets do as they're told, don't they?"

"Stop touching me, Marco." I turned and met his eyes, giving him some of his hard back. "Don't touch me."

After a long beat, his hand fell away. "Raise that voice, Z, and I won't have to touch you again."

I turned back to the fight. Everything had changed. Amir was in charge now, sending Grizzled back to the ropes. He landed blow after blow on Grizzled's sides and belly. The muscles in Amir's back flexed and strained under his artful, athletic movements. He was so light on his feet, when Grizzled came after him, Amir dodged most of his hits easily.

I clapped for him first and quietly said his name. There was no way he heard me, but I couldn't put any more power into it. I was too tense, too afraid, and nothing going on in front of me made me want to cheer.

But I felt Marco's eyes on me and the pressure I was under. Amir was beating a man to a pulp, and for some reason, he needed my voice to encourage him to do it even harder.

My heart stopped when Grizzled seemed to have gotten a second wind. He came after Amir, landing a solid right hook to his jaw. Amir spun, and for a split second, our eyes connected.

I cupped my hands around my mouth and yelled at him, because in that moment, I didn't want him to lose. "Come on, Amir! You can do it!"

He only let Grizzled land one more punch before he began to systematically destroy him. Punching, punching, punching until Grizzled was bloody and wobbling. It was brutal, interminable, and breathtaking all at once. Amir's golden skin shined with sweat, but he showed no sign of flagging. He bounced on his toes, jabbing, dodging Grizzled's few feeble punches, and once more, took a split second to sweep his eyes over me.

Then he threw a punch that made Grizzled spin like a ballerina, making it clear this match was finished. The referee jumped back into the ring, speaking to Grizzled, perhaps asking him if he was done. He nodded, and the ref grabbed Amir's hand, holding it in the air.

Marco and Julien jumped up, cheering at the top of their lungs, so I followed suit. Well, I didn't cheer at the top of my lungs, but I yelled along with them, calling Amir's name.

He looked right at me, sweat and blood mingling on his face and bare torso. His hair was even darker, and his expression was feral. Something stirred low in my belly, and this time, it wasn't fear. I shouldn't have found him attractive...well, ever, but especially not now. Not when he'd just viciously attacked another man, even if the other man had signed up for it. But dear god, there was something so primal about the way he'd fought and now stood victorious, his legs spread wide, his sleek chest rising and falling in rapid pants, that made me press my thighs together and stifle a whimper.

I swore he saw my reaction to him. He hadn't taken his eyes off me, and there was something telling in the twitch of his lips as he stared. I was in his snare until Reno rushed the ring, taking his brother's attention for himself.

Amir left the ring a minute or two later. Julien, Marco, and I followed. The door to his dressing room was open. Amir stood on the far side of the room, wiping his face with a white towel, leaving streaks of blood. When we entered, he only had eyes for me.

"Everyone out. Zadie, stay," Amir growled.

The traitors who'd had my back during the fight were ghosts as soon as Amir had told them to vanish—another reminder

Julien and Marco weren't my friends. The click of the door shutting behind me served to drive the point home. They'd locked me in here with him.

He prowled toward me, hands flexing at his sides, something wild in his glare, like he was more animal than man. Heart hammering, I backed away until I hit wall. He kept coming until his bare chest was flush with mine. His hand came to my throat, ringing it in a firm circle.

"You were holding his hand." He dipped down, touching his nose to mine. "What the fuck are you doing, Zadie? Why are you making me crazy?"

"I didn't mean—"

"Fuck what you mean." His hand tightened, leaving me just enough room to suck in a breath. "I wanted to jump out of the ring and drag my best friend into it so I could beat the shit out of him. Because *you* touched him. *You* let him hold your hand. And then...and then I hear your sweet voice yelling my name, and it's all I can do not to kill that bitch so I can get to you. What the fuck are you doing, Zadie?"

Amir squeezed my throat harder as his mouth crashed into mine. When I gasped for air, he slid his tongue between my parted lips and licked me all over, owning me, claiming every inch with violent lashes.

My nails dug into his shoulders hard enough for him to let up on his grip. He continued his assault, his kisses anything but loving or passionate. This was his alternative to hitting me. His hard, unyielding mouth was my punishment.

Somewhere in the back of my mind, I knew I hadn't done anything wrong to deserve punishment, but my inner protests were weak. Because Amir's mouth on mine made everything else fade.

His hands were just as furious, squeezing my breasts, my butt, my hips. Over my clothes first, then diving under, rolling my nipples between his fingers and shoving a hand down the back of my panties.

He tore his mouth from mine, panting hot breaths against my lips. "Down on your knees, little mama."

"Wha—?" My mind was at war with itself. Desire and logic clashed with one another. I knew Amir's mouth. He'd used it in a different way on me, a passionate, giving way. My body was remembering that and responding to him now, even though all he was doing was taking and passion had been replaced by violence.

"On your knees. Show me who you belong to." He pressed on my shoulders until I was sinking down to the rough concrete floor. With his hand on the back of my head, he held me steady while he rubbed his clothed erection along my lips.

Feeling him like that was a cold bucket of water on my head. Panic clogged my throat. I didn't want this. I wasn't his. I didn't want him in my mouth. Not this way. Not with concrete cutting into my skin through my jeans, dozens of people milling about just outside the thin door, and Amir too blind with anger and adrenaline to even know who I was.

I peered up at him, tears welling in my eyes. "No," I whispered, pushing at his hips.

He rocked his erection against my lips again and held my face there for a long beat until he groaned. And I knew then I had to find my voice. I'd come to Amir for protection, not to be used and ruined. I wouldn't let him take another piece after Drew had already taken so much.

"Amir," I slapped at his stomach and shoved off him, falling back on my butt, "I don't want this. I said no!"

I didn't scream, but he heard me. He nearly leapt back from me as though I'd physically hurt him. His eyes were crazed as they swept over me huddled on the ground.

His head jerked to the door. "Get out, Zadie." His tone was so low and threatening, it sent ice through my veins. "Get the fuck out of here right now."

I scrambled to my feet and ran for the door, yanking it open and flinging myself into the hall. Julien was there, leaning against the opposite wall. My momentum sent me crashing into him. He held my arms, keeping me steady on my feet.

"Whoa, whoa, what's going on?" he soothed. "You okay?"

"I had to—" I bit my bottom lip to keep tears from flooding out and stop myself from saying what had gone down in that room. Julien wasn't my friend. He was Amir's. I had to keep telling myself that. "I'm fine. He's just in a bad mood and isn't so nice."

"Well..." heels clicked behind me, causing me to turn, "I can always turn his mood around."

Julien groaned at the pretty brunette in the pink dress pushing the door open. "Vanessa, Jesus, come on. Have some pride, dude."

She winked at me over her shoulder. "You might not want to stand there, babes. My man tends to get loud." Then she disappeared inside the room and closed the door behind her.

Spinning away from Julien, I fell against the wall next to him. He stroked the side of my hair in a way that told me if circumstances were different, he *would've* been my friend too.

"We'll roll out soon," he said.

"Sure." As soon as Amir was finished with my replacement. "I never want to come here again."

Julien held his hands up. "You're gonna have to talk to him about that."

I nodded, resigned, and suddenly achingly exhausted. "What a strange friendship, to have no power."

He shifted so he was in front of me, peering down. "That's bullshit. I have no say over what you and Amir agreed to. That's your thing, and I'm not interfering. The rest, though? Nah, we're equal. He knows if he tried to pull his dominance show on me, I'd piss on his bed and in his shoes to show him who the real king of the house is."

I sputtered. "Like an angry cat?"

Julien cocked a crooked grin. "Exactly. Cats are fucking terrifying."

A cacophony of crashes came from Amir's dressing room. Seconds later, the door was flung open and he stormed out, stony faced, with a hoodie and track pants now on. He charged by us without pause. Julien and I turned to each other, then back to where Amir had disappeared.

"Yeah, we gotta go." He raised his hand like he was going to touch me then dropped it. "Just stick by me, okay?"

Vanessa strode from the dressing room, a seriously pissed-off scowl on her pink, puffy lips. When she made eye contact with Julien, she flipped him off, then shot me a snarl before plowing her way down the hall in the opposite direction of Amir. Maybe she didn't appreciate his treatment either.

"Come on, Z." Julien pushed me ahead of him, keeping me there the whole way out of the warehouse. When we made it outside, he stepped away from me, giving me a wide berth like I was a leper.

Amir was leaning against the SUV Marco had driven us in, no one else around. They were all inside, watching the fights.

"Where's Marco?" I asked.

Julien shrugged. "Probably placing some bets on the next fight. Unlike you, he likes to watch grown men beat each other bloody."

Amir straightened as we approached, taking in the ridiculous distance Julien was keeping from me. Ignoring his foul expression, Julien clapped him on the shoulder and gave him a half hug.

"Nice job tonight, man. You had me worried for a second when Ishkov got in that jab to your temple at the beginning."

Amir handed him the keys. "Reno wanted a show. I gave him a show. Let's get out of here. I'm toast. Need a fucking drink then bed."

The ride back to campus mostly consisted of Julien making jokes, Amir grunting, and me shrinking in the back seat, wishing I'd never thought of this brilliant plan in the first place. I had no idea how I'd thought it would go, but not this. Never like this.

Julien pulled up to the curb in front of my dorm, and I hopped out as soon as it stopped moving, calling my thanks over my shoulder. When I started for the stairs, Amir was there in front of me, his arms folded across his chest.

"You okay?" He was gruff about it, but the fact he was asking took me aback.

I tucked my hair behind my ear. "I'm fine."

"I get jacked after fights. I had no business putting my hands on you." His midnight eyes gleamed, but there was no apology there.

"Okay," I whispered.

"Okay." He rocked back on his heels. "Go inside, Zadie."

"Good night, Amir."

It wasn't until I was walking down the hall to my room that I finally took a full breath. I was okay. Amir had manhandled me and scared me, but he hadn't hurt me. I was whole and un-harmed. My lungs inflated a little more with each affirmation I told myself.

They shriveled to dust when I got to my door and there were flowers and a note waiting for me.

"No, no, no," I hissed. "Not tonight."

With shaking hands, I scooped up the folded paper and twin daisies, taking them inside. Given it was Saturday night, Elena was out making trouble somewhere, and Helen was off with Theo, so I was alone. And for once, I was relieved.

I shoved the flowers deep in the kitchen trash can and took the note to my room. My hands were still trembling when I unfolded it.

Pretty girl, pretty girl
Won't you give me a whirl
You look right through me
But I'm determined for you to see
I can be the man for you
if you ditch the one you're talking to
     • *D*

With a strangled sob, I tucked the note in my drawer and threw myself face down on my bed. Why? Why did I have to be the one he fixated on? Couldn't he have found someone else?

I could've pinched myself for thinking that. I'd never want anyone else to go through what I did for the year Drew stalked me. These poems were child's play compared to the cow's heart speared with a kitchen knife he'd left on my doorstep. Or the time I'd tried to go on a date and he'd slashed the guy's tires. It was nothing compared to him showing up on my porch over and over and over until my mom wanted to move, my dad, the hippy pacifist, looked into buying a gun, and I turned so far inward, it took me another year to open up again.

I refused to curl up like a scared animal again. That was why I was with Amir. That was why I'd go back, even after tonight. I might not be a scared animal, but I was his pet, and for better or worse, he wanted me, so he'd keep me safe.

· · · · ● · ● · · ·

Amir held me as he tasted me. The first swipe of his tongue between my legs sent me to another plane. I should have been shy with him, but I was someone else. We were somewhere else, where only this bed and our bodies existed.

I touched his hair, and he growled, licking me even deeper, showing me in no uncertain terms how much he liked it. My fingers threaded through the soft spikes of black jutting from his scalp. His fingers dug into my thighs and ass, holding me open.

I should have said no one had ever done this to me before, but I thought he probably knew. He planted his tongue in my entrance, and it felt like he was planting his flag, claiming me as his.

I came so hard, stars flashed behind my eyelids. And then Amir was on me, holding me against his chest, nuzzling my neck, murmuring how beautiful and sexy and delicious I was. The exact right things I needed to hear after allowing myself to be so vulnerable with him.

His erection dug into my hip. I slid my hand down, pressing my palm against the bulge. He groaned into my throat, rocking his hips into my hand.

"I want you, Zadie." He cupped my throat, propping himself up so he could peer down at me.

"I want you too." I reached up to stroke the dark stubble on his cheeks.

He leaned into my hand, letting his eyelids fall halfway closed. "Let me feel you from the inside. Show me if your cunt is as soft and warm as the rest of you."

His harsh words, the way he gritted at me, should have sent me back to reality. But I liked his blunt desire. The way he wanted me was written all over him, and he did nothing to conceal it.

"I want you," I repeated.

Amir's phone chimed. With a sigh, he swiped it from my nightstand and held it above his head to read the text. I was angled so I could see the screen too.

Reno: *On my way to pick up the money myself. Bitch gonna learn her lesson tonight.*

Above it, maybe an hour ago, Amir had texted his brother Helen's location. Bile rose in my throat. Worry gnawed at me from every angle. Here was my crash to reality, and it was as painful as my bones cracking on the pavement.

With a long sigh, Amir switched off his phone and tossed it back on the nightstand. "I need to head out soon." Then he got on his knees and ran his hands down my sides, giving me a look of longing so intense, it took my breath away. "I could fuck you fast. Make it good for you and fucking great for me, because anything with this body would be great for me, but when I'm inside you, I want to take my time with you, and tonight isn't going to be that night."

I scooted back until I hit my headboard, pulling a pillow in front of me so I wasn't so exposed. "It's not?"

He shook his head, and with his eyes on mine, he adjusted his erection in his pants. "No, little mama. Not tonight. I'm gonna take your number with me, and we're gonna meet up when we both have the time to fuck until we get our fill. That's gonna be soon. You with me?"

I shook my head hard. "No. No, I'm sorry. I lost my mind for a while."

He jerked like he'd been hit. "You...lost your mind?"

"Yes. I lost my mind." What was going to happen to Helen? What kind of monster had he led to her? "I would never...not with you."

Even though he made me feel safe and forget every bad thing that had ever happened to me. Even though my body fit in his arms like I was made to be there. Even though I let him get closer to me than I had ever let any other man. Even though my heart would crack just a little bit more when he walked away.

Amir ran his hand over his mouth, his gaze drifting around my room until it came back to me, hard and unyielding. There was something else there too, but he shuttered it as quickly as it had appeared.

"Guess we both lost our minds." His eyes swept over me, and something like disgust curdled in his beautiful, dark features. "Can't stand girls like you. Can't fucking stand them."

Then he was off the bed, snagging his shirt and phone, and I was doing everything in my power to hold back my tears. I'd come so close to letting him be my first, and in many ways, he had been my first. What had I been thinking?

Amir wasn't some misunderstood rebel. He wasn't a soft-hearted criminal. He wasn't the white knight who'd swoop in and save the day. That wasn't the story I'd stepped into.

Amir was a villain, and I was the idiot girl who'd fallen for him so quickly, I had to stop myself from asking him to come back even as he walked away with my heart squashed under his boot.

He did turn back, but when he opened his mouth, I wished he hadn't. "You see me out, Zadie, around campus or otherwise, turn the other way. What happened here tonight was an exception. You come near me, I won't be nice."

I nodded. "I understand."

After a long look, my captor was gone, and I knew I'd never be the same.

I'd fallen for a villain, after all.

CHAPTER NINE

Zadie

SUNDAY MORNING, AMIR SENT me a text.

MyCaptor: *Take the day off.*

Monday and Tuesday, he sent me two more.

MyCaptor: *Don't need you today.*

MyCaptor: *Have a thing going today. Don't need you at the house. I'll let you know when I want you.*

"Oh my god, what's so fascinating on your phone?" Elena groaned, grabbing for it after I checked it for the tenth time.

"Nothing." I stuffed it in my messenger bag to rid myself of the temptation. "Sorry, I was just waiting to hear from my mom."

She picked the cheese out of her veggie wrap. "That's fine and all, but I'm needy, Zadie. If I don't have enough attention, I have a tendency to become destructive."

We were having dinner at a table Elena had chosen in the center of the dining hall, and more than one person continually glanced at her or out and out stared. After living with her for a semester, I already knew she was rarely without attention. One of the reasons I liked her was because she was unabashed about who she was, including the facets of her personality that many people—okay, most people—would consider flaws.

I offered her a grin. "Eli's coming to visit with my mom this weekend. I'll bring him by the suite. He'll give you all the attention you need."

She threw down her cheese. "Okay, no. I do have standards, and sixteen-year-olds do not meet them. Not that baby bro isn't adorable, but...no."

I giggled imagining the heartbreak Eli would go through if he knew Elena had called him adorable.

"Tell me what kind of attention you need then. My phone is gone, it's just you and me."

She tossed her wrap down then picked up her napkin to twist it between her fingers. "I'm thinking about breaking up with all my friends."

My smile fell away. "Okay..."

Her eyes met mine, and she must have seen my rising hurt, because she waved her hands in a flurry. "Oh my god, obviously I don't mean *you*. I have more couth than to sit across from you and share that I'm *thinking* of breaking up with you. If that time ever came, I'd go out in a blaze of glory, not over a crappy veggie wrap in the dining hall."

Before she could explain, Helen set her tray down on our table with Theo beside her, and their friend, Lock, on Theo's other side. Where Theo was handsome, Lock was rugged and built like a mountain. He looked like he belonged in a forest chopping down trees rather than the pristine, palm-tree-lined Savage U campus. They both made me nervous and too shy to do anything other than offer a brief smile.

"What's happening?" Helen asked. "I feel like we interrupted something."

Elena picked up her wrap again. "That's because you did. You could wait until we're done talking, snatch."

Helen flipped her off. "No one wants to hear your business, bitch."

Elena arched a brow. "Then why are you sitting here?"

"Z's here. I can't leave her alone with you for long or you'll turn her into one of your pod people friends." Helen shuddered. "Living with one of you is my limit."

Elena unrolled her wrap completely and began to dismantle it. "Do you think living with you is a dream? You could *try* not to corrupt Zadie. I saw you teaching her how to make shanks out of my toothbrush."

Helen snorted. "Didn't I tell you toothbrushes make terrible shanks?"

"Yeah." All eyes swung to me. "It wasn't your toothbrush, El. It was actually your comb, and I was the one who asked Helen for a tutorial."

Theo was the first to crack, slapping the table as he laughed. Lock let a deep rumble of amusement roll through him. Helen grinned at me, and Elena sent a sharp elbow jab to my ribs followed by a kiss to my head.

For a girl who'd completely stepped away from forming any attachments after Drew took over my life, it was a little overwhelming...but nice. Nice to feel normal, liked, make them laugh with silly, makeshift prison weapon jokes.

"Anyway," Elena tossed her shiny blonde hair behind her shoulder, "I was telling Zadie I am done with my friends. They're just..." She made a snarly face.

"Is that brand-new information?" Helen asked.

Elena tore off a piece of her wrap. "Obviously not. They're vapid and boring half the time, but our parents are friends and blah, blah, blah. *Boring.* I just can't do it anymore."

"Why not?" I asked.

Elena blended in with her pretty blonde friends. She had the same money, social status, clothes, looks, but to me, she stood apart. Not that she wasn't capable of evil. But beneath it all, she was good. It was just that there were layers of thorns and brambles to get to that part of her. The other girls, at least the ones I'd met and lived with freshman year, didn't have that same core. I hoped she was beginning to see that too.

"I was at this dinner thing with some of them...actually, it was a dinner with some guys from your frat, Theo."

Theo raised his hands. "I just live there. I'm not one of them."

Elena lifted a shoulder and went on. "Well, they're guys you know at any rate. They were talking about some stupid movie called *Dogfight* where they throw a party and the guys compete to invite the least desirable date. I don't know, I haven't watched it."

Helen groaned. "Don't tell me they're going to throw a party like that."

"That's their plan. It was just...gross. The whole thing." Elena shuddered, and my stomach flipped. Those poor, poor girls. "What really got me was the girls I was with were laughing about it and cooing over these assholes like they were so fucking clever, when really, they were just cruel. Like, I'm not usually rah-rah sisterhood or anything, but are we really at the point where we're cheering guys on for misogyny?"

"Careful, girlie, next step is burning your bra," Helen said dryly.

Elena cupped her breasts and gave them a jiggle. "Oh, god, can I? Let the tits breathe."

"Which guys?" Theo brought the subject back around.

Elena flicked her fingernails. "The usual suspects. Ryan, Sean, Dylan, Deacon, Owen...a few others. I didn't write down names or anything, but I think most of the house was involved."

Lock made a rumbling sound, but he didn't say anything. He studied his food as he methodically shoveled it into his mouth, pointedly not looking at anyone, but we were all looking at him.

"What's on your mind, man?" Theo slapped his arm.

Lock swallowed, wiped his mouth, then slowly turned his head to Theo. "Nothing."

Theo folded his arms. "Nothing? Right." Then he addressed us. "At the end of the semester, I'm moving out of the frat house and getting a place with Lock. So yeah, my ties will be cut with those guys. I encourage you to do the same, El."

She folded her napkin into a triangle. "Believe me, I'm done with those boys. The girls will be more of a slow extraction." Then she grabbed my arm. "We should move in together too. Abby asked me, but I'll just tell her you and Helen needed a third roommate, and since I felt sorry for you guys, I agreed."

Helen's head jerked back. "I did not agree to that."

"But it's a great idea, right?"

"No," Helen replied. "I can't afford it, so no."

Elena pursed her lips, then her eyes alighted. "We'll pay on a sliding scale. We'll each contribute based on our parents' income. Equity, babes. I'm all about the equity."

"You could rent a house by ours, baby," Theo suggested.

Lock pushed back from the table so abruptly, his chair made a loud screech. "I'm out." Then he lumbered off, his tray looking like a playing card in his big hand.

Elena's narrowed eyes followed his wide back and something about her deflated when he disappeared. It was strange, but now that I thought of it, Lock never hung around when Elena was nearby.

I touched her hand. "I'll live with you, if you're serious. I'm kind of over the dorm."

Helen sat up straight. "What? No. I'm not leaving you alone with her."

I met her gaze and raised a brow. "I guess you're going to have to live with us."

Helen sighed and let her head drop onto her arms. "God, I guess so."

· · · ● ● · ● · ● · ·

By Wednesday afternoon, I hadn't received a text from Amir at all, so I decided to take that to mean he still didn't want me at the house. It was just as well, since I had an exam coming up. I headed straight to the library after my last class, intent on burrowing in and studying for the next few hours.

I found a spot on one of the upper floors in a low traffic area that was quieter than any other part of the library. There were a few students at tables divided to make cubbies. I snagged a cubby on the end of the table, the girl beside me hunched over her computer with headphones covering her ears.

I read, highlighted, and took notes. Then I went back and quizzed myself. Doing well in school was important to me, but it didn't come naturally. I had to work my butt off for my grades. Because of everything with my stalker, my grades slipped my senior year of high school. I'd only made it into Savage U by the skin of my teeth. Having a mom, dad, and stepdad who were alumni also helped. A lot, I suspected. But that meant I didn't take being here for granted. Slacking off wasn't an option. Even if I could, I planned to one day work as an accountant where precision mattered.

Fortunately for me, I took pleasure in studying. I liked sitting in the cool library, snuggled up in my hoodie, with nothing to distract me. I relished the moment information clicked and settled in my brain. And there was nothing better than getting my exam back with a big fat *A* on it.

I had accepted I was a nerd a long time ago. I didn't try to fight it.

After a couple hours, I needed to stretch my legs, so I left my stuff and took a walk through the aisles, inhaling the delicious scent of old books. Once my blood warmed up and my mind cleared a little, I wandered back to my cubby. It was evening now, and many of the people who'd been studying when I'd come in had cleared out, including the girl who'd been sitting beside me.

It wasn't until I sat down again that I noticed a folded piece of paper on top of my notebook. My stomach instantly churned with dread.

It might be nothing.

It was silly to try to convince myself of that when all I had to do to find out was unfold it. I just...didn't want to.

I did anyway.

Zadie, Zadie, Zadie, can't you see
Your bright blue eyes hypnotize me
I just like your hips that sway
Guess that's why I follow when you run away
Zadie, Zadie, Zadie, can't you see

Your soft, thicc thighs hypnotize me
I just love your sweet girl ways
Guess I'll show you one of these days
  • *D*

I would have laughed at how terrible the poem was—and how un-Drew-like it was—if I hadn't been so utterly horrified. Someone was here, watching me, even now. The quiet library, filled with corners and blind spots and shadows, suddenly felt ominous instead of peaceful. I threw my things in my messenger bag as quickly as possible.

"Zadie." A quiet whisper, barely audible, but I heard it. Someone was calling for me. God, I wasn't even sure this was Drew anymore. Did it matter? "Zadie, wait."

My heart pounded with terror. I had to force my leaden legs to move. I would not be the dumb girl who waited around for the bad guy to show up—especially not when the bad guy was *telling* me to wait.

Black closed in on the edges of my vision. Panic disoriented me. I rushed down an aisle, only to come to a dead end. This wasn't the way to the exit. Where was I? Someone was behind me, footsteps approaching.

I turned, forcing my feet to move faster, even with my chest feeling like it was caving in. Why? Why were they doing this to me? Was this Drew? Was it someone else? Was I losing my mind?

No, no, the poem was still in my hand. It was real. And my name, I heard it. I hadn't imagined it. Someone was coming for me. Someone wanted me afraid. They wanted to get to me. And now, I was cornered. The only thing in front of me was more walls, and to my left and right were endless rows of books. God, where was the exit?

I can't breathe. I can't breathe. I need a door. Someone, please, give me a door.

Sweat beaded on my forehead and upper lip. If someone was coming behind me, I couldn't hear them over the galloping rhythm of my terrified heart.

Ahead of me was my answer. I lunged for the door, throwing myself inside and yanking it closed behind me. This wasn't an exit. I was standing in blackness, but the heavy smell of cleaning products told me I was in a closet. There was most likely a light switch somewhere along the wall, but I didn't dare move. If I stayed here, if I didn't make a peep, they wouldn't find me. They'd go away, and I'd be safe. At least for now. I'd find the exit. I'd call Helen or Theo or even Lock. Yeah, Lock was big. He'd walk me back to my dorm. He'd scare anyone away who meant to harm me.

I just had to be quiet. Only for a little while.

My reassurances meant nothing when the doorknob jiggled. My hands flew to my face, as if it were some type of protection, but it was all I could do.

He'd found me. After all this time, he had me where he wanted me, trapped. I might as well have given myself to him on a silver platter.

"Zadie, what the fuck?"

My heart stopped. The door clicked shut. My knees turned to liquid, and I fell.

CHAPTER TEN

Amir

IN THE PITCH BLACK, I caught Zadie a second before she hit the ground. When my arms clasped around her, she squealed a tortured, strangled sound that barely made it out of her throat.

"No," she moaned. Her hands made weak claws, hitting and scratching at my chest with kitten-like strength. Her entire body was racked with tremors.

"Zadie, come on, mama. You're okay." I held her tight against my chest, instinct telling me that was what she needed, even though I had no clue what had her so fucking spooked.

A keening noise that shot me straight through my sternum came from her, and she kept fighting, even as her hits grew weaker.

"Listen to me." I threaded my fingers in the back of her hair. "Fucking listen. I'm not going to hurt you. No one's going to hurt you. Talk to me. Tell me what's going on."

"No, no, no, no. Please no." Her voice was tiny and pleading.

Jesus Christ, had I done this to her? I knew I'd fucked up, but was this the result?

"You want me to let you go? Tell me if you want me to let you go."

"No," she cried, clinging to me instead of fighting me.

"Okay." I lowered my forehead to the top of her head and squeezed my eyes shut. "Okay, Zadie. I need you to breathe. You're safe. I'm not going to hurt you. No one's going to hurt you. You're as safe as can be. We're in a closet in the library. You're safe. No one's going to hurt you. Breathe for me. Nice and slow."

I kept going, repeating myself. Her shallow pants had gone deeper, slowing incrementally. Her hands had opened, sliding to clasp around my neck. I no longer had to hold up her entire weight. She still leaned on me, and I liked that, so I wanted her to keep doing it. Quivers ran through her muscles. Her face was shoved against my chest. But she was calming and letting me help her get there.

"You know where you are?" I asked softly.

She sucked in a shuddering breath. "Closet, in the library."

"You know who I am?"

"Amir."

"Are you safe?"

She made a choking sound. "I don't know."

"You're safe." My fingers slid through the back of her hair in a rhythmic motion. "Am I going to hurt you?"

"I—I don't know."

I shook my head and rubbed my lips on her crown. "I'm not going to hurt you. No one is."

"You're not going to hurt me," she repeated.

"That's right. I'm not going to hurt you. No one is."

"You said that," she whispered.

"I need you to believe it. Do you believe it?"

"I believe it right now."

The waver in her answer brought me to a stop. I grew still as I turned it over in my mind. She either believed I was going to hurt her or someone else was. Quite possibly both.

"What were you running from? What had you so spooked?"

She shook her head and whimpered, "He's out there."

"Who? Someone bothering you? You tell me and I'll take care of it."

"You can't."

"Zadie." I gripped her jaw and pushed her head back. In the dark, I could barely make out the shape of her face, but if I knew her—and I fucking did—her puffy bottom lip was poking out in a pout. "I'll give you that since you don't know the things I've done and *will* do to keep those I consider mine safe."

"And I'm yours?"

"You know you are."

"A pet." Her chin trembled in my hold. I pressed my thumb to the center of it, holding her like that until she stopped shaking.

"A pet I care to keep in one piece and safe." Bending, I ghosted my lips over hers, then whispered a vow into her mouth. "You lay it on me, I'll do what I need to do so I don't ever find you hiding in a supply closet again, shaking like a fucking leaf because you're so scared."

She didn't answer. Not that question at least.

"Why are you here, Amir?"

"Finding you. You didn't show. Did you forget about our deal?"

A heavy sigh deflated her. "I didn't hear from you. I didn't think you wanted me there."

"Julien and Marco are starved. They miss you."

"You didn't tell me to come."

My thumb stroked the jut of her chin. "I didn't tell you not to, which means I wanted your pretty ass at my house, cooking in my kitchen. Do you know how angry I was when four o'clock came and went and my pet didn't appear?"

"No, I don't."

"*So* angry, Zadie. I had to come find you."

"I wasn't hiding. I mean, I wasn't then."

"Are you going to tell me why you're hiding now?"

A tremor racked her body, and even though she was already in my arms, she stumbled against me. "I need to go home."

"I'll take you, but you're not leaving this closet until you tell me what the fuck is going on."

She slid her hands down from my neck to my chest and tried to shove me back. It did no good. "Please, let me go. I don't want to do this."

"Start talking and I'll let you go."

"*Please*. I just need to be in my room. I need to go."

If I took her to her room, she'd be locked away and I'd never get my answers. Aside from that, I had a visceral need to keep her close until I made sure she was okay and I found a way to kill the thing that had made her this afraid.

"Here's what's going to happen, Zadie. We're going to leave this fucking closet, grab your things, and go to my car. Once we're in there, locked and secure, you're going to tell me everything, then I'll decide if I want to drive you home or take you back to my place so you can do all the chores you've been slacking on this week."

She gasped, then a beat later, slapped my chest. "I haven't been slacking. You told me not too—"

I covered her mouth with my hand. "I'm fucking with you. Needed to see that spine of steel. It's still there—that's how I know you're going to be all right."

With little protest, Zadie allowed me to lead her out of the closet. She stuck close to me, gripping the back of my shirt while I had an arm circling her shoulders. We found her bag abandoned in one of the aisles I'd followed her down, a folded piece of paper beside it. Once she had both, we made our way out of the library to the parking lot behind it. The whole time, Zadie's body shook, and her head swiveled right and left, checking her surroundings.

Some fucking punk had scared her tonight. They obviously had no idea who she belonged to. This would not stand.

In my car, Zadie hugged her bag to her chest and clutched the folded paper in her hand. I blasted the heat in order to warm her up and smooth out her trembling muscles.

"What's on the paper?" The way she was holding it, I figured it had to do with what was going on.

"A poem," she croaked.

I stilled. "A poem someone wrote for you?"

"Yes. He left it for me when I left my desk for a few minutes."

I plucked the paper from her hand and unfolded it. It took me a second to wrap my head around what I was reading, then it made me equal parts amused and pissed off.

I hit the paper against my open palm. "Do you know what this is?"

"Bad poetry?"

I snorted a laugh. "If you consider Biggie Smalls a bad poet, then yeah."

Her brow furrowed. "I don't follow."

"Whoever wrote this must be a fan of nineties' rap. They reworded Notorious B.I.G.'s song, "Hypnotize." It's fucking awful, but no doubt that's what they were going for. You have no idea who left this?"

Her teeth dug into her bottom lip. "I thought I knew, but now, I'm not so sure."

Leaning closer, I gripped her chin, tilting her face back and forth. "This isn't the first."

She shook her head. "No. But tonight...he was there. I heard him calling my name. That was when I ran away."

"You said you thought you knew who left it. Tell me who."

"Um..." she shoved a hand into the side of her hair, "I don't know if you remember when I told you I had a stalker. I'm sure you don't, but—"

"How could I forget that?" At that moment, I'd wanted to bend time, travel back to before Zadie met that kid and put a bullet in his brain so none of the bullshit he pulled on her had ever happened.

"Dragon slayer," she whispered.

"Yeah." Bracing my elbow on the console, I got in her face. "Are you saying he's here? He's leaving you bad poetry and not back in Oregon...I don't know, chopping wood and shit?"

"I thought so." She rubbed her lips together. "I've gotten a few. They're all kind of innocuous. I wouldn't have thought much about them, except Drew used to leave me poems all the time. His were typed on special homemade paper, though. And they were...well, they were sick but well written."

"You're shitting me."

Zadie's eyes widened with alarm. Given she'd been having a panic attack less than an hour ago, I probably should have gone easier on her, but she drove me out of my goddamn mind.

"No, I'm not."

"You're *shitting* me."

"I'm not." Her voice quivered.

"This guy has left you multiple notes and you haven't told me?"

"Why would I tell you?"

She asked the question with so much sincerity, I knew she didn't get it. She didn't understand what being mine meant. Her situation was different, since it was a punishment, but that didn't make her any less mine.

"Are you my pet?" I asked in a calm, steady tone.

"Yes." No hesitation. At least she got that.

"Do I own you?"

"I don't—um..." *There* was the hesitation I'd been looking for.

"Zadie..." I tugged on her chin, drawing her face alongside mine so I could speak low in her ear. "Do I own you for now?"

She finally nodded.

"Then you'll always tell me when someone or something threatens your safety." With her chin in my hand, I forced another nod out of her.

"Well..." she tucked her hair behind her ear even though it was already there, "I'm scared of you, so—"

"You should be. I'm not a good man. But you still have to come to me with shit like this. I'm bad, Zadie, but I'll be *your* biggest bad when it comes to anything that threatens you. What will I do with a broken pet?" I clicked my tongue on my teeth. "No, I need my pretty little pet whole."

Her soft jaw tightened. Zadie was sweet, kind, and she went along with the law I laid down without much argument, but under her surface, she was bucking against me. She held it in, unlike the night in her dorm room when she told me she'd never be with me, that sleeping with me was akin to losing her mind. And hell, she'd been right, but I'd wanted it to happen anyway. The image of her soft and pliant and writhing beneath me was forever burned into memory. Even now, when I was pissed at her for a multitude of reasons, I was picturing her like that, and my dick thought that was reason enough to punch at my zipper. It didn't help she smelled like berries in the rain and her angry panting reminded me too much of the sounds of her coming.

"He's left a few notes. I don't know if it's Drew or someone else. My lawyer in Oregon said the restraining order still stands. She's also checking in with the officer who handled my case. I haven't heard back from her yet, but I'm…" She exhaled a ragged breath.

"Fucking terrified?"

"Yeah," she breathed. "I don't know if I want it to be him or someone else."

My fingers flexed on the steering wheel. "Better the devil you know…"

"Right."

"You don't keep anything from me again, Zadie. You're mine. What happens to you is my concern. You get me?"

She nodded in my periphery. "Okay."

"I'm gonna take you back to your dorm now. Take the night to get your head straight. Julien and Marco can starve."

Shifting in her seat, I felt her eyes on the side of my face as I drove. "What about you? Are you starving too?"

That voice. God*damn* that voice. It had gotten in my head too. When she wasn't angry, when she was just talking to me like anyone else, she sunk me. Her words were crystal clear, like a glacial spring, but there was nothing cold about them. She wrapped every syllable in a fleece cocoon. It probably wouldn't make sense to anyone else, but I felt the warmth in her words. More than that, her voice was sweet in a way that wasn't put on. It was just her. Pure Zadie. Like a sexy-ass preschool teacher or something.

I didn't like her having this effect on me. Not when she didn't mean it or want it. I shoved away the desire to keep asking her questions so she'd keep pouring her honeyed words into my ear. No one had power over me, especially not little girls with soft bodies and angelic faces. Never going to happen.

"Nah, I've been eating elsewhere. It's all good," I replied, knowing the implications in my response.

"Oh." She shifted again so she was looking straight out the windshield. "Good."

I pulled up to the curb in front of Zadie's building. She scrambled to gather her things, but before she could escape, I wrapped my fingers around her arm. She looked at me over her shoulder.

"Need you back at the house tomorrow. I'll pick you up after your last class."

Her eyes flared with surprise. "No, you don't have to. I—"

"It wasn't an offer. I said I'll pick you up."

One nod. She gave in easily. She must've been really afraid if she was agreeing without a fight. Why did that make me want to lock my doors, drive her to my house right now, and keep her in my room until whoever was fucking with her marched themselves into an early grave?

"I'll see you tomorrow," she whispered.

"You will. Now, get the fuck inside and text me a picture of you in your bedroom. I want face—not feet or pillows. Face, Zadie."

She threw herself out of my car and made a beeline inside. I sat there, waiting for her text. It took five minutes, then there she was, sitting on her bed. Scrunched nose, rosy cheeks, pouty bottom lip. No cleavage, no body, and still, my dick pressed against my zipper.

Me: *Good girl.*

Zadie: *Goodnight, Captor. Thanks for the rescue.*

I tossed my phone onto the passenger seat, done with this girl. If I looked at her picture for another second, I'd find a way to get to her, get her on her back, and finally sink into that pretty pink pussy of hers.

If that happened, if I allowed myself to give in to all the urges I had when it came to Zadie, I had no doubt I'd be well and truly fucked.

CHAPTER ELEVEN

Zadie

JULIEN WAS KEEPING A close watch on me. He'd done the same when I came back to the house the day before, sitting in the kitchen with me the whole time I cooked. He was cute and needy and it made me laugh.

"I want you to teach me how to make biscuits," he announced, raking hungry eyes over the steaming biscuits I'd just taken from the oven.

I arched a brow. "Do you? If you know how to make them, why should I keep coming to make them for you?"

He snapped his fingers. "Good point, Princess Z. 'Cause I know nothing I make is ever going to live up to your cooking, even if I learn from the master herself."

I bit back a grin. "So, you want to remain helpless?

"Hell yes I do. I think I'm going to hire you next semester."

I walked to the island where he was sitting, propping a hip on the stool next to him, and waved my wooden spoon. "Or we could just be friends. I like to cook for my friends. You may or may not know this about me, but I don't actually have aspirations of becoming a housekeeper or personal chef."

I thought he'd laugh, but he gave me a close inspection, sweeping over my face and the hand holding the spoon.

"You'd wanna be my friend after all this?"

I lifted a shoulder. "We'll see. You have a couple months to win me over. Sometimes I don't like you very much, you know."

My blunt honesty surprised even me. When I first met Julien, I'd been intimidated. He was just as devastatingly attractive as Amir and Marco. His shaggy, sandy hair, sharply carved features, and crystalline green eyes would have sent most girls' hearts into overdrive. I wasn't immune, and guys who looked like him always drove me deep into my shell. But over the last couple weeks, he'd shown me a kindness that had caught me off guard, dragging me right back out of my shell. I still found him devastatingly attractive, but I wasn't attracted to him. I didn't wonder what his lips felt like or how his hands would feel on my body. He was just Julien. Hot, friendly, Julien. Unless he was doing Amir's bidding. Those were times I *really* didn't like him.

Julien winced at my answer. "No doubt I'll give you more reasons to hate me as time goes by."

"I don't hate anyone, not really."

He scratched his chin, shooting me a crooked grin. "You don't hate Amir?"

I shook my head. God, if I were to hate anyone, it would be...okay...well, Drew would be on top of the list, but Amir would be there somewhere too.

"No. My mind tends to go more toward fear than hate. That's just how I work."

"Are you scared of Amir?" he asked.

I was...a lot of things when it came to Amir. I didn't hate him, not at all. Everything I felt for him was so mixed up and swirled together, it was impossible to sort the fear from the longing from the desire from the anger. I couldn't think straight when it came to him. He'd pushed me down to my knees and rubbed his dick on my lips without my permission, but he'd also held me through a panic attack and promised to protect me. And when I first came to him, I'd known he would, even though we'd only met once. There in my room, the hours we were stuck together, I saw the kind of man he was. Captor and savior all rolled into one.

"Sometimes I'm scared, yeah." I tapped the spoon on his arm. "Why are you so interested in how I feel about Amir?"

"I'd like to know that too."

I whipped around, finding Amir leaning one shoulder on the doorjamb, his arms folded over his chest, a hint of a frown marring his otherwise impassive face. His dark, stormy gaze flicked from Julien to me, his brow furrowing until there was a deep crevice down the center.

"Curious, dude," Julien replied. "Next, we can talk about Marco, then circle back to me again."

I turned back to him, and he winked at me, which made me roll my eyes.

"Remember how I said I don't like you sometimes? This is one of those times," I hissed.

Julien laughed at my hissing like I was a tiny, cute kitten. Amir didn't laugh, but then, he rarely did. At least not when I was around. He stalked into the kitchen, straight to me, and braced one hand on the back of my stool, the other on the counter in front of me, boxing me in.

"Since I missed the beginning of the conversation, why don't you enlighten me, Zadie?" Amir's hiss *was* effective. Voice dropped low, he sounded like a sleek jungle cat preparing to pounce.

I tipped my head back to meet his midnight eyes. "I told Julien I don't hate you but sometimes I'm afraid of you. I don't think that's a secret."

"No." He slowly shook his head. "A couple days ago, we discussed how you *should* be afraid of me." He picked up one of the ringlets that had formed around my face from the steam while I was cooking. "But I'm surprised to hear you don't hate me. I would hate being someone's property."

I raised my chin higher. "You think of me as your property. I know I'm not. I also don't know what hating someone feels like, but I don't think it's this."

He exhaled a hard breath. "You...don't know what hate feels like?"

Julien chuckled. "Are you surprised our personal ray of sunshine doesn't know what hate feels like?"

Amir leveled his friend with a cutting glare. "'*Our*'?" Without looking at me, he cupped the back of my head. "Zadie is mine. She's not giving you any sunshine."

He was so freaking ridiculous, I couldn't hold back a giggle. When Julien heard me laughing, he snorted so hard, he started coughing. Amir straightened, folding his arms over his chest again, while Julien and I burst into laughter. Marco wandered in, a bemused look on his face, and sidled up to Amir.

"What's going on?"

Amir glanced at him, then us. "No fucking idea."

Of course, that brought on a fresh wave of giggles. Julien bent in half, his forehead on the granite, while I covered my mouth, attempting to stifle some of my laughter, but it was no use. Amir was so growly and pissy for no actual reason, and it tickled something inside me.

"They laughing at you?" Marco asked.

"Yeah. It seems like it," Amir replied.

"You mad?"

Amir stared at us, and through my teary eyes, I swore I saw his mouth quirking. "Nah. I know Julien won't be laughing when I don't let him eat any biscuits for dinner."

Julien shot out of his chair, stone-faced sober. "I let a lot of shit slide, but that's never gonna happen."

Amir grinned wide. "Really? Are you going to stop me?"

Marco slapped his chest. "There's going to be a mutiny up in this ship if you get between me and Zadie's cooking."

Without warning, Marco darted for the oven. Amir caught him around the middle, hauling him back toward the island. Amir took Marco's elbow to his chest, then he grabbed Marco's elbow, bracing it at his side. Marco tried to spin out of Amir's grasp, but Amir caught his other elbow, pinning him in place.

Julien darted for the sink, grabbed a sponge, and hurled it straight for Amir's head. When it bounced off with a wet slap, he dropped Marco's arms to wipe the sudsy water from his forehead.

"You fuck," he growled through a feral grin.

Marco picked up the sponge and pegged the back of Julien's head as he retreated to the other side of the island. Meanwhile, Amir had a kitchen towel in his hand, using it like a whip on Marco's legs and Julien's torso. The three of them were wild and messy, cussing and shouting insults. I couldn't stop the giggles, even as I crouched down so I wouldn't end up with a sponge to the head.

This was the first time I'd seen Amir playful—Marco too, for that matter—and it was an incredible sight. He looked younger, freer, and there was a brightness in his midnight eyes that was never there. Right then, I was the furthest from hate I'd ever been in regard to Amir.

I pinched the back of Julien's arm when he came close to me. "Don't worry. If he takes all of them, I'll make you your own batch next time."

Chuckling, Julien patted my crown. "That's my girl."

Silence descending over the kitchen. Amir's grin vanished, and I instantly knew I'd said the wrong thing. For a moment, I'd forgotten I was a pet and not a person to him. They could joke with each other, but I wasn't allowed to join in.

He dropped Marco, who'd taken on the expression of a man watching a train wreck, and held his hand out to me.

"Time to go, Zadie," Amir bit out.

"Okay," I whispered. I hadn't unpacked my messenger bag, so it was simple to slip it over my shoulder to make a quick escape. Amir took it from me as soon as I stood and strode out of the kitchen without a backward glance, clearly expecting me to follow.

"Sorry, Z," Julien murmured.

"You'll be all right," Marco added, but yeah, he still had that train wreck look.

I gave them a wave. "See you guys later. And don't let him eat all the biscuits."

Amir was waiting for me in his SUV. I climbed in, clutching my bag in my lap. He was silent as we took the short drive back to campus. It wasn't a comfortable silence by any means. The weight of it was so heavy, it was unbearable. I couldn't keep doing this, not for the rest of the semester. My stomach hurt from the tension emanating from Amir in waves.

Taking a deep breath, I forced out the scrap of bravery I contained. "I don't have feelings for Julien, you know. Not like that."

His hands tightened on the wheel. "Okay."

"If you'd rather I come and go without speaking to anyone, I can do that. Just tell me so I know what the expectations are. I don't want to upset the balance in your house. I'd hate to think I'm causing a rift between you guys."

He huffed. "You're not gonna cause a rift."

"Um..." I bit down hard on my lip, "well, good."

Instead of pulling up to the curb in front of my dorm, he turned into a spot. With the SUV in park, he draped his arm over the wheel and turned to me. His eyes here half lidded, lazy, careless, like he hadn't just been irate with me.

"You give a shit, huh?"

I sat up straight. "Of course I do."

He cocked his head. "Why aren't you into him?"

"What?"

"Julien. Why aren't you into him? He's nice, funny, easygoing. Girls like the shit out of him. You get along with him. You talk to him. So, why aren't you into him?"

There was no heat behind his question. Not even a fraction. If anything, there was confusion, like he was genuinely perplexed why a woman like me wouldn't want Julien.

I thought about my answer carefully but quickly. "I don't think he's my type."

His eyes grew narrow. "You have a type?"

"Maybe? Based on my first boyfriend, who was a street racer, then Drew, who's absolutely bananas, then you...I guess I go for guys likely to spend time in jail."

His laugh was dry. "I'm on your list? Pretty sure what went on between us was all down to the circumstances."

I bristled at his easy dismissal, as if I couldn't discern for myself who I was attracted to. I wasn't a girl who crushed a lot, nor did I fall into bed with just anyone.

"I wouldn't have almost given you my virginity if it was only circumstance. I know my own mind and who I like. My picker could be a little choosier but—"

Amir's hand covered my mouth. "Shut up, Zadie."

I blinked at him, patiently waiting for him to tell me why he was mad at me this time.

"You're a virgin?"

I nodded, still muzzled by his hand.

"You said you missed fucking." He got closer, his nose almost touching mine. "You were going to let me inside you. If I hadn't picked up my phone, I would have been inside your pussy."

I nodded again.

"What the fuck?" he breathed.

I shrugged.

He finally dropped his hand down to my chin. "You're not kidding, are you?"

"No, I'm not kidding at all. I was caught up in you that night." I licked my dry lips. Amir followed my tongue's path with his thumb, making me shiver. "I said I missed fucking because I...wanted something that had been taken from me because of Drew. I missed something I hadn't had because of him."

"What the fuck, Zadie?" He didn't sound mad anymore, just confounded.

"I don't know, Amir. You made me like you, *despite* the circumstances." I brushed a strand of hair from my forehead. "But it doesn't matter anymore. I just...I don't want you, Marco, and Julien fighting anymore. So, I'll just keep to myself and won't cause any problems. Okay?"

He exhaled heavily through his nose while pinning me with a hard stare. "It doesn't matter anymore, huh?"

If he kissed me right now, I would kiss him back, and not because I was his pet. The swirly, heady feeling he'd given me as my captor had never gone away. It had just lay dormant until I was in his presence again. I was such a cliché, the good girl who fell for bad boys.

"Amir…"

I didn't know what he wanted me to say.

"Zadie,"—he pinched my chin between his fingers—"get the fuck outta my car."

The way he said it, it was like he was reciting a love poem to me. Like a coo in my ear first thing in the morning. Soft, lilting, almost a song.

"Okay. I'll see you tomorrow then."

"Nope. I don't need you tomorrow. I've got plans at night." He shook my head gently. "Be good. Text me from your room."

He let me go, and I ran inside. Helen and Theo were snuggled on the couch, and I assumed Elena was out since it was Friday and she was always out on Fridays. I tossed a wave at the two of them, then closed the door to my room and pressed my palm to my thundering heart.

I didn't linger like that, though. Sitting on my bed, I snapped a picture of myself, rolling my eyes slightly to the side so he would get the message that I thought this whole tradition was silly.

MyCaptor: *That's my pretty girl. Don't like the eye roll, but the rest is perfection. What a nice pet I have.*

Me: *Good night, Captor.*

MyCaptor: *Night, Zadie.*

· · · • · • · · ·

My stepbrother was a giant. At sixteen, Eli was at least six and a half feet tall, with boats for feet and baseball mitts for hands. Every time I saw him, I was taken aback for a few minutes until I accepted reality: he was my baby stepbro, but he'd always be way bigger than me. As such, he enjoyed palming the top of my head and moving me around like I was a stuffed animal and he was the claw in an arcade game.

My mom, on the other hand, was model slim, long legged, and pixie faced. She was dwarfed beside Eli. Seeing their mismatched heights across from me in the diner booth made my heart go pitter-patter. I *really* needed this visit. One hug from my mom, and all my troubles were a distant memory. She clung to me a little tighter than normal, which told me she'd needed the visit just as much.

We were having breakfast at the T, which was in Savage River's cute downtown area. Mom and I planned on doing some shopping after. Plying Eli with food was the only way to get him to agree to hang.

"Have you heard from your dad?" Mom asked while cutting her pancakes.

"Yeah. We talked a few days ago." I laid my fork down on my plate and patted my mouth with my napkin. "He joined a foraging club, so that's how he's spending his weekends lately."

Eli's dark brow pinched. "What's he foraging for?"

"Morels and mushrooms. He's out tromping through the woods, digging up mushrooms. It's very on brand for my dad," I explained.

Mom laughed softly, and I couldn't miss the wistfulness in her eyes. "That sounds like Keith. I'm glad he's found something he's enjoying besides smoking and worrying."

I wasn't a kid who'd grown up with screaming matches and angry words. My parents had loved and respected each other.

They were vastly different, but for a time at least, they relished each other's differences. And then…well, everything fell apart.

"Wait," Eli scratched his head, "are they, like, magic mushrooms?"

I snorted a laugh. "No, they're really just regular mushrooms. Dad's club tromps around the forest, picks mushrooms, then takes them back to someone's house and they cook. It's very wholesome, but I'm certain there's copious weed and wine for the last part too."

Eli chuckled. "That, I could be into."

Mom slapped his huge arm. "Hey, dude, I'm not your mom, but I am *a* mom, who doesn't want to hear her teenage boy say stuff like that."

Eli hung his head, but his eyes lit on me. "Sorry, not-mom."

I snickered at his faux contrition. "You're such a good boy, Eli."

He made a ring with his fingers over his head. "See my halo? I'm an angel."

Mom shook her head. "Oh my god, why did I always think I wanted to have two kids? I was very obviously mistaken."

After breakfast, we wandered around Main Street, going in and out of shops. Mom bought both Eli and me a stack of books from the book shop. Once he had his, he found a bench to read on while we went into a clothing store. I kept catching sight of him through the window, and even though he was reading, there was something about the curl of his shoulders that filled me with worry. Since my mom was deep in conversation with the clerk without any sign of ending anytime soon, I went outside and sat beside my giant of a little stepbrother.

He looked up from his book when I patted his knee. "What's the story, morning glory?" I asked.

His mouth quirked. "Don't know. Why don't you tell me the tale, nightingale?"

"How's Max, Eli?"

My mom continued to be vague and cheerful when it came to her husband's prognosis. She'd done the same thing when she and my dad were divorcing, so I didn't trust anything out of her mouth when it came to big, potentially disastrous happenings. She did it to protect me, but I didn't need protection, not in this case. I needed the truth.

With a heavy sigh, Eli closed his book and slid it back in his bag. "What's your mom told you?"

"She's remaining optimistic." I flicked my hand toward the store I'd just come from. "You know her. She keeps it all tucked away until she can't."

He nodded, but his movements were sluggish, as if the burden he carried made his movements difficult.

"She's taking really good care of him. My mom would have freaked out. I mean, she is freaking out and she kind of hates my dad, you know? But Felicity is so steady, all the time."

"My mom's good that way. She does better when she has a task to focus on." I bumped his arm with my shoulder. "You didn't answer my question, though. How's Max?"

Bending forward, he clutched his head in his hands. "He's sick. Really, really sick."

I laid my hand on his back. "Is it the chemo? Is that making him sick?"

"Yeah, I don't know. There was one morning Felicity had to run out to pick up a prescription so it was just me and my dad. He started gagging and coughing and couldn't stop. I stood there, Zadie. I didn't know what to do. My dad was doubled over, barely able to take in air, and I just stood there."

He choked out the last few words, and I heard his tears, even if he wouldn't show me.

"Eli...he's okay. He recovered from that incident, he doesn't blame you, and I'm sure he hated you seeing him like that as much as you hated seeing it."

"I should have helped him."

"You will. Next time. You'll be better prepared, right?"

The deep, mournful sob he let escape brought tears to my eyes. I laid my head on his shoulder, murmuring words of comfort, telling him it would be okay, that I would be there for him however he needed me. Keeping his face hidden, he swiped his tears away. Eli might have been a giant, but he was really just a kid, and this was a lot. Even if Max recovered, living through this illness, seeing his dad wasn't invincible, would forever change Eli.

"I think he's going to die, Zadie."

"Babe..." My heart crammed in my throat. "Is that...? Mom said his prognosis is—"

"I don't know what the doctors are saying. My dad is just ...sometimes, I think he's fading." He got up from the bench and tore down the sidewalk, and I chased after him. I couldn't leave him alone, not like this.

"Eli, stop!" I called. "Please, just wait for me."

He slowed down enough for my short legs to catch up with him. I grabbed his forearm, tugging until he stopped. His cheeks were rosy. His eyes were watery and bloodshot.

"It's okay to be scared," I whispered.

He shook his head sharply. "Felicity and Dad don't need to deal with my stuff on top of everything else."

"Then call me. Text me. Ask Mom to drive you to see me. No matter what, I'm your big sister, and I'm here, okay? I really mean it."

He stared at me for a long time, his eyes so wet, they drew my own tears to the surface. Then he let loose a pained exhale and wiped his eyes with the heel of his hand.

"If he dies, promise me you won't go away." His nose twitched, and he looked at the sidewalk. "Promise we'll still be family."

I threw myself at him, wrapping my arms around him as tightly as I could. He curled around me, returning my hug with the same kind of fervor.

"I'm your *sister*. Your kids are going to be my nieces and nephews, and I expect you to be my kids' favorite uncle. That doesn't go away, no matter what." I pinched the skin on his back. "I'm mad at you for asking me that."

His laugh was closer to a sob, but that was okay. At least he was laughing and hugging me and not crying and running away.

Just as suddenly as I'd thrown myself at him, I was yanked backward, out of his arms, into the chest of someone else. My skin prickled when a low, menacing voice whispered in my ear.

"Zadie Night, you've been a bad, bad girl."

CHAPTER TWELVE

Amir

I HAD A PROBLEM.

I reacted first, thought second.

Driving down Main Street, seeing my girl chasing after a big dude and then throwing herself at him, I didn't think. I parked, flew out, and reacted.

And I fucked up.

"Hey! Get off my sister," the big dude hollered.

Zadie twisted her head to meet my shocked eyes. "Amir, meet my brother, Eli. My little, sixteen-year-old brother."

Zadie's face was blotchy, her eyes red, tears at the edges. When I looked up at her brother, I saw the same. If I'd taken a second before flipping the fuck out at seeing Zadie in another man's arms, I would have realized this wasn't a man at all. Eli was tall and wide, but there was no mistaking he was still a kid. A kid who was clearly going through something rough. Something Zadie was going through too. Something she hadn't told

me about. Fuck, I didn't even know she had a brother or that
he was coming to visit her today.

"I apologize." Tipping my chin down, I met Zadie's eyes
again. "I'm sorry. I wasn't thinking."

"What's going on?" Eli demanded. "Who are you?"

"Eli—" Zadie started in warning, but I cut her off with a
squeeze to her waist. Then I shifted her to my side, keeping my
arm firmly around her shoulders.

I wasn't someone who took kindly to demands, but in this
case, I didn't mind. Eli was looking out for his sister, and I was
the stranger who'd ripped her from his arms. If I had a sister
like Zadie, I'd burn it all down for her. I got the feeling if Eli
didn't like what I had to say, he just might try to douse me with
gasoline and strike a match. So, today, he'd get my patience and
respect for looking out for Zadie the way she deserved.

"It's okay, man. I'm Amir, Zadie's boyfriend. I hope you can
understand, I saw my girlfriend in another man's arms and
lost my mind for a minute." I stroked her shoulder with my
thumb. "I really am sorry, man. Someone forgot to tell me she
was seeing her brother this morning."

Zadie stiffened, but she didn't put up an argument. No
doubt she'd rather me call her my girlfriend than my pet in
front of her brother.

Eli frowned, his eyes flicking back and forth between us.
"Does Felicity know you have a boyfriend?"

"Not yet. It's new, and with everything happening, I
haven't..." She looked up at me, scrunching her nose. "I
haven't told my mom about us yet. Sorry."

I tapped the end of her nose. "That's okay, baby. You'll tell
her soon."

Eli tipped his chin. "You can tell her now. Here she comes."

I grinned down at Zadie, who did not look amused. In fact, it seemed like she was snarling, but on her, it came out so cute, there was nothing threatening about it. "I get to meet your mom today?"

Her expression crumpled. "Be nice, please?" she whispered.

The sorrow behind her eyes sobered me. "You got it, mama. Best behavior. Promise."

We turned around to greet the tall, thin, older version of Zadie. Same sweet, beautiful face, shiny chestnut waves, bright smile. And when she spoke, she had a slightly deeper version of Zadie's honeyed voice.

"Hey, kids. Did you make a new friend?" She stopped in front of me, her gaze bouncing from my arm around her daughter to my face. "Who might you be?"

I held out my hand. "Amir Vasquez. I'm Zadie's."

"Oh, I like that." She slipped her hand in mine, giving it a firm shake. "Felicity Elks. My daughter is a secret keeper apparently."

"Mom, I was going to tell you, but it's new. I knew you'd want to meet him, but it's too early, so—"

"She thought I'd freak out. You know, too much, too soon." I smiled at Zadie. "But she doesn't get there's never enough of her."

I could tell she wanted to step on my foot, but with her mom and brother watching with keen eyes, she only returned my smile.

"He thought I was hitting on Zadie," Eli added, smirking at me. The little shit wasn't going to let me play it off, which I also respected.

Felicity's mouth gaped. "What—?"

"Yeah,"—I rubbed my nape—"not my finest moment. I was driving by, saw my girl with another guy, and reacted. I'll be groveling for a while, but at least I got to meet the two of you."

Felicity pressed a hand to her chest. "You're adorable, Amir. So adorable. I think I like you."

A laugh burst out of me. "No one's ever called me adorable."

"Not even when he was a baby," Zadie added. "He was born with a menacing scowl."

I shook my head at her. "You don't even know how right you are."

Zadie raised her eyebrows. "Don't you need to get going? I thought you were busy today."

"Actually, no. Not until tonight. I have the whole day free." I had planned on spending it studying, but that had lost its appeal the second I'd tucked Zadie under my arm and claimed her as my girl.

"Well, we were about to take a tour of campus. Zadie was going to show us where all her classes are, then I have to hit the university shop to buy some swag for my husband. I promised I'd bring him back a hat." Felicity reached around and patted my arm. "If that doesn't sound too boring, you are more than welcome to join us. I'm sure Eli would appreciate not spending his entire day with just two women."

I gave Zadie's rigid shoulders a squeeze. This girl wanted me away from her family, but I was already hooked on my role as her doting boyfriend. Now wasn't the time to bow out, even if she poisoned my dinner tomorrow. "There's really nothing I'd rather do."

· · · · ●· ● · · ·

A few hours later, I was fully immersed in the Elks-Night family. Eli was chill as hell, and Felicity was as sweet as Zadie, but without the shyness. Although, around her mom and brother, Zadie blossomed. I got the feeling she felt truly comfortable and safe with them. Several times throughout the day, she'd be laughing, enjoying herself, then she'd catch my eye and her light would dim.

We'd be talking about that, because I didn't like it at all. If she was giving other people her light, I wanted it too. That light should've been mine.

I also learned that Felicity's husband, Max, was seriously ill with leukemia. Felicity put on a brave smile when she was explaining his treatment plan, but there was a stillness that fell over the three of them that told the truth: they were all afraid of what was to come.

Now, we were in the food court of the student union, grabbing a coffee before her mom and brother had to head out. Zadie and I were in line to order while Felicity and Eli hunted for a table.

I was being stared at. I'd caught Zadie's eyes on me several times, always with a pensive stare.

"What?" I murmured. "What's going on in that head of yours?"

She twisted her lips. "I'm thinking you're either a sociopath and you've been faking it with my family all day, or underneath all your armor, you might be a decent guy."

"The only thing I've been faking is our relationship." I slid my hand along the small of her back, dipping down into her back pocket to cup her ass. "I've thoroughly enjoyed playing your boyfriend, though."

Her eyes narrowed. "You feel me up whenever you want anyway."

"Not nearly as much as I want. I should get a gold star for how much I hold back with you."

She rolled her eyes, then made the outline of a star in the air with her pointer finger. "You get an invisible star. It's the best I can do."

I snatched that shit out of the air and tucked it in my pocket.

"You know what I liked about today?"

"What?" she asked.

"The way your mom and Eli looked at me because they thought I was with you. There were no expectations beyond treating you right. And when they saw me treating you right, they were all smiley and bright." I lifted a shoulder. "I don't know. The way I grew up, people I knew, none of us had that. So yeah, it's been cool to get a taste of it."

She opened her mouth, then closed it right away, turning her head.

"Nah, Zadie. You have something to contribute and I want to hear it." With my knuckle, I hooked her under her chin and turned her head toward me again. "You have something to say?"

"Not really." She chewed on her bottom lip, averting her eyes.

"Talk, mama."

Huffing, her big blue eyes flicked up to mine. "I was just thinking you act like having people who support and care for you is a pipe dream, but, Amir, you're here. You're in this school because you're incredibly smart and you work hard. You could have a girlfriend with a nice family if you wanted. But I don't think you want that. If you did, all you'd have to do is snap and it would be yours."

It was our turn to order, so I had a minute to mull over what she'd just thrown at me. My knee-jerk reaction was to say she didn't know shit—and she didn't. With my own two eyes, I saw what she was brought up with. She had hard times, but she had a thick layer of insulation around her, even if she didn't realize it. When Zadie looked at my life, it was through that lens, not mine.

When we shifted to the next counter to wait for the drinks, I stood behind her, splaying my hand on her stomach, and dipped my mouth to her ear.

"You think Felicity would want me around her pretty little daughter if she knew how I make money? How my brother makes money?"

She let her head fall back on my shoulder but kept her eyes from me. I really didn't like when she kept her eyes from me.

"I won't pretend to know anything about that, nor do I want to. But I think Felicity wouldn't have to know either. Moms don't have to know everything. It's better for them."

"Really?" My lips skimmed her velvety ear. "You keep secrets from your mom? Scandalous."

Her laughter was a feather to the back of my knees, nearly bringing me down without even trying. "If I'd told her I was held hostage last semester, do you think I'd still be enrolled here?"

I nipped at her lobe. "You're never going to let that go, huh?"

This time, her laughter was more like an anvil to my chest, hitting me hard and not letting me up. Jesus Christ, this girl could laugh. Anything she did with that mouth was magic.

"No, I guess I'm not." She grinned up at me. "In ten years, when you're a fine, upstanding businessman, I'll swing by your office with a cup of coffee so we can reminisce about the time you held me as collateral. Or I could pop into your wedding and give a to—"

I covered her mouth with my hand. "I don't like the joke anymore."

She turned her head and pressed her forehead to my throat, catching me off guard. It felt conciliatory, even though I was the one crossing lines. My hand dropped, curling around her chest. We stood there like that, wrapped around each other, for another minute, until our order was called. She didn't say a word, and neither did I.

I didn't know what that minute was, but I had no doubt everything about it—the closeness, the peace, the utter calm—would stay contained within those sixty seconds.

At the table with Felicity and Eli, everything was the same again. Felicity showed us what she'd bought for her husband, even though we'd all been there when she made the purchase. Eli and I talked college sports—Savage U's teams weren't shit, but he followed them religiously anyway, especially baseball, which was his game. And Zadie had gone back to keeping her eyes from me.

I tapped her hand. "Have you shown your mom the latest note left for you?"

Her eyes rounded. "No, Amir—"

Felicity leaned forward in her chair. "What note?" Her gaze whipped from me to Zadie. "Zadie, what note?"

She shook her head. "It's not a big deal, I promise."

"You haven't told your mom?" I already knew she hadn't, but I didn't agree with the decision. Her mom might have been going through the heaviness of her husband's illness, but Zadie needed her too. If she wouldn't ask for her mom's help, I'd take that decision from her.

"Why don't you tell me, Amir?" Felicity set her coffee down, leveling me with a steady glare.

"Someone's been leaving Zadie poems and flowers. She suspected it was Drew, but given the last poem, she's not sure."

"Zadie," Eli ground out. "How could you not tell us?"

She rubbed her forehead. "Because I could be freaking out over nothing. You guys have enough going on, I didn't want to add one more th—"

"Stop it." Felicity slapped the table. "Don't you dare say another word. I know what my enough is, and I have plenty of capacity to deal with my daughter. I need you to tell me everything so I can have the information to decide which direction we need to proceed."

Zadie's furious gaze cut to me. Her fingertips were going white from gripping the edge of the table. I pried one finger loose at a time, cupping her small, soft hand in mine.

"Tell your mom," I urged.

She tried to yank her hand away from me, but I wasn't letting go. Not until she did this. She was right. Her mom didn't need to know everything, but she did need to know this. As my pet, it was my job to decide the best way to protect her. I'd be her physical shield but dealing with cops and lawyers was outside my wheelhouse. Felicity had the capability of handling that area, but she had to know what needed to be handled first.

Each word out of Zadie's mouth was reluctant, but she laid out the basics, skipping over the library incident. I let that slide for now. Her voice was devoid of emotion, but I felt it in the twitch of her muscles, her clammy palm, the rapid rise and fall of her chest.

Felicity started typing on her phone as soon as Zadie was finished talking. "I'm taking care of it. Don't worry, baby. If it's Drew, we'll fry his ass. If it's another dipshit, we'll handle him too. You aren't in this alone." Her gaze shifted to me. "Thank you for telling me. It's obvious you're taking care of

Zadie and looking out for her. If she didn't have you, Eli would be carrying her to our car and she'd be coming home with us."

Eli looked at his sister. "I'm still considering it."

I laid my hand on his shoulder. "Nah, man. She's good with me. You take care of your dad and Felicity. I've got my girl."

Zadie huffed and twisted her hand, but I held it tight. Oh, she was mad, mad. But I didn't really give a shit. Keeping what was going on a secret was only going to endanger her.

Felicity's mouth was strained. "Thank you, Amir. I don't think I can explain what it was like for Zadie and our family during the height of the stalking. Drew used to show up in restaurants, at shops, when Zadie was out with friends at movies. She became so afraid of running into him, she wouldn't leave the house, and when he began leaving her presents at our front door, her room was her only safe space." She touched her fingertips to her mouth. "That's how I know you're protecting my girl. She must feel it, because two years ago, she would have been in her bed, scared of the world."

It was a good thing none of them could see what was going on in my mind. If they could, they'd be afraid of *me*. I'd witnessed Zadie's terror in the library, but hearing her mom lay it all out for me only added another layer to the fury I carried for a guy I would hopefully never meet.

"I hear you, Felicity. Zadie is covered. This, I promise."

After all that was settled, we were about to part ways, so I asked for a few minutes with Zadie to say goodbye. I pulled her with me around the corner into a small group study room that wasn't in use. I kept walking until her back hit the wall and braced my hands on either side of her head.

"You had no right." Her words came out shaky with anger.

"I did, Zadie. You're mine, aren't you?"

She lifted her chin. "I'm yours at your house. That doesn't spill over into my life. I didn't agree to that. My mom...do you understand her husband might be dying? Do you?"

I worked hard not to slam my hand into the wall. "Do *you* understand if this guy gets to you it would kill her? How's she supposed to deal with her daughter being hurt, raped, dead, when her husband is dying? Tell me, Zadie. You want to do that to her? What about Eli? You want to hurt the kid who looks at you like you hung the moon?"

Tears welled in her eyes. "Shut up, Amir." Her hands came to my chest, giving me a weak shove. "Just shut up."

Bringing my hand off the wall, I cupped her jaw. "This is me looking out for my pet. You might not like it, but I don't give a fuck." Dipping down, I touched my lips to hers. She gasped against my mouth, and it was all I could do to walk away. "I have to go tend to some business."

"Okay," she whispered.

Those tears were still in her eyes, even if she wasn't letting them fall. I couldn't walk away and leave it like this. Not until I made sure she really understood. "I need you to tell me you get why I did what I did with your mom."

Her pouty little mouth pressed into a tight line, and she gave me a sharp nod. "I don't want her to hurt or worry."

"I think she'd tell you that's her job."

Some of the tightness left her mouth, and the corners curled into a slight smile. "She probably would."

Uninvited warmth spread across my chest. What the fuck was that about? "Come a little early tomorrow."

"Ten?"

"No." I brushed my lips over hers again. Couldn't help it, the sweetness was addictive. "I'm going out tonight. It'll be late. Make it noon."

She turned her face away from mine. "Have fun then."

I grinned. Oh, this girl didn't like the idea of me going out. Interesting. "I said it's business, didn't I? My kind of business goes late."

"'Kay."

With a groan, I pulled back, grabbed her hand, and tugged her away from the wall. "Be good, Zadie. Don't drive me crazy."

I left her with her family after Felicity hugged the shit out of me and Eli clapped me on the back. The illusion was over, the job was done, so why the hell did I feel like I was leaving something important behind?

CHAPTER THIRTEEN

Zadie

As soon as I opened the door to my suite and Eli caught sight of Helen walking around the kitchenette in a tiny pair of shorts and a tank top, he tripped over his own oversize feet and nearly landed on his face.

Helen allowed him some dignity by pretending she hadn't seen him lose bodily function over her.

"Well, hello, Zadie's cute family." Elena strutted out of her room in leggings and a sports bra. Eli's swallow was audible, poor guy.

My mom hugged them both, cooed over their hair and clothes, and got all the dirt while Eli studied his feet as carefully as he could.

"Did you have a good time on Main Street?" Helen asked.

Mom pressed her hands together under her chin. "Oh yes, we definitely did. Well...Eli was bored to tears with all the shopping I did, but he survived. And you'll never believe who we ran into."

My stomach dropped. Oh crap. She was going to say it. Why hadn't I anticipated this?

Elena pursed her lips. "Hmmm...I don't think I can guess. You'll have to tell us."

"Zadie's boyfriend. Oh-em-gee, he's so cute." Oh god, she said it.

Both Helen and Elena hit me with accusatory stares, then they checked in with each other to ensure neither knew.

"Wow," Helen said with all kinds of false cheer. "No fair. Zadie hides him from us."

Oh, I was in for it when my family left.

Elena folded her arms. "Right? It's almost like we don't even know he exists."

Mom hugged me around my shoulders. "Oh my gosh, I know it's new, but if you haven't seen them together, you *have* to. Amir treats my girlie like the queen she is. He was all precious with her, pulling out her chair, holding her hand everywhere we went, and, oh, the way he looked at her. It gave me goose bumps."

Amir *had* been far too good at pretending to be a devoted boyfriend. As much as I wanted to believe he had it in him to really be that way if he wanted, the truth was, he'd probably seen a romance movie once and absorbed the traits. I was leaning toward deciding he was a sociopath.

"Amir?" Elena turned to Helen with a pinched brow. "Isn't that the guy who—"

Helen nodded. "Yep."

They both looked at me again. I hoped my expression was pleading. They could grill me all they wanted when my family was gone, I just needed them to play along for a few minutes.

Elena whipped me with a narrowed gaze. "Helen had a crush on Amir in high school."

Mom covered her mouth. "Am I talking out of turn? Did you guys not know Zadie's dating him?"

"It's new," I murmured.

Because she was a cool, cool girl, Helen waved off my mother's worries. "No, I knew. Zadie ran it by me before anything happened. My crush is ancient history, and it definitely wasn't reciprocated. But Zadie's so sweet and careful about my feelings, she doesn't bring him around the suite, so we don't get to see them together."

Elena crossed to me and hooked her arm around my neck. "You'll have to bring your man by for inspection. It's one thing for Mom to approve. It's a whole other for your friends to give him the stamp."

"Helen has a boyfriend," I blurted. "His name is Theo, and she wants to tell you all about him."

My mom was a little bit of a golden retriever—easily distracted and sought out happiness to rub herself all over. And since she and Max were basically still newlyweds, she couldn't get enough of other people's love stories. Therefore, her attention shifted to Helen and away from me. While she bombarded Helen with questions about Theo, Elena hissed at me, motioning for me to join her by the sink in the kitchenette.

"Don't even think about leaving this suite until you spill, girlie." Elena tapped my nose. "I hope the ass you're tapping is worth the third degree you're about to get."

"Vulgar," I whispered.

Her mouth twitched with amusement. "Tramp," she whispered back.

I gasped. "Am I...am I a tramp now? That's kind of cool."

She snickered. "By the way, your stepbro knows we can see him staring, right? Like, does he think he's under an invisibility cloak?"

Poor Eli was hovering by the door, studying Helen from his vantage point. When his eyes swept to Elena, she casually looked away, as if she had no idea he was being a creeper.

"He's young." And he would keel over and die if he heard me say that.

"I know." She shrugged. "It's cute, which is why I won't call him out for it. I'm just saying, he could use some lessons in subtlety."

"He'll get it one day. I like that he's not smooth and cool yet."

"Yeah," she tapped her chin with her perfectly manicured fingernail, "you're right. There's charm in innocence since it's so rare these days. I mean, I thought my sweet little roommate, Zadie Marie, was the picture of innocence, but look at you now, hooking up with criminals."

"My middle name isn't Marie."

Elena's straight white teeth bit into her bottom lip. "That's the only correction you're making?"

I shook my head. "Can this wait until my mom leaves? I'll explain."

She picked up a piece of my hair, rubbing it between her fingers. "Fine. But don't use this time to come up with a bullshit story. I'll be disappointed in you."

With that heavy warning in my head, I joined my mom and Helen, drawing Eli into the conversation as much as he was willing. All too soon, it was time for them to head back home. I made promises to visit as soon as my head was above water with school, and my mom said they'd come back next month if I couldn't find the time. She hugged me tighter than usual, and Eli did too. Today had been a break for us all. They were going back to the reality of a sick husband and father, and

I was staying here, with my stalker and my captor...and two roommates who were about to demand answers.

In the doorway, my mom squeezed my hand. "First thing Monday, I'll make calls about Drew. He's not going to get to you, baby."

I nodded. "Thank you. I'm sorry I didn't tell you."

"Absolutely not. You don't ever have to apologize to me. You're my kid. You don't get that as your mom, it'll always be my job to take care of you, no matter how old you get. I know you have Amir now, but it's still my job, one I love having."

Another hug from her, and a promise to give Max my love, then she and Eli were gone.

Elena and Helen were waiting for me. I perched on the love seat beside Elena, not really sure what I was going to say.

"I'm not really dating Amir," I started, and the stark relief in Helen's exhale sent shock waves of guilt down my spine.

"What does that mean? Because, unless your mom's delusional and you were just playing along, she saw you and Amir together today," Elena said.

I licked my parched lips, but it did no good. My mouth was desert dry. "You know how I got that poem?" The girls nodded. "Well, I've gotten a few, and this isn't the first time someone has sent me poetry."

I told them the whole, sordid story of Drew. Besides Amir, they were the first people I'd shared my stalking trauma with, and I found it was somewhat freeing to spill it all out. I'd been so incredibly isolated during Drew's year of terror, both by his design and my choice, that once I was finally away from him, it had taken me a long time to realize I didn't have to be alone. A lot of the time, I was still convincing myself of that.

"Holy fuck." Helen launched at me, hugging my neck fiercely. "I'm so sorry, baby girl."

Elena piled on top, nuzzling into my chest. "Tell me his name. My father knows people. We'll ruin this bastard."

"Oh my gosh, I love you guys, but I can't breathe." I pretended to cough and choke, but truthfully, I liked our kitten pile.

Helen squeezed onto the love seat with us, me between them. "Okay, so I understand why the poems freaked you out, even if they're not from Drew. But why Amir? What the hell does he have to do with any of this?"

Sighing, I pushed my clammy palms down my thighs. "That night, when he and I were here alone—"

"When he held you at gunpoint," Helen added.

I turned to her. "He put the gun away. Well...he put it on the coffee table. He never pointed it at me."

"Semantics," Elena dismissed dryly.

"Right. I'm not saying what he did was right. I'm only explaining that we had a lot of time to talk, so we did, and somewhere along the line, I told him about Drew. He...wasn't happy about that happening to me and made a promise that if Drew ever bothered me again, he'd protect me."

"You're kidding." Helen shoved at my leg. "You went to Amir for protection?"

"Sort of, yeah. We made a deal that I cook for him and his housemates every night and he watches out for me."

That was the very sanitized version of our deal. I feared if I told them I was Amir's pet, they'd lock me away and try to deprogram me. But I was entirely of sound mind. I'd known exactly what I was doing when I'd accompanied Elliott to the party that night...I just hadn't predicted how it would work out.

Helen snarled. "Okay, I hate everything about that. You're like his servant or something?"

Elena got out her phone. "One text to my dad, and he'll ruin Amir right after he brings down Drew. Just say the word."

"I'm fine, I promise. His housemates are really nice, and half the time, Amir isn't the worst."

Elena arched a brow. "And the other half? Is he the devil himself?"

"No. He's...what you'd expect, I guess. Dark and angry."

Helen shot up straight. "Has he hurt you? Do I need to pay him a visit with my bat? I will fuck him up."

"No." I shook my head hard. This was the exact opposite of what I wanted happening. "Please don't. I swear, he hasn't hurt me. He can be a real a-hole, but he hasn't touched me like that."

Helen settled slightly, but her body was still taut, like she was ready to grab her bat and beat the living hell out of Amir if I gave her a single hint it was what I wanted.

Elena kicked her feet out, resting them on the coffee table, her ankles crossed. "That doesn't really explain why your mom thinks Amir's your boyfriend."

My sigh was heavy. This was a little trickier to explain without alarming them. The last thing I wanted to tell them was the way Amir had gone bananas seeing me in Eli's arms. That sounded like a lot more than a deal, even in my own head.

"We happened to run into him and he just told my mom we were together. So, now she thinks that, and I'm okay with it because it gives her peace of mind."

"Your mother has peace of mind that you're with Amir?" Helen snorted. "That's so fucking funny. He's not even a drug dealer with a heart of gold. He's just a drug dealer."

"He's not just a drug dealer. He's in his junior year in the business school and wicked smart." I wanted to kick myself for jumping to his defense, but there it was.

"You're kidding me." Elena leaned around me to speak to Helen. "Did you know he goes here?"

Helen threw up her hands. "Absolutely no clue. Then again, the only time I dealt with him was when I was picking up product, handing him money, or being threatened. You know, when he told me he'd burn down my trailer with my mom and sister inside if I didn't pay him the money he owed me, that kind of fun stuff. So, forgive me if I don't see his other facets. My opinion of him is skewed from the times he threatened to kill my family and made me believe he meant every word of it."

My heart twisted painfully in my chest. I wouldn't debate whether he meant it or not. It wasn't my place to defend Amir. Even if it was, I couldn't say with any certainty he wouldn't have followed through on those threats.

"I know. He's not a good guy. He'd tell you that himself." I wrapped a loose thread from the hem of my T-shirt around my finger. "I guess that's why I feel certain he'd defend me against Drew. I...maybe I'm being stupid and I'll regret going to him, but it is what it is now. I promised him a semester, so I'm going to give it to him."

Elena patted my knee. "You made your choice, I'll respect it, but, babe, if you want out, tell me. I'm not kidding about my dad. You might believe Amir's scary, but he's got nothing on Gil Sanderson. He will make Amir's *ancestors* regret ever existing."

Goose bumps pricked my skin. "I believe you, El." And it scared me to even contemplate someone coming after Amir like that, even if he deserved it. Even if he'd done terrible, unforgivable things.

"You're not going to fall for him." Helen wasn't asking a question, she was demanding a promise. I really hadn't wanted to lie to either of them. Stretching the truth was one thing, but

out and out lying? No, that wasn't me. But I was in a corner I
saw no way out of—a corner Helen had backed me into.

So, I lied.

"I won't fall for him. Don't worry, Hells."

But maybe it wasn't a lie. I wouldn't fall for him now because
I already had. Four months ago, when he'd tucked me in his
lap, listened to me, and swept me away in all he was.

· • • ●• • ● • • ·

For the first time, I felt no dread when I climbed the steps
to Amir's house. Nerves had replaced my usual reluctance. I
didn't know how Amir would treat me today now that he
didn't have my family as an audience, but I hoped we wouldn't
go back to the way things were before.

It was eleven thirty when I opened the door with the key
Amir had given me last week. I was a little early, but I expected
the boys to be up and at least lounging around, having a lazy
Sunday. Instead, I was greeted by silence.

I didn't know what to do. Were they even here? I trailed
through the downstairs, not finding a single soul or any sign
of life. The three of them weren't exactly the neatest, often
leaving plates on the counter, but there was none of that.

With a sigh, I ventured upstairs, keeping my steps light just
in case they were actually still asleep. Marco's door was first,
but it was sealed up tight. I didn't dare try to peek in. Julien's
room came next, and his door was partway open. I stuck
my head in, and my cheeks instantly burned bright. He was
splayed on his back in the center of his bed, wearing only a pair
of black briefs. I squeezed my eyes shut. The last thing I needed
in my head was the vision of the ridges of his V disappearing

into the low band of his underwear, even though it was now a little too late.

I hurried to the end of the hall. Amir's door was closed, but I decided to take a chance and slowly pushed it open. I got halfway when it creaked and I regretted every decision I'd ever made in my life. In the dimly lit room, the form on the bed stirred. I didn't know what to do. If I pulled the door closed, it might squeak again. If I left it open, he'd know I'd been there.

"Zadie."

My forehead hit the door. "Hi."

"Are you going to stand at my door forever or come in?" Amir's voice was low and gritty with sleep. "Get in here, mama."

I entered his room, closing the door behind me, and warily approached his bed. He was on his back, one arm slung over his forehead. When I was close, his other arm shot out, grabbed the back of my legs, and drew me close until my knees hit the side of the mattress.

"Zadie," he croaked, "whatcha doin' here?"

"It's almost noon," I whispered. "You told me to come."

He grunted, trailing his fingers up and down the back of my thigh and under my skirt. His blankets covered him from the waist down, and on top, he was wearing a button-up shirt.

"Did you sleep in your clothes?" I asked.

With a groan, he felt his chest, then let his arm flop. "Yeah, fuck. I came home and crashed." His eyes fluttered open, focusing on me standing above him. "Whoa. I like that."

"What?"

"Your pretty face being the first thing I see when I open my eyes. Fucking nice."

He threw back the blankets and sat up, swinging his legs over the side of the mattress. I tried to back up, but he caught my hips and kept me close, pressing his face into my stomach. At first, I just stood there in shock. When he rubbed his face back and forth, I brought my hand up, gingerly combing through his short hair. His moan was soft, but filled with bliss, so I continued, each of my strokes more sure.

We stayed like that for several long minutes. My hands in his hair, his face pressed against my belly, arm circling below my butt, the barest hint of sweetness filtering through the air. His breath warmed my skin beneath my T-shirt, but I shivered anyway.

"Need to go take a shower." He gave my butt a squeeze. "You wanna make me breakfast?"

"Yeah." I scratched his nape, drawing another moan from deep in his chest. "I'll make you something. Go."

He planted a kiss just below my belly button then rose to his feet. I took a step back, watching as he unbuttoned his wrinkled shirt, revealing his lean, golden torso dappled with dark hair. He tossed it on the bed and shot me a smirk before striding across the room and closing himself in the bathroom.

My hand shot to my chest, covering my fluttering heart. How did he do that to me? Without a single word, he made me feel more for him than I had for any other man. It didn't make sense, but I was helpless, and I had been since the beginning.

Well, I couldn't stand there pining over him forever. The fact was, no matter what my feelings were, I was still his little pet, and I had a job to do. I'd strip his bed, throw his linens in the laundry, make breakfast for the boys, then remake his bed.

Throwing myself into action, I picked up the shirt he'd tossed aside, catching a whiff of the sweetness I'd smelled earlier. That was strange.

I brought the material near the collar to my nose, taking a deep inhale, and nearly choked. That was not a good smell.

Not at all. Cloying florals and irritating spices clung to the inside of my nose, making my stomach churn. I threw the shirt down on the bed, disgusted.

Why would that scent be on Amir's shirt?

Morbid curiosity got the better of me. Climbing onto the bed, I lowered my face to the sheets. There was nothing on the far side, but where Amir had lain when I walked in, there was more of the same overly sweet scent.

Oh. Oh no.

Ripping the sheets from the corners of the mattress, I coughed so hard, I nearly gagged. There was no denying Amir's clothes and sheets were covered in cheap perfume. He'd been out last night, and I guessed I now knew what he had done for at least part of it.

Thoroughly put in my place, I pushed away the feelings that couldn't be dealt with right now and carried the load of sheets out of Amir's room like a good little pet.

That was all I was. A toy. A pet. Something to own. I really, *really* had to remember that.

CHAPTER FOURTEEN

Amir

MY HEAD WAS THROBBING again, but unlike my chronic headaches, this time, I'd done it to myself. There was a time when I'd enjoyed myself at Reno's version of a business meeting—a private room at Savage Beauties with enough strippers for each of us to have two in our laps if we wanted. Those days had come and gone, though. The routine was stale. Now, I had to drink myself stupid to get through the night.

I deserved to feel like a sweaty ass crack with all the ways I'd abused my body last night. Thank Christ I finally washed away the scent of desperation, cheap perfume, and the beer someone had splashed on me. I'd been too far gone to take care of it last night, but fresh from the shower, I felt like a brand-new man.

My boys were up and moving about by the time I made it downstairs. Julien was bugging Zadie—from more of a distance before I got pissy with them both—and Marco was slumped at the kitchen table with one of his regular fucks sitting beside him, typing away on her phone. I pulled up a seat on his other side, keeping watch on Zadie cooking and Julien running his mouth.

Marco's mouth turned up in a smirk. "You look like dog shit."

I gave him a once-over. "Pot, kettle, man."

"No way. I didn't imbibe half as much as you. Julien and I had to carry you into the house. You were toasted."

I rubbed the center of my forehead. "I took it too far." I glanced at the girl. "Cover your ears, sweetheart."

With an eye roll, she tugged her hood over her head, unfolded herself from the chair, and stalked into the kitchen to check out what Zadie was doing. I kept my eye on her to see if she'd talk any shit to my pet, but she just peeked at the stove, then propped a hip on the counter, adding herself to Zadie's audience.

"What'd Reno have to say?" Marco asked.

"Remember when we caught Schiffer pushing scripts and he mentioned Reno isn't in that line?"

Reno dealt in street drugs, always had. Mostly weed, but also coke and MDMA. That wasn't his primary money earner, and since I handled most of that end, he let me decide what products we were going to push. I'd seen enough bugged-out meth-heads to be certain we didn't want to go there. For a time, I'd had a lucrative side business selling performance enhancers to athletes, but I'd stopped that. The end of college was hurtling closer, so I was slowly pulling back, easing my way out.

And Reno was having trouble with that.

"Yeah, I remember."

"He wants me to find a source for scripts, specifically Oxy. He's all buzzed about it. Wants it to happen soon." I cupped my forehead, pressing hard at my aching temples.

"You're not going there." Marco wasn't asking. He wasn't involved in my business, had never wanted to be, and he couldn't stand that I was pushing for my brother.

"No, I'm not going there," I agreed. "Having a calm conversation with my brother is next to impossible. Add in a chick grinding on his dick while shoving her tits in his face, and it's a no go. So, I drank that shit away. I'll have to deal with him in time, but last night wasn't it."

Marco clucked his tongue. "Just another fucking way to reel you in. You see that, right?"

"I see it."

As soon as I had my college diploma in my hand, I was out of the business. Going legit and all that. Reno knew and had known from the very beginning. He had his thing, and I was going to have mine. He'd agreed to my conditions before I'd started working for him. I was in my second semester of my junior year now, and the end looked all too real. I sensed his low-level panic. And when Reno panicked, nothing good came of it.

Case in point, he was all hyped to move into pharmaceuticals, with me at the helm. That wasn't happening. He was my brother, I'd throw down for him, I'd take care of business for him, but I was not getting pulled any deeper, not when it was nearing time to walk away.

Marco's girl came back, slipping into her seat. Julien followed, holding two platters filled with pancakes, eggs, and bacon. Zadie trailed behind him with a bowl of fruit. They set everything on the center of the table, and Julien took the last chair, wasting no time in serving himself a heaping helping of everything.

I grunted. "You're going first?"

He waggled a brow. "Yep. I set the table *and* I carried the food. I automatically score higher on the scale than you bitches."

I'd give him that, even though he was annoying the shit out of me.

Zadie hovered beside the table, gnawing on her bottom lip. Her eyes were trained on the table. Her fingers fidgeted with the hem of her shirt.

"Did you eat?" I asked her. "I guess it's lunchtime. Did you eat lunch, mama?"

She shook her head. "No, but that's okay. I'll grab something at the dining hall."

"Considering you're staying for a while, I don't think that's a great plan. Take a seat. Grab a plate."

She looked up, scanning the table. "There are no seats. I'll just si—"

I scooted back from the table and patted my thigh. "Here's your seat. Come here."

She didn't have to move for me to notice how utterly stiff she was. Her shoulders were so rigid, they were nearly around her ears. This was a far cry from the girl who'd woken me up this morning. I didn't like it. Not at all.

I slapped my thigh harder this time. "Move your ass, pet, and put it in my lap. *Now.*"

Marco's girl drew in a sharp breath. She'd been around a few times and knew damn well not to utter a word. As for my boys...well, I felt their attention on me, but mine was solely focused on Zadie, who was slowly rounding the table.

When she got close enough, I tugged her into my lap, where she perched like a bird on a high wire, ready to fly away at any moment.

Nah, I definitely didn't like that.

"Relax," I murmured, sliding my hand under her hair to cup her nape. "You're not going anywhere, so pretend you like me and lean into me."

She released a breath, and some of the tension eased from her shoulders, but most of it remained.

"It's gonna be like that, huh?" Squeezing her nape, I whispered in her ear. "Gonna act like an uptight princess all of a sudden?"

She shook her head and turned so her nose grazed my cheek. "No. I'm just uncomfortable."

"Mmm. Maybe you just need some food in you." I picked up a forkful of eggs, holding it up to her mouth. "Eat."

She hesitated before parting her lips and accepting the offering. I liked that, seeing her lips wrapping around the tines of the fork. Me being the one to offer her nourishment, Zadie taking it into her body. My dick swelled behind the loose fabric of my joggers. No doubt she felt it growing thick and hard under her thigh.

We continued like that through breakfast, one bite for me, one for her. She never relaxed, never leaned into me, and it was driving me out of my mind. She'd been sweet when she'd showed up this morning, and all I was getting now was bitter.

"This was the shit, Zadie." Marco wiped his mouth and fell back in his chair, rubbing his stomach. "Thanks, girl."

"Yeah, I hope they're paying you enough." Marco's hookup dragged her fork through the syrup on her plate. "Please don't tell me you're cooking for these fools out of the kindness of your heart."

Zadie shook her head, her fingers clutching the edge of the table. "No, I'm not cooking for them out of the kindness of my heart."

I slid her hair to one shoulder and nuzzled the crook of her neck. She shivered. "Zadie's my good girl, and she's very much appreciated. Don't worry about what she gets paid."

Zadie was like a board in my lap. All her soft had gone rigid. Her head was bowed, avoiding not just my eyes, but everyone's. It bothered me. Really fucking bothered me. And I had no idea how to get it back.

The girl shrugged. "I'm just sayin'—"

I was not in the mood for anything this girl was *just sayin'*. My head pulsed with pain. The only person I was in the mood for was Zadie, and she was very clearly not in the mood for me.

"Marco, is there a reason there's a stranger at my table talking to my girl? Questioning my shit? 'Cause if there is, I'd like to know."

Marco turned his hand over. "I don't know why she's questioning your shit, but she's gonna stop right now." He wrapped his hand around her wrist and tugged until she stood up. "Come on, baby girl. Time to hit the road."

She followed him willingly, sliding her hand up the back of his shirt. He was tipping his head down to hers as they turned the corner. I had a feeling it wasn't quite time to go yet. Marco would handle her, it just might involve his dick in her mouth—and knowing him, she'd tell him thank you for the deposit when he was done.

I let my head fall against Zadie's back, closing my eyes and rubbing it back and forth. It felt better, just doing that, feeling her warmth through the thin layer of her shirt, her sweet berry scent soothing my aching skull.

"Headache?" Julien asked.

"Yeah. I thought I was going to kill it with breakfast, but it's settled in."

Julien had been around me long enough to know the deal with my headaches. He got up, filled up a refillable bottle with water, shook out some pain pills, and brought them to me. Zadie tried to shift out of my lap, but I held her there with my hand anchoring her hip while I swallowed the pills and guzzled water. It would help, but it'd take a while.

"Go back to bed, man," Julien urged. "You went way too hard last night. I'd almost say it serves you right to feel this bad but..." He shook his head, trailing off.

"But you're not a sadist?"

He chuckled. "Nah. Now, get your ass in a dark room until it fades." He got up from the table, grabbing the plates and platters.

"Let me help you." Zadie tried to push to her feet, but I kept her in my lap, rolling my forehead on her shoulder. "Amir, stop. I need to clean up."

"I've got it, princess." Julien grinned at her over his shoulder. "You saved my stomach this morning. Washing a few dishes is the least I can do. Now, take my boy to his room and force him to rest."

I nipped at her ear. "I think that sounds like a really good idea. Take me to my room, princess."

"I need to remake your bed." She lifted her chin but kept her eyes down.

"Then let's go do that."

My bedroom was blissfully dark. When I closed the door behind me, it was quiet too. Zadie's shoulders stiffened at the sound of the door clicking shut, but she moved forward, making my bed with efficiency that in no way surprised me. I watched her from the doorway, enjoying the way she looked in my room, like she belonged.

When she finished, she stood by the foot of the bed, her hands clutched in front of her. "If that's all, I'll leave you alone. I didn't get any studying done yesterday, so—"

"No, that's not all. Get in bed with me." I winced at the sound of my own damn voice. Jesus, if I could have extracted my brain from my skull, I would have. That held more appeal than the sharp, stabbing pain.

Zadie stepped forward. "Is it that bad?"

"Yeah. It's that bad." I pushed her back until her legs hit the bed. She sat down, swinging her feet onto the mattress and scooting over to make room for me. Stretching out beside her, I rolled to my side and shoved my face into her cleavage.

Berries. Rain. Warmth. Zadie.

"Talk to me, mama."

"About what?"

"Anything. Tell me a story. I don't know. Just talk."

Her small hand rested on the center of my back, barely there. "Okay. Um...I've always thought it was kind of funny when you called me 'mama.' When I was born, my parents fought over what to name me. My dad wanted Sadie, but my mom liked Zadie better. She said it was more unique and had pizzazz." Zadie giggled, and yeah, I could picture Felicity saying exactly that. "She won because...well, she'd just given birth and that trumps everything. But my dad, he's a little bit of a ballbuster, so he started calling me grandpa out of spite."

"Grandpa?" I murmured.

"Mmhmm. He's Jewish, and *Zayde* is the word for 'grandpa' in Yiddish. My mom hated it so much, but the nickname stuck. To this day, when I talk to my dad, that's what he calls me. I don't know if he remembers my actual name."

"Don't think I'm going to call you grandpa."

"No, I wouldn't want you to." Her hand glided up my back to the base of my head. Fingertips pressing into my scalp, she rubbed up to my crown then back down. "Does this feel okay?"

"Fuck yeah. Keep talking."

"Zadie doesn't mean grandpa. I don't want you to think my mom would have done that to me. It's just an alternate spelling of Sadie, which means princess in Hebrew. Sometimes my dad would call me 'princess grandpa' to drive her really nuts. It's really no wonder they're divorced." She sighed. "More?"

"Keep talking, princess."

Her fingers were working magic on my scalp, scratching and rubbing in smooth, rhythmic motions. My head was resting on her perfect, magnificent tits, and my arm was circled tight around her middle, trapping her against me. The pain in my head hadn't eased, but her lilting whisper made it bearable.

"My dad is the most gentle man I've ever known. He hates seeing suffering and will do anything to end it. A bleeding heart, my mom says, but I don't know. I think he just has an exceptionally *good* heart."

The beat of her heart thrummed against my ear. Steady, easy, soothing in its predictable pattern. When I got headaches, I always preferred complete silence. That was before I'd known what it was like to lay my head on a soft, pretty tit and listen to an angelic voice talk-sing me a story about her really nice dad.

"We lived in this big, old house in Oregon that had a shed in the back I still think is haunted. A mama raccoon moved in one year and had her babies. My mom wanted to call animal control because, of course, mama kept digging through our garbage, but my dad wouldn't hear of it. When the babies got bigger, they moved on, but something went wrong, and a baby got left behind. I guess because it was missing a paw."

Her cool fingers trailed down the side of my face, soft as feathers, then back to my forehead, cupping it firmly in her palm. I almost shuddered from how good it felt. She had no fucking idea what kind of relief she was bringing me.

"My dad couldn't leave the baby there. He scooped it up, held it in front of me, and said, 'Grandpa, meet your sibling, Charlie.'" She giggled softly. "Charlie was adorable and snuggly. Dad hand-fed her and built her all kinds of contraptions to keep her busy. It was an utter disaster, but we both loved her too much to admit defeat until we had no choice. Dad found a wildlife rescue sanctuary for her to live, and he ended up volunteering there. He still does, even though Charlie is long gone. He calls me all the time to tell me about the animals that come in. 'Grandpa, your new sibling, Arthur, has arrived.' My mom never understood it, but I did. I think because I'm just like him. I can't stand to see anyone suffer. It physically pains me, even if it's a stranger. Even if it's my captor."

My mouth curled at the edges. I liked everything about her story, and I heard her message loud and clear. She wasn't comforting me now because she liked me, more like it was a compulsion, part of her nature. She should have known by now I had no problem taking full advantage of her nature if that meant I got to have my head on her tits and her hands rubbing my head.

"I like your dad," I said.

She exhaled. "Yeah, I do too. I don't know yet if I'll go back to Oregon when I'm done with school, but I can't imagine always living so far from him."

"Not a Cali girl, Zadie?"

"I don't really fit in here."

"It's a big state."

She breathed out a laugh. "That's true." She slid her fingers through my hair. "I don't really know what I'll do. What about you? Are you a Cali boy, Amir?"

"Can't picture myself anywhere else. I don't think I'd fit in at a wildlife sanctuary in Oregon."

"It's a big state."

That made me laugh. "You trying to get me to move to Oregon with you, mama? Is that what this is?"

"No, I'm not that naive."

"What's that mean?"

"Nothing." She cupped my forehead again, spreading warmth all over my pain. "Shhh. Close your eyes. No more talking."

I wanted to argue with her, but there was a railroad spike driving through my skull every time I spoke, so I took orders, shut my fucking mouth, and closed my eyes. I'd done nothing in my life to deserve this kind of treatment, and truth be told, I'd stolen it for myself.

I didn't feel the least bit guilty about it either.

My conscience was so clear, I fell asleep with my head on Zadie's tits, her hand in my hair.

When I woke up, she was gone, the sheets cold. I didn't like it, but she'd be back. And I'd decided I wasn't letting her go at the end of the semester.

She'd be pissed I was reneging on our agreement.

But what did she expect? Everyone knew there was no honor among thieves, and I had every intention of stealing my soft little princess and keeping her as my own.

CHAPTER FIFTEEN

Zadie

DEACON TOOK THE SEAT next to mine, and I groaned. Not inwardly either. It had been a long, long week, and I was out of patience. This guy wasn't taking a hint. He was annoying, but he was relatively harmless, especially when he broke away from his laughing bros.

But I was at the end of my rope, so my normal empathy was frazzled into near nothing.

"Hey." He grinned at me, and even that annoyed me. "TGIF am I right?"

"Mmm."

"Do you have plans this weekend?"

"I don't know." I opened my laptop, tilting it away from him before typing in the password.

What I wanted to do this weekend was lock myself in my room and do all the homework I'd been neglecting over the last couple weeks while I played pet to Amir and his crew. I wouldn't get to do that, though. Not in the way I needed to recharge. I was at Amir's beck and call.

The sacrifice I'd been making for Amir's protection had seemed worth it in the beginning. My time, my pride, my energy were all things I could give up so I wasn't terrified of my own shadow—so I could leave my dorm without being constantly afraid.

That was before I realized how much it would wound me to come face-to-face with the reality that Amir did not reciprocate my feelings for him on any level. Before I had to smell another woman on his clothes. Before I had to contend with a bitter jealousy raging through my system I'd never once felt.

"There's a party tomorrow night and—"

I turned to Deacon. "Please don't finish your sentence." I didn't like him. I thought he was kind of terrible. I still didn't want to have to reject him.

His expression was genuinely perplexed. "Why not?"

My sigh was heavy with exasperation. "Just don't, okay? You should sit with your friends. I'm not in a chatty mood."

He twisted in his seat to face me. "See, this is the problem with you, Zadie. I hear you rejecting me, but you're so adorable and polite about it, it makes me like you even more. You're not like other girls—"

I cringed hard. "That's not the compliment you think it is."

He chuckled. "I don't think you're hearing me. I'm trying to say something nice to you."

"It's not a compliment if you have to put down other women to give it."

"Ah, a feminist." He bobbled his head like he'd uncovered an important truth. "I can dig that."

My nose scrunched. "That's not what feminism is," I murmured.

He leaned closer. "What?"

"Nothing." I shook my head. "I'm sorry, but I'd rather not talk anymore. It would make both of us more comfortable if you sat with your friends."

Deacon stilled, staring a hole into the side of my head. "I don't get you. If you had any idea what I gave up—you know what? Never mind. You're obviously having a bad day, so I'm not going to push you."

"Thanks." I loaded as much sarcasm into that one word as I was physically capable of.

"I'm not a bad guy, Zadie. I know I can be a dick, and I showed you the worst of me, but I think a girl like you could bring out the best. You're a quality girl, and I'm a quality guy. I'm just asking you to keep an open mind, because I think you're adorable and sweet. I can't *stop* thinking about you, actually."

His declaration of infatuation, or whatever it was, gave me the chills. Goose bumps sprouted up and down my arms. Fortunately, he got up and moved to sit with his friends, who earned their laughing boy nickname by cackling at Deacon until our professor called the class to order.

This wasn't the first time I'd asked myself if Deacon could be the one leaving the poems for me. I'd received another one this week, the same terribly written rhymes carefully typed on white paper. I hadn't told Amir or my suitemates or even my mother. It was as though my throat couldn't push out enough air to form the words. At least not those words. I'd spent so much of my life talking about my stalker—to my parents, therapists, the police, lawyers—I thought maybe I was just done.

I didn't want my biggest personality trait to be the stalker girl. Was that too much to ask?

Probably.

I'd spoken to my mom every day this week. The detective who'd worked on my case had retired, so there were a million hoops to jump through to speak to someone. Finally, she'd gotten a new officer to agree to look into my case and Drew, but according to her, he didn't seem to be moving with any urgency.

As soon as class finished, I gathered my things, eager to escape. But then what? I had to trudge to Amir's house and enter a whole new level of hell.

Since he'd fallen asleep on me over the weekend, he'd been more attentive than ever, watching me like a hawk. Sitting in the kitchen while I cooked. Studying my every move. I didn't know what was behind this escalated intensity, but I hated it...because I loved it.

When I stood up and slung my messenger bag over my shoulder, Deacon was waiting for me a few rows down. With a sigh, I walked down the steps, resigned. I couldn't leave this classroom without walking by him, and I had a feeling he wouldn't leave me be as requested.

Sure enough, he fell into step with me, down the steps and into the hallway.

"Are you ready for the test Monday?" he asked.

"No, not at all," I replied honestly.

"Do you...do you want to study together?"

I glanced at him, taken aback by the earnestness in his question. "That's a nice offer, but I do better on my own. Thank you, though."

His smile was tight. "Got it. Thought maybe a study sesh would be more your speed than a frat party."

I had to laugh at that. "You're right, it would be. But I really do prefer to study on my own. I can't concentrate when there are distractions. If I could be in a sensory deprivation tank, all the better."

Deacon chuckled as he held the door open for me to exit the building. "I don't know, might be hard to study without any light."

My laugh was softer this time. "That's true. I guess I would need one sense in my tank."

We were both laughing when Amir stepped into my path. His bunched fists were at his hips, his midnight eyes were on me.

"Oh, hi," I stammered.

He held his hand out. "Come on. I'm driving you."

"All right." My fingers twitched, but I wouldn't let myself slip my hand in his. Not when I so desperately wanted to.

Amir took matters into his own hands, transferring my messenger bag from my shoulder to his, then wrapping his fingers around my wrist and tugging me into his side. He turned us both to face Deacon, then he curled his arm around my shoulders. For his part, Deacon blanched, but he didn't back off. He stood there, legs wide, chest puffed, as if he was ready to take Amir on if he needed to. As if he had any chance.

I slid my palm across Amir's chest. "Let's just go. I'm tired."

"Are you okay, Zadie?" Deacon asked.

"I'm fine," I assured him. I may not have liked Deacon, but I would never want him to face Amir's wrath. After witnessing his viciousness in the ring, I wouldn't wish that on my worst enemy.

Okay, maybe Drew. *Maybe*. But I wouldn't watch.

Amir's muscles flexed and rippled under my hand, then he tipped his chin to peer down at me. "Do I need to do something about this situation?"

I shook my head. "No. It's fine. I promise. There's no situation."

His head snapped back up to scowl at Deacon. "You see this? This is mine. Remember that, kid, and we'll be fine." Then he stalked off, and since I was attached to him, he dragged me with him, forcing me to scramble to keep up.

"Can you please slow down? My legs are much shorter than yours."

He immediately tempered his pace, slipping his hand from my shoulder to cup the side of my neck. He kept his touch gentle and light, despite the tension bleeding from his muscles. "I did not enjoy seeing you sharing a laugh with that asswipe."

My mouth gaped. "I'm not allowed to laugh now?"

"That's not what I said."

"He said something funny, so I laughed. I didn't accept his proposal to become his personal house pet next semester or anything."

"No."

"No what?"

His hold on my neck rose to my jaw. His thumb pressed against my bottom lip. "No, snarkiness doesn't suit you. Not from this sweet mouth. Stop."

He was right, it didn't, but I was completely out of sorts. And maybe I was more than a little angry and fed up with...well, everything. So, if some snark came out, it was only fair, and I didn't want to be called out on it.

"I'm sorry I can't be sweetness and light every second of the day. I'm human, Amir. Sometimes I'm in a bad mood. Sometimes all of this gets to me, okay?"

"All of what, mama?"

He used that voice on me. The lacquer-coated one that made my stomach feel like it was on fire.

"Everything. You, the poems, school, Max. I guess I'm tired. I know you don't care. I know I have to suck it up, and I will. I promise I will. But—"

Amir swung me around, backing me into the side of his SUV. I hadn't even noticed we were in the parking lot until that moment.

"If you could do anything right now, if you didn't have any of this shit going on around you, what would you do? How would you spend your Friday night?"

I considered his question carefully, flipping it over in my mind to see if it was a trick. "Last semester, I spent most of my Friday evenings with Hells and Elena having dinner and sometimes watching a movie. They always went out after, and I'd stay in my room studying and listening to music. And I *know* it sounds boring, and maybe it was, but I want a little bit of that boring back. I wasn't worried or scared. I could just *be*. I'd like a night like that, where I can just *be*." I brought my hand up to his chest, pressing into the heat emanating through his Savage U T-shirt. "I don't know if I'll get that back."

"You will." He leaned into me, bringing his face close to mine. "I'd give you that if I could."

Lips parting, I sucked in a breath. "That's a nice thing to say."

"If I take you back to your dorm now, give you the night off, what will you do?"

I was both elated and miserable at the prospect. I needed the distance from Amir he hadn't been giving me this week, but I didn't want it. My mind was at war with my stupid, stupid heart. My mind would win, though. All I had to do was remember those perfumed sheets, and my mind would stomp my heart into a bloody pulp.

"Homework. I really, really need to catch up."

He shook his head. "Jesus, what a waste. Friday night and my pet wants to do homework."

"It's not that I want to, it's that I have to. We're not all as naturally gifted as you, Amir."

His mouth twitched, giving me a small grin. "That sounded like a compliment."

I pushed on his chest, but of course he didn't budge. "You know how smart you are. Don't be coy."

He'd had me read over his analytics paper on Wednesday before he turned it in the next day, and it had been perfection. My little nerd soul had longed to throw it down on the floor and roll around in all the ideas and analysis printed on those five sheets of paper.

Stupid Amir and his big intellect. He could have just been hot, but no. He had to add in smart and make himself irresistible to a girl like me.

Perfumed sheets.

Pain. Blood. Gore.

There, that's better.

He trailed his hand down the side of my hair, toying with a ringlet. "If I didn't have to do a job for Reno, I'd take you out. Give you the kind of Friday night you should be having."

"Why do I think our ideal nights out differ greatly?"

"You deserve to be shown off, Zadie, not locked away in your room. You can have a lazy Sunday. You can be boring when you're forty. What you won't be doing anymore is hiding. Not when I can be with you." He hooked his arm around my waist so our bellies were flush. "You dance?"

"In my bedroom," I replied.

"You dance." His lids lowered. "You're gonna dance with me."

"Is that part of my job?"

"Does it need to be to get your sexy ass in a dress and grinding on my leg?"

I swallowed hard, but it did nothing to clear the thick coating in my throat. "I don't know," I whispered. "I don't...I've never done that."

He took a handful of my butt and squeezed. "I know that. Believe me, I know that. I'm gonna make it happen for you, Zadie. All the things you haven't done because of that piece of shit, I'm going to give them to you."

Perfumed sheets.

"So, it's part of my job?"

The heat in his eyes dimmed. He let go of me to take a step back. "Does that make it easier?"

I nodded. "I need to remember what we are."

"We are what I say we are." Taking me by the shoulders, he swiveled me around then opened the SUV door and practically shoved me inside, copping a feel as he went.

The drive home wasn't quiet, but Amir didn't speak. He cranked up the sound system, drowning out the silence with explicit rap. I thought he'd pull up to the curb and dump me out, but he turned into a spot and put the SUV in park.

Reaching across the console, he unbuckled me, grabbed my wrist, and tugged. "Get over here, mama," he gritted out. The heat was back, but this time, it was a raging fire, and I feared it was directed at me.

I should have run. I should have done anything other than crawl across the console. But I didn't. Amir took me by the waist and guided me to sit sideways on his lap, like he'd done that first night. And the second.

He might have been angry, but he stroked my face so gently, I didn't feel any of his wrath.

"What are you doing tonight?" he murmured.

"Staying in and studying. What are you doing tonight?"

He exhaled through his nose. "Work."

Work probably meant more perfumed sheets, or maybe bloody clothing and bruised knuckles. Quite possibly both.

"Have fun," I whispered, unable to keep the melancholy out of my voice.

He canted his head, studying me, really taking me in. "I'm taking you out tomorrow. It's part of your job, if that's what you need to hear."

"Okay." At this point, it *was* what I needed, to keep what was happening with him compartmentalized. It was the only way I'd walk away at least somewhat whole.

His thumb pressed into the corners of my mouth. "What's this about? Why does it look like you're sad?"

"I told you, it's been a lot lately. Too much." I blinked at him, then let my eyes fall. "I need...I don't know. I don't know what I need, but I just...I don't know."

He stared at me for another long beat, then he did something so unexpected, I went with it. Cradling the side of my head in his wide palm, he pushed me down until I lay on his chest and wrapped his arms around me.

And it was...a hug. Amir was hugging me. The backs of my eyes stung from how tender the gesture was. I didn't even know he *could* be tender, yet here he was, holding me when I needed it badly.

The scent of his warm spice invaded my nose. His calm heartbeat thrummed in my ear. Fingers trailed up and down my arm and along my spine. It was so nice, so sweet, so perfect, I would have thought I was dreaming, if not for the fact that I didn't have nice dreams like this anymore. Not lately at least.

My tight, stressed body relaxed as the minutes ticked by, and I melted into Amir's embrace. Then he kissed the top of my head, and my heart shuddered so hard in my chest, it felt like my sternum was close to cracking.

I couldn't do this. This wasn't wise.

I lifted my head. "I should go in."

"Yeah." He took my jaw in his hand, pulled me close, and touched his lips to mine. "Get out of my car, Zadie." His lips ghosted over mine again, then his head fell back on the rest, and he watched me under half-mast lids.

"'Kay." I forced my limbs to move, retreating to the passenger seat to grab my messenger bag. With one hand on the door, I looked at Amir. "Thank you."

He lifted a shoulder. "Don't like you sad. I didn't know that about myself until now. But yeah, I don't like it."

There. There he went saying things that would inevitably lead to my heart breaking. I should have punched him. Instead, I smiled. His gaze lowered to my lips while his turned up ever so slightly.

"Who knew you could be kind of sweet?" Swinging open the door, I hopped out onto the pavement, then spun around, looking up at Amir. "I'll see you tomorrow."

I kissed my hand, then waved a goodbye, closing his door behind me.

I had always known Amir was dangerous, but there in the front seat of his vehicle, he'd given me a glimpse of how *truly* dangerous he was.

Chapter Sixteen

Zadie

Like déjà vu, I arrived at the boys' house early on Saturday. I was a little more trepidatious, but still hopeful, than I'd been the previous weekend.

The house was quiet. I didn't know what I should do first. Despite the shift between us over the last week, I hadn't gotten over the sting of the perfumed sheets to chance waking Amir up again. So, I killed some time by dusting the living room, which was really an excuse for me to sit at the piano and run my fingers over the keys. Touching them without playing a note only took the slightest edge off my yearning to play, but it was something.

I wandered back into the kitchen to brew a pot of coffee. Marco preferred his iced, so I poured him a mug and placed it in the fridge to cool so he could have it when he woke up. Then I set out the mugs I'd noticed Amir and Julien using most often so I'd have them close at hand when they were ready for their coffee.

Hadn't I become the good little house servant? Jeesh. If my mom only knew she was shelling out big bucks in tuition for me to learn how to properly fold fitted sheets.

A creak in the hallway floorboard alerted me to someone approaching right before they appeared in the doorway. I flinched when the person turned out not to be one of my three boys.

"Oh." Vanessa stopped short when she noticed me. "Hey."

"Good morning," I squeezed out. My throat had become tight at the sight of her bed head, smeared mascara, and bare legs—because she was wearing a T-shirt and nothing else. Vanessa, the girl from the fight who'd volunteered to take my place on her knees in front of Amir, had spent the night here.

She shrugged and continued across the kitchen to the coffee maker. I scooted down the counter, giving her access. She chose the mug I'd set out for Amir, filled it halfway with coffee, then moved to the fridge to add a heavy dose of creamer.

Taking a sip of her coffee, she propped a hip on the counter across from me, eyeing me over the brim.

"So, what's your deal? Amir said you're like his servant or something?" Vanessa took one long sweep of me with her eyes, then dismissed me by studying her fingernails.

"Or something," I replied.

This girl's presence made my stomach hurt. On one level, I understood what it meant, but I was having trouble accepting it on every other level. If I did, I wouldn't be on my feet anymore. I wouldn't be able to stand in this kitchen and hold my head up.

The shirt she was wearing was Amir's. The same Savage U T-shirt he'd been wearing yesterday when he'd talked about taking me dancing. It shouldn't have been a gut punch, but it was. Oh, it was.

Vanessa looked at me and curled her lip. "Stare much? God, don't be a freak." She rolled her eyes, taking a long pull of the coffee *I* had just made.

I wished I could have been mad. Mad would have been easier than scraped and raw. If I left now, I'd be okay. I just needed air and perspective. This only hurt because I was here, in this house. When I walked back into my life, this would shrink down until it was barely anything.

Resolved, I opened my mouth to tell Vanessa goodbye when Amir came sauntering into the kitchen wearing just a pair of lounge pants, rubbing his taut, golden belly, and yawning. His eyes landed on me, and his mouth morphed into a smirk.

"Hey, mama. I was disappointed not to see your face first thing like I did last weekend." His voice was gritty with sleep and entirely without shame, even though his hookup was standing across the kitchen from him. "Seeing you in my kitchen makes up for it, though."

When I didn't respond, Amir stopped in his tracks to look me over. When he got to my face, his mouth parted, and a deep furrow ran between his brows.

"Zadie? What's up with you?" His head whipped to Vanessa. "Did you say shit?"

I would deal with the consequences later. My feet became unglued, and I strode toward the archway that led to the hall where I'd left my shoes. I had to get out of here. I couldn't stand to see Amir with *her*. How sad was that? Falling for my captor and being jealous when he didn't fall back. I couldn't believe myself.

Amir was faster than me, darting into the hall to block my path to the front door. "What the fuck?"

He reached for me, and I flinched, backing up a step. "I need to go."

"No you don't. You're staying right the fuck here and talking to me."

He came at me, arms out. I dodged, going right. I'd leave my shoes behind. Maybe that was crazy, but I just needed to leave. I had to get out of here before he figured out why I was upset. Before he saw the green-eyed monster riding me like a wraith.

"Let me go."

He didn't. As soon as I moved, he was there, coming at me, and I knew he would never let me leave. Panic took my logic and ground it into dust. I whirled around and ran in the opposite direction, taking the stairs as fast as I could. Heavy footsteps beat the wood behind me, but I didn't falter. My only endgame was to get away.

I rushed through the first doorway and shoved the door closed. Only, it didn't close all the way. Amir came crashing through, then *he* closed it, flipping the lock to drive the point home that he'd caught me.

I backed up until my legs hit his mattress. The second I took my eyes off Amir to check for an alternate escape, he pounced, driving me onto the bed. I rolled to my stomach, clawing at the comforter to pull myself to the other side, but Amir landed on top of me, straddling my hips and leaning over my back. I tried to get my knees under me, but he had me pinned to the bed.

"Let me go," I whimpered. "Please. I need to go."

He stroked the side of my hair, pushing it back off my face. My cheeks were flaming with half embarrassment, half fury. I couldn't let him see me like this. I *wouldn't*, so I pressed my face into the bed. But that was a mistake. I was instantly engulfed in Amir's warm spice, and it went straight to my head, making me dizzy.

"The fuck, Zadie?" he murmured. "You gotta calm down. I'm not letting you go, so you need to relax and tell me what the fuck is the matter."

"No, get off me!" There was no strength behind my demand. He had me here, trapped in his room. My captor. If he wanted to shove my face in his conquests, he could and would, and I would just have to bear it. It was my own damn fault for falling for the villain. I knew better, but here I was anyway.

"I'm not getting off you. Not until you talk, and even then, I might not. I like it here." He rocked his hips forward, and there was no mistaking the bulge rubbing my butt. "Talk, mama. Right the fuck now."

"I can't," I mumbled miserably.

He brought his face close to mine, rubbing his cheek against my ear. "Zadie...give me something to go on here."

"Get off me."

"No." His weight lifted, and for half a blissful second, I thought he was letting me go. Then he grabbed my shoulders and rolled me to my back. His hands came down on either side of my head, caging me in. I squeezed my eyes shut. He growled. "Fuck, Zadie, you're killing me. I thought we were friends."

I shook my head. "We're not."

"Did Vanessa say shit?"

My breath hitched of its own volition. Amir stilled. Neither of us spoke, but we didn't need to. He heard me, and I felt his understanding.

"Please," I pleaded.

"No." He skimmed his nose along mine. "I need your words. I can't fix it if I don't know what's wrong."

I shook my head. "You can't fix it. It's my head that's the problem. I just need to go. Then it'll be better. Please, Amir."

He cupped my cheeks, keeping me still. "Open your eyes."

I squeezed them tighter.

"Open, Zadie. Right the fuck now or I will redden your pretty ass."

My eyes flew open. He didn't laugh at me like I thought he would. He stared at me hard enough to see straight through me. But still, he wasn't getting it, and that made me mad. How could he not see how I felt? How could he not understand what it was like for me to stand in a room with him and the girl he fucked last night?

"I don't want to be here," I whispered.

"Too bad." He pressed his forehead to mine. "Talk. Tell me why you were liking me yesterday and now you can't even look at me."

"Because..." He wouldn't let me turn my head. His eyes burned into me. He was all I could see, smell, feel. It was too much. I wanted out and away, and since he wasn't allowing that, I snapped. "Because I hate changing your slutty sheets and seeing that girl in your shirt. I hate everything about it, and I need to go. Please, please let me go."

Amir reared back, giving me breathing room. I would have been relieved if he hadn't laughed at me. Full and hearty, his shoulders shook.

"My slutty sheets?" He peered down at me, grinning wide. "What the fuck does that mean, mama?"

I dug my heels into the bed, pushing myself up the mattress. I got maybe a foot before Amir followed, pouncing on me again. Frustrated, I slapped my hand down on the blanket and balled it in my fist, yanking hard.

"These slutty sheets. I hate them. I hate that you want me to change them after you've had another girl in them. I know you don't care, I know I'm your pet, but I hate them, and if

I have to smell that perfume again, I'll throw up all over your expensive, slutty sheets."

Amir caught my wrists, cuffing them together over my head with one hand and holding my face with the other.

"What is this?" His eyes searched mine until light shone through his midnight. "Is this jealousy? Are you jealous, Zadie? You think...what? I had Vanessa in this bed last night?"

My nose scrunched at her name on his lips. "She's wearing your shirt. I know you had her in your bed. It's none of my business, but I—"

"What shirt?"

I scowled at him. "You know what shirt. Your Savage U shirt. The one you were wearing yesterday."

He pressed his thumb to my lips. "You're jealous."

He wouldn't let me turn my head, so I averted my eyes. "No." My denial was so damn weak.

"You are, mama, and I like it." Reaching over my head, he brought his pillow to my face. "Smell this."

I sniffed, and all I was hit with was Amir. Warm, spicy Amir.

He tipped his head down to the foot of the bed. "Look down there. Tell me what you see."

Black fabric was carelessly tossed on the far corner of the bed. The longer I stared at it, the more it dawned on me what it was. My urge to escape tripled.

"Tell me what you see," he ordered softly.

"Your shirt." My throat was five times too small, barely squeaking out my response. *His shirt was on the bed. That meant...*

"Mmhmm. The same Savage U shirt half the campus owns. Including Marco." He ran his nose along mine. "Did my sheets smell slutty?"

"No. Not like last weekend."

His laugh was barely a breath. "Strippers. They bathe in that shit then rub it all over you, even when you're not asking for it."

That didn't make me feel better. "'Kay."

He lowered his chest to mine, and his fingers flexed around my wrists. "Come on, mama, tell me how jealous you are. You want to be the only girl in my sheets? You want me to smell like you, baby? Give me those words. I need to—"

My teeth sank into his chin, giving him a sharp bite, then I fell back onto the bed and mewled. I couldn't take it anymore. I'd lost it. With Amir on top of me, the heat of his skin warming mine, his scent invading me, his lacquered words coating my ears...it was far too much.

He stared at me with wide, shocked eyes.

"Zadie,"—he released my wrists and slid his hand under my head—"you bit me."

"You won't stop talking."

His fingers curled in my hair, and he tipped my head back. Then he shifted, shoving my legs apart with his knees to fit himself in the cradle of my thighs and ruck my skirt up to my waist. His cock was rock hard, and when he lowered his hips to meet mine, he rocked against my core. My panties and his thin pants were the only things separating us. And I *felt* him. I mewled again, bucking my hips, but that only drove him against me.

"Tell me you're jealous," he gritted out.

I would never say it. Never, ever. I looped my arms around his neck and tugged until his mouth was close enough for me to latch on to. I bit his bottom lip, then licked the spot where my teeth had been. Amir groaned the second my tongue touched his skin and answered back with his plunging between my lips.

I'd unleashed him without meaning to, but even as I lost my mind in his dominating kiss, I knew there was no going back. Mistake or not, this was his show now.

He yanked at my hair, tipping my head back farther, taking my mouth to its limit. He bit and sucked, licked me everywhere. I nipped at his lips and sucked on the tip of his tongue. He must've liked it when I did that, groaning and grinding his erection into me.

He had my shirt up, under my chin, the cups of my bra down, and his mouth on my nipples. He suckled one, then the other, drawing them into beaded points.

"Beautiful tits. Never forgot the taste of them," he murmured as he raked his eyes over them. "These are my tits now, aren't they?"

"Yes," I whispered. I would have agreed to a lot—even though I was mad at him and didn't really believe it—to keep his lips fastened to my nipple.

My breath got stuck in my throat when he slid his hand between our bodies, pushed my panties to the side, and trailed his fingers down my folds. At my entrance, he swirled the tip of his finger around, dipping in slightly before traveling to my clit and applying firm pressure.

My eyes flew open, finding his staring back at me. His mouth and mine were grazing, barely touching, but still connected. Each time his chest rose, mine fell. Our air mixed and swirled until I couldn't tell if I was breathing or he was.

His fingers worked between my legs, touching me like he'd done it a hundred times and knew exactly how I liked it. I'd been soaked before he started, worked up from his body on top of mine, but now, I was drenched.

"Yeah, jealous, mama," he murmured against my lips. "This pussy's been mine since the first time I touched it, hasn't it? You've been waiting for me to come claim it."

"Stop talking," I rasped. He was far too close to the truth.

"I'm sorry for making you wait." He snagged my bottom lip between his teeth then sucked it into his mouth. "This pussy's angry at me, but I'll make her better."

Without warning, he sat back on his knees, yanked my panties off, and dove down to feast on me. His lips latched onto my clit, sucking and flicking his tongue. My mind raced to keep up, but it was no use. Once his mouth was on me, my mind was out of the equation.

My spine arched. I clawed at the sheets beside me. I wanted to claw at his shoulders and scalp, to push him off me or tug him closer. He laid claim to my body without asking if I wanted to be claimed. But he'd been right. I *had* been waiting for him to come back to me. Despite everything, I'd longed to feel his mouth between my legs again since he'd walked out of my room.

Amir held on to my hips, pulling me tighter to his mouth. His fingertips dug into my flesh. I whimpered and sighed as heat rushed down my belly, settling in my clit. His tongue took the heat and used it to make a spark, igniting me. Each pass of my clit stoked it higher and higher, until I burst into flames for him, crying his name, singing my pleasure to the ceiling. And he kept at me, sucking and licking until I was nothing but ashes, helpless in a pile in the center of his bed.

And then he was over me, rolling a condom on without taking his eyes off mine for even a second. He didn't give me time to come down or think clearly. Not before he fitted the head of his cock with my opening and notched it inside. He stopped there, exhaling a heavy breath over my lips, then pushed in a little more.

"Amir...what..?" I could have protested. A big part of me wanted to. This was way too fast, and I wasn't sure I was over being mad at him. But if I asked him to stop, would he? Moreover, would I even be able to ask?

He tapped my lips. "Quiet. I only want to hear my name out of these lips. Get out of your head."

My inner walls rippled with a leftover wave of pleasure, making him squeeze his eyes shut and tighten his grip on my hips.

"*Fuck. Shit.*" His eyes opened and glared at me with something like accusation.

"Was that bad?" I wasn't so naive not to know he *liked* the way I felt around him.

"I'll show you bad. Open for me," he said through clenched teeth.

My legs spread wider, like I couldn't help following his command. He hitched one of my legs up, pressing my knee almost to my chest, spreading me so he could sink inside, inch by inch. I whimpered as his body speared mine, creating space for himself in my core. A space that was only his, now designed to fit his body.

Tears pricked my eyes from the pain, from the magnitude of the act, from the relief that it was finally happening, from the person it was happening with. His eyes tracked the one tear that trickled down my temple as he held still as deep in me as he could get.

"You want to be the only girl in my sheets?" He wiped the tear away. "Is that what you want?"

My lips parted. Only a wisp of air escaped.

Shaking his head, Amir started to move, retreating slightly, then pushing back in. He was holding back, going slow for me, letting me get used to how incredibly full he made me. That surprised me. I'd rarely known him to be gentle.

"Touch me," he murmured. "Touch me, Zadie."

When I stayed frozen, he took my hand and brought it to his shoulder. Then he grabbed my other hand, placing it on his cheek.

"Fucking touch me," he ordered softly. "Move with me. Show me you want my sheets smelling like berries and not anything else."

Once my hands were on his hot skin, something in me flipped. The floaty feeling of watching myself from above disappeared and I came crashing into my body. I dragged my palm along the scruff of his jaw, to his nape, holding on to him there. My other hand ran along his shoulder, down the sinewy muscles in his arm, to his back. He made deep, pleasured sounds as I explored his skin. I hoped that meant he liked my hands on him, because I couldn't get enough of the feel of him.

"Is this good?" I asked.

He glared at me, frowning like he was angry with me. Then his hips reared back until he was barely in my body.

"Is *this* good?" He slammed inside, taking my breath, my guts, my eyesight away.

"Amir," I whimpered, clinging to his taut biceps.

"Don't ask me if having your hands on me is good. You're smarter than that, mama. You feel my cock in you. I know you can feel how hard you make me. Tell me you know." He drove forward, hitting me so deep, stars sparked behind my lids. "Tell me you're mine."

I nodded, bringing my hands up to cup his neck. "I know, I know. I feel it."

He dropped his head so his nose grazed mine. "Tell me you're mine. Tell me."

"I'm—"

He swirled his hips, finding a raw, flaming nerve inside me. My spine bowed, and my neck arched back. Amir slipped his arm around my middle, holding me in that position while he fucked me with determined precision, rubbing that magic spot until I released a tremulous scream.

He kept holding me, grunting into my neck as he rode my body like a wave. Over and over, he thrust into me, drowning me in everything him. I wrapped my arms around his shoulders, letting him take me where he needed to go.

His movements became more frantic, the noises escaping his lips desperate. I held him tighter. He said my name like an exaltation, plunging in deep and staying there. My walls clamped around him, hugging him as he pulsed.

"That's right, baby girl. That's right," he murmured as his movements slowed. Hot lips dragged along my neck, then teeth grazed my pulse. "Mmm...good little pet."

My eyes fluttered open. Heart stuttering in my chest, my arms fell to the side.

Pet. I'm his pet.

Oh no. What had I done?

CHAPTER SEVENTEEN

Amir

THE SOFT, PLIANT WOMAN in my arms turned rigid at the flip of a switch. My cock was buried deep inside her, my arms wrapped around her, yet she was already gone. I lifted my head, and hers turned to the side.

"Zadie."

She sighed. "I'm okay."

"Zadie." Fingers curling around her jaw, I turned her to me. "Whatever's going on in your head, cut that shit out right now. You just gave me a gift. Don't act like that doesn't mean something."

Her eyes narrowed. "You took it."

Sweet voice, rotten words. Fuck that shit.

"Oh, I took it? Is that how this is going to play out?"

Her lips parted, but before she could speak, the fire in her eyes died out. "No. I don't know." She pushed on my shoulders. "Can you get off me? Please?"

"No." I rocked my hips, still hard as steel in her hot little pussy. I'd need to pull out soon to get rid of the condom, but not before she stopped retreating. "Tell me you gave it to me."

Her teeth clamped down on her lip. The same teeth that bit me and made me lose my shit. I sure as hell hadn't planned on ending up in bed with Zadie this morning, much less fucking her as hard as I did for her first time. But the second those teeth touched my skin, I became frenzied for her.

"I gave it to you," she whispered.

"Regret it already?"

She chewed on her lip for several hideous beats before shaking her head. "No."

That didn't satisfy me in the least, but I had to pull out to deal with the condom. Zadie winced as I left her body, curling into herself the second I was no longer on top of her.

Condom tied in a knot, I tossed it on my bedside table and rolled to my side, pulling Zadie into me. She tipped her head back, her brows furrowing as her eyes darted around my face.

I reached down to cup her pussy. "Sore?"

She nodded. "A little."

I kept my hand there, and she didn't bat me away. "What the fuck's going on in your mind? You don't regret it, but you're looking at me like I murdered your dog."

She wet her bottom lip and sucked in a breath. Her hand reached down to settle over mine between her legs. "I don't regret it if that was you," she lowered her voice, "fucking your girl. If that was you fucking your pet, then I made a big mistake."

My mouth twitched at the dirty words coming from her sweet, rosy lips. She made it cute and sexy. I'd have to coax more dirty talk from her so I could hear her whisper it while I took her. Yeah, I was going to have to do that. And soon.

"Told you you were mine, Zadie," I replied.

"Then you called me pet." Her lips pursed into a sweet little pout. Oh, my pet was mad at me.

"You are my pet, but that's not a bad thing." I touched my lips to hers. "That means I'll take care of you. I'll make sure you have everything you need. Means I'll bite the head off any motherfucker who tries to touch you."

She shook her head. "I don't like that. I don't want to be your pet and change your slutty sheets and—"

I slammed my lips to hers, cutting off her stream of bullshit. This girl had no idea. None. She squirmed, but that was her only form of protest, allowing me to sweep my tongue into her mouth, flicking her tongue against mine.

I rested my forehead on hers. "There is no one else, mama. You've got me wrapped up in you. That girl downstairs slept in Marco's bed last night. She hasn't been in mine in months, and even when she was, she never spent the night. The perfume on my sheets last weekend was from my shirt. No one was in bed with me. Yeah, I had strippers rubbing up on me, and I let it happen because I was wasted. Won't happen again. If you're mine—and you are, I just need the words from you—then we're gonna be slutting the sheets up together. No one else. I don't share, and you keep giving me what you just gave me, I won't even *see* another girl, much less touch one."

Her nose scrunched. "Oh."

"Yeah, oh. Now, I need you to talk, because I just laid it all out for you. You have to give me more than 'oh.'"

She trailed her fingers up my arm to rest on my neck. "I'll be yours if you'll be mine. I won't share either. And smelling that perfume on your sheets...that hurt, and we weren't together. If that happens again, I won't stay, even if I want to."

"I don't like you threatening me with leaving."

Her brows rose. "Imagine coming to my bed and finding it smelling like cologne. Imagine it. Tell me you wouldn't walk away."

"You really want me imagining something that will make me homicidal? Because that's what will happen if some asshole finds his way into your bed. I know my pet, my loyal, beautiful pet. You'd never invite someone there when you're with me. So I find the scent of cologne in your sheets, I'll know something horrific happened, and I'll tear apart the world to find the—"

She pressed her fingertips to my lips. "I'm sorry I asked." Then she giggled. The sound traveled through the little bit of air between us, landing like a stone on my chest.

"Don't say shit like that to me, mama. I'm not levelheaded when it comes to you."

"I've noticed." Her cheeks glowed red, and if I wasn't mistaken, she seemed happy. "I should get dressed. I didn't make breakfast yet and the boys are probably starving."

I propped myself on my elbow, tracing the rounded curve of her cheek. "Things have changed. You get that, right? You don't have to cook and clean, Zadie."

She bit her bottom lip, eyes drifting to the side. "But...I want to. Not every day, and I'll skip cleaning, but I do like cooking for you. It makes me happy to do it. Unless you don't like my cooking..."

Dry laughing at her obvious fish for a compliment, I gave it to her. "Best home cooking I've ever had. Marco and Julien would revolt if I told you not to cook for us anymore."

"Then it's settled."

The two of us threw on our clothes, Zadie spent some time in the bathroom, and we headed downstairs. Julien was slumped over the kitchen island, staring into his mug of coffee. Vanessa and Marco were nowhere in sight. Hopefully he'd gotten her out of here. I'd make it clear when we were alone she wasn't welcome in this house anymore. Marco could get her dank pussy elsewhere.

"Good morning," Zadie chirped.

Julien's head shot up. He took in her wrinkled clothes, wild curls, swollen lips, and looked at me, all mellow and light on my feet. One look, and he got it. A slow smile spread across his face. I gave him shit, but Julien was my boy. I didn't have to say the words for him to know I'd been wanting Zadie for a while now. He didn't have to say a syllable for me to know he was happy it had finally happened.

"All right, all right. About time." His smile fell. "Does this mean no more dinners? I don't think I can survive on dollar ramen anymore. I can't fucking do it, Zadie."

She peeked around the open refrigerator door. "Don't worry your pretty little head for even a second. I'll still be here."

Julien grinned at me. "Your girlfriend called me pretty."

"Yeah." *Girlfriend.* Motherfuck, that was a head trip. I met Zadie's eyes over Julien's head. They were bright, sparkling, and her cheeks had taken on a permanent blush. "She can compliment you all she wants. It's you who has to watch that shit. Maybe don't even make eye contact. Even better, address her as Ms. Night."

Zadie laughed as she passed me with an armload of veggies and eggs. "If you address me as Ms. Night, I'll poison your food," she singsonged.

Julien threw out his arms. "I thought you were saving that for Amir."

She looked at him over her shoulder. "Who told you I don't have enough for all three of you?"

Laughing, I pulled up a stool beside Julien and joined him in watching my girl cook. Fuck, she was pretty. It grated on me to see her and Julien having an inside joke, but at the same time, I liked that he liked her. We had both been with enough low-quality women the other couldn't stand. No fucking need to repeat those mistakes.

My phone vibrated with a text from my brother and reality struck. As much as I wanted to toss Zadie back into bed and lick the pain away from her sweet pussy, I had a job to do. I had money to collect, people to deal with, and Reno to answer to.

I'd give myself an hour of this. My girl, my house, my kitchen. An hour of being the guy who deserved a girl like Zadie. Who got to have lazy Saturdays. Who wasn't beholden to a power-drunk brother who'd sooner blow up the whole town than rein in his reckless brutality.

· · • • • • • • · ·

I walked into Reno's warehouse, one of his guys by my side. When I collected money, I took backup, but I never involved Julien or Marco. They were as clean as I could keep them, and they'd stay that way.

Reno wasn't in his office, but I opened up his safe to drop my weekly deposit. He'd count it later. He trusted me implicitly, but when it came to his money, he didn't leave room for error. That was the one thing he was on top of. Money was god in his books, and he'd sacrifice anything to get more of it.

Blood was his sacrifice of choice. Not his blood, though.

I found him in a room in the back, the place where he took those who made him unhappy. He was pacing around a bloody man tied to a chair. Reno's knuckles were cut up, his forehead sweaty. He'd been at this for a while.

When I caught his attention, he grinned. "Yo, man. Your runs go good?"

"Yes. No problems." I nodded to the man who was too swollen to identify. "What's up with him?"

Reno flashed a wicked grin and gripped the man's hair, yanking his head back. "Joshy asked for an extension on his loan. You know I'm a reasonable guy. I allow one extension, which I think is more than generous. Joshy's on extension number three. Joshy obviously thinks I'm a little bitch. I had to do a little work to relieve him of that notion."

"Hmmm." I tucked my hands in my pockets and rocked on my heels. "How much does he owe?"

Reno chuckled. "That's the funny part. Joshy was down to the last five hundred. He was so close to the finish line, but he had to go fuck it all up." He bent down, getting in the bloody man's face. "Not gonna do that again, are you, Joshua?"

Bloody Man grunted in what I assumed was affirmation. I wouldn't want to get on Reno's bad side, not because he was so scary, but because he did not give a single fuck. Violence didn't bother me, but it delighted my brother. He'd barely made it out of high school because he kept getting in fights over the slightest provocation. He'd even punched a teacher, the idiot.

When he finished beating the shit out of Joshua, we went to his office where he counted out the money I'd collected, just as I knew he would.

"How's it going?" he asked as he put the cash back in his safe. "How are classes?"

"Good. A lot of work."

He sat down in his chair, shaking his head. "My baby brother, the genius. You're gonna go straight and make more money than I ever will."

I turned my hands over in my lap. "That's the dream. We'll see."

He leaned forward, steepling his hands under his chin. "Nah, you will. God didn't give you that intellect for nothing."

I narrowed my eyes. "What's with the flattery?"

That made him rock back in his chair and laugh. "Fuck you very much. I can't admire my kid brother?"

"I know you. I know you want me to get into pharma. If you're trying to butter me up, it's not happening. I can't take on anything else, and this summer, when I'm interning, I'm going to have to cut back. You support me going legit, then you need to drop the talk of me diversifying my product."

He turned serious. "I heard you the last time. I'm bringing in Eddie on that front. He has contacts in TJ we're going to work with."

I pressed my fingertips to my eyes. "I don't want to know, all right? Just don't get yourself killed."

"How can I when I'm immortal?"

That had me grinning at him. "Is this like the time you convinced me you could fly and fractured your arm in three places?"

Reno's brain didn't work the same as other people's. His sense of danger was pretty much nonexistent. So when I asked him to prove he could fly when I was seven, he took me by the hand, walked me to the nearby park, climbed to the top of a huge tree...and he flew. The asshat was lucky to survive that stunt.

He rolled his eyes. "That tree grew ten feet after I climbed it. The wind changed directions. Someone put lead in my boots. There was kryptonite in someone's pocket. A witch cursed me."

I chuckled as he spouted off all the excuses he'd given me when he'd crash-landed with an arm bent the wrong way.

"I don't give a fuck what anyone says, those were good times," he said.

Huffing, I let my head fall back. There was a lot of bad in my brother. *A lot*. I was under no illusions about who he was as a person. But the asshole had always been a good brother. When he talked about me going legit and being successful, pride seeped through every word. I didn't know if he really cared about anyone else on earth besides me. I never saw it if he did.

Marco and Julien didn't get why I stayed. Why I kept working for Reno when the risks weren't worth it. This was why. Times like these when we were just two brothers who grew up with no one to count on but each other.

"Yeah, we made our own good times," I replied.

Our parents had been around, but they were pretty indifferent to us. It'd been just me and Reno most of the time. That kind of history was pretty much impossible to turn my back on.

"Are you going out tonight?" he asked.

"Nope."

"No?" He raised a brow.

"I've got my girl."

He cocked his head. "The pretty thick one? What was her name?"

I nodded. "That one. Zadie."

"And she's yours?"

"Yep." Now this...this, I was proud of. My chest was full of it. "She's mine. My nights out are going to be different."

His shoulder shook. "Guess the missus doesn't like you having girls park their asses on your dick, even if they're getting paid to do it."

"Nah. And I'm not interested in anyone else's ass on my dick. Not when I've already got the finest one I've ever had in my bed."

He hummed, swiveling in his chair. "She seemed like a good girl. Does she know what you do?"

"She has an idea."

As far as I was concerned, Zadie knew enough about this side of my life. She didn't *want* to know more, nor did she need to.

"Be careful," he warned.

"I will."

I'd be very careful with her. I had a lot of ugly in my life, but she was pure beauty, the kind that didn't belong in my world. But I had her. She was mine. Like Marco and Julien, she was my clean in a lifetime of dirty. There wasn't much I wouldn't do to ensure she stayed that way. Not much at all.

CHAPTER EIGHTEEN

Zadie

"PLEASE TELL ME WHERE we're going."

"I won't."

"But I asked so nicely."

Amir slid a sly smirk my way. "You always ask nicely, Zadie. Because you're a good girl. A sweet, nice girl."

I made a face at him that he didn't see since his eyes were on the road. "I can be mean. Watch what happens if it turns out you're taking me to...I don't know, a monster truck show."

That made him laugh. "Way to ruin the surprise. When we get there, your ass is going to be spanked."

I pressed my legs together involuntarily. "If you're really taking me to a monster truck show, you're going to get spanked too."

He cupped himself. "Keep talking dirty to me, mama, we'll never get to the monster truck rally."

I groaned, covered my face with my hands. "I can't tell if you're being serious and I hate it."

"I'm always serious," he replied.

"I know." I peeked at him through my fingers. "Which is why I'm really scared right now."

This was the night out Amir promised me, only it was happening a week later. Last Saturday…well, we hadn't made it out of his house.

I climbed into Amir's SUV. He took one look at me, and his head fell back on the rest. His eyes squeezed shut, and he exhaled heavily through his nose.

"Hi." I hadn't been shy with him in a long time, but that was before. I had never had a huge attachment to my virginity, but I felt different. Not like I'd given away a piece of me, more like I'd taken back something that had been stolen. So, it was important. Kind of monumental. I couldn't help attaching emotion to it, and by proxy, to Amir.

And of course, he couldn't stand the sight of me. It had only been eight hours we were apart, and now this. It was like I physically pained him.

When he didn't reply, I put my hand on the door. "Okay…well, I think I'm going to go back inside. It's already late anyway and—"

His hand clamped on my thigh in a flash. Leaning across the console, Amir put his face in mine. "Do you honestly think you're going back to your dorm right now?"

His lashes were so thick, it seemed he had double the amount of an average human. They only served to intensify the heat he emitted in his glare. Why he was glaring at me, I had no idea.

I leaned in too, but instead of glaring, I nibbled his chin. "Stop looking at me like you're angry."

He pressed his thumb to my lips. "Are you going to bite me every time you don't like something I'm doing?"

"Maybe. You still haven't said hi to me. That's making me feel extra bite-y right now."

His lips twitched. "Hi, Zadie Night. You look so breathtakingly beautiful and mind-numbingly hot, I forgot my manners."

"What?"

He jerked his chin. "You heard me."

I touched my fingers to his cheek. "No one's ever said anything like that to me before. I'm processing."

He did the thing again, closing his eyes and breathing heavy from his nose. I didn't know what that meant, other than he might have found me annoying. I should have kept my biting ways to myself, but since they were exclusive to Amir, I didn't quite know how.

Finally, he put the truck in gear, driving with determination through campus. At the main entrance, he went the opposite way I had expected, and soon, we were pulling up to his house.

"Did you need to pick something up?" I asked.

"No. I changed my mind." He turned the car off and climbed out, stalking around it to open my door. "Get out, Zadie."

He said it gently, so I didn't bristle. I let him take my hand, helping me hop down to the curb. With his long fingers splayed on the base of my back, he nudged me along the path to the front door and inside.

"We're really not going out?" I asked.

"No. We're not." He wove our fingers together, dragging me through the house. But I didn't want to be dragged, and since I wasn't a pet anymore—not strictly one anyway—I put up a protest.

Twisting my hand, I pulled free from his grip and stopped walking, fists at my hips. He whirled around, frowning at me like I'd murdered his kitten.

"Don't take you away from me."

My fists tightened. "Don't drag me around like a dog!"

He ate the space between us, slid his arm around my waist, and pulled me against his chest. "I'm fifteen seconds from losing my mind. If I don't get you in my bedroom right now, I'm fucking you right here. I don't know where Julien and Marco are, but I can't promise they're not here. If I get you in my room, I can calm down and take it slow, like I know you need. If I do it here, I can't promise to be soft."

"What?" I breathed.

He dipped his face to the curve of my neck, inhaling along my shoulder and throat.

"Have you seen yourself tonight, mama? You look like a little fallen angel, all tits and ass and soft and naughty." He rocked his hips, prodding my belly with his hard cock. "You feel that?"

I nodded, lost for words. How was this real? How was I affecting this beautiful man so profoundly? It wasn't fake. He wasn't pretending. My flirty black dress with the deep V and ruffled hem—perfect for the dancing I'd been promised—had stolen his carefully guarded control.

Heat pooled in the tender area between my thighs.

"I feel it," I answered.

"Let me take you upstairs, Zadie."

I nodded. He took my hand in his, brought it to his mouth, and dragged his lips across my knuckles. And when we got to his bedroom, he calmed down and took care. We went slow, and it was different than the first time. Amir and I got lost in each other, touching, tasting, making love. Because that was what it had felt like. Something separate from sex or fucking.

Something kind of beautiful.

Since that night, we'd spent a lot of time in Amir's bed. I never slept there. I couldn't until I told Elena and Helen we were a couple, and I just wasn't ready for that. They wouldn't approve, and if I were honest, I was still holding my breath, waiting for this to blow up in my face any day now. I'd rather not prove them right when it did.

We drove for longer than I'd expected, and I still had no idea where we were going. I was promised dancing, but that was all I knew. If I ended up at a hoedown at a monster truck show for real, I was walking home.

Somehow, I didn't picture Amir, in his sleek, tailored black pants and button-up shirt, enjoying monster trucks. Just a hunch.

When we drove through a quaint beach town, I *really* didn't know what to expect, and Amir wasn't spilling. He parked, tucked my arm in his, and led me down a small boardwalk next to the sand to the entrance of a restaurant surrounded by tiki torches.

Live music floated on the ocean breeze, and as the hostess showed us to our table on a patio by the beach, my stomach fluttered with excitement.

A band was set up on the far side of the patio, playing music that sounded like it had come straight from the tropics. Beyond them, a large bonfire was burning on the sand. Couples were dancing on the beach, having made their own dance floor.

"Wow." When I finished scanning my surroundings, I brought my gaze to Amir's, finding him already watching me. "I love this."

"Better than monster trucks?"

I laughed, my cheeks heating with pleasure. "Yes. Unequivocally. Please never take me to a monster truck show. I will never forgive you."

He took my hand, running his thumb along one of my fingernails. "One day, you're going to have to tell me what you have against monster trucks. Seems like a deep-seated thing."

I smiled at him, at the side of himself he was showing me. Instinctively, I knew he hadn't shown this side to many people, so I would guard it as carefully as a lit match on a windy day.

"Have you been here before?" I asked.

"No. I asked around."

"I thought you'd take me to a club to dance."

He nodded. "I would take anyone else to a club. And we'll do that too. The thing is, I'm not in a place with you where I trust myself to be cool when there are other men around you, looking at you, seeing you move in one of your sexy as fuck dresses."

I swallowed hard. "I might be a terrible dancer. You don't even know."

"I know. I've had you in my bed, mama. I know how that body moves."

Fortunately for my wet panties, a waiter came by to take our order. When he smiled at me, Amir nearly came out of his chair. I would have laughed except I could tell he was genuinely struggling with his blind jealousy. And since I had felt that way only a week ago, I understood the plight.

As soon as the waiter left with our order, I scooted my chair over so I was right beside Amir, twisted my arm around his, and entwined our fingers. He took my leg and draped it over his, trailing his fingers up the inside of my thigh then back down to my knee.

"When does it get better?" I asked.

"What? When does what get better?"

"With your past girlfriends...when did you get to that place where you could be cool? A week? A month?"

His brow furrowed. "Never."

"Oh." I wasn't the table-flipping type, but, man, I had to suppress the urge to flip the table in front of me. Thinking about Amir being possessive over other women turned me into a furious ball of rage. "Okay, well—"

"Hey." He took my chin in his free hand, turning my face to his, running his nose along the length of mine. "Never because I haven't cared enough about another girl to make her mine. This is all new territory to me. I can't promise I'll ever be cool."

"Are you...?" I pressed my lips together, gathering my thoughts. "Are you telling me you've never had a girlfriend?"

He stared back at me, unblinking. "That's what I'm telling you. I never planned on having one, not while I'm in school doing what I do for Reno. Relationships can be messy. They'd take my mind off what I need it to be on."

"Oh." My shoulders curled inward.

"Don't tell me you planned on me."

I sucked in a breath, pushing down my hurt feelings. "No, I didn't."

"Take that frown off your lips. I told you I don't like when you're sad. I can't stand it." He pressed his thumb against my mouth. "I never planned on a girlfriend because I didn't know you existed. You're so fucking easy and unmessy. Like a dream, mama."

And just like that, my hurt feelings were gone.

"That's incredibly sweet." I aimed to kiss his cheek, but he turned, giving me his lips instead. It was quick, but just as sweet as his words. "I hate to contradict you, but I come with a lot of baggage."

"That's other people. You aren't making the drama. I'm talking about *you*, Zadie. There's nothing messy or conniving or shady about you. You don't manipulate. Fuck, I trust you, and the number of people I trust, I can count on one hand. I think you might be a little whack for being into me, but I'd say that's in the plus column."

I giggled even though an inkling of guilt wormed its way around my stomach. I wasn't manipulative, but *I* had manipulated my way into Amir's life and under his protection. I guess that made me shady and conniving too—the exact type of girl he didn't want.

But things had changed now. We were different. I would *never* do anything like that again. I'd acted out of desperation and need, and only because I knew I wouldn't hurt him. I didn't have that in me, not when it came to Amir.

"I'm not denying being a little whack, considering I'm sitting here, holding hands with my captor."

Amir huffed a laugh. "You think Katie Holmes ever saw the dealer again?"

I scrunched my nose. "You mean, after *Go*? Probably not. His name was Todd. Todd the drug dealer." I shuddered. "No, definitely not."

"So, if my name was Todd, we wouldn't be sitting here?"

I had to bite my lip to hold back a smile. "Again, definitely not. You're lucky you have a good name."

He touched his lips to mine. "Definitely lucky, princess."

"I'm princess now?"

"I've been thinking about the story you told me about your name. Something occurred to me later. Something I'd forgotten."

I leaned closer, my breasts flush with his bicep. "Tell me right now. I demand it."

"Bossy." He grinned into another light kiss. "You know what Amir means in Arabic?"

"I don't."

"It means prince."

My breath hitched. "You're kidding."

He shook his head. "I'm not. You and me, we're some kind of prince and princess out of a twisted fairytale."

"I don't know about twisted. The captor and the princess is pretty classic."

Amir's brow lowered over his intense gaze. "This is what I mean about you. I see us being together as something twisted, because a guy like me should never have anything so pure and sweet. But you, my sweet little mama, look at us like something that makes sense, something inevitable."

"I don't know about inevitable. But I'm okay with us having different outlooks. I probably could use a little cynicism, and I'll be happy to shower you with puppies and rainbows."

He reared back, hands up in defense. "The fuck? Do not throw puppies at me."

Laughing, I grabbed the front of his shirt and yanked him to me. He wrapped his arms around me, pulling me right into his lap. Even though we were in a restaurant, surrounded by other people, I decided not to care since he didn't. Not one little bit.

· · · · ● · ● · · ·

My toes were sinking into the sand. My body was sinking into Amir's. His hands were on my rocking hips, knee between my legs, pressing against my core. He led our pace, stirring our bodies to the rhythm of the sultry Caribbean music. We weren't alone, but it felt like it, the way we were wrapped in each other.

Amir could *dance*. He'd led me out here after we finished our dinner, and we hadn't taken a break since. He took charge of us both, leading me the whole way. The way he moved, fluid and confident, had me aching for him, to find somewhere dark and take him inside me. At the same time, I never ever wanted this night to end.

The music slowed but remained just as sexy. Amir spun me around and bent his knees so my butt was cupped by his hips. Under the light of the moon, we rocked together. His hands were all over me, running down my sides, over the curve of my stomach, faintly touching my breasts. I reached up and threaded my fingers together behind his neck, giving him full access to all of me.

We weren't alone, not by a long shot, but we were so lost in each other, we might as well have been. Everything faded. My troubles, our differences, the secrets neither of us were willing to touch. We were whittled down to two bodies, breathing and moving, touching and feeling.

"You're so fucking sexy, mama." His teeth scraped my earlobe. "

Tipping my head to the side, I pressed a kiss to the underside of his jaw. "You're sexy too."

I felt his smile on the curve of my neck. "Yeah? You think I'm sexy?"

"Mmhmm. I don't think many men can dance like you do."

He took my hand and spun me in a dizzying circle. We ended up with our chests flush, our hands clasped between us, his other so low on my back, his fingers brushed my ass, and my hand curled around his neck.

I'd definitely never had such a romantic moment in my life. Every inch of my skin prickled with awareness of the man holding me. My insides were thrumming. How could I have this? Dancing on the beach with the exact person I wanted to be with. This entire night was so far removed from my life two years ago, I would have thought it was a dream, except I would have never been so audacious to dream something like this.

Above us, lightning cracked the inky sky. I might have jumped had Amir not had his arms around me.

A fat drop of rain landed on my shoulder, followed quickly by another and another.

"Is it raining?" I asked, incredulous the weather would dare interrupt our perfect night.

He dropped his forehead to mine, heaving a sigh. "Damn. I didn't even think about checking the weather."

There was something about the way he sagged with disappointment that made my heart swell. He cared about giving me this. It was important to him.

"I would dance in the rain with you." Once I realized the truth of my words, the raindrops smattering on my shoulders and head weren't such a big deal. The night was warm, and my skin was heated from being so close to Amir, I didn't mind the rain one little bit.

The sky took that as a challenge, because a moment later, it opened up with a deluge so powerful, we were soaked to the bone in an instant. This, I conceded in my head, was a lot less fun.

We ran, hand in hand, along with the rest of the crowd.

Unlike them, I was laughing and not the least bit upset. When Amir heard me, his steps slowed until we were standing still beside his SUV.

He cupped my smiling face. "Why aren't you upset? Your dress, your hair, it's all..."

"It's wet, and I can't find it in me to care." I rose on my toes, catching his chin with a kiss. "Dance with me for a little bit longer."

Amir studied me with eyes darker than the jet-black sky. Then he spun me in tight circles before pulling me into his chest with a wet smack and rocked me to the beat of the rain slapping the ground. His smile was indulgent and fevered as I laughed. I'd never danced in the rain with anyone, and it made perfect sense that my first time would be with Amir. He was quickly claiming all my first times and turning them into something so much more than I ever could have imagined.

I tipped my head back to the sky, letting the rain drop on my face. Amir held me against him, and I felt his eyes on me, watching, always watching.

His hand scraped up my back to tangle in my hair, pushing my face forward so our eyes met. His gaze was bright, but somewhat frenzied.

"Hi," I whispered just loud enough to be heard above the falling rain.

"You're so fucking mine," he declared in a tone so ferocious, my toes curled.

His mouth descended onto mine before he gave me a chance to agree, but the words bounced around in my head.

I'm so fucking yours.

CHAPTER NINETEEN

Amir

WE WERE IN THE back seat of my truck. Rain poured like a waterfall onto the roof, locking us in to our own private cave. No one could see in, not that anyone was out anymore.

Zadie's top was down, her skirt around her waist, thighs on either side of mine as she rode me. She held on to the seat behind me, rolling her hips and pushing herself down on my cock.

I was losing my mind. Hell, maybe I already had, going in deep with a girl like this. But goddamn, who would blame me? She rode my cock like she couldn't get enough. My sweet little Zadie, all wild, desperate to take me. And her soft ass slapping my legs, tits bouncing in my face, the taste of her on my lips, I was just as desperate.

"You my good girl, Zadie?" I snapped my hips up, hitting her deep, making her gasp.

"Yes," she hissed.

"Tell me." Both her hips in my hands, I pushed her down and rose to meet her. Her eyelids fluttered, but she kept them open and focused on me.

"I'm your good girl."

"Mmm, yeah you are." I trailed my hand along her spine, making her arch into me. Leaning forward, I closed my lips around her pretty pink nipple, suckling gently, the way she liked. My girl could go hard on my cock, but she needed soft here. When I gave her what she needed, she rewarded me with the sweetest cries, my whimpered name, her utter physical devotion.

I switched to the other side. Her fingers wove into my short hair, holding me to her. Insides clamping around me, trying to pull me over before I was even close to ready.

Popping off her tits, I gave her thigh a light smack. "No. You're not ending this."

She shook her head. "I don't want it to end. I can't help it. Your mouth on me, I can't, Amir. I don't have any control."

I hummed, holding her hips again. She fucked like she danced, fluid, loose, easy. Like she was boneless, pouring her body over mine. I'd never had it like this, like her. I knew I'd love being inside her, but my girl took it to the next level. And it was all mine. She hadn't learned tricks or techniques from some other dick. Zadie gave me what she wanted to give me out of instinct. That only made everything she did sexier.

"Slow down, mama. I'm gonna rub your clit until you come, then I'm gonna fuck you hard." Her inner walls clamped down on me. I slapped her thighs. "What'd I say?"

She stopped moving. Her swollen lips parted, and a mewl broke free. "Please."

Releasing my hold on her, I dragged my palm down her curved belly to the slick heat between her legs. She held mostly still, gently rocking toward my hand as I circled the pad of my finger around her clit.

"You're so wet."

She nodded. "For you."

"Were you wet when we were dancing?"

"So wet."

"Did you feel how hard I was?"

"It made me even wetter," she confirmed.

"What would you have done if I had lifted the back of your dress and fucked you right there? Right on the beach, where anyone could have looked our way and seen us?"

Her breathing stuttered. The hand braced on my chest clenched. "I would have been worried, but then I would have gotten lost in you like I always do. I would have screamed your name so everyone knew how much I liked it."

I pressed harder on her clit, making her writhe. "That's hot, mama. I like talking about it." Cupping the back of her neck, I tugged her ear next to my mouth. "But you know I'd never do that, would I?"

"No," she whispered.

"Why not?"

She didn't even hesitate half a second. "Because I'm yours."

"That's right. I don't share this pussy. These pretty tits are only for my eyes. I own your cries."

She rubbed her cheek against mine. "And I own your cock. No one else can see."

"You do own my cock." I slid my hand up, tangling it in the back of her hair to tip her head back. "Now, come on it. Show me how much you like when I fuck you."

Swirling my fingers around her clit, I raised my hips, hitting her deep and staying there. Zadie's cheeks pinkened. Her nipples tightened. Chest rising and falling in rapid bursts, her face contorted into pained rapture. She moaned my name, clawed at my chest, and I became undone.

The feel of my girl trembling with the pleasure I gave her and my name on her swollen lips snapped all my control. I threw her down, draped her leg over the back of the seat, the other on my shoulder, and went at her. She was still coming, so tight I had to fight my way through. Jesus Christ, those sleek, flexing walls sucked me in and didn't want to let go.

Zadie's head thrashed. Her nails dug into my chest. I couldn't stop looking at her, the flush of her cheeks and chest, how pretty her tits looked when I had her folded in half, the way her eyes went hazy, like she was on another plane.

She was taking me with her, and her cunt was so perfect, so welcoming and sweet, I'd follow her into hell if it meant I could keep fucking her for the rest of my tortured eternity.

My innocent, shy Zadie gave me something no one else had. This was mine and mine alone.

And in the back of my head, the thought rang out, *no one else is ever going to have this. This will always be mine and mine alone. Always.*

I spilled inside her while her eyes were locked on mine. Somewhere inside my chest, there was a crack. Small, but deep, it hurt but was a relief at the same time.

It was too much. Too fucking much.

I shoved my face in her neck, taking in her berries and rain.

"Need to take you home," I murmured.

She nodded, slowly stroking my hair. "Okay. Let's go home."

· • • • • • • • • •

When I pulled into the driveway at the house, Zadie touched my arm. "I thought you were taking me home."

"I did." Having zero desire to hear her protests, I turned off the car and hopped out, circling to her side. She was still sitting in her seat, chewing on her lip. "Get out of my truck, mama."

She scrunched her nose. "It's late. I should go back to my dorm."

"Think it's pretty clear I disagree. Come inside. I'm not sending you back to your dorm with my cum inside you. That's not what this is between us. I let it slide last week, but that's done." I held out my hand to her. "Come on."

She placed her hand in mine and allowed me to help her out of the SUV. When she was standing in front of me, she pressed her palm to my chest. "If you think I don't want to be with you, you're wrong. Things are just so new and a little complicated."

I brought her knuckles to my mouth and grazed them along my lips. "Nah. Nothing's complicated about this. I take my girl to dinner and dancing, she ends her night asleep in my bed. That's how it is."

She sighed, leaning into me. "We need to talk about this."

"I'll talk...when you're in my bedroom, wearing my T-shirt."

Zadie relented, following me inside, where it was quiet. It was rare for any of us to be home this early on a Saturday, and yeah, midnight was early. Marco and Julien were probably out, finding trouble, while I'd brought my trouble home with me.

After a hot shower and gentle fucking against the tiles, I slipped one of my black T-shirts over Zadie's head and let it drape over her body. She wore it well, tight at her tits, loose in the middle, hugging her hips. It did nothing to cover her ass, but I didn't have a single problem with that.

In my bed, she turned on her side, tucking her arm under her head. Her fingertips trailed down the center of my chest. Our feet were tangled in a knot.

"I don't know how to tell Helen and Elena about this," she whispered.

"Just tell the truth."

She gave my chest hair a sharp tug. "That might work with Elena. Helen, though? No."

"I don't give a fuck what your girls think, Zadie. All I care about is what you think. Are you gonna let them influence you?"

My gut twisted. There was a good chance they could talk Zadie out of being with me. There was no love lost between us. Helen, especially. I'd known her peripherally since high school. Maybe before that. I couldn't remember. And she'd known me too, saw and heard about the things I did. *Still* did. There was no world where she'd merrily give Zadie her blessing. Helen's opinion of me didn't matter. What she said to Zadie about me and how she twisted my image did.

"Influence me? No, they won't, but it won't make me happy to have you at odds with my friends. That's why I want to make sure and know—"

I pressed my thumb to her mouth. "No. There's no making sure."

She bit my thumb, snarling, her little nose wrinkling up. "Don't shush me, Amir. I was trying to say I want this thing between you and me to be solid before I rock the boat. I don't know what that really looks like. Maybe it just means a little more time together, so when Helen comes back at me with all the bad about you—the bad I already know—I can tell her all the good only I get to see. She's important to me, and so is Elena. I don't want to be at odds with them."

"So, I'm your dirty little secret until...when? How long?"

She leaned in and kissed my chin. A small gesture, but it was Zadie. She liked to kiss me there, and I more than liked when she did it.

"I'm really happy." Her words were delicate and sweet, like spun sugar. "Can't this be enough for now? When I think of how much we've shifted in such a short time, I get overwhelmed. I need—"

"What? What do you need?"

She rubbed her lips together, then took a breath. "I need you to cut me a little slack. Okay? Nothing about you and me is wrong or dirty, and I don't want you to be a secret. You know, my mom already knows about you. Can't that be enough? For right now?"

It wasn't enough. Zadie drove me to distraction. The only way I was able to function was knowing she was mine. And that was low-functioning because I needed that public claim. All the little fuckboys who looked at my sweet girl like she was a possibility had to receive the message Zadie Night wasn't an option. Not to touch, not to talk to, not even to look at if they'd like to keep their eyes.

"Fine."

She kissed my chin again. "You don't sound like you're fine."

Hooking my arm around her, I drew her to my chest. "I'm not going to pretend to be pleased with the situation, but I'll live." I touched my lips to her forehead. "Go to sleep, mama."

"Don't be mad at me."

I frowned at her. God, she really had no idea. None. "I don't think I'm really capable of being mad at you."

"I'll make it right, I promise."

She might. Most likely, I'd lose patience and make it right for us both.

CHAPTER TWENTY

Zadie

I WOKE IN AMIR'S arms. He was kissing and sucking my neck, humming against my skin. At first, I kept my eyes closed, blissful in the state between asleep and fully awake. His lips were so soft, but when he sucked, my toes curled.

"Mmm...I like mornings with you," I murmured.

"Yeah?" He latched on to my pulse, sucking a little harder, at the same time his hand slipped between my thighs. Bare from the waist down, he had nothing impeding him, and he took advantage, dipping into my opening with a warm finger, swirling around my clit with another.

He made me come within minutes, before I had ever opened my eyes. Then he curled around my back, holding me close, sliding inside me.

"You like that?" he asked softly. "Do you like waking to me kissing you? Getting my cock inside you before you leave the bed?"

"Yeah." I took his hand from my belly and kissed his fingertips. "This is perfect."

"We could have this, mama. All the time."

I twisted my head around to find him staring down at me intently. Reaching up, I ran my fingers along his scruffy cheek. "We will."

He didn't reply. Instead, he shoved his face in my neck and rolled my body so I was almost on my front. His mouth latched to the curve of my neck, biting and sucking while he moved faster inside me. I let myself sink into the feel of him and block all the rest out. I'd wanted this moment, dreamed about him holding me, touching me, kissing me, since he held me captive. Now that I had it, and the reality of Amir and me together was a hundred times better than anything I could have imagined, I wasn't going to overthink and ruin it.

The way he moved inside me made it impossible to think coherently anyway.

He may not have been happy with my choices, but he treated my body like a treasure. Any self-consciousness I should have had rightly felt fell away with my thoughts. His tightly muscled body riding my rounded curves was the most carnal feeling in the world. He kept kissing me, grinding into me, rolling my nipples around between his fingers, murmuring sweet, filthy words in my ear, and I was a trembling wreck. I said his name, he answered with mine.

The end came quietly, but no less consuming. We held tight to each other, staying attached for as long as we could before he had to pull out. I turned over, watching him pad to the attached bathroom. I hadn't thought I was into men's butts before I saw Amir's. His was tight, round, and dimpled on the sides. If I didn't think he'd go ballistic, I'd bite it.

Hmmm...maybe I'd chance it one day.

He came back wearing a pair of basketball shorts, stopping at my side of the bed. He trailed his fingers along my breasts and stomach, dipping one in my belly button.

"What time is it?" I asked.

"Early. Thought you'd want to sneak back to your dorm."

I caught his hand before he could wander between my legs. "That was surprisingly thoughtful considering you didn't want me to leave last night." I pushed my borrowed shirt down and sat up, smoothing my palms along his bare sides. "Did I kick you while I was sleeping? Hog the covers? Snore?"

He grinned, pushing my hair back from my face. "I don't know. I had the best night of sleep I've had in...I don't know. A really long time." He nudged my chin with his knuckle. "I don't want you leaving, but I'll let you this time."

I held back from rolling my eyes. "That's magnanimous of you, Amir." I kissed his stomach, then pressed my cheek to his warm skin. "That night of sleep changed you."

I felt his laughter through the muscles in his stomach. "Come on, funny girl. I'm taking you home before I change my mind."

· · · · ● · ● · · ·

Like every Sunday morning, Elena was on our couch, reading the newspaper, her ankles crossed on the coffee table. It was her one habit that didn't fit anything I knew about her, but she had done it almost every morning we'd lived together. When I had asked, she said she'd been reading the paper with her father since childhood. Back then, it was the comics, now the financial section was her favorite.

She lowered the paper when I opened the door. "Hmmm."

"Good morning," I whispered.

"No need to whisper, you floozy. Helen's at Theo's."

I sank onto the love seat opposite her. "I'm not...I didn't..."

Her eyes raked over me in last night's rumpled dress with Amir's T-shirt slung on top, stopping on my neck. "Hmmm."

"Elena—"

She folded the paper, set it down beside her, and scooted forward, bracing her elbows on her knees. "Please don't lie to me. Tell me you won't answer, but don't lie. Your neck is covered in hickeys." My hand flew to the side of my neck. Crap, I hadn't even looked. "And you're wearing a man's T-shirt. Not to mention you didn't sleep here last night. If you try to tell me you fell and hit your head and neck, got temporary amnesia, and spent the night in the hospital, I'll be very disappointed."

My mouth twitched despite being caught red-handed. "I spent the night with the guy I'm seeing, but it's new, so..."

Her head bobbed. "Noted. I'm happy you're getting laid. Every girl deserves a good dicking now and then."

My teeth dug into my bottom lip. It was on the tip of my tongue to tell her it was Amir. But then I remembered how pissed she'd been when she found out about our whole *Go* situation last semester and decided to hold off. I wasn't ready for our bubble to burst.

"It was really good," I agreed.

She patted my knee. "I'm happy for you, but I'm also seething with jealousy since my sex life is beyond pitiful. How about we don't go into detail, okay? I'm two seconds from saying fuck it, shaving the back of my head, and learning to love eating pussy. The orgasms have to be better when they're coming from a woman, right?"

My eyes went round. I had no answer to that. Fortunately, she didn't want one, picking up her paper and moving back into position like it had never happened. I took that opportunity to escape to my room.

The first thing I did was go in the bathroom and inspect the damage Amir had done. I gasped at the reflection of my bruise-mottled neck. Amir's sweet kisses didn't seem quite so sweet anymore.

I snapped a picture and texted it to him.

Me: *Why?*

MyCaptor: *Pretty.*

Me: *This isn't nice. The whole side of my neck is black and blue. I bruise really easily.*

MyCaptor: *I'll remember that next time. Did I hurt you?*

Me: *You didn't. You annoyed me.*

MyCaptor: *Annoyed I can live with. Hurt, nah, not so much.*

Me: *I'm not hurt. I'm going to shower. Xoxo*

MyCaptor: *XXX*

· · · · ● · ● · · · ·

"If you keep staring at me, I'm going to think you want to fuck."

My teeth dug into my bottom lip to hold back a grin. Amir was studying, and I was too...sort of. It was hard to concentrate when he smelled so good and the sun streaming in through the kitchen window hit his bare chest, highlighting the golden tones of his skin. And when he glowered at me over his textbook, he got a spark in his midnight eyes that reminded me of the North Star.

"I want you to study." I closed my book. "I know how difficult Krasinski's class is."

He nodded to my book. "And you're not studying anymore? You're going to sit there and distract me?"

I snarled at him. He chuckled. I'd yet to figure out how to intimidate this man, but that was okay. I didn't really want to.

"I need to stretch my legs. I can't think if I sit for too long."

Normally, if I was engrossed enough, I could study for hours without moving. But nothing was more interesting to me than Amir. Luckily for me, he was a much better student than I was. Instead of going to the library during the week, I'd taken to coming to his house. Julien and Marco were usually out, so it was quiet. Just the two of us. Alone, with lots of beds and flat surfaces and perfect sunlight.

I never thought it would turn out that *I* was the problem.

Amir ignored me while I stared. At least...I thought he was ignoring me until his shoulders started shaking.

"What's wrong?"

He put his book down, laughing silently. "You, mama. You keep looking at me. Weren't you going to take a walk? Stretch your legs?"

"Can I play the piano?"

That was my second favorite thing about coming to Amir's house. The first was pretty damn obvious since I was mildly obsessed with him.

The piano belonged to Julien, and he had no trouble sharing it with me. That was...after he'd watched me play and deemed me fit enough to use his prized possession.

He cupped his forehead. "Zadie...I want to say yes to every fucking thing you ask, but I really need the quiet for now. Why don't you go watch TV in my room for an hour? Then I'll give you as much attention as you want."

"Fine." Lifting his hand to my mouth, I nibbled his index finger. "I'm going to check in with my mom."

His brows rose. "Nothing?"

Officer Ryder was continuing to be less than helpful. If not for Max's illness, I didn't doubt my mom would have flown up to Oregon to do her own investigating.

"We'll see." I held up my phone. "I'll be in your room. Take your time. I'll just be snooping through your things."

His laughter followed me out of the kitchen.

I flopped back on his bed, texting with my mom for updates. Ryder had told her Drew's parents were giving him the runaround, but he would be "following up." My mom wouldn't leave him be until he did, that was for sure. The upside was I hadn't received any more notes, and nothing like the library incident had happened again. That didn't mean I wasn't still on edge any time I wasn't with Amir or my friends. Since Drew, there hadn't been a time where I'd ever fully relaxed.

I must've dozed off, because the next thing I was aware of was Amir's mouth on my jaw, working his way to my neck.

"No hickeys," I mumbled.

"Mmm." He had me trapped beneath him, holding my arms over my head. "Sleepy, mama?"

I opened my eyes to his and shook my head. "Not anymore."

He sat back on his knees and flipped my skirt up around my waist. My panties came off easily after that. He placed my legs on either side of his knees, spreading me wide. Then he looked. His eyes raked over my core, studying me like a piece of art.

I started to reach for him, but something black on my arm stopped my movement.

Amir. Amir. Amir's girl. Property of Amir. Amir. Amir.

His name was down the length of my inner forearm in stark black. In small letters and large, he'd branded me.

"What is this?" I asked. "Tell me this isn't Sharpie."

His fingers slipped inside me, making me gasp. "It's Sharpie."

I held up my other arm, but all he'd drawn on that one was a small heart with an *A* in the center.

"What did you do?"

He curled his fingers, hitting that spot on my inner walls that made my eyes roll back. And they did, because I couldn't help it, but I tried to squeeze my legs closed to push him out of me. Amir kept up his treatment, caressing me from the inside, adding his thumb to my clit from the outside.

"Stop it," I whispered. "I can't believe you."

"Really? You can't believe me?"

My eyes shot open. My glare would have had more impact if I hadn't been panting. Or maybe not. Amir didn't find me intimidating in the least.

"Why?"

"Because,"—shifting, he braced one hand beside my head until he was over me again—"my beautiful, sweet, angel of a girlfriend likes to walk around campus like she isn't taken. She likes to go to sleep at night without me. She's mine, but no one knows it."

He thrust his fingers in and out of me. There was no anger behind his words or the way he touched me. Amir was bringing me to pleasure even while he was disappointed in me.

"I don't like any of those things," I protested weakly. "*I* know I'm yours."

"That's right, mama, you *are* mine. You fell asleep in my bed today. When I lay my head on that pillow tonight, I'm going to be smelling your shampoo, missing your fucking soft little body next to mine. I'm sending you home with my name on your arm so you don't forget, because I never do."

He dipped to run his tongue along the curve of my bottom lip and groaned.

"Sweet, even when she's angry," he murmured.

My thighs clenched as pressure built in my belly. If he wanted to make me come, I'd take it. There was no going back now anyway. He wouldn't stop, and my body would murder me if I tried to make him.

My hips rose and fell with his fingers sliding, curling, driving into me. Lips parted, I panted his name, "*Amir, Amir, Amir.*"

And then...he stopped.

My eyes flipped open.

He smirked down at me, withdrawing his fingers. "Tell me when."

"I don't know." I rubbed my thighs together, but it wasn't enough. "Soon."

From his subtle flinch, I knew that answer wasn't enough either. He'd given me more than a week, but I wasn't there yet. I didn't want to see Elena and Helen's faces when they discovered I'd been keeping this secret.

Amir's nose trailed over mine as he sighed. "Do you know how beautiful you looked when I walked in here and found you sleeping? So incredibly beautiful, it hit me in the gut. All I could think was how much you're mine. You won't let me claim you the way I want, so I claimed you like a toy, Zadie. You've got my name all over you so the other kids know you belong to me. *That's* how out of my mind you drive me."

"I'm unequivocally yours, Amir."

But that also wasn't enough. I didn't have the words to reassure him. I'd shown him over and over how strongly I felt for him, but I hadn't done the one thing he'd asked. I would, and soon, but just...not yet.

He fell back on the bed with a sigh, and I followed, kneeling between his legs.

"Zadie." He drew my name out like a curse.

He was hard beneath his sweatpants. I freed him, pulling them down around his hips, and slid my palm up his length. He rocked into my hand, the tip already leaking. Gathering the moisture in my hand, I rubbed it into his skin, all the way to the root and back up again.

"I'm yours, Amir."

Dropping down, I took him in my mouth. His fingers automatically tangled in the sides of my hair, pushing it away from my face so he could watch me. He always, *always* watched me, just as I watched him when he was between my thighs. This was more than quick and dirty pleasure, though I wasn't denying it was that too. This was connecting on a level words couldn't touch. I was showing him how important he was to me. Setting his pleasure center stage and reveling in giving it to him. This was just for us. Not a show for anyone else. What happened here was between Amir and me, and it was all that mattered.

His length slid along my tongue, as deep in my throat as I could take him. Amir let me set the pace and depth, rocking with me, but never pushing. Because he pushed me a lot, but never when I was giving him this, which only made me want to do it even more. And I wanted to do it a *lot*. I loved the way he felt in my mouth, the sounds he made, how surprised he was each and every time I let him finish in the back of my throat.

Amir grunted, reached down for me, grabbed me by the hips, and flipped me around. I was straddling his face before I knew what was happening. He lapped at me, making feral sounds when my taste hit his tongue.

"Oh god, I'm close."

"Put me back in your mouth. We're coming together this time." His fingers dug into my flesh, pulling me down on his lips.

I bent forward, taking him in my mouth again. It was messy this time, my rhythm erratic. He was distracting me, bringing me back to the edge, and from his jerky movements, he was getting close too.

We kissed and licked and worshiped each other until we were tumbling, tumbling. Amir spilled on my tongue, and I fell apart on his lips. As soon as we were both done, he gathered me in his arms and crushed his mouth to mine. Then he rolled out of bed, tugged up his pants, and walked out of the room.

Oh no. He was so mad at me. I ran my fingertip along his name on my arm. Tears pricked the back of my eyes. Before they could fall, he was back, carrying a bottle and a bag of cotton balls.

He climbed on the bed, poured the rubbing alcohol on the cotton ball, and held his hand out. "Give me your arm."

I complied, and he wiped the cotton ball over each *Amir*, erasing them from my skin. My heart thudded in my chest with each one that disappeared. He was concentrating, wiping the ink away with meticulous care. When my arm was blank again, he reached for the other one, but I jerked back, holding it to my chest.

He raised his head, brow furrowed. "One more."

"No." I touched my thumb to the small heart with the *A* in the center. "I'm keeping this one."

"Okay." He screwed the lid on the bottle and reached behind him to place it on his bedside table. Back against the head-board, he looked down at me sprawled in his bed. "I shouldn't have done that."

"Written on me?"

"No." He took my arm, rubbing this thumb on the lone heart. "Erased them."

I sat up and straddled his legs. "You did because you take care of me."

He grabbed two handfuls of my ass and planted me over his cock so we were chest to chest. "You take care of me too. You just drive me crazy. I'm not going to be patient forever."

"I know you won't, but I appreciate you being patient with me now." I nibbled his chin, followed by a kiss on his lips. "I really, really appreciate it."

He exhaled through his nose, fingers toying with the curled ends of my hair. "Did you talk to your mom?"

"Yes, and no news."

His brow went heavy over his dark eyes. "I don't like that shit. They don't take this seriously, do they?"

"Not really. They were more concerned with the growing meth problem than me. They only took action the last time when I woke up to Drew in my bedroom. That was after almost a year of him watching me and following me."

And even then, he'd gotten a slap on the wrist and counseling. That and a restraining order were all he'd had to answer for a year of terror.

"Fuck." He drew me closer, if that was possible.

"I'm not scared. Not right now." I draped my arms around his shoulders. "How did studying go? I'm afraid to ask if you need help."

He narrowed his eyes on me. "Any shit I said to you that first week gets thrown out. I was out of my head having you in my space."

"It's forgotten. Now, tell me about Krasinski. Is his class still as close to going through boot camp as I remember?"

Amir talked to me about his classes, the internship he was going to ask Dr. Krasinski to write him a recommendation for, the paper he was writing. I told him about the final paper I wrote for that class, the one I got a ninety on, the highest grade Krasinski had ever given on a final paper. He told me he was going to take me down, but I heard the pride behind his teasing.

For that space of time, I felt like a normal college girl, falling hard for her boyfriend. Her hot, caring, smart as hell boyfriend. Then he dropped me off at the dorm. I slinked out of his truck only when I was sure no one I knew was around to see, and it all came tumbling back.

Amir was still all those things, but he was also all the bad Helen and Elena would inevitably point out. But Amir and I were getting to a solid place where I could truly defend my choice to be with him if I needed to. I hoped it wouldn't come to that. That my friends would accept my happiness at face value.

If they didn't, I would fight, to keep Amir, but to keep them as well.

I just wasn't confident I wouldn't lose.

CHAPTER TWENTY-ONE

Zadie

"My father doesn't believe in renting," Elena declared.

Helen rolled her eyes. "Renting isn't like the Tooth Fairy. It's a real, tangible thing. You can't not believe in it."

Elena rolled her eyes right back. "Obviously he knows it's real. Don't be purposely obtuse."

"Don't be purposely classist," Helen tossed back.

I took a bite of my sandwich, wondering how Elena and Helen were going to survive another year of living together when they couldn't even get through a meal in the dining hall without going at it. Although, I wasn't sure either of them would like me once I told them Amir and I were together. I'd put it off for another week, but the end was almost here. I'd give myself this weekend, then I'd tell them.

"It's my *dad*, not me," Elena groaned. "And I had a point of bringing that up."

"What? What's your point?" Helen challenged.

Elena wagged a perfectly manicured finger at her. "My point is, I mentioned to my father that I wanted to start to look at houses for the three of us to live in. He balked at first, then came back with the idea of investing in rental properties near campus."

Helen's face flushed. Her red lips parted. "So, your dad is buying you a house?"

"He plans on buying a few as investments. We'll live in one. It's honestly very cool. My dad won't be a slumlord or anything, and he's agreed to allow me to help fix up a few of them."

Helen snorted. "You're going to do manual labor?"

Elena held her hands out. "Look at these nails. Are these the nails of someone who does manual labor? No. I'll be *designing* the improvements."

"I think it's a great idea," I interjected. The two of them could go back and forth forever, and while they amused me, Amir was picking me up in a half hour, so I couldn't sit here with them all night. He was already impatient enough to get me. I'd just texted him I was still at dinner and he sent me a scowling emoji back.

"I don't think college students need *designs*," Helen drawled.

Elena arched a brow. "Oh? So I should just let the contractor choose the new tiles for the bathrooms? And the cabinets in the kitchen?" She snapped her fingers. "One second, those sound like *design* choices, which I will make. What's your problem? I told you we'd pay equitably. I don't get why you wouldn't want to have a nice place to live."

Helen started to say something else, but my attention was pulled away when someone took the empty seat beside me. Cold dread pooled in my stomach and spread through my veins like ice.

"Can we talk?"

Elliott Schiffer had his arm draped around the back of my chair and was leaning into me, creating a false intimacy between us.

"Hey." I leaned back, hitting Helen's shoulder. "How are you?"

His brow furrowed. "Forget me. I'm worried about you. Are *you* okay?"

I hadn't heard a peep from Elliott since he'd offered me up as a human sacrifice. Not a text or call. Nothing. And that was good, because I had no doubt Amir would follow through on his threats and eviscerate Elliott if he caught him even looking at me.

"I'm fine. You should go, though."

"I miss you, Zadie. I shouldn't have done what I did. I realize what a good thing you and I had and—"

I frowned at him. "We barely kissed. I'm pretty certain you don't know my last name or where I grew up. I don't know—"

"I know your last name is Night." His eyes shifted to the side, then back. "I don't remember where you grew up, if you ever told me, but we can get to know each other. How much longer do you have to do this *thing* with him?"

He brought his hand up from my chair to graze my shoulder. I shivered, the dread in my belly turning to revulsion. I tried to pull away more, but since Helen was beside me, I had nowhere to go.

It didn't matter anyway.

One second Elliott was looking at me with sad, puppy-dog eyes. The next, his head was slammed down on the table.

Amir had arrived.

I jumped up with a yelp, my chair clattering to the ground behind me.

"The fuck, Schiffer?" Amir leaned over him, pressing his reddened face against the table. "You have short-term memory? What did I say?"

"I was checking on her," Elliott screeched. "Making sure you haven't hurt her!"

Amir's head whipped to mine. "You, don't move."

I held my hands up, pleading for him to listen. "Amir, he didn't—"

He snapped his fingers at me. "Need you to be quiet, mama. We'll talk after I deal with this asshole."

Helen and Elena surrounded me, both laid hands on my shoulders. Amir grabbed Elliott by the scruff, hauling him from his chair. Elliott barely put up a fight, allowing himself to be shoved several feet away.

Amir jabbed the air. "No more warnings. If I see you near my girl again, I will follow through on all my promises. Reno won't be happy with your shit, and you don't even wanna know what happens when he isn't happy."

Elliott bowed over and over as he backed toward the door. The dining hall had gone quiet. It felt like a hundred pairs of eyes were on me, though they were most likely looking at Amir and Elliott.

As soon as Elliott was out the door, Amir stalked toward me with his hand out.

"Come on. Time to go."

Helen was rigid beside me, her arm like an iron band around my shoulder. "She's not going anywhere with you. I'm not afraid of you *or* your woman-beating brother."

Amir tipped his chin, his eyes only for me. "You gonna correct her, Zadie?"

My chin was trembling. I couldn't bring myself to speak. I didn't quite know what to say to any of them. I wanted Amir, but I hated this. I couldn't lose my friends. I was supposed to have the weekend to prepare. I wasn't prepared!

"Your deal is null and void," Elena added. "Now, shoo, weirdo."

Helen laughed under her breath, and I almost did too, but only because it was absolutely absurd to hear Elena call Amir a weirdo. Like we were kids. Like he wasn't dangerous. Like he wasn't the villain who rarely went anywhere unarmed.

Amir shook his hand at me. "Right now, Zadie. Come."

Helen shoved me behind her, getting in Amir's face. "Dude, catch a clue. Zadie only agreed to be your little slave because she wanted protection from her stalker. She doesn't like you, she just knows you're demented enough to kill anyone who would deign to threaten something or someone you own."

"Helen, no—"

Elena clasped my hand, holding me back. Helen wasn't listening to me anyway. She had her own reasons to be angry with Amir. Mine were just the tip of the iceberg.

"Whatever you think is going on between the two of you isn't real. She's hanging around you for one thing, and one thing only: protection. That was always the point. But she doesn't need you. She's got me, Elena, Theo, Lock. We have her back. So you can crawl back into your fucking hole, dude. You're nothing. A girl like Zadie would never be with trash like you."

Amir's eyes were on me the entire time Helen spoke. I shook my head, but I still couldn't form words. I just couldn't force them out. Because what she was saying wasn't entirely untrue, but it also wasn't true at all.

"Zadie?" Fury filled every cell of Amir's body and overflowed, rising into the air around him like smoke. Jaw clenched tight, hands fisted, legs spread wide, he looked like he was prepared for battle.

Helen pushed forward. "Did you not hear me? Get over yourself. Zadie does not need you. If she had told us what was going on from the very beginning, she never would have come near you. Get out of here."

Without another word, Amir spun on his toe and stormed out of the dining hall. I found my voice when he pulled open the door.

I shook Elena's hand off. "I need to go after him."

Helen tried to stop me, but I tore my hand away and marched forward, my short legs moving at a panicked clip.

Pushing outside, my heart was lodged in my throat. Amir was across the courtyard, his long legs carrying him faster than I could catch. Sucking in a breath, I yelled for him.

"Amir!"

His feet came to a stop. I darted for him, and he turned when I was halfway there. The furious expression he wore drew me up short. He wasn't just mad at Helen, he was mad at me.

"Tell me you're not with me for protection," he barked. "Tell me that was a lie."

"I'm with you because I like you." I took a step toward him. "I like you *so* much."

"You're not answering my question, Zadie." His head cocked. "Why were you at that party?"

"Amir..." Oh, why did he have to ask me that?

"Just fucking answer me. Tell me now how deep the deceit runs."

I sucked in a breath, hoping he would listen. "I came to the party hoping I would see you. I didn't know what Elliott was planning on doing, and I didn't have a plan other than putting myself in your orbit."

"Was that kid your boyfriend?"

I shook my head. "I told you he wasn't. I told you that from the very start."

He scrubbed the scruff on his jaw. "And I didn't listen. God-*dammit*, Zadie. Why? You could have straight up asked me. You didn't have to—" He cut himself off, shaking his head with an expression of disgust. "You fucked me so I'd keep you longer?"

Something inside me crumpled. In all the times Amir had been mean to me, he'd never made me feel like this. Like I was disposable or a piece of gum attached to his shoe.

"No," I replied miserably. "How could you ask me that?"

He pounded his chest. "*I'm* the one who was deceived here. Don't act all injured. I don't even know you. I thought you were my sweet girl. My honest girl. And it's all a lie. No wonder you didn't want to tell anyone about us. None of it's real to you, is it? You'll ride my dick as long as I protect you?"

Tears welled in my eyes. Not from what he was saying, but from the place I knew those words were coming from. I'd hurt him. My dishonesty had brought us here, and I couldn't stand the injured look on his face.

"It was an excuse!" I cried.

He went still, peering at me from narrowed eyes. "What does that mean?"

I licked my dry lips and let loose everything I'd been holding back. "It means I haven't stopped thinking about you since you left my suite almost half a year ago. I saw you three times on campus, and each time, you looked right through me like I didn't exist. When I started getting those poems, I was scared. I was really, really terrified. And I remembered your promise."

Whatever we are to each other when I walk out of your door, you'll tell me if this guy comes back.

I slapped my hair out of my face. "Of course I remembered your promise. I remember everything about that night. You let your brother hurt my friend, and yet...I wanted you. I knew you didn't want me, but I thought if maybe you were protecting me like you said you would, you'd really see me again like you did that night and maybe you'd want me too. So, it was an excuse. All of it. It was an excuse to see you, to be near you. And that's it. I manipulated everything so I could spend time with you."

I laid myself on his altar. Sacrificed my pride for the truth. I would never want Amir to think I was using him as a shield. He was so much more than that, and those blossoming feelings I'd had at the start had bloomed into something so huge and bright, he'd had to be blind not to see. Even if he was blind, he had to *feel* the way I was so obviously into him. I'd never tried to hide it.

Amir stared at me. He stared and stared, his chest heaving like he'd sprinted for a mile straight. He opened his mouth a couple times to speak but shook his head and closed it again.

Finally, he raked his hand through the side of his hair and nodded to the ground. "I gotta think. Go find your friends, Zadie."

I was rooted to my spot. He lifted his head, his brow pinched tight. "*Go*, Zadie. Get out of here."

As much as I didn't want to, I knew I had to give him this. If he needed time to think this over or forgive me, I'd let him have it.

"I'm really sorry I wasn't truthful. I hope this isn't the end." I spun around and stumbled back to the dining hall. Elena and Helen were waiting for me outside the doors. They must have heard the whole thing, since Amir and I hadn't exactly been quiet

I thought they'd hate me and shut me out, but as soon as I was within reach, they both enfolded me in their arms and guided me back to our suite. They didn't make demands for explanations, though I sensed that was coming.

In our suite, Elena pushed me down on the love seat, and Helen went to the kitchen to get drinks. She came back with three glasses of the sangria Elena's mother had had delivered to us a few days ago, thrusting the fullest one into my trembling hands. I took a sip, then a longer pull. A much longer pull.

Helen rubbed my arm. "It's time to talk, girlie."

I set my glass on the coffee table and accepted my fate. I'd been flying too close to the sun for too long. This burn had been inevitable.

"Amir and I have been officially together for a couple weeks."

Helen didn't flinch. Elena made a sour face, but she stayed quiet.

"I lied to you, and I'm really sorry. The night he was holding me as collateral, things happened between us, and I...well, I was mad he was complicit in what happened to you, Hells. So mad. And I get that me being with him now makes me disloyal to you. If you tell me you can't be friends with me anymore if I continue seeing him, I'll—"

She touched my arm. "Don't finish that sentence. I don't want to know what you would have said. I won't tell you not to see him, but, dude, I need to know you're fully aware of who he is."

"He's a criminal," Elena said dryly. "That's who he is."

Helen kicked back beside me, staring Elena down. "I hate to agree with Elena, but yeah. Amir is a criminal. His brother is a monster. You have no business getting mixed up in that world."

I chewed on my bottom lip to stop my knee-jerk desire to jump to his defense. "I went in with my eyes open. I've spent months thinking about him, about why I had feelings for him and how to deal with them. When I started getting the poems, I thought about Amir. Not that he'd sent them, but how safe I'd felt when he'd held me that night. Which is crazy, right? Because he had a gun, he forced me to stay, but it's just how I felt. How I still feel. So, I used that as an excuse to seek him out."

Elena shook her head. "I'm not happy you lied straight to my face."

My lungs burned with shame, radiating through my entire chest and up my throat. It was the worst feeling. This wasn't me. I wasn't a liar.

"I'm really, really sorry." I clasped my hands together in my lap, my head bowed. "I don't know what else to say except I haven't had friends in a long time. I didn't want to lose you guys."

Helen nudged my foot with hers. "Jesus, girlie, you're not going to lose us. But lying and hiding something as big as Amir Vasquez being your boyfriend isn't cool. I hear you, you get that, but I might need to be mad for an hour or two."

Elena sniffed. "More like a day or two." Then her eyes narrowed. "You know that dude showed up tonight so you couldn't deny him."

I scrunched my nose. "Amir?"

She nodded. "Yes, Amir. He walked into the dining hall to stake his claim. I'm going to guess you were surprised he showed up."

So much had happened, it hadn't even occurred to me. Amir had been supposed to pick me up in front of the dorm, but he'd known I was having dinner in the dining hall. He had forced the issue, and here we were.

The truth was out, but I didn't know if he'd ever look at me again. On that thought, I drained half of my sangria and wiped my mouth with the back of my hand.

"He wasn't happy I was keeping him from you," I told them.

Helen studied me for a long beat. "He really treats you right?"

I nodded. "We started out rocky because of how things ended last time. But he...yes, he's really so good to me. I don't know how to explain it, but I have never been comfortable with another man the way I am with him."

Elena popped a brow. "And the sex is amazing."

I giggled softly. "It is."

"Tramp." She rolled her eyes, but I knew Elena now and understood she was being affectionate in her own twisted way.

Helen clicked her tongue. "I really don't like you being in that world, Z."

"Helen," I admonished gently, "the first day I met you, you took me with you to collect drug money. I think you, of all people, should allow me and Amir both some grace."

She flinched at the reminder. "I shouldn't have brought you along. I own that. But I was dealing out of desperation. What's Amir's excuse?"

My brows fell heavy over my eyes. "What do you mean? I...um..."

Elena sat forward, looking at Helen. "She doesn't know."

Helen frowned at me. "Hasn't Amir told you about his family? I mean, besides his woman-beating brother."

I shook my head. "No. I know his uncle owned the warehouses and left them to Reno, but I guess I thought he grew up like you."

Elena snorted. "Nope. I didn't know Amir in high school, but Miguel Vasquez has served as part of my father's legal team for years. And his mother, Dr. Farrah Abadir, has worked on half the faces in Savage River, my mother included."

My mouth fell open in shock. Why hadn't I asked about his background? Why had I assumed he did what he did because he *had* to? I felt so stupid.

Helen folded her arms. "Your boy's family is rich-rich. A plastic surgeon mommy and a lawyer daddy, and their two boys are living a life of crime. They must be proud."

"I didn't know," I whispered.

Helen knocked my foot again. "I'm sorry I had to be the one to tell you, dude."

My stomach churned the same way it had when I'd rode the Ol' Yeller roller coaster three times in a row at the Oregon State Fair when I was twelve. I had to swallow again and again to keep bile from rising.

"It's good you did. It feels like everything is out there now." I gave her a weak smile. "Can we talk more later? I kind of want to bury my head under my covers for a little while."

They let me go, and even though things weren't quite back to normal, I was pretty certain I wasn't going to lose them. Not if I kept being honest with them.

Phone clutched in my hand, I pulled my covers up to my chin. Every night when Amir dropped me off, I always texted him a picture of me. If I didn't do it within a minute or two of me leaving him, he'd call. My chest pinched with the knowledge he wasn't going to call tonight. He might not call me again.

I wouldn't be the one to give up, though.

I took a picture of myself and texted him.

Me: *I'm home, thinking about you. Wishing we could talk, but I understand you need space, so I'll give it to you. Xoxo.*

I fell asleep waiting for his reply.

· · · · ●· ● ● · ·

I dreamed he came and we danced on the beach. Even in my dream, I was sad and clung to him so he couldn't walk away. My ringing phone pulled me away from the feel of his hands on my hips. I tried so hard to stay, but my eyes fluttered open, and I was back, alone in my room.

My phone was next to me in bed, my mom's name on the screen. It was already ten in the morning. I'd crashed early last night and had slept *hard*.

"Hi, Mom."

"Hey, baby. Did I wake you up?"

"Mmm. Sort of, but that's okay. I'm being a bum."

She chuckled. "Well, now's the time to be a bum, before real life starts. Although, you know I'm still a big fan of lazy Sundays."

I smiled despite the misery weighing on my chest. "Where do you think I get it from?"

"I taught you well. As we speak, Max and I are bumming on the sofa. Eli hasn't emerged from his room yet. He's got another hour before we drag him out."

I gasped. "He's a growing boy. You have to let him sleep until at least noon."

"Eleven is my limit."

"How's Max?"

"He's okay. We're getting through." The phone became muffled, but I still heard Mom telling her husband I was asking about him. Then she came back. "Max says if you worry about him for longer than a minute a day, he'll ground you. I'm not sure he has the authority to do that, but he seems pretty adamant."

"Tell Max we'll discuss this when I visit you next."

She cleared her throat. "There was a reason for this call, baby."

At the switch in her tone, I sat up, swinging my legs over the side of my bed. "Yes?"

"I finally got answers from Officer Ryder about Drew. He made some calls, including to Drew's parents. They didn't want to tell him anything, and it took a few conversations before they finally admitted his whereabouts."

My nails dug into my knees as my heart thrashed. "Is he here?"

"No, he's not. Drew was admitted to a mental health facility ninety days ago. It's a long-term treatment program. They didn't tell Ryder his full diagnosis, but they admitted Drew had a bad psychosis episode and harmed himself severely. He...um, tried to end his life with his father's table saw and lost a hand. I don't know if it makes you feel better to know he isn't the one who has been sending you—"

She kept speaking, but I had folded in at the news of what Drew had done to himself. I'd been angry at him for so long for what he'd put me through, but I couldn't help the rapid rush of sympathy that punched me in the gut. What kind of mental state had he been in to use a table saw on himself? And to lose a hand?

"Zadie? Zadie? Honey, are you there?"

Tears dripped down my cheeks. Oh god, what had he done to himself? Even if he got the help he needed, he'd never ever be the same.

The phone was taken from me, then Amir was in front of me, crouching down, wiping the tears from my face. He spoke to my mom, telling her I was okay, he had me, listening to her for a minute before he said goodbye.

He placed the phone on my nightstand, then urged me to lie down. He stretched out next to me, pulling me into his arms. I didn't know what this meant, why he was here, but my thoughts were too filled with the tragedy that was Drew to try to figure it out.

Amir stroked my hair and held me. He didn't speak or rush me. He gave me exactly what I needed.

And I thought, this was what Helen and Elena didn't see. They didn't know he could be like this. I loved that this side of him was solely mine, but a little part of me wished they could see so they would understand.

"I'm okay." I lifted my head from his chest, taking in his tired eyes and the frown lines around his mouth. "It isn't Drew."

He barely moved, only the slightest tip of his chin. "Felicity told me. Fucking awful."

"Yeah." Shuddering, I let my gaze trail over his unhappy face again. "What are you doing here?"

His frown deepened. "Did you think I'd really stay away?"

"I hoped you wouldn't, but I wouldn't have blamed you."

He pushed my curls off my face and cupped my jaw. "I was so..." His jaw clenched and unclenched. "I was going to say angry, but that's not it. Disappointed is more what I felt."

I flattened my palm over his heart. "I understand."

"You don't." He rubbed his thumb along the underside of my mouth. "I was disappointed because of my ego. Once I had some space, gave myself a chance to really take in what you'd said, I got pissed." When I opened my mouth to apologize once again, he pressed a finger over my lips. "I got pissed at myself for walking away from you the first time. For saying ugly shit to you I didn't mean because you called me out on something I wasn't proud of."

"You mean telling Reno where Helen was?"

His eyelids lowered. "Mmhmm. I told him that to appease him. So he didn't go apeshit and make good on all his threats. I was stupid not to think he'd go there. And maybe I didn't give enough of a shit about what would happen if he did. So, when you, the pretty, sweet, sexy as hell little angel, called me out, I reacted because you were right. And I. Did. Not. Like. That."

"And now?"

"And now, I'm gonna say thank you for pushing me. You looked past the ugly I showed you. I don't know why, but I'm not gonna question it because I don't want you rethinking me." He pushed the strap of my tank top down and pulled me close to touch his lips to my shoulder. "You were never with that asshole?"

I shook my head. "I told you I wasn't. I heard him talking about your brother's parties and I suggested he take me. I thought you would probably be there."

Amir's frown shattered and re-formed as a grin. Low laughs vibrated his chest. "You really are devious, aren't you, mama? I like that you have that in you."

"I don't know about that. I'm just lucky my very poorly thought-out plan worked out."

He took my face in both hands. "You thought I didn't want you, but I *couldn't* want you. Not after I left you in your bed. Do you see that? You're still too good for me, but I'm way too weak to give you up now."

Grabbing his hand, I brought it to my mouth and bit down hard on his fingertip. He stared at me, nostrils flaring, but he didn't jerk away. "Stop saying you're not good enough. You're insulting me because I chose you."

His mouth quirked. "No one's perfect. You're close, but you have fucking terrible taste in men. You said yourself you like guys who will likely wind up in jail."

I snarled at him. "Please don't joke about that."

"What? That I might end up in jail? You know what I do."

"I do. I just don't know why you do it. I thought I did, but I was wrong."

His brows pulled together. "What's that mean?"

"It means I naively thought you were like Helen. Doing what needed to be done to rise above what you were born into. But that isn't you. Helen told me. She told me who your parents are. I don't know why I never asked you about them. I guess I thought you'd tell me if you wanted to."

His jaw hardened. "I wouldn't have. I don't talk about them."

"Okay. You don't have to," I rushed out. "But tell me why you're working for Reno. Please?"

Sighing, he threaded his fingers in my hair, then brought my head down until our foreheads met. "It's my brother, mama. Maybe you don't get that because your brother didn't come along until you were already grown, but there's no breaking that bond. He needs me, so I'm there."

This was the first time we'd talked about what he did for Reno. Like I'd assumed he'd grown up poor, I also assumed there was an end date to his job. Maybe even an end date to his relationship with his brother. Or maybe I'd just buried my head in the sand because it was easier than facing the real answers.

"He's going to need you forever?" I asked.

Amir tipped my head back. "He's always my brother. Even when he's a piece of shit. That's not changing. Will I always work for him? If that's what you're asking, then no. I won't. But that comes later, after I graduate."

"Another year," I murmured.

"Now you know, but nothing's changed for you, Zadie. Nothing between us will be any different except now all our secrets are out in the open. What I do for Reno is separate. It won't touch you. It won't touch us. I need you to hear that, because I'm not going to discuss it with you. It won't be up for discussion ever again."

His hands in my hair were gentle, his words delicate and soft, but his message was unyielding. When it came to Reno, Amir was and always would be an unmovable brick wall. If I pushed, he wouldn't be happy.

My relief at having him back, at being forgiven, overrode the screaming protests in my mind.

"If you get arrested, that affects me."

His eyes bored into mine. "I'm not getting arrested. I've been doing this too long. I know how to be safe and keep the important people in my life clean and away from all of it. I'm not giving you up, so you need to accept this is the way it's going to be. I will bend and discuss and maybe even compromise on occasion, but not about this."

I nodded. "Okay."

I let it go, and I let Amir back in. I might regret it one day, but on *this* day, I was too relieved he came back to me to feel anything else.

CHAPTER TWENTY-TWO

Amir

I SPENT ONE SEMESTER in a dorm and vowed never again. Even with how cushy the suites were at Savage U, I'd been claustrophobic.

But once Zadie let me into her room, I had no desire to leave. Then again, her room contained *her*. It smelled like her, and everything was soft and girly...like her.

We'd spent the day kissing and talking and quietly fucking. One of her suitemates left food for us by the door, so we ate, kissed, fucked, and talked some more.

She showed me the last poem she had received, more than two weeks ago. This time, someone had bastardized an Eminem song. I was beginning to think, and Zadie was too, these poems were from some kid with a crush. Some socially awkward geek thought my girl would be impressed by pitiful love notes.

It was late, near midnight, and I was starving. "Is there any food in that little kitchen out there?"

"There's some snacks." She ran her palm along my stomach. "Are you hungry? Do you want me to go get you something?"

"I'm good. I'll find something to eat. You look too good in that bed for me to let you out."

She was comfortable here, even sweeter than she normally was. That might've been because we'd broken down most of the walls between us.

I wandered out into the quiet living area to the minuscule kitchen, opening cupboards. They had one stocked with snacks, and I grabbed some granola bars. My stomach was going to be eating itself by morning, but I wasn't going anywhere until the sun rose.

I found a bottle of water in the fridge, stacking it on top of the granola bars. I turned to go back to Zadie's room and found Helen standing in her own doorway, arms folded over her chest.

"You should let her go."

I set the bars and water down and mimicked her stance. "Not an option. And not your business. She's not a child. She can make her own decisions."

Helen stalked across the small living space, stopping a foot from me. "Zadie isn't a child. She's an incredibly intelligent woman. She's also good. I don't know many good people, and I have a feeling you don't either." Her fingers curved into a claw near her middle. "I have this instinct to preserve that goodness because it's so rare. But you...well, you're going to suck it away. Because I know you, dude. You might like her and want her, but when it comes down to it, you're a leech. You're going to suck and suck her goodness out until you're fat with it and she's a shell."

"That's what you think?"

Her eyes narrowed. "That's what I know. I'm not going to let you do it, you know."

I clicked my tongue. "You're so wrong."

"Am I? I don't think so. But let me tell you this: if you in any way hurt her or cause her harm because of the way you choose to live your life, I will burn your goddamn house down. And I mean that both literally and metaphorically."

"Nothing's going to happen to Zadie." I swiped a hand across my jaw. "I appreciate your concern for her, which is why I'm going to let the threat you just laid down slide. But just because I'm with your friend does not mean you have a free pass to disrespect me. You need to think before you speak to me."

She rolled her eyes and slowly raised her middle finger. "Get over yourself, Amir."

I couldn't even hold back the laugh that burst out of me. "Get the fuck out of here, Helen."

"You're in my suite, dick."

"That's right." I scooped up my snacks and water. "And I have a girl waiting for me. Nice catching up."

Zadie was sitting on the edge of the bed when I came back to her, worrying her bottom lip with her teeth, asking me a question with her big blue eyes.

I tossed the granola bars and water to the side to cup her head and tilt it back. Every time I looked at her face, at the way round and soft played with smooth and angled, I got caught up in her. It was a true fact, I'd never seen anyone prettier than Zadie. After a day in her room, no makeup, only a little sleep, she still looked like this. Sexy, pretty, sweet...fucking everything.

"No worries, mama. Helen was just explaining how it is."

"How is it?"

"You have a good friend."

I pushed her back on the bed and crawled over her, caging her body with mine. But it felt like I was the one who was caged. My skin was two sizes too small, my insides restless, pacing, needing, always fucking needing around her.

"Take your clothes off."

Her lips fell open. "Again?"

"Open your legs. I need to eat."

I sat back on my knees, giving her room to slip her T-shirt over her head. Since that was all she had on, she was naked in seconds, legs open for me.

The first time, I'd asked her to show me her universe, and she had. But it was mine now. I was the pioneer who saw pretty, bare land and claimed it as my own. Those pretty, puffy pussy lips were the door to my kingdom. I got down on my belly to explore my newfound home.

She was slick under my lips. Hot and sensitive, her hips rose to meet me at first contact.

"Amir...oh god, I don't think I can come again, baby."

I flicked my tongue on her clit, which had already swelled up so nicely for me. "I need you to do it for me, mama. This is going to be my orgasm. I need it. Are you going to deprive me of something I need?" I licked her clit again, and she shuddered.

She lifted her head to watch me between her legs. My girl surprised me with how much she liked to watch me work. Her delicate fingers threaded through my hair. Our eyes connected as I opened my mouth to suck on her pussy lips the way she liked. She might have thought she couldn't come again, but I knew this body. I knew what she could take. The tremble that shook her over from head to toe told me how right I'd been.

I kept my eyes on her while I ate her, feasted on her, sucked up the sweet nectar that leaked from her and ran down her folds. Her eyes stayed open until the very end, then she was holding my head against her with both hands, her thighs squeezing, her spine arching as she came apart at the seams.

She was still shaking when I flipped her over, gripping her hips to draw them up. She tucked her knees under her, offering herself to me, and I *gladly* accepted, sliding into her heat for the fourth time that day. It might as well have been the first. I had to stop, get hold of myself, gain control.

"Fuck, mama. Fuck, how do you feel so good? When I'm with you, inside you, I lose myself. It's like my first time."

She rocked her hips, drawing me impossibly deeper. "Move," she mewled. "Please?"

Sweat beaded on my forehead as I reined in my desire to go hard and fast and pump her full of my seed. I looked down, but that was a mistake. The sight of Zadie's plump ass and hips spread out nearly sent me over the edge. There was no end to my desire. Having her the first time had cracked open a plastered wall, revealing a bottomless well of need. It went on and on. Maybe one day I'd be sated, but for now, I was nowhere near that point.

"This ass..." I smoothed my palms along her exaggerated curves to her breasts, cupping them. "These tits..." and down to her dripping cunt, rounding my fingers on her clit. "This fucking delicious pussy..."

"I need you," she breathed.

"That's all you have to say." I rocked forward and retreated, even though pulling out, even by a few inches, went against my every instinct when it came to her. Then I thrust forward, enveloped in her impossibly hot and soft walls, and all was right.

Using my thumbs, I spread her cheeks to watch myself plunge in and out of her. My cock was coated with her pleasure, all shiny and slick. She let me take her raw, the only woman I'd ever wanted to go there with, and there was no going back for me. Nothing would ever come between us.

"Tell me how it looks." She pushed back so when I thrust, we collided in a loud slap. "Tell me what you're seeing."

"You're wet, mama. So, so wet, you're dripping all over my cock." I rubbed a thumb over her other tightly closed hole. "I like this, it's so tempting. You want me to take you here?"

I dipped down, only entering her with the tip of my thumb. She pushed against me harder, releasing a low moan.

"Yeah, you like that, don't you? You like the idea of me owning every hole?"

She moaned again in response, her fingers curling to grip the sheets.

"*Yeah*, you like that." We'd talk about it until we were both there, then I'd follow through. I'd own Zadie because she damn sure owned me.

Sliding my hand up her spine, I gripped her nape, the other hand holding her hip. I'd talked us both into a frenzy. My smooth plunges became frantic, hard thrusts. She answered by rearing back, her ass slapping against my hips.

She whimpered as her walls fluttered and clamped down, sucking me in so deep, my choices were taken from me. The only thing I could do was unload, painting her insides with my seed.

Knees giving out, she collapsed onto the mattress, and I followed, half on her back, half on the bed.

She threw a granola bar at me, glancing off my shoulder.

"That wasn't very nice." I touched my lips to her nape. "Didn't I make you feel good?"

Turning her head, she peeked at me from one eye. "You have drained me dry. I have nothing else to give."

Her words were uncomfortably close to Helen's, and they dug into my brain. "I think it was you draining me."

She shifted to her side so we were face to face and trailed her fingers along my hairline.

"We're good, you know."

I nodded. "I know."

"We have time. We don't have to fit it all in in one day."

"You think that's what I've been doing today?"

"I don't know." She pressed her palm to my chest. "I'm not complaining. I guess I was feeling it too. I mean, I always feel like I want you to fling me into bed." I grinned wide, and she shoved my mouth gently. "But that was heightened today, right?"

"Right. And for the fucking record, I always want to fling you into bed. Or against the wall. Or over the back of the couch."

She pushed on my lips again.

"What did Helen say to you?"

"She was being protective. Telling me you're too good for me. Everything I already know."

Zadie's mouth twisted to the side. "Can I tell you a story so you might understand a little about me, then you'll stop wondering why I hate you saying you're not good enough or I'm too good?"

"Please tell me a story, little mama. I always want to understand you better."

With a long exhale, she began. "My mother had an affair with Max for six months before she left my dad."

My brows shot up. "For real? Felicity?"

She nodded. "My parents were miserable at the end. When everything with Drew happened, instead of turning to each other, they turned away. My dad smoked weed, researched guns, stalker laws, vigilantism...he let the situation consume him. I don't know if my mom even tried to get to him. She leaned on Max, though. He was her college boyfriend, her first love. I don't know why they broke up back then, but I don't think the feelings ever went away. Anyway, they started an affair, he came up to Oregon, she traveled to California, and my dad spiraled. I don't even know if my mom was hiding where she was going, you know? I guess she got consumed too."

"Aw, fuck. Were you angry at her?"

She bit her bottom lip, taking her time to answer. "I was at first. Of course I was. Our family was already broken, and she'd shattered us. But my dad, he didn't fight for her. He accepted she was leaving with barely any reaction. And I...well, I met Max and saw them together."

"Yeah?"

"It was the first time I really saw my mom as a whole person. Not just my mother or my dad's wife, you know? I saw she was human, that she'd had a life before me, a life outside of me, and would continue to have a life when I left home. She messed up—god, did she mess up. I don't like what she did to my dad, but I don't like what he did to her by pulling away. The thing is, even though I'll never understand why either of them responded to my crisis the way they did, I *love* them. They're human and fallible, but they love and adore me. They've always been devoted to me as my parents."

"They hurt you."

"Yeah." She kissed my chin, then my lips. "They hurt me, but that's human too, isn't it?"

"Not if I can help it."

She laughed softly. "Well, you can't. I'm going to be hurt because it's part of life. You hurt me, I hurt you, but we're better for it. When you were my captor, you scared me until you didn't. Until I saw you as a person and not just the man with the gun. I don't like what you do, I don't agree with it, and I think you're way too smart to lower yourself the way you do, but that doesn't make me better than you. It also doesn't make me think less of you. People mess up. They mess up over and over. That doesn't change who they are. They are not the sum of their mistakes. I still love my mom, I love my dad, and now I've grown to love Max and Eli like family. And I—"

She clamped her mouth shut, but her cheeks were glowing red. I wanted to hear what she'd stopped herself from saying, but I let it go for now. She'd already said a lot.

"You're a good girl, Zadie Night." I tugged her against my chest, enclosing her in my arms. Like always, I had an urge to keep her trapped with me and never let her go.

"You're not the villain you think you are, Amir Vasquez." She patted my chest. "But that's not the point. I'm telling you I'm just as flawed as you and my parents. My mother betrayed my dad, but I've chosen to look past it for selfish reasons. By all rights, I should be angry at her, I shouldn't accept Max, but I do, and it didn't take long for it to happen."

"Zadie..."

This girl really had no idea. She thought she was flawed because she forgave her mother. The mother who adored her. God, Drew had done a mindfuck on her. He'd warped her perspective so much, she didn't see straight. If I could have taken a table saw to his other hand, I would have. That motherfucker didn't deserve to have any extremities.

"And you, Amir...I've chosen to look past things with you I never could have imagined myself looking past, also for selfish reasons. Because I want you, and I had to give up everything I wanted for too long."

I took her face in my hands. The prettiest fucking face in the world. "You don't have to give me up."

If she *ever* thought she had to, I would find a way to rewind the world again and again until she changed her mind. Zadie giving me up wasn't a possibility. Not now.

She scrunched her nose. "I just told you I'm not going to."

Zadie might not have thought I was a villain. Perhaps that was debatable, and I sure as hell hoped I was redeemable. But the fact was, I wasn't a misunderstood bad boy with a heart of gold. It was gray at best, and only beat for a handful of people.

Right now, it was thundering for Zadie.

"Not gonna give you up either, mama."

CHAPTER TWENTY-THREE

Amir

AT THE END OF commerce, my brain always felt swollen in my skull. Dr. Krasinski had earned his reputation as both a hard-ass and the best teacher at Savage U. He took the semester he had with his students and forced as much information into them as humanly possible.

I'd never been more challenged, but I'd never gotten so much out of a class. When I wasn't with Zadie or doing my shit for Reno, I was studying and writing for Krasinski.

I walked down the steps of the lecture hall, my brain still buzzing with all I'd heard over the last hour. Zadie and Julien had taken this class last semester, but they'd undersold it in a big way. I was going to have to talk to them about that when I got home this afternoon.

"Mr. Vasquez." Krasinski stepped into my path. "Do you have a minute?"

I kept my expression impassive. This could be really good or really bad. I hadn't done shit to make it bad, but that didn't mean it wouldn't be.

"Yes, I do," I replied, stepping off to the side with him so the flow of students could continue to the exit.

"I received your email last week. I've been doing some thinking about your request."

Krasinski was the recommendation I needed to land a coveted internship at Sparta Inc., the largest import company in Southern California. They took on exactly five interns a year, and my ass planned to be one of them.

"I'm curious about your thoughts," I said.

He crossed his arms and rubbed his well-trimmed gray beard. "You've impressed me so far this semester. The insights in the last paper you turned in were fresh and showed an expert grasp of the material. You've also brought a lot to the discussions we have in class. But I have some qualms."

Fuck. Shit. Fuck.

"That's unfortunate. Can I ask what they are?"

He paused, staring at me for a long beat. "I'll be blunt, Mr. Vasquez. I asked around about you. While your past teachers all had positive feedback, there are murmurs. No one knows anything concrete, but there's a shadow that follows your name. I don't need confirmation from you whether you know what I'm talking about. I'll assume you do."

I remained impassive, all while feeling the fire at my feet grow hotter and hotter. The chickens had come home to roost, and I shouldn't have been surprised, yet I was.

When I didn't respond, not even with a nod, he went on. "I'd like to consider my recommendation over spring break. I know you need an answer from me, and I will give it to you when classes are back in session, if not before. But for me to associate my name with anyone, I need to be certain, and to be blunt, I'm not certain about you. To be even more blunt, one arrest on your record for the things you're rumored to be involved in will kill most opportunities in the line of work you plan to go into. Imagine an import business like Sparta trusting their operations to—"

He cut himself off, but the message was received. A company who imported goods from overseas wouldn't hire someone with a black mark on their record for peddling dope. It was too risky, no matter if the black mark was well in their past. I'd just have to make sure that never happened.

"Thank you." That was the only thing I could say. "I hear you. I want you to know I take my future extremely seriously. If you decide to give me the recommendation, I will do everything in my power to make sure you don't regret it. Thank you for considering it."

There weren't many men I'd defer to, but Krasinski was one. Not just because of what he could do for me, but because I truly respected him. For the way he taught, but also for having this conversation with me. Given what he'd heard, even if it was half-truths, it couldn't have been easy for him to say.

It was like pouring acid in my ears to hear.

Fuck.

· · • • · • • · · ·

By the time I walked across campus to my truck and drove home, I was still wrapping my head around my conversation with Krasinski. I didn't like being told what to do, but he hadn't. He'd simply been honest about the consequences of the way I made money. He'd held up a mirror and said, "Look at yourself, you dumb fuck."

But I was already pulling back as much as I could. I'd made a promise to Reno I couldn't break. I *wouldn't* break. My word was all I had in this world, and I'd given it to him.

Fucking shit.

If I screwed over Krasinski, assuming he gave me the rec, there was no going back.

I was stuck here, caught between the present and the future. My future.

I'd just have to be even more careful. Delegate. Lay as low as possible to outrun the shadow behind me.

And I had to survive the next week, waiting for my answer from him. I wouldn't even have Zadie here to distract me for most of it. She was flying to Oregon on Monday to visit her dad for a few days. I only had the weekend with her, and I intended to claim every second of it.

As soon as I opened the front door, I was assaulted on every level. Warm, garlic-scented air, fast-paced music from the piano, Zadie's high, smooth voice singing a Melanie Martinez song. This wasn't an uncommon occurrence anymore. Two weeks had gone by since Zadie and I had spent all day and night in her room, and something had shifted between us. The near choke hold I'd felt compelled to keep on her had loosened without me noticing. When she and Julien interacted, I didn't have to fight off my need to fuck her in front of him to show him who owned her, because all of us knew. I owned Zadie, and she owned me right the fuck back.

Rounding the corner into the living room, I first found Marco kicked back on the couch. He tipped his head to the piano, where Julien and Zadie were side by side, playing together. When she discovered he was the pianist of the house, she'd begged him to let her play our piano. Since neither Marco nor I especially appreciated his music, he'd been giddy to share it with her.

My girl turned her head, the grin that was already on her face brightening. I stood there as she sang about training wheels, moving her fingers over the keys without looking. Julien's floated over the keys like butterflies. From my uneducated ear, he had mad talent. He'd played for as long as I'd known him. Zadie, of course, sang and played like an angel. Watching her and my best friend happy, making music, my other best friend enjoying the sounds, soothed the bitter, angry mood I was in.

I couldn't say I didn't have an ounce of jealousy boiling in my blood. That wouldn't be true. But I trusted the two of them, so I let it slide and allowed their friendship to cement. I planned on having Julien as a part of my life until we went to the grave, and with the way Zadie had reached into my chest and wrapped her soft little hand around my heart, she just might be there too.

The song came to an end with a dramatic pounding on the keys from Julien. I stuck two fingers in my mouth to whistle my appreciation. Marco gave a slow clap from his place on the couch.

Laughing, Zadie hopped up from the bench and threw herself at me. I caught her, pulling her into my chest, needing her soft more than I realized. I shoved my nose in her hair, taking in her berries and rain and the silk of her curls.

"Hi," she murmured against my chest.

"Hey, mama. You're a sight for sore eyes."

Julien got up from the bench with his arms outstretched. "Don't I get a hug too?"

I cocked my head at Marco. "He looks lonely over there. Go ask him."

Julien bolted across the room and launched himself into Marco's lap. Marco shoved him off, sending Julien sprawling to the ground. Zadie swiveled in my arms when he knocked the coffee table onto its side.

"He's impervious to damage," I told her. "He falls, and he bounces. Been that way since he was a toddler."

Julien sprung up and took a bow. "I think I stuck the landing."

"Fucking aces, man," Marco agreed.

I buried my nose in Zadie's hair again. "What's cooking in the kitchen, mama?"

"I'm roasting garlic right now. In a little bit, Marco and I are going to make risotto."

I turned her around to face me again, holding her shoulders. "Marco? As in the Marco who lives in this house? The kid who can't make toast?"

She nodded, grinning. "That Marco. He claims he can't cook, so I told him I'd teach him. When I get back from Oregon, we're conquering salmon."

"Have you domesticated us? Is that what's happening here?"

She gave an innocent shrug, but I saw through her. Zadie wasn't required to cook for us anymore, but she still did a few times a week because she liked it. What she didn't do was change my sheets. I'd learned my girl could hold a grudge, and every so often, she brought up my slutty sheets, even though she was the only one who'd been in them in a *long* time. So I changed them now, and she watched.

Utterly domesticated. It came with copious blow jobs, a plump ass parked on my dick pretty much any time I wanted it, and a sweet girl who touched my face as she was falling asleep, so I wasn't even complaining.

I pulled Zadie into the kitchen, backed her into a cabinet, and took her mouth. She responded immediately, curling her arms around my neck and rising on her toes so she could get to me. Lips parting, she invited me inside, and I went, sucking on her tongue and lips, licking her mouth. I'd needed this, to sip from her sweetness, drink her nectar, remind me of what was vital.

"Mama...you taste too good," I rumbled against her lips.

"I like when you taste me like that."

"Can't get enough." I took a breath, staring down at her. "I'm going to take you dancing tomorrow."

"Okay." She blinked up at me like she was trying to remember where she was. She got that look when I kissed her for a long time. She lost her sense of place and time entirely. This fucking girl. "The same place? I loved that night."

"No." I took her chin between my fingers. "We'll go back when there's rain in the forecast. Need to get caught in the rain with you again."

She huffed a laugh. "We could just have Julien spray us with the hose."

My forehead wrinkled. "You want him being there when I fuck you?"

She shook her head fast. "No, I do not. I'd never be able to look at him again."

I grinned at her, my shy Zadie, only wild for me. "I'm taking you to a club. Gonna show you off."

Her teeth dug into her bottom lip. "Really?"

"Yeah. Really." I pushed her hair behind her ear. "Did Deacon give you any trouble today?"

"No. He doesn't even look at me anymore. I imagine being glowered at by you a few times a week wasn't something he wants to continue. And I *really* doubt he had any desire to get up close and personal with you."

I scoffed. "Me? I'm a lamb. Nothing to be afraid of."

It'd been a month since Zadie had last received a poem. She'd relaxed, but her guard was always up. I'd caught her checking over her shoulder more than once or running her hands over her arms to smooth out goose bumps. The only thing that was stopping me from eviscerating this Deacon fuck was Zadie begging me not to. There wasn't much I'd deny her. As long as Deacon kept away and quiet, he wouldn't be hearing from me. But if he even *thought* about taking another shot at her, all bets were off. There was only so far a man could be pushed before he had to step up and say *enough*.

Zadie nipped at my chin. "I'm not afraid of you."

"Good." I tapped her forehead with mine. "You have nothing to be afraid of when you're with me."

Her pretty blue eyes narrowed slightly. "Are you going to tell me why you looked so angry when you first got home? Did something happen?"

I exhaled through my nose. Normally, I liked that Zadie was attuned to me and my moods, but this wasn't one of those times. Discussing what Krasinski had said to me would only lead to her worrying or questioning my job. Both options were unacceptable to me.

"I had to remind myself I didn't want to rip Julien's head off for being so close to you. That's all."

"That's all?" Two words so loaded with skepticism, I almost buckled.

But this topic wasn't for Zadie, and that was for her own good.

"That's all."

CHAPTER TWENTY-FOUR

Zadie

AMIR'S WARM BREATH AND cold lips brushed my skin, making me shiver, which was a difficult task since I was hot from dancing and being pressed against him for the last hour. I was still pressed against him, though now he had me draped across his lap. We'd just sat down in a private booth in the VIP lounge of some club in a beach town not far from Savage River.

"Cold?" he murmured beside my ear.

"Your lips are," I replied.

He took my chin in his hand, tipping my head to the side to touch his lips to mine. It didn't end in a touch. His tongue teased the seam of my lips, parting them to sweep inside. He licked the vodka and cranberry juice off my tongue, humming with satisfaction at the taste of me. His hands took my hips, pulling them back until my ass was on top of his growing erection. I pressed down on him, teasing him, while searching for friction too. Dancing with Amir turned me on. The way he moved, the way he held me, set my skin alight. I loved that he wasn't afraid to really get into the music. He didn't just grind on me. My man had real moves.

"*Fuck*. I have to stop kissing you before I come in my pants."

The way he said it, he sounded genuinely tortured. His desire for me gave me a heady buzz of power along my skin. I never imagined being the reason a man would lose control, especially a man like Amir who held his reins so tight, they were practically embedded in his fists.

"Don't do that." I nibbled his chin. "Your cum is mine."

He sucked in a harsh breath. "Jesus, Zadie. I'm already on the edge and you say shit like that? You want me to take you right here? I'm almost to the point I do not care who sees."

I didn't believe him. I mean, I did believe he wanted inside me, but not the other part. Amir would never be at the point he didn't care who saw me.

It was just as well, because we weren't alone anymore.

"Yooooo, what's good?" Julien threw himself down on the opposite side of the booth, Marco following with Vanessa clinging to his shoulder like a barnacle. Unfortunately, she looked nothing like a barnacle in a white dress that was so skintight, I almost felt I was seeing her naked.

Jealousy swam in my stomach like an anaconda, so big and fast, I had to press a hand to my middle so I didn't get sick. This was a woman Amir had slept with. A woman whose hip bones were visible, stomach didn't roll when she sat down, a woman who—

Amir gripped my nape, crushed his lips to mine, and drowned me and my thoughts in a soul-destroying kiss. He only stopped when Julien cheered for us, yelling over the music, "Unh, unh, get it, get it."

I hid my hot face on Amir's shoulder while he talked to his boys like nothing had happened. Any time Vanessa tried to grab his attention, he flat out ignored her. I wished she wasn't sitting with us, but at the same time, I was glad she was. Amir wasn't being subtle about his disinterest in her, and though I didn't love the idea of her feelings being hurt, I also wanted her to understand Amir wasn't an option for her anymore.

Eventually, she got up to leave, hesitating for a moment like one of us would stop her, but not even Marco asked her to stay. I didn't like her, but when she flicked her long hair behind her shoulders and swayed her hips, I couldn't say I didn't watch her perfect butt bounce as she made her exit.

Julien shook his head. "Dude, you have to get better taste."

Marco gave a lazy shrug. "Easy pussy is easy pussy. At least I know she's not gonna catch feelings since her heart already belongs to another."

Amir held his hands up. "Not to me. She left that shit on my doorstep and I let it freeze. It'd be nice if she didn't have a presence at the house anymore, but I'm not gonna tell you what to do."

Marco shrugged again. "All right. It's no skin off my back. Plenty of other bitches."

I brought my head up to ask Julien what his type was when a man appeared at our table. He was dressed like most of the men here, in a button-down and fitted jeans, but he was strung out, jittery.

"Hey, man." He addressed Amir, white-knuckling the end of the table. "Can I talk to you?"

"No. You need to walk away, César."

He leaned over, and up close, I saw the sweat beading on his upper lip, the red rimming his nostrils, the broken blood vessels in the whites of his eyes. "It'll just take a minute. I'll buy your next round, okay?"

"No." Amir shifted me from his lap onto the bench then pushed out of the booth, rising a head above the other man. "You don't approach me. That isn't how this works."

The man backed up a step, wringing his hands. "I know, I know. I apologize. I'm just in a bad way, and I need—"

Amir's hand came down so hard on the guy's shoulder, he staggered. "Don't say another fucking word. I said no. The disrespect you're showing me by approaching me in public and speaking to me out of turn is so fucking audacious, I can barely believe it's happening. You're lucky I'm in a good mood, kid. Damn lucky."

The guy bowed his head, but he didn't move away. I couldn't hear what he was saying, but his mouth was moving, moving, almost like he was chanting. His entire body was moving, bouncing knees, scratching arms, twitching shoulders. He definitely seemed to be in a bad way.

Amir closed in on him, bumping his chest, and only then did he stagger back. His mouth kept moving, and though I couldn't hear his pleas as Amir herded him away from us, I knew from the expression of anguish in his eyes that was what they were.

Julien clucked his tongue. "Junkie trash."

Marco's nostrils flared. "Stupid fuck. Now Amir's never going to sell to him. He should've gone to the corner if he needed a hit that bad."

They bantered back and forth about the man, César. How his desperation stank. That he was about to lose his house because all his money went up his nose and into his veins. He'd *already* lost his kids. They were laughing at how low he'd fallen, that he'd let himself get there.

"Cognitive dissonance." It tumbled out of my mouth, only a whisper, but Julien stared at me, leaning closer.

"What'd you say?"

I lifted my eyes to his. "I said cognitive dissonance. You're making fun of César for being hooked on drugs, but you live with the man who sells them to him. He's your best friend." I touched my forehead. "I mean, I do it too, but I guess I didn't find anything about what just happened funny."

Julien reached across the table, laid his palm on my wrist. "You're not wrong. I'm always gonna be on Amir's side, but I get what you're saying, Z."

Marco scrubbed his mouth and exhaled, turning his head to the side. "Insensitive," he muttered.

"I'm not trying to police you guys," I rushed out. "I swear, I'm not. That was more about me realizing something. I shouldn't have said anything."

My stomach lurched with feelings that weren't happy ones, and I didn't know what to do with them. I couldn't talk to Amir about how much I'd hated that scene. He'd told me in no uncertain terms his job wasn't up for discussion. And that man...I didn't know anything about him, he might have been a rapist or a serial killer, but the anguish in his eyes would stay with me for a while.

Marco turned back, his dark eyes blazing into mine. "You have to be a lot tougher than that, Zadie. That shit was nothing. Do you hear me? He keeps his business separate, but it bleeds. If a low-life junkie's gonna make you sad, then you need to walk, because you're going to be facing a lifetime of sad."

My mouth fell open as Julien pulled his hand away from my arm to slap the hell out of Marco's. I slumped back against the booth, willing myself not to cry. This wasn't the time or place. I had to think, but I couldn't do that here, with the giant, bickering men across from me, the bass rattling my bones, three drinks swimming through my blood.

Amir slipped back in the booth, straightening his sleeves, then wrapped his arm around me. His mouth touched my cheek, sliding up to my ear.

"I'm sorry, mama. You didn't need to see that."

I nodded, curling into him. "Can we go soon?"

He peered down at me. "What's wrong? Did something happen while I was gone?"

"No, I just got tired all of a sudden. If you're not ready, I can wait. It's okay."

Amir lifted his chin to Marco and Julien, who'd stopped bickering when he'd showed, and were now watching the two of us with warring expressions. Julien's was soft, almost wistful. Marco's lip was curled in the barest sneer, making him seem dubious, and I knew that was aimed squarely at me. He probably viewed my doubts as disloyal, and maybe he was right. I certainly didn't like where my mind had gone tonight.

"We're heading out," he told them. "See you in the morning."

Within minutes, we were out of the club and in his SUV. Amir kept one hand on me during the drive back to his house, like he was afraid I'd get lost. The thing was, I was already lost. I couldn't forget that man's anguish, and I hated it.

I was truly my father's daughter, helpless in the face of suffering.

"What happened to him?" I asked.

Amir started at my sudden question, his hand flexing on mine. "I had security remove him. I hope he went home and slept it off, but knowing what I do, he's probably looking to score somewhere else." In my periphery, his head turned to study me for a second before he focused on the road again. "Were you scared?"

"No. I think I'd say surprised."

He scoffed lowly. "Me too. That never, *ever* happens. He must've seen me tonight and gotten desperate enough, he took a chance. The people I deal with know discretion is my top priority, and that scene tonight was anything but discreet." He slammed the heel of his palms against the steering wheel. "Goddamn motherfucker little bitch."

Amir roared, and I did my best not to cower. His anger wasn't at me. It probably wasn't even wholly at that addict. Nevertheless, I'd been a victim of a man's anger over things not going the way he wanted, so it was hard for me to exist in this too-small vehicle and not be afraid.

Panting, Amir grappled with my hand until our fingers were woven together. I squeezed, both for him and me, and he squeezed back even harder.

"That never should have happened. Never. He shouldn't have come near you." He brought our joined hands to his mouth to kiss my knuckles one at a time. "I'm sorry, Zadie. I'm so fucking sorry."

I nodded in the dark. "I know you are."

• • • ♦ • • ♦ • • •

In his bedroom, Amir undressed me like a delicate doll, slowly lowering my dress until it pooled at my feet, following the fabric with his lips on my skin. He seemed to understand I needed this from him. For him to prove he could be gentle and loving, even after he'd exploded with hatred in his truck less than half an hour ago.

He kneeled in front of me, cupping my hips in his hands, rubbing his lips back and forth on the curve of my stomach.

With my eyes closed, I threaded my fingers through his hair and let my head fall back. His mouth was warm now, the ice from the club ancient history. He kissed me from hip to hip, then lower, dragging my panties down a centimeter at a time. His mouth dragged from my belly button to the top of my slit. Tongue darting out, he wedged it between my lips then sucked. I exhaled a soft gust of breath, tipping my hips toward him.

Amir urged me onto the bed, staying on his knees between my open legs. His hands were splayed on my inner thighs, keeping them spread. I was on my elbows, watching him look me over, licking his top lip as if he was eyeing his favorite dessert.

He lowered his head, and though I knew he wanted to bury his face and devour me, he took his time. Laving, touching, kissing me everywhere, not only my clit. He drew my pleasure out to maddening lengths, then took it further. This man, *my* man, was worshiping at my altar.

My fingers curled into the sheets next to me. Each pass of his teasing tongue had me lifting my hips for *more*. Could anything be better than this? I didn't think it was possible.

"Amir," I whispered. "Oh god, baby, I love what you're doing."

His eyes met mine as he pulled my clit into his mouth. There weren't many things more intimate and raw than maintaining eye contact with him while he sipped at my pleasure like it was life-giving. But we did this. We always looked at each other. Amir didn't try to hide how much he loved my body, and I couldn't bear looking away from him.

Until I had to.

A bolt of heat shot down my spine, lifting my hips off the mattress and throwing my head back. My stomach tightened until all I could do was rock into his mouth, seeking relief from the pressure. And he gave it to me, so beautifully, I had to cry his name to the heavens.

"Amir...you...I...*please*, Amir!"

He slid one hand up, pressing it against my thrashing heart, while he licked me through my pleasure and all the aftershocks.

He climbed to his feet when I was finally done, and I sat up, intent on helping with his clothes too. His nimble fingers unbuttoned his shirt in seconds, sliding it off his sinewy, golden arms. My fingers were frozen on his belt. Lip between my teeth, I got caught up on the tight, lean muscles of his stomach and my favorite trail of black hair that ran from the middle of his chest all the way down. Leaning forward, I dragged my tongue along the trail. Amir's fingers tangled in the back of my hair, holding my face to his abdomen.

"Beautiful fucking girl." He tipped my head back and stared down at me, motionless. "My beautiful fucking girl."

"My beautiful fucking man." My hands unfroze, working his belt open, then his zipper. Reaching into his briefs, I freed his thick, swollen cock and lowered my head to take it in my mouth. He held on to my hair, not allowing me to go very deep. I swirled my tongue around the tip, needing to show him the same precious treatment he gave me.

"Zadie," he groaned. "I want that, mama. You can give me your mouth all you want any other time, but right now, I want to hold you while I'm inside you."

He tugged me away from his cock, holding my face in both hands. He stared down. I peered up. The corners of our mouths tipped at the exact same time.

I loved him. I had fallen in love with this violent, corrupt, loving, beautiful man. It didn't make sense, but I did, I loved him.

And when he lay on his side, draping my leg over his hip, slowly sinking inside me, I considered he might love me too. If not now, then one day. Because when he held me like this, when his eyes locked on mine, more warm and searching than I'd ever seen, I believed he could love me.

Amir's mouth covered mine, his tongue slipping between my lips and licking me in the same languid motion his hips rocked into mine. All thoughts of violence, love, consequences, desire, blood, life, fled from this space we shared, until all we were left with was us. Two bodies meeting, finding pleasure and comfort in each other. He fucked me well into the night until we were both breathless and spent, wrung out on each other.

After, Amir continued treating me like a princess, helping me clean up and kissing me sporadically. He tugged his shirt over my head. He'd told me he liked how they were tight on me in places they were loose on him, so I couldn't bring myself to feel self-conscious when his tees didn't hang on me like they did Vanessa.

I sat against the headboard, watching him pull on a pair of basketball shorts that hung so low on his hips, my mouth went dry. He caught me looking and chuckled at my blush. Bending over me, he tipped my chin with his knuckle and took my mouth in a slow, thorough kiss.

Amir took the spot beside me in bed, pulling me down so we lay face-to-face again. He caressed my cheek in an achingly sweet way I felt to the tips of my toes. I didn't think he even realized he was capable of being this gentle with anyone before me. I'd given him so many of my firsts, willingly and with pleasure. He gave me this first without being aware, but I'd treasure being the first—and hopefully only—girl he took such great care with.

"No one ever held me when I was a kid," he whispered, like he was telling me a great secret, and maybe he was. I had a feeling this wasn't something he'd said out loud before.

"I'm really sorry," I whispered back, snuggling in closer.

"My brother loved me. He wasn't my parent, and he's never really been right in the head, but he's always loved me."

My heart was being strangled with his words. "I'm happy you had him."

He went quiet for a long moment, caressing my cheek and sweeping over me with his gaze. "Our parents were busy. Kids were on their checklist, something to be done. Once we were here, they checked us off, then checked out. We had nannies, but they weren't fucking Mary Poppins, you know? But Reno...I don't know how to explain it except to say he kept me human. Without him, I think I would have checked out too. He started stealing for me, candy, toys, character T-shirts. Shit most kids had, but not us. He knew what it was like not to have it, so he got it for me."

"He didn't want you to feel like he felt."

"Right." Amir's jaw hardened, and his gaze went distant.

"What character shirts did he steal for you?"

That brought him back to me. His mouth quirked into something close to a small smile. "Pokémon was my shit back then."

I smiled back at him. "You had to catch them all, huh?"

"Yeah." His thumb traced the curve of my smile. "I don't even know why I'm telling you this except I want you to understand."

I nodded. I knew why he was telling me. Tonight had been ugly, an ugly Amir wasn't going to be able to kiss better or smooth over for me. He needed me to know why he couldn't turn away from that ugliness, even if it hurt me and other people in the process.

"Thank you for telling me, baby," I murmured.

His lips touched my forehead. "Like when you call me baby."

And then he tucked me under the thick cover, pulled me onto his chest, kissed my lips, and whispered good night.

· · · · ● ● ● ● · · ·

I hadn't fallen asleep. It had been maybe an hour or two since Amir had drifted off. He'd kept me close. Even in his dreams, his arms never loosened.

My thoughts were keeping me awake. My trip to Oregon was coming at both the best and worst time. I needed to see my dad, to touch the huge, old trees that filled our backyard, take a hike, remember who I was.

But I liked who I was here too. I didn't want to run away from that. It was just that I was seeing falling for Amir had been flying a little too close to the sun. He lived a lot of his life in the jet black of midnight, but he, himself, was bright. The kind of bright I couldn't resist. Except now I was feeling a little singed and raw.

A shadow passing under the door caught my eye. I didn't know why it drew my attention, since there were two other people in the house and it could have been either of them, but something in my gut screamed at me. Something wasn't right.

The distant sound of breaking glass sent my heart pounding.

Drew?

No, he's not here. Drew is in a hospital in Oregon. Maybe it's nothing. Maybe Julien broke a glass in the kitchen. It's probably nothing.

I couldn't settle. Couldn't convince myself everything was okay. So, I eased out of bed and tiptoed to the door. As slowly as I could, I cracked it open, peeking into the hall.

And I found someone peeking back at me.

I froze, my gaze locked with one that was wild and crazed. In the back of my mind, I recognized this man, equally frozen at the opposite end of the hall. *César.*

His arm unfroze. He reached into his pocket, pulling something small and silver out. A *snick* sounded, and the object flashed silver. My mouth opened—to scream, to gasp? I didn't know—but nothing came out.

Because that was a knife.

This wasn't the first time I'd woken to a man in my home who wasn't supposed to be there, holding a knife. My dad heard him before he could act, but my dad wasn't here tonight.

And this man, he was crazed in a completely different way than Drew had been.

Two things happened at once. From behind me, Amir snapped my name. In front of me, the man started toward me, knife raised. I couldn't be sure which action got me to move, but the next breath, I slammed and locked the door.

"Someone's in the house," I whispered.

"Zadie?" Amir sounded only half awake. "Come back to bed."

A crash against the door made my shoulders jump, and I repeated myself. "Someone's in the house!"

Amir pulled me away from the door and shoved me behind him onto the bed. Flinging open his bedside table, he pressed the combination of his safe and pulled his gun out. The muscles in his shoulders were bunched as he checked it over in a hurry.

Spinning to face me, he jabbed a finger at me, leveling me with a menacing stare. "Don't move off that bed. Whatever you hear, you stay in here. I'll send Julien in. You lock the door and do not come out until I'm back."

I nodded, fear taking my voice. Everything had gone quiet in the hall. To me, that was even more terrifying than the pounding. At least then I knew where he was. Now, he could be anywhere, and Amir was going out there.

Julien slipped into the bedroom, locking the door behind him. He paced back and forth, tugging at his hair, then slammed his palms on the wood. He probably hated being stuck in here with me. If I could have spoken, I would have told him he didn't need to stay, that he should help Amir. It would have been a lie. I didn't want to be alone.

I tucked my knees under my chin, holding them tight to stop the shakes from racking my body.

Julien stopped pacing, taking me in, and exhaled, approaching the bed. "Amir and Marco are handling it. I know you're scared, but you don't need to be. Anyone who breaks in and makes all that noise doesn't know what the fuck they're doing."

I nodded, trying to take in his assurance and wrap it around my stuttering heart.

"Okay," I rasped.

"Just wait for Amir. Okay, Zadie?"

Just wait for Amir.

CHAPTER TWENTY-FIVE

Amir

THE HOUSE WAS DEATHLY quiet when Marco and I returned two hours later. One of Reno's guys had come by, swept up the shattered lamp in the living room, and boarded up the broken panel of glass next to the front door. It'd be fixed in the morning, but for tonight, my gun was staying out and ready.

Marco went to his room, probably straight for the shower. That was where I was headed too.

Julien was in the hall outside my bedroom, hands on his hips. "Did you take care of it?"

"Yeah. It's done." I jerked my chin to the door. "How is she?"

"She was terrified, but she wouldn't talk. Fell asleep a bit ago. She's been quiet."

I squeezed my eyes shut. This wasn't what Zadie needed. I'd promised her this part of my life wouldn't touch her, and in one night, it'd touched her twice.

I hit Julien's shoulder. "Thanks for looking out for her. I appreciate it, man."

He dipped his chin, waving me off. I slipped into my dark bedroom, letting my eyes acclimate, finding the small lump on Zadie's side of the bed. Her hair spilled over her pillow, only her forehead visible atop the covers.

Relief coursed through me at finding her asleep. I crept into the bathroom, shutting myself in. In the unforgiving light, I examined my hands, flexing my stiff fingers with a wince. My knuckles were swollen, a couple bloody. They needed to be bandaged, but first I had to deal with the rest of me. My white undershirt was splattered with blood, same for my dark-gray basketball shorts. I dropped them on the floor and turned on the shower, letting it heat.

Hands gripping the edge of the counter, I let my head drop forward. Tonight had been so fucked. *So* fucked. The only thing right about it was Zadie, and she probably wasn't going to like me very much when she woke up in the morning.

I'd make her like me again. I'd done it once. I could do it a thousand times over. I'd make her feel safe, prove to her none of this would seep outside of my carefully insulated other life. This was an anomaly. It. Would. Not. Touch. Her.

The door behind me crept open, and Zadie's reflection appeared in the mirror. Our eyes connected there. Hers were wide and worried. Something she saw in mine made her gasp and rush forward.

I turned my head to look at her. "You should be sleeping. Go back to bed. I'll be there in a couple minutes."

"What happened?"

I wasn't ready for this. The words weren't straight in my head. "You need to go back to bed, Zadie."

She picked up my hand, sweeping her thumb over my battered knuckles. Then her attention dropped to my clothes on the floor, the blood spatters easily visible.

"Why was he here? How did he find you?"

There was no way out of this. I could lie, refuse to answer, shut her down, but I didn't want to. Not with her. And as sure as the sun would rise, Zadie wouldn't accept it.

"César, the guy from the club—he thought I kept product in the house, so he followed us to find out where I live. Convinced his cousin to help him break in to steal from me while we were sleeping. They were both high off their asses, so a shit idea sounded reasonable."

She nodded. "Are they alive?"

My heart stopped beating. Those ugly words coming from her pretty lips drained the life out of me. *Fuck. Shit. Fuck.* What was I doing to this girl?

"They're alive. I'm not a killer."

Big blue eyes rose to meet mine. They were shiny with unshed tears. She wouldn't let them fall, not if she didn't want them to.

"Are they walking?"

"Zadie..."

She licked her lips. "What did you do to them? Tell me what you did." Her thumb pressed on my injured knuckle. "You have to hit someone really hard to come back with hands looking like this, don't you? Where did the blood on your shirt come from? What part?"

I moved fast, circling my arms around her. "You don't want to know any of that."

"No, no!" She pushed at me hard, but I held fast. She wasn't getting away. "Tell me. Tell me what you did. I need to know who you are. What did you do? Who are you?"

"I'm not going to do that."

She was breaking me, this girl. My soft, sweet girl couldn't take any of this. She felt it deeply, even though César had deserved everything he got. Jesus, he'd broken into my *home*, carrying a knife and rope. That wasn't some innocent. We were lucky his cousin had been so damn bumbling, he'd knocked over a lamp and alerted Marco and Julien. Zadie too. I'd been so comfortable in bed, dreaming about my girl, I might have slept through getting my throat slit.

"Tell me, Amir. I won't let you hide this from me." She pounded at my chest with closed fists, fighting my hold as hard as she could. "Let me go, let me go!"

"Never. Not going to happen."

I walked her out of the bathroom, throwing us both down on the bed and trapping her beneath me. My fingers wrapped around her wrists, cuffing them beside her head. She stared up at me like I was a stranger.

"I'm not doing this with you, mama. I took care of what needed to be taken care of. That will never happen again. You're safe with me. This house is safe. No one is going to touch you. I know you saw things that upset you, and I'm going to make it right, but that will *not* be done by telling you every detail of how I dealt with the problem tonight."

She turned her head to the side, keeping her eyes from me. I did not like that.

"Zadie." My hands flexed around her wrists. "Fuck, Zadie, I know you're mad, but—"

"This isn't the first time a man broke in while I was sleeping," she whispered to the wall. "I got used to feeling safe with you. I made a mistake."

My sternum rendered in two. It was so painful, I couldn't breathe. My head dropped to her cheek, eyes squeezing shut.

"You didn't make a mistake. I took care of it. This isn't like Drew. It's done, Zadie. He won't be back. No one will touch you. People in my world don't know where I live. Helen was one of maybe three or four people, and that's only because I know her. I don't have product here. I don't keep money here. You're safe, Zadie."

She'd stopped fighting. Her limbs were limp. Her head lolled to the side. "I'm really tired."

Shut down. She wasn't willing to listen tonight, and I got it. As much as I wanted to, I couldn't force her to trust nothing like this would ever happen again. And, fuck, did I want to.

"Okay. You need sleep. It'll look different when we wake up. You'll see I have you."

"I'm going to sleep now."

I pulled back, even though it went against every instinct I had, but I had no choice. As soon as I did, she tugged the covers over herself and curled up on her side. I stood there, watching her for minutes. She didn't move or say another word. Even after I took the fastest shower known to man, she hadn't moved.

I lay down in bed beside her, pulling her against me. She was too stiff to be asleep, but neither of us spoke. Sleep wasn't coming for me either, not with a board on my window and the sad, scared girl in my bed.

It was going to be a long night.

· · • • · • • · · ·

I couldn't say how, but I fell asleep sometime around sunrise. When I woke up a couple hours later, the sheets beside me were cool and empty. I shot out of bed and took the stairs two at a time, skidding into the kitchen.

Zadie was at the island, a throw wrapped around her shoulders, sipping from a mug. Julien had a hip propped on the counter, peering into the toaster. Marco was at the table, shoveling eggs into his mouth.

I strode into the kitchen and kissed the top of Zadie's head. "Did you sleep?"

"Not really." She raised her mug. "Hence, cup two of coffee."

"Didn't think I'd fall asleep."

She knocked the side of her head into my arm. "I'm glad one of us did."

"Wish it had been you." Pressing on the underside of her chin with my fingertip, I tipped her head back and studied her face. "Even tired, still the most beautiful girl I've ever seen."

I leaned down, brushing my mouth over hers. Her lips were almost hot, and I got a taste of her coffee. Tangling my fingers in the fall of her hair, I brought her closer, taking the kiss just a little deeper. We weren't alone, but even more, I was on fragile ground with her. Too fragile to push beyond her limits.

"I slept like a princess." Marco dropped his plate in the sink with a clatter. "Thanks for the concern, brother."

"Hey." Julien's spine snapped straight. "Were you forgetting something?"

Marco scratched the side of his head, staring at him for a beat before his eyes widened.

"Nope. I was not walking away from my dirty dishes." He spun in a tight circle to the sink. "Just practicing my dance moves for you, Z!"

Then, my boy, who never let anyone tell him what to do, proceeded to rinse his plate clean and stack it in the dishwasher. He even went so far as to wipe out the sink.

Utterly domesticated.

Zadie blew him a kiss on his way out. He winked back at her.

"Don't give him my kisses," I grumbled.

She gave me the barest smile. "Would you mind taking me back to my dorm? I really could use a long nap, and I think I'll sleep better there."

"You're leaving tomorrow."

Everything in me did not want to let her go. She'd be gone for five days as it was. Things between us needed to be settled before that happened. I had to know without a shadow of a doubt she was coming back to me before I allowed her to step on that plane.

"I know, but I'm tired and my brain is fuzzy. I just need to be in my room for a while."

"All right. I'll take you and come back at noon to pick you up." Taking her mug, I placed it on the island and drew her from her stool into my arms. She buried her face in my chest, hugging me tight. That made it easier to give her a few hours. Not easy. Zadie leaving me was never easy.

"I just need some sleep," she murmured into my chest.

She wore my shorts and T-shirt on the ride back to her dorm, looking adorably disheveled. Looking like a girl who just rolled out of my bed and I wanted to toss her back in it.

I stopped at the curb. She unbuckled and leaned her body across the console, crushing her mouth to mine. Before I could say "fuck it" and drive her back to my house, she tore her mouth away and darted out the door, waving as she ran up the steps to her dorm.

We weren't right. We weren't fucking right at all. My girl wasn't getting on a plane and flying away from me until we got back to where we were last night.

• • • • •• • • • • •

It was three hours later, still an hour before I was to head back to pick up Zadie. Julien and I were kicked back in the living room, both too spent from the night before to do much other than watch a movie on TV. Meanwhile, Marco was killing it at the gym. He was the most laid back of the three of us, but the kid did not take a day off from working out, even when he was running on a couple hours of sleep.

Fuck him and his eight-pack.

My head was beginning to throb. I needed to get up, swallow back some painkillers and guzzle water so it didn't develop into the kind of headache that had me locking myself in my dark bedroom, unable to do much except ride it out. Of course, the last one of those I'd had, Zadie had helped me ride it out, and it hadn't been even half as bad as they normally were.

My phone vibrated. I flipped it over on my leg to check the screen. A text from Zadie.

Zadie: *I decided to change my ticket and fly back to Oregon today. I should have told you I was going today, and I'm really sorry I didn't, but I thought you would force a conversation on me I am not ready to have. I need space and time to reconcile my mind with what happened last night. I know I'm not okay with it, but I can't see beyond that and what that means for us. I'm sorry I couldn't say this to your face. The plane is about to take off, so I have to turn my phone off. I'll text when I land, but I really need space, so I'm asking you not to call. Xoxo*

I read it, reread it, and reread it again. I couldn't believe she'd snuck out on me. My Zadie, my sweet little Zadie, had lied to my face and snuck out like a fucking thief in the night. She wasn't wrong, I would have forced a conversation, but god-fucking-dammit, we were adults. We *needed* to have a conversation.

My forehead pulsed. *Shit.*

"You look ready to murder your phone." Julien craned his head to read the screen. "Who sent you a paragraph? Princess Z?"

"She's gone."

"Gone where?"

"On a flight to Oregon."

He shook his head. "Nah, she's leaving tomorrow. What'd she say?"

"She changed her ticket. Needs to get her head on straight."

Julien sank back against the cushions, rubbing a hand over his mouth. "Pussy move to leave without telling you first."

There was no thought before I made my next move, whipping around and gripping him around the throat. I pressed him deep into the couch, hovering over him.

"Don't ever disrespect my girl like that again. You hear me? That's *my* fucking girl."

His hands went up in surrender, and I let him go, falling back to my seat. The throbbing vein in my temple was more like a rope, lassoing my head as tight as it could get.

"I'm sorry, man. I love the girl. In general, she's as high quality as they come. But I don't like her leaving you high and dry like this."

I squeezed my eyes shut. "She hates violence."

"She knew who you were."

"Knowing and experiencing it firsthand are two different things."

He clicked his tongue on his teeth. "Marco told her she was too soft for you. Her running away at the first sign things get tough pretty much proves it."

I cracked an eye. "When the fuck did he say that shit?"

"Last night, at the club, when you were dealing with César the first time."

"Marco needs to not run his mouth to my girl."

"He wasn't wrong, though. You're not changing, we all know this. *She* knew this from the jump. So why get in deep with you if she couldn't handle it?"

"Fuck." I squeezed my temples, trying to dull the ache. "Everything is wrong."

"Maybe this is good, though. You've been all up in each other's business for months. A few days apart will put it all in perspective."

"I don't need perspective."

He sighed, then the cushions shifted as he got up. "Sit your pathetic ass there. I'll get you some meds."

· · · ● ● · ● ● · · ·

The next time I opened my eyes, I had another message from Zadie. It was hours later. I'd crashed on the couch after Julien had dosed me.

Zadie: *Hey, I'm here at my dad's. Everything smells really fresh. I had forgotten how fresh the air is here. I know you're probably angry with me, and I'm sorry. But I wanted to let you know where I am.*

Me: *Send a picture.*

The picture she sent was of the top of her head, massive trees towering behind her. Green and lush everywhere, and in the distance, a range of mountains.

Zadie: *My backyard.*

Me: *I am mad at you. Really fucking mad.*

Zadie: *I know, but I had to go. I can't think clearly when I'm with you. All I want is to be with you and consequences don't matter. Give me this time, okay? I'll text you pics, but I really don't want to get into this while I'm here.*

Me: *I don't like you taking my choices.*
Zadie: *I know you don't.*
Me: *I really don't like you taking my girl from me.*
Zadie: *I know that too. I'll text tomorrow. Xoxo.*
Me: *XXX*

I threw my phone down on the floor and closed my eyes. But when I did, I saw the beauty Zadie had come from. The beauty she'd run back to when things had gotten too ugly here. The conversation hadn't happened, so why did it feel like I'd already lost her?

CHAPTER TWENTY-SIX

Zadie

My heart was broken a thousand different ways.

Leaving my dad and Oregon hurt. The week I spent with him had grown tendrils of homesickness around my heart that hadn't been there before. Boarding the plane and saying good-bye to the trees and the mountains and my father had squeezed my heart until a piece of it was left behind.

But it had already started chipping away before I'd even set foot in Oregon. It had been so incremental, I'd only noticed the subtle pain in my chest, not what was truly happening. I couldn't say for sure when it had started, but I could point out the times I'd known for certain I'd broken a little more.

When Amir shut down any conversation about his job for Reno.

When I lied to my roommates.

When Marco called me soft.

When Julien and Marco laughed at an addict.

Amir *taking care* of César at the club.

César's desperation.

Amir's swollen knuckles.

The blood on his shirt.

His refusal to answer my questions.

Knowing he would not give this up. Not for me, not for anything.

I stayed in Oregon longer than I'd planned because I couldn't face the inevitable. So, Monday came, and I was scrambling to keep up in my classes. My mind just wasn't on campus today and paying attention was next to impossible. Fortunately, I didn't seem to be the only one still on spring break mode. Half my professors took it easy on us and reviewed the material they'd already covered rather than moving on to something new.

My last class was the one I shared with Deacon and his group of laughing boys. He'd mostly left me alone recently, only occasionally saying hi. Since the anonymous notes had stopped at the same time his attention had been pulled back, I had to assume he was the one who'd been sending them all along.

I had no idea why, nor did I ever need to know. As long as they stopped, I didn't care.

Today, when I had no patience and only wanted to get through my class so I could hide in my room a little bit longer, had to be the day he chose to wait for me at the end of class and fall into step with me.

"Hey," he greeted.

"Hi."

"Did you have a good spring break?"

"Mmhmm."

"Yeah, me too. I went to Cabo with my family and some friends. Have you been?"

"No. I've heard it's nice."

"It is. Killer surfing. Did you go somewhere?"

I adjusted my bag on my shoulder, curling my fingers around the strap. "I visited my dad in Oregon."

"Dope. Is that where you're from?"

"Mmhmm." The door was straight ahead. Surely he'd leave me alone then.

"So, are you really outdoorsy? I don't know why, but when I think of Oregon, I'm thinking forests and plaid and that kind of shit."

"The area I grew up in is pretty much like that. And yes, I like being outdoors. Does that qualify as outdoorsy?"

He chuckled, nudging my shoulder with his. "I don't know. Does liking to surf and golf make me outdoorsy?"

I snorted a soft laugh. "Who's to say?"

Deacon held the door for me. Outside, I planned to continue on my way, but he said my name and I stopped, peering over my shoulder.

"Are you with that guy?" He caught up to me. "The scary one?"

"I don't know any scary guys, so I don't know what you mean." I bit my bottom lip, refusing to rise to his bait. He didn't know anything about Amir, so calling him scary rubbed me the wrong way. Even though he wasn't wrong. "I have to go. I'll see you next time."

He reached out, but only grazed his finger on my arm before I yanked it away. "Hey, would you—?"

"Did you send me notes and flowers?" The question was blurted out before I even knew it was coming, but once it was out there, I wondered why I'd waited so long to ask.

Deacon's mouth flapped open and closed, then he nodded. "Uh...yeah."

"Why didn't you sign your name?"

His brow furrowed. "What do you mean? I did."

"No. You signed 'D.' Why?"

"Uh..." he rubbed his crinkled brow, "I didn't think I had to, not after the first one I dropped in your bag. I assumed you would know they were from me."

"In my bag? What do you mean?" I hadn't gotten a note from him in my bag, and I'd certainly never seen one with his full name on it.

His eyes drifted to the side then snapped back to me. "It was like two months ago? Beginning of the semester. I didn't really think you'd want to talk to me, but I wanted to talk to you. My boys convinced me to leave an apology note. I don't know, you got up to talk to the prof, I think, so I dropped it in." His head cocked. "You really didn't get it?"

"I have no idea what you're talking about." I dropped my bag to the ground, taking my computer and notebooks out. I had a tendency to throw everything in there, including receipts and random jots, so the bottom was lined with a mess of wrinkled papers. In that, since I knew what I was looking for, I spotted a folded paper, the same kind the poems had been written on, and pulled it out. I unfolded it, read Deacon's short and pompous apology, and there was the bottom. Instead of a 'D' like he signed his poems, he had written 'Deacon Forrestor.'

I nearly fell back on my butt. Pulling myself together, I tucked everything away and stood, waving the note at Deacon.

"I never saw this.".

If I had...god, if I had, I never would have gone to Amir. Everything between us wouldn't have happened. I would have pined from afar for who knew how long. That would have hurt, but nowhere near the constant ache I was carrying now.

His shoulders slumped. "Fuck. No wonder you've been looking at me like a serial killer."

Like a stalker.

"I don't think that, but the seemingly anonymous poems on my doorstep were creepy. And the library..."

"The library. Yeah, I got out of there as soon as your scary dude appeared." He groaned. "Let me take you out for a drink to apologize. Or dinner. Or coffee."

"You know, you really scared me."

He made a sound at the back of his throat like a creaky door. "I'm...did I? Fuck. You kind of ran away in the library, and I guess...I *scared* you?"

"You terrified me."

Deacon actually flinched. He stared at me like I was speaking a language where he only understood every third word. Was I the first person to call him out on his behavior? Perhaps other girls—less traumatized girls—found his relentless pursuit charming.

"Zadie!"

My head whipped around at the bark of my name, knowing exactly who I'd find. Amir was marching toward me, hands fisted at his side, eyebrows pulled into furious slashes over his eyes.

"That's the scary guy," Deacon mumbled.

He sure was. I knew he wouldn't hurt me, but I still didn't love being the object of his rage.

Leaving Deacon and his utter cluelessness behind, I walked toward Amir, meeting him in the middle of the path between buildings. My heart thumped hard in my chest. I loved this man. I'd *missed* him like crazy. But as much as I wanted to, I wasn't walking into his arms. I was preparing to walk away, because he was making me.

He took me by the shoulders without a single word, guiding me to the parking lot. At his SUV, I wrenched away from him.

"I can't go with you," I said.

"The hell you can't. Get in the truck, Zadie."

"No."

He raised both hands, shaking as he stopped himself from touching me. "I'm so fucking pissed at you right now. If you don't get in—"

"What? You'll what?" It wasn't a challenge. I said it gently. The last thing I wanted was to hurt him more than I already had.

He groaned with frustration, thrusting his hand through the side of his hair. Eyes flicking to mine, his chest rose and fell, rose and fell, as he struggled to find his control.

"Were you going to tell me you were back?" he finally asked.

"Yes, of course. I just needed to get my head straight."

His hand fell to his side with a heavy thud. "Wasn't that why you were in Oregon? Why you snuck out on me, refused my calls, refused to talk about anything real over text? Your head's looking pretty straight to me, Zadie. It's time to talk. The conversation is overdue."

I sucked in a quivering breath. He was absolutely right. I was only stalling by avoiding him. The outcome of our talk was a foregone conclusion. I needed to get it over with so I could start learning to live with the pain I would walk away carrying.

"I love you, Amir."

He staggered back a step, hitting the door of his SUV. He gave his head a shake, as if he was trying to clear it.

"What?" One word, loaded with so much astonishment, I had to wonder when the last time anyone had told them they loved him. It made me doubt myself for a moment, doubt my convictions, the decisions I'd made.

I nodded. "I do, I love you. But I can't be with you if you're working for Reno. The things you do, I just can't overlook it. I know I told you I could. I really thought I could, but after everything, I know I can't. It's not in me." I touched my chest, which should have been caved in with how battered I felt. But I was whole, and I'd still be whole after this.

His wonder evaporated, leaving a guarded, angry man, holding himself back from exploding. "So, this is an ultimatum."

"No." I bit the inside of my cheek to give myself a different kind of pain to concentrate on. "It's not an ultimatum. You've already told me you won't choose me. I won't ask you to."

He threw his arms out. "And that's it? You expect me to go along with this?"

I wrapped my arms around my middle to stop myself from hugging him. It was unnatural for us not to touch. Even before, when we weren't together, Amir always found excuses to put his hands on me. From his bunched muscles and tightly clenched fists, he was holding himself back as much as I was.

I hated myself for doing this, and I *really* wanted to hate him for making me do this, but I just couldn't.

"I don't want this, but I can't be with you anymore. I'm sorry I ever came to you." I bit my cheek again. "I'm sorry I can't be the girl you need."

His jaw ticced as he stared me down. "It doesn't seem you know what I need, Zadie. Not if you're pushing this bullshit on me."

My exhale was ragged, like air passing over broken glass.

"Then I guess I should say you're not the man I need." Copper flowed on my tongue from the wound I'd bit into the inside of my cheek.

Amir flinched like I'd struck him. "Fuck that. Try again."

"I love you, Amir."

He flinched even harder. "Untrue."

"I do. I love you. This is absolutely destroying me. I'd rather go through a thousand years of Drew than do this."

His nostrils flared as his body listed in my direction. If he touched me, this was over. I would fall into his arms with relief. At the last moment, he pulled himself back, steeling his spine.

"Then don't do it. My job with Reno doesn't touch you. It's separate. It has nothing to do with you and me."

I shook my head hard. "That isn't true and you know it." I pressed my hand to my mouth to steady my quivering chin. "I love you, and I do not want this to be the end. But I can't be with you while this...violence has a stranglehold on you."

"Stop fucking saying that."

"Will you quit? Right now, will you tell your brother you can't work for him anymore?"

He rubbed the top of his head, looking at me. I looked right back, seeing the defeat in his eyes. He wanted a battle, but he'd already chosen sides, and I'd laid down my weapons. It was over.

"No," he answered.

I nodded once. It was what I'd already known. "Then that's it."

His palm slammed into his door. "I never should have let you go. I knew you'd come back fucked. You didn't let me make it right."

"I'd made my decision before I ever left."

His mouth twitched, like he was holding back from what he wanted to say with all his might.

"I love you, Amir, but I can't be with you anymore." Suddenly cold, despite the warm spring sun, I rubbed my palms up and down my arms. "In a year, when you're finished working with Reno, maybe we can try again."

Every muscle on his body went rigid as he stared at me. I'd never seen him more furious.

"A year? You want me to wait around for a year to be with you again?"

I shook my head and choked out a response. "No. Of course I don't want you to wait." I pressed my hand to my burning cheek. "I know you're angry with me now, but maybe you won't be then. And if we're both single, we could try again. I just—" I sucked in a deep breath. "I very much don't want to walk away from you forever. Because I love you, and I will miss you."

Amir stepped forward, bringing his face only inches from mine. His midnight eyes were flat, not the endless night sky I was used to seeing.

"If you walk away now, it's done. You could be my queen, Zadie. You could be my everything. But if you walk, if you're so fucking weak and disloyal, you can't stick with me when shit gets real, you'll be nothing to me. There's no going back from that."

He was *so* mad. I saw it in every breath, every jerky movement. I didn't know if he loved me the way I loved him, but I was certain he cared for me very much. I was even more certain I was hurting him. Maybe not as badly as I was hurting myself, but badly for sure.

I drew in every ounce of my courage. Fortified my walls with my convictions. Reminded myself who I was and what I believed in.

Then I let my eyes fall over Amir's face. I wished my last glimpse of him could be when he was laughing at me or giving me one of his smug grins. The angry man in front of me wasn't *my* Amir.

But I was letting him go so it would be easier to walk away from him when he was like this. Not easy. I couldn't imagine a scenario where this would be easy.

"I love you, Amir."

His breathing hitched, and he started to hold his hand out to me.

He'd misunderstood.

"Goodbye."

I turned and walked away.

"Zadie!" He launched my name at me like a grenade, filled with pain and burning anger.

My steps stumbled, but I righted myself and kept moving. This was right. I couldn't be true to myself if I stayed, no matter how eviscerated it made me to walk away.

Amir didn't chase me. I knew he wouldn't, but I both worried and hoped in equal measures he would.

He didn't. It was over. It should have been over before it even began.

CHAPTER TWENTY-SEVEN

Amir

I WALKED INTO MY house. Everything looked the same. Same scuff on the wall. Same worn-out rug on the floor. My friends in the living room, laughing over something stupid on TV.

It was wrong. All of it.

Life didn't get to be the same when I was upside down.

I had woken up this morning with the decision to find my girl, bring her back here, and make her beg for my forgiveness—which she would, and I would give her gladly.

This morning could have been a thousand years ago. I was a different person now.

My world was controlled. I held the reins. Shit went my way because I made it so. People listened to me, deferred to me, did what I asked, what I told them to. No one walked away from me. They watched me walk when I was well and truly ready.

I wasn't anywhere near ready to walk away from Zadie. Hadn't I been thinking about keeping her forever?

God, who was that naive kid who thought he controlled his world?

I didn't control shit.

Fuck Zadie for asking me to do something she damn well knew I couldn't. Fuck her for throwing around love like it was so damn easy to turn on and off.

Julien came out of the living room, headed in the direction of the kitchen. He stumbled over his feet when he spotted me frozen by the front door.

"Uh...hey." He approached. "Did someone die? You look like someone died."

"Nope."

"What's up, man?"

I had enough presence of mind not to throw my backpack across the room. My laptop and school shit were in there. When I got over this, which I damn well would, I'd regret destroying the things important to me.

With a calm I pulled out of my deepest reserves, I set my things down, kicked off my shoes, and passed Julien to head into the kitchen. I grabbed a bottle of water out of the fridge and drank until it was gone. By the time I crushed the bottle in my hand, Marco and Julien had both arrived.

Concerned. They were concerned about me.

Well, fuck that.

"Zadie walked."

Julien started. Marco crossed his arms, a storm brewing on his face.

"She broke up with you?" Julien asked.

"Yep. Had a feeling it was coming when she snuck off on me." I pulled up a seat at the table and sank down in it. "She confirmed it today."

"And?" Marco took the seat across from me. "Is she into someone else?"

Julien grunted. "Zadie would never."

I shrugged. "I don't even know what Zadie would do. Thought I did. Thought I had a loyal girl. Seems like I was mistaken."

"What the fuck did she say?" Marco demanded.

I slowly turned my head to him. My friend was indignant. Pissed off for me, and he had no idea what had happened, just that I was wronged.

"She said she loved me."

Marco stared at me, blinking slowly. Julien leaned forward, his elbows on the table.

"Let me try to remember her words." I pretended to think, but they were imprinted in my brain. It didn't take much to call them up. "She said she can't be with me while this violence has a stranglehold on me. She said maybe in a year, when I'm not doing my job anymore, if we're both single, we can try again."

Julien spread his hands on the table. "So, it's the job? The job she knew you had before this started? Did she give you an ultimatum?"

I shook my head. "No. No ultimatum. She asked if I'd quit. I said no. She said it was over. That was it. I have to fucking accept this girl, who says she loves me, won't be with me." I scoffed at it all. "What a farce. That's not love. That's more of her manipulative bullshit. Telling me she loves me before she walks away? Nah. Nah, I don't buy that."

Marco lifted a shoulder. "If she can't deal with violence then she was right to walk."

My gaze whipped to him. "She doesn't need to deal with violence. I keep my Reno business separate from my life. That doesn't touch the people I care about. I'm careful. You and Julien aren't a part of any of it. It could have been that way for her. But she walked, so she'll never know."

Marco straightened, staring at his palms on the table. "I'm sorry, man, but that's bullshit."

Julien slapped his arm. "Dude."

"No, no," I held my hand out, "I want to hear this. Go on."

Marco lifted his head. "You've convinced yourself Julien and I are separate, but that's bullshit. Everyone in that life knows our faces. They know our names. If they wanted to get to you, they could easily go through us. Hell, if the cops showed up at your door, don't you think we'd be hauled in right along with you? It's not like my hands are clean. I help you out all the damn time. You don't ask. I have your back, always. But saying we're separate? That isn't true by any means."

"Cognitive dissonance," Julien murmured.

Marco nodded. "Zadie wasn't wrong."

My brow pulled together so tight, it felt like my skull might crack. "What the fuck?"

"That night, at the club, Julien and I were laughing at how pathetic César was. She said it was cognitive dissonance, to see him as weak and look down on him for being an addict, but stand by you when you were the supplier," Marco explained.

"You told her she was too soft," Julien said.

He nodded. "Hell yeah I did, and I stand by it. We both know Amir isn't walking away from Reno and that life. Zadie was gonna see a lot of ugly if she stayed. Turned out, she saw more of it that night when César came to the house."

My shoulders were bunched so tight, I couldn't lower them. "Why'd you say cognitive dissonance to me?"

Marco leveled me with a steady, open stare. "Because you keep telling yourself you have two lives and they never meet.

You've told yourself that so often, you believe it. Even when the evidence is waving red flags in your face, you stick to the story you've told yourself. The truth is, Julien and I are in deep with your life. Jesus, man, I helped you fuck up César and his cousin that night. How is that separate? Explain it to me."

I had nothing to say. Even if I did, I wasn't sure I could speak, not when the barriers I'd constructed in my mind were being swept away by the barrage of truth Marco had just dropped on me.

Julien folded his arms on his chest. "I sat in your room with her that night. She was shaking so hard, I thought she might crack a tooth. That level of terror can't be faked. I see why she walked. I'm sorry she did it, but I see why."

My head was roaring. The cracks in my skull weren't there to let the light in. No, those bitches were ushering in the pain. And it wasn't just there. My chest and gut felt like they'd been pummeled with brass knuckles.

"You can see why?" I'd gone dead calm. If I moved too fast, my head would snap off. "You understand why my girl left me? Is that what the fuck you're saying to me?"

"I'm saying she was scared," Julien replied just as calmly. "You didn't see the height of her terror, but I did. She's only my friend, and I don't want her to ever have to go through that again. She's a lot more than a friend to you. You care about her, want her safe. She wasn't safe with you that night, and the reality is, you can't promise to keep her safe. We all know it."

"Fuck," I grunted.

Julien went on, even though I really wanted him to shut up. Needed him to shut up.

"I don't see this as being disloyal to you, Amir. I get why it feels that way, but I don't think it is. To me, it's her putting herself first. Knowing what she can handle and what she can't.

Asking to try again in a year, when you're done, tells me she walked strictly because of your job, not because she doesn't want you." He ran his hand through the side of his hair. "Zadie's a good girl. Not the right girl for you, though."

"I decide that." My fist came down heavy on the table. "I get to decide who's the girl for me."

Julien held up his hands. "I'm not trying to decide anything. I'm going to miss the hell out of her, and I *really* liked seeing how good she made you feel. But fuck, man, I think it's pretty obvious, given the current situation, you two were a mismatch. We all know you're never quitting on Reno. You told her that. There's no path forward for you two."

If I'd let his words absorb, I would have detonated and Julien would have been caught in my explosion. So, I didn't take them in. I stared at him, at the view out the window to the backyard, inhaled the faint scent of burnt toast from the morning, soaked up the warm sun streaming through the glass, and rolled everything he said into a ball, tucking it in the back of my mind for when I could handle thinking about the truth in it all.

Marco got up from the table, opened the cabinet that housed the liquor, pulled down a bottle of tequila, and grabbed three shot glasses. He sat down, filled the glasses, and passed them around.

He held his up. "You heard our thoughts. Now, it's time to turn it all off."

Yeah. Turning it all off sounded like exactly what I needed. I tossed back the shot, reveling in the burn of my throat, and slammed my glass down. "More."

He filled my glass. I swallowed it. "More."

The same. "More."

The burn barely made a dent after that one. "More."

He kept pouring. I kept drinking.

Until finally, *finally*, midnight came, and with it, all the bright faded, and so did I.

· · • • •• • • · ·

It took three days for me to crawl out of my hole. Three days of going to class half drunk and mostly hungover. Nights of drinking until the light was blotted out and all I was left with was black.

On Thursday, Marco poured the fresh bottle of tequila down the drain. "Enough."

"I say when it's enough." But I had no power behind my protest. First, because I felt like shit warmed over. Second, because he was right. Getting obliterated three days in a row was really fucking enough.

"Smoke a blunt if you need some relief. Your liver will thank you," he said.

"I don't need relief." I just didn't want to think. Thinking meant making decisions. I wasn't really ready to do that.

He propped himself against the fridge and crossed his arms. I was bent over the island, cupping my head in my hands.

"Ready to talk it out?" he asked.

"Nah."

"All right. I have shit to do. Just telling you I'm here if that's what you want."

I lifted my head. Marco was walking out of the kitchen. "There isn't anything to talk about, right? I have to get out."

He stopped midstride. "What?"

"I have to get out." I pounded the heel of my hand against my forehead, still foggy from the past three days of fucking myself up. "You were right. I've wrapped myself in my own bullshit so tight, I believed it, even when it was obviously untrue. I'm taking chances with you, with Julien. I've got Krasinski doubting me and my future because of my connections to Reno's business. I've got junkies breaking into my house. I've got my girl—" I shook my head. I wasn't going there. Not right now.

"*Can* you get out?" Marco asked.

I closed my eyes, exhaled through my nose. "He's not going to be pleased. I'll have to empty out a lot of my savings to appease him." I opened my eyes and focused on Marco. "Tell me, brother to brother, is this the right move?"

He didn't hesitate. "Without a doubt. If he lets you go, this'll be the best move you've made in a long, *long* time."

Zadie had been the best move I'd made in a long, long time. But I told myself this particular move, getting out of my promise to Reno a year early, couldn't be about her. It had to be about me, my future, and my two best friends who were my brothers.

When this was done, when I got free and clear of the stranglehold of violence—maybe she was right, maybe that was what it was—I'd go to her. She'd be back at my side where she belonged, and she'd never fucking leave again. But I needed to be clean, without any ties, before I did that. I wouldn't give her any room to protest, since I wasn't going to accept any.

"He'll let me go. I might have to fight. I'll definitely have to pay. But he'll let me go."

He might let me go crawling and bloody, but I didn't care. As long as the chains were broken, it'd be worth it.

CHAPTER TWENTY-EIGHT

Zadie

A WEEK PASSED. IT had been empty and full all at once. I ached for Amir, for what we could have had and what we *did* have. But I was also angry at him for choosing to stay in that life. I would never understand his choice, and I didn't want to.

I was never alone. Not when I cried, studied, or stared out the window on a cloudy day I hoped might turn into rain. It didn't. Elena, Helen, Theo, and even stoic Lock were always around. I was always being hugged and touched and reassured.

I hadn't told them about the break-in, just that Amir and I split because of our differences. I guessed I was protective of him, even though it was over.

I'd made it through a weekend of no Amir, no Julien, no Marco. Because I missed them too, but I couldn't have them either. I saw Julien once on campus. He gave me a sad wave, then he turned the other way. It wasn't a surprise, but it stung like a thousand hornets.

Not hearing a single word from Amir stung even worse. It was more like shrapnel lodged under my skin, though. He'd let me go so easily, with barely a fight. It was what I needed, but it still made me feel disposable.

Monday was a trudge through my classes. By the time I got back to my dorm, all I wanted was to crash on my bed and turn off my brain for a while. I opened the door, finding Elena on the love seat and an all too familiar blonde taking up the one opposite.

"Hey." I started by them, keeping my head down so I didn't get caught up in a conversation I really didn't want to participate in.

"Hey, Z. We'll be out of here soon." Elena knew how I felt about Kayleigh, one of my roommates from freshman year who'd been absolutely horrendous to me.

"Oh my goodness, Zadie, is that you?" Kayleigh jumped up and surrounded me in her cloud of sugar-lemon perfume. "I totally forgot you're El's roomie. So fun. It's good seeing you." She air-kissed my cheek and gave me a tight smile.

"You too. Have a good visit." Well, that wasn't so bad. Maybe she'd grown up some since I'd lived with her. Or maybe she was just on her best behavior in front of Elena.

I retreated to my room, closing the door quietly, and collapsed on my bed. But I was either a glutton for punishment or too curious for my own good, because I got right back up a moment later, cracked my door, and peeked out.

"—going to die when I tell you this. Remember the party the Pi Sig boys were planning?"

Elena made some kind of disgruntled sound. "Cretins, all of them."

Kayleigh giggled. "I don't know, I think some of them are really cute. But that's not really the point. See, their Dogfight party is this weekend, and almost all of them have secured their dog dates except Deacon. His buddies sent him after this girl, but Deacon ended up liking her and said she was too pretty for him to win the ugliest date contest."

My arms prickled with goose bumps at hearing Deacon's name.

Elena patted her mouth like she was yawning. "Wow, I'm bored. Misogyny makes me sleepy."

Kayleigh giggled again, but it was less sure this time. "Oh, I know you think the party is lame, and I guess it is. I wouldn't have brought it up, except you'll never believe who the girl is." She leaned forward like she was telling a secret but didn't lower her voice at all. "It's Zadie! Deacon is totally a chubby chaser. His boys are *dying*."

"What?" Elena went as rigid as I felt.

"Isn't that crazy? I mean, she is cute, so Deacon's right, she wouldn't win him the grand prize, but can you even believe it? He's so into her, he writes her the corniest poetry, and it's just the funniest thing I've ever heard."

Elena rose to her feet. "Get the fuck out of my suite."

I couldn't see Kayleigh's face from my angle, but I imagined her looking really stupid. And scared. If Elena Sanderson was pissed at me, I sure would be.

Kayleigh unfolded from her seat, hands on her hips. "Are you kidding me? Are you actually mad at me because I—"

A loud crack stopped Kayleigh from spitting out whatever horror she'd had on the tip of her tongue. Elena blew on her red palm like a smoking gun and feinted a lunge in Kayleigh's direction, sending her stumbling back a step.

Elena casually checked her fingernails for chips all while eviscerating Kayleigh. "One day, Prada willing, you will have an original thought in your vapid head, and I hope it's the realization that you will never be as good as Zadie. You'll never be as pretty or hot, but above that, you will never be liked for simply existing. I know you've been around her and spent a year living with unbearable jealousy because you sensed—though you couldn't possibly understand, because again, vapid—Zadie is special and you never will be. You're ordinary and boring and frankly, a piece of shit. So, please, Kayleigh, take your rotten snatch, busted extensions, and wretched veneers, and see yourself out of my suite."

"I can't believe you s-s-slapped me," Kayleigh cried as she moved to the door.

"Oh, believe it. I've done much, much worse, and I'm always game to top myself." Elena slammed the door shut on Kayleigh's back and dusted her hands off. "*Au revoir, salope.*"

Elena sauntered into the kitchen, filled a glass with water, and took a long drink. I pushed out of my room, red faced. She opened her arms, and I rushed into them, both of us squeezing tight. I got the sense Elena wasn't much of a hugger, because she did it a little too hard, but I liked it anyway.

"Everything I said was true," she murmured.

"Thank you for saying it."

I didn't cry. I wasn't sad. I'd heard worse things, and being called chubby really wasn't untrue, so I couldn't bring myself to care about that anymore.

"I really don't like that girl."

I let out a wet laugh. "No, me neither. I don't think she's actually jealous of me, though."

Elena pulled away, holding on to my shoulders. "Agree to disagree, sunshine."

I tried to smile, but I couldn't force it. "I think...I think I need to do something about that party. I can't let it happen to the girls who got invited."

"You're right. And obviously, *I* can't let you take that on yourself." She let go of me, picked up her phone, and started tapping. "Helen will be back in a minute. Once she's here, we're going to fuck up some Pi Sig boys and make them wish they were never born."

I crinkled my nose. "I don't think I can fuck anyone up."

She patted my head. "Obviously we're not going to break bones or anything. It will be the *threat* of breaking bones that does it."

"Give me a minute to gather my thoughts. I think...I think I have an idea that won't require breaking bones."

I wasn't immune to being hurt. The little confidence I had was a fragile thing, something hard won after everything I'd been through. Hearing Kayleigh talk about me, about how Deacon and his friends viewed me, made my confidence waver. The girl I was when I came to Savage U freshman year would have crumbled. But I was so much stronger now, and I was pissed off.

Who were these boys to decide who was attractive? What gave them the right to traumatize girls for fun? How did their self-importance get so grand, they assumed they could hurt people and not face repercussions? If I'd accepted an invitation to that party, I would have been destroyed to find out the true reason behind it. How does someone recover from something like that?

I wasn't going to run and hide. Those laughing boys wouldn't be throwing a party this time.

· · · · ● · ● · · · ·

Helen, Elena, and I marched across campus, each of us with a bat in hand. Elena had bought us all pink bats. Helen absolutely refused to carry hers. Her bat was an old wooden one, scuffed from the times she'd used it, and Helen didn't play baseball, so...

We had a plan. Whether my bloodthirsty roommate stuck to it was yet to be seen, but we had one.

My courage fled as soon as the frat house came into sight. Laughing boys lined the front porch. If I'd been alone, I would have turned right back around and ran home to hide in my room.

Elena and Helen had no such qualms. They charged forward, bringing me with them.

One of the guys stepped out of the group to speak to us. "Can I help you?"

Helen pushed open the front door and stalked inside without acknowledging him. Since Theo lived here Helen knew her way around. Not that she would have let that stop her.

Elena paused with her bat on her shoulder, cocking a hip, scanning the guy from head to toe. "No. I don't think you can, buddy. Try helping yourself to a haircut that doesn't look like it originated from a TikTok trend then maybe we'll talk. I put strong emphasis on *maybe*."

The guy sputtered. Elena ignored him, grabbed my hand, and pulled me along with her. Helen was waiting for us at the base of the stairs. As soon as she saw us, she continued her mission, storming up, us following.

Deacon's door was cracked. Helen pushed it open with her bat, covering her eyes with her hand.

"If your dick is out, I'm going to scream."

Elena peeked over her shoulder. "I think his dick is away. I forgot my magnifying glass to be sure, but if I can't see it, it's not there, right?"

Helen dropped her hand from her eyes and waved at Deacon, who was frozen on his bed, his laptop on his lap. His eyes were on me, even though I was only peering at him from between Elena and Helen.

"Zadie? What are you doing here?"

My friends shifted, allowing me into the room, and pulled the door shut behind me. This was my show unless I needed them. Gathering up the courage that had tried to do a runner, I found my words.

"I know about the party. The Dogfight party."

Deacon shut down his laptop and sat up straight. "I was never going to invite you to that. You don't fit the...um, criteria."

I swung my bat back and forth between my fingertips. "What's the criteria?"

His mouth twitched. He swiped at it with his hand, glancing at Helen and Elena as they wandered around his room, picking up things from his dresser and desk.

"You know I like you. Christ, you've seen the poems. I've never written a poem my whole life, but I think you're really pretty. And sure, you've got some extra pounds, but it doesn't even bother me. Not on you."

I shook my head, frowning at him. "What's the criteria, Deacon?"

He exhaled, shoving his fingers through his floppy brown hair. "I guess it sounds bad, but it's not really. The girls don't ever find out. The prizes are awarded after. And honestly, you should see some of the dogs in the engineering department. They probably feel lucky to have been asked out for once in their lives."

Helen bent down, getting in his face. "Do you actually hear yourself?"

He scooted back, giving himself some space, craning his neck to see me around Helen. "I know you think I'm an asshole, but I promise, I was never going to invite you to that."

Elena bent down on his other side, even more in his face than Helen had been. "You said that, Deke. Is all the misogyny addling your brain? Or is it as naturally puny as your dick?"

Helen cleared her throat. "Actually, the last time I paid Deacon a visit, I got a front-row view of his erection. You know life isn't fair when this douche has a decent-sized hard-on."

Elena shrugged. "I heard he finishes in two pumps so it's a waste."

Deacon leapt to his feet, angry now. "You need to get the fuck out of my room. I'll call campus security if you don't." He swung around to Helen. "And don't think I won't have you banned from the house. It won't be so easy to visit your boyfriend then, will it?"

Helen crossed her arms. "Yeah, I don't think that'll be happening."

I strode forward so I was closer to Deacon than I would have liked, but it was time to shut this down. "You need to cancel the party."

He glared at me, then he sputtered a laugh. "Now, why would I do that? What makes you think I even have the power to do that?"

"Are you saying you have no power?" I gave him a pouty look and batted my eyes a little. It wasn't something I'd done before, so there was a chance I looked stupid, but from Deacon's softening eyes and the curl of his lips, I didn't think so. "Who should I talk to then? Who planned the party?"

"The leadership committee planned it, but you don't need to talk to anyone else, Zadie. It's just a laugh, no one gets hurt. If it bothers you, I won't even attend."

If it bothered me? Oh, this guy was clueless. But I wanted him to keep talking, so I continued my pouty lip thing, adding in a little nibble to the bottom one. Deacon visibly shuddered.

"The leadership committee? Are you a part of that?" I asked.

"No, that's Ryan, Sean, and Owen. Next year I will be, though." He puffed out his chest. "I'll be the one making decisions."

Not if I could help it.

Elena tapped her bat against a frame on Deacon's wall. It held a Harvard scarf that looked vintage. "This is cute. Looks like someone's grandpa was an Ivy Leaguer. I bet you really let the fam down when you came to Savage U."

Deacon instantly tensed and flew into action, rounding the bed. Helen popped in front of him to block his access to Elena.

"Don't touch that. It's irreplaceable," he seethed.

Elena tapped her bat a little harder. "So, you'd be super sad if I broke the glass and wrapped this old thing around my neck?"

He tried to dodge around Helen, but she held her bat up, getting in his face. "What do you want? I told you, I can't cancel the party. There's nothing more I can do."

Elena arched a brow. "Oh, I think you can do a lot." She reared back and whacked the glass, instantly shattering it. Then she pulled the scarf off its matting and swung it around in her hand. "Jeez, this thing is scratchy."

"Put it down," he screeched. "That belonged to my grandfather. It's more than fifty years old. It's fragile."

"Cancel the party," I said. "Cancel it or I'll go to President Whitlock."

He glanced at me over his shoulder, red faced and wild eyed. "I can't do that, Zadie. I've been patient with you because I like you, but it's wearing thin. Gather your army of cunts and exit my room. Well, you can stay if you want to be nice, but these bitches need to make a swift fucking exit before I lose my shit."

He started to push Helen out of the way. She was a tough girl, but she wasn't big, and... well, Deacon was pissed. But I had enough. We could go. I pressed the button on my phone, stopping the recording, and ensured it was sent directly to the cloud.

"We should go." I held up my phone. "I have enough."

Deacon spun all the way around, the scarf forgotten. "What are you talking about?"

Elena sauntered right by him, scarf in hand, to his desk. His eyes were on me, so he didn't see her opening his drawers and drawing out a long pair of scissors.

"I asked you nicely to cancel the party. Since you're un-willing, I'll be sending the recording I just made to President Whitlock. Elena and Helen will also act as witnesses to every-thing we heard." I crossed my arms, meeting him square in the eyes. "And if you don't stop harassing me during and after class, including in the library and my suite, I will hand over all the notes you've left me to the police and request a restraining order. When I leave this room, I want nothing more to do with you, Deacon Forrestor—not that I ever wanted it in the first place. And in the future, when a girl tells you no, that's the final answer. Being creepy and writing terrible poetry will not change that."

Before he opened his mouth, Elena giggled. "Whoopsie!" She'd sliced the scarf clean in half. "I guess my hand slipped." She dropped the scarf and scissors, picked up her bat, and swiped everything off Deacon's desk. "Damn, slipped again."

She skipped right past him to the door like a preppy Harley Quinn, giving him a crazed wave as she exited. I knew it was more for show than anything, to keep him on edge and distracted as Helen and I escaped, but I couldn't say she didn't scare me just a little too.

Deacon was hot on our heels as he ran toward the stairs. "Fucking bitches. I'll destroy you. You're so fucking fucked, you pigs. You fucking filthy cunts. You're dead."

He chased us all the way outside where we were intercepted by two very big, very strong, very angry men. Luckily, they were on our side.

Theo shoved Helen behind him. "We'll talk about this later."

Lock grabbed my bicep in one hand, Elena's in the other, and moved us behind him. When Elena tried to sneak right back in front of him, his arm shot out, blocking her.

"Stay, Elsa, or I will spank your ass red," he growled so low, only the three of us heard.

Elena froze, cheeks flaming, staring at Lock like he'd both lost his mind and pushed a button she hadn't known existed. He turned his back on her. She continued staring.

Theo was having a word with Deacon and a few other guys I didn't recognize. Deacon was being held back and quieted by the guys with cooler heads as Theo calmly explained his father, President Whitlock, would be hearing all about the Dogfight party from him personally.

I let Theo handle it from here, because I'd done it. *I* was the one who'd come up with this plan. I tricked Deacon into spilling everything about the party, including dropping names. And I was the one who would be taking this stupid, backward frat down. Buh-bye, laughing boys.

Pride surged through my veins. I'd stood up for myself and other girls. For once, I hadn't sought out a man to help or hide behind. My own bravery had taken me by surprise—and I was high off it. If this was what taking a stand felt like, I'd do it more often. I'd suck it up, find my voice, and use it.

Helen tucked me under her arm. "You did good, Z. These boys are toast."

"You were pretty scary." I elbowed Elena. "And you...remind me not to meet you in a dark alley."

She glared at Lock's wall of a back. "Does he really not know my name? Are you kidding me?"

Helen and I made eye contact. She laughed first, and once she started, I couldn't stop myself. For the first time in a week, I was happy. Genuinely light and not weighed down by heartbreak.

Everything was going to be okay. Maybe not right now or even soon, but I'd get there.

CHAPTER TWENTY-NINE

Zadie

By the time Friday came along, action had been taken. Pi Sig was on the verge of losing their charter. The leadership had stepped down and left the frat. And Deacon had been voted out by his brothers. Since Theo lived in the house, he gave us the latest updates as soon as they happened. And that was only what was going on inside the frat. The university hadn't come down with a decision yet, but there was a chance all the guys involved would be expelled.

As a private university with *very* famous and powerful alumni, Savage U really didn't like scandal. Pi Sig had already been on thin ice because of the cheating scandal several members had been involved in last semester. Hopefully this would be the straw that plunged them into icy water.

Despite all the things going right, nothing was *truly* right. My high had dissipated, leaving room for my ache for Amir to return. It didn't help that I'd seen him twice this week. He'd been studying in the student union once, a frown pulling his entire face down. Maybe he'd sensed me watching, or maybe it had been a coincidence, but he'd raised his head and found me immediately across the room.

The second our eyes had clashed, my knees had nearly collapsed. The longing, the bitter sadness, the desperate pining, came rushing back, and I had to hold on to a chair to stop myself from crawling to him and begging him to take me back.

The next time I saw him, he'd been walking with Julien and Marco. That time, he'd been laughing. And maybe seeing him happy and living his life was worse than the scowl in the dining hall. It seemed like he'd moved on like we'd never happened.

That wasn't really fair, since I'd laughed and smiled and had happy moments. They just...didn't reach all the way into my soul like the ones I'd had when we were together. There would never be anything like dancing in the rain and making frantic, sweet love in the back of his truck. Nothing.

My friends decided to take me out. And since I'd spent way too much time hiding in my room, I agreed. Even if I held out hope that Amir and I might find our way back to one another a year from now, I couldn't put a pause on my life for that tiny inkling. Plus, I was tired of moping.

Elena got me dressed in skinny jeans and a low-cut black top, then Helen applied red to my lips. By the time we got to the bar, I had something like a strut going on. It was nothing compared to Elena's, but it was something.

That all came to a halt when I saw pretty, slutty-sheet Vanessa exiting the bar as the three of us were about to enter. Her shoulder smacked against mine, hard enough for it not to have been an accident.

In the past, I would have let it go. But I had become the Zadie who stood up for herself. I wasn't going to be pushed around by Vanessa or anyone else.

"Hey!" I rubbed my shoulder and crinkled my nose. "That wasn't necessary."

She stopped, cocked her hip, and gave me a slow once-over. "I'm surprised to see you here. Shouldn't you be supporting your man?" She snapped her fingers. "Oh, that's right. You haven't been around for a couple weeks. Amir finally came to his senses and dumped your dumpy ass."

I let her insult slide, though Helen and Elena bristled on either side of me. "What do you mean? Supporting him how?"

She rolled her eyes. "The fight tonight. Wow, you really are out of the loop." She smirked at the girls she was with, who were equally pretty, flat stomached, and scantily clad. "I guess I'll be seeing myself right back into Amir's loop. You know how he gets after a fight."

Vanessa winked, and if a wink could be evil, hers was. Helen yanked me away from the entrance so I didn't have to watch Van and her girl gang walk away.

"Are you okay?" Helen asked.

When she asked, I took a quick survey of myself and found I was definitely not okay.

"He's fighting," I breathed.

Helen's jaw tightened. "My friend, Gabe, used to fight for Reno back in high school. They're no holds barred. People get legit hurt at those things. What is Amir thinking?"

Despite the warm evening, my teeth started to chatter. "He likes it. The violence, he likes it. He's never going to stop." I swiveled to Elena. "Can you drive me to the fight? I need to see it. If I see it, see him like that, I'll be able to let go. I'll remember who he is and what he's not willing to give up. Please?"

Helen and Elena exchanged a glance over my head, then El focused on me.

"Okay. But as soon as you see him, we're leaving, coming back to this bar, and getting hammered. Then it's done. No more Amir. He was never worth it, but seeing the sad he's put you through, he's yesterday's trash."

· · · · ● · ● · · ·

The warehouse was at capacity. Hordes of sweaty, bloodthirsty men were crammed together, waiting for the next gladiators to take the center stage.

The three of us stood between two sets of bleachers, surveying the area. My heart was in my throat, pounding to a panicked rhythm. I didn't know why I was so worried. Amir had proven again and again he had no trouble handling himself.

Nevertheless, as I stood between my friends, I was worried. Really, really worried, and I couldn't even say why.

"Promise me we'll never have to come here again." Elena kicked the dirty floor with her sparkly heel. "I think I have hepatitis."

Helen was taut and on guard, scanning the crowd. "We're going to stay right here. No sitting down, no talking to anyone. As soon as the fight is over, we're leaving. If I sense we need to leave before that, neither of you is going to protest. Got it?"

Elena and I bobbed our heads. Helen had ten times the street smarts than either of us and more experience with crowds like this. If she wasn't comfortable here, I had to ask myself why the hell I thought it would be a good idea to drag my two friends along.

Before I could dive deep into my very unwise decision, the next fight was announced. Vasquez versus Ishkov. Amir was fighting Grizzled again.

As the crowd roared, I closed my eyes and leaned into Helen. She curled her arms around me, letting me hide for a moment. I wouldn't be able to hide for long. I was here to see. My eyes had to be fully open so I could move on.

When the bell rang, I opened my eyes again, slowly turning back to the ring. There he was. This violent stranger I couldn't seem to stop loving. The man in the ring with him, Ishkov, seemed to have grown three sizes and become even more grizzled. Yet, he was light on his feet, dancing circles around Amir, landing testing jabs on his middle.

I gagged on the bile rising in my throat when Ishkov landed a solid right hook against Amir's jaw. The way his head whipped to the side made my entire body sway in the same direction. My eyes rolled to the side, to the crowd that couldn't get enough of this, then they landed on Julien, who was sitting on the other side of the room beside Marco, staring back at me. He gave one hard shake of his head and mouthed, "Go."

He might as well have punched me in the gut. Julien didn't even want me in the same warehouse as Amir. I'd lost them all. That wasn't a surprise, but it was finally solidifying in my mind.

"I'm sorry," I mouthed.

He shook his head again. "Go."

Helen hissed. Elena made a strangled sound. My attention snapped back to the ring, where Amir was pummeling Ishkov. He was going after him like he hated him, slamming his taped fists into the man over and over. Ishkov barely budged, dodging and guarding, but not showing any signs of pain.

It wasn't the brutality of the hits, but Amir's dead-eyed determination that nearly sent me to my knees. I didn't recognize him, but maybe that was a defense mechanism. How could I love a man who turned off everything except his desire to hurt and win? But I did. I did love this man, and I'd known who he was when I fell.

A sob ripped through me, and it might as well have been the entire universe tearing. Blood flew from Ishkov's face, splattering on the ground. My broken heart sprayed a matching pattern.

We were over. We were really through.

Elena took me in her arms, murmuring unintelligible words of comfort. I clung to her, hiding my face, but needing to stay until the bitter end.

"Oh shit," Helen hissed. "Oh shit, oh shit, oh shit."

I had to see. I had to know. My eyes flew open, but what I saw was worse than I'd been braced for. Ishkov had recovered and was coming after Amir with a renewed strength. He landed blow after blow, his fists slamming into Amir's body like a cannonball.

It was a horror show, one I couldn't turn off. The body I loved, that had been over me, under me, inside me, all around me, was being beaten and bloodied. I couldn't process what I was seeing, only that Amir was losing, and he was losing badly.

A solid punch to his head sent Amir spinning around until he was facing in our direction. His eyes rolled around in his head for a beat before he focused, and when he did, he was staring right at me. The look of absolute devastation that appeared on his face sent a shock wave down my spine. He was yelling, screaming, "No, no, no, no, no!" I couldn't hear him, but there was no mistaking what he was saying.

I took one step, reaching out for him even though I was way too far away to touch him. He raised his arm to reach back, and that was when Ishkov came at him, slamming his fist into Amir's jaw, severing our fraught connection.

Helen grabbed me around the waist, pulling me close to her side. "We have to go. Something's going down here. We need to leave."

I remembered my promise, that I would leave when she said, but my feet still dragged as she and Elena got us out of there, bundled into Elena's car. I realized I was rocking myself as we sped away from the warehouse district, back to our pristine, brightly lit campus.

"Did you get bad vibes?" Elena asked as she pressed the accelerator, defying the speed limit.

"Yeah. I was checking out the crowd, the dudes who were frothing at the mouth when Amir started losing, and it dinged that part of my brain—the caveman part that reacts lightning fast to danger. I don't know, but my gut was telling me we needed to get out." Helen twisted in the front seat to check on me in the back. "Are you okay?"

I shook my head, pressing my lips together to stop from crying. "No."

Helen sighed, reaching back to take my hand. "You want to go back to the suite, eat mozzarella sticks, and watch a shitty movie?"

"Yes, please," I whispered.

Amir had been losing. But Reno wouldn't let him get really hurt, would he?

God, I hoped not. Amir had to be Reno's exception. The one person he cared for. Even if we never spoke again, I couldn't bear the possibility that Amir wouldn't walk away from that fight.

So, I convinced myself nothing was wrong. Everything was all right. I was fine. He'd be fine. All of it was fine.

CHAPTER THIRTY

Amir

MY WORLD WAS A dizzying flash of lights, swirls of movements, sounds that were nothing more than crashing waterfalls and ringing bells. There were hands on me, lifting, carrying, digging into broken places—skin, bone, spirit. And then I was down, on something that might have been soft, but to my live-wire nerves, it might have been a bed of nails.

I struggled to open my swollen eyes. Vulnerable. I didn't like being out of it, but I couldn't bring my mind around yet. Over the raging whoosh in my ears, I heard Julien and Marco's voices. They were close. It was their hands on me, wiping blood, sweat, grime. Adding bandages to the worst of my cuts. I hadn't seen myself, but there was no way bandages were enough. My face split multiple times under Ishkov's relentless hits. His knuckles were knives, so sharp and precise, they sliced through skin.

Someone trickled water into my mouth, wiped my eyes and forehead, slapped my cheeks a little to bring me around. This time when I tried, I got my eyes open. Julien and Marco were hovering over me.

"There he is, Sleeping Beauty finally rejoins the land of the living." Julien's words were light, but there was no humor behind them. He was pissed at me for the decision I'd made that had brought me to this moment.

"I'm good," I grunted. "Help me sit up."

Marco grabbed my hand, slowly pulling me upright. My ribs were on fire, but that was no surprise since I'd heard the crack as they'd broken.

"If you pass out, I'm not helping you up again," Marco warned.

The world tilted from side to side. Once I was sitting, but after some slow breathing, it went steady again.

"I'm good. Just feel like I got run over by a truck." As the fog lifted, I glanced around the room. "I'm ready to go."

Julien put his hand on my shoulder. "No. Sit here. Make sure you're not going to keel over the second you stand up."

People came in and out of the room while I got my shit together. Before Julien was ready, I climbed to my feet, moving like an old, arthritic man. I tossed on a hoodie and pulled the hood over my head.

Outside, we started down the sidewalk to my truck, but Reno's voice had us spinning back around. He came jogging up, a deep frown furrowing his brow as he looked me over.

He clapped me on the shoulder. I winced at the hard contact, but he didn't notice. "You're all right, man. Shake it off. You just made me a shitload of cash. A *shitload*. Are you sure you want to retire?"

A whip lashed at my forehead. "Never been more sure of anything."

That was what tonight had been about. Reno wasn't happy with me, but I hadn't given him a choice. Let me walk from the business, or I'd walk from him, and it wouldn't be pretty. Not that allowing myself to be beat to shreds was pretty. It sure as hell wasn't, but it was Reno's price, and I'd paid it in blood.

He clicked his tongue against his teeth. "So serious. Always so serious, my baby brother."

I grunted. "This is it, Reno. The last time."

He rose to his feet, holding his hands up. "All right, all right. I heard you. You're straight as an arrow. You've told me enough times over the last two weeks. Pussying out on me for a girl." He scoffed, running his hand over his mouth. "Never thought I'd see the day."

A girl.

More fog lifted. Her face came back to me. It was only a split second, and I still wondered if she'd been a vision. But no, if I was going to imagine Zadie, she'd be smiling at me, not gazing at me like she'd finally seen beneath my veil and the monster had been revealed.

"What was Zadie doing here tonight?"

I didn't know who I was asking. The fucking universe? Was I living in a cosmic joke? It felt like it. I'd spent two weeks extracting myself from every strand of my part in Reno's business, and it was all supposed to culminate tonight. Then I was going to go to her. Tell her it was over, and she was mine.

"I don't know, man," Julien said. "I saw her while you were in the ring. I tried to get her to go, but she wouldn't."

Reno busted out with a deep chuckle. "Oh shit, the girl you were getting out for, the one who can't stand violence, she was here tonight?" He slapped his leg, laughing harder. "What the fuck are the chances?"

"Slim," I mumbled. "Who told her about the fight?"

There was no way she showed up here by chance. She'd avoided me like the plague on campus. Twice I'd seen her, and both times, she'd fled as soon as we'd made eye contact. Both times, it had taken everything in my power not to chase her down and fuck some sense into her. Because nothing about being apart from Zadie made any damn sense. She had to know that. She had to see it.

Reno patted his chest. "You know it wasn't me. It's fucking poetic, though. You think she's gonna take you back now, brother?" He laughed like this was a joke. Like I'd just paid in blood for some shits and giggles.

"That isn't helpful," Julien barked.

Reno's grin fell away. He really didn't have a sense of humor. The dude only laughed at his own jokes.

"Are you trying to say something?" He took a step toward Julien. I moved into his path, teetering on the edge of the sidewalk. "Move, Amir. I'm talking to your funny friend. He says I'm not helpful. Not fucking helpful, when I practically raised you, gave you a job, helped you buy the house his pussy ass lives in."

Julien ground his teeth behind me. He didn't think much of Reno. Neither did Marco. But Marco could keep his mouth shut when he needed to. Julien hadn't mastered that skill yet.

"You don't need to talk to him," I said. "We need to go home. I'm barely standing here. I'm toast, man."

"Whose fault is that?" Julien couldn't fucking help himself.

Reno's body went taut. He started to reach into his jacket pocket when bright lights coming way too fast down the street caught everyone's attention.

"Oh shit."

Almost as soon as the truck came into sight, it veered onto the sidewalk, heading straight toward us. Reno dove away,

Marco made a run for it, but I could not get my body to move. And then it was too late. Even if I moved, I couldn't avoid being hit.

It happened in a blink, but I managed to have a million thoughts.

Zadie was nine hundred ninety-nine thousand of them. Her face, her sweet smile, her scent, her laughter while she danced in the rain, her pouty lips, her kindness, her love. She was my last thought before I went flying and searing pain in my side took over all my synapses, leaving no room for thought or memories.

And then it was chaos. A crash. A thump. A wet smack. Squealing tires. Broken glass. Screams. Fucking gut-wrenching screams.

I crawled across the sidewalk, clutching my ribs. Marco was there, ahead, in the middle of the street. Where was Julien? Where was he? He'd been behind me, hadn't he?

"Julien?" I croaked. Nothing louder would come out of me. I couldn't get my lungs to fill. But I kept crawling, crawling, needing to get to Marco. He had to know where Julien was.

Reno ran past me, to the truck that had crashed into a light pole barely half a block away. A few of his guys were behind him, barking words my ringing ears couldn't register.

But Marco...he was crouched over something, his phone to his ear. What was Marco looking at? Where the fuck was Julien?

"I need an ambulance. Someone's been hit by a truck. He's hurt. Really hurt. You gotta get here now. There's a lot of blood. He's not moving." Marco was talking to someone on his phone. Who was hurt? It's just been the four of us. I was hurt, but I didn't need an ambulance. I just needed to find Julien.

"Julien?" *Where are you?*

Marco raised his head, and then shook it. "I don't know if he's gonna make it." He clawed at the sides of his hair. "I don't know what to do. I don't think I should touch him."

I made it to him, and at first, I couldn't understand what I was seeing. It was Julien on the pavement, but it wasn't. Because Julien was fine. He was on the sidewalk. This Julien was broken, bent wrong, his face flayed open on one side. And the blood, it was every-fucking-where.

"Julien?" *Where's the real Julien?*

Marco was shaking, his hands hovering over the man on the ground. "He pushed you out of the way. Why didn't he go with you? He pushed you, but he just stood there. He could have dove with you. Shit. Shit, shit, shit. He's not going to die. He can't."

This couldn't be Julien. Not my friend, my brother. He always landed on his feet. He fell, he bounced. That was what we always said. He was impervious to damage. That was why this couldn't be Julien. Fucking Julien.

But it was. It was, it was, it was.

That was Julien's blood soaking the ground. Julien's shoes on the other side of the street. Julien dying on the gritty street.

Fucking Julien.

CHAPTER THIRTY-ONE

Zadie

UNKNOWN NUMBER: *Is this Zadie?*

I stared at the message. I'd meant to turn my phone's sound off before falling asleep, but I'd passed out after a crying jag, so that hadn't happened.

It was six in the morning, and I was awake, wondering if I should reply. As always, curiosity won out.

Me: *It is. Who's this?*

Unknown number: *Marco. Got your # from Julien's phone. Wanted to let you know he's in the hospital. He got hit by a car. He's in a coma. Shit is rough right now, but I thought you should know. He doesn't have a lot of friends, no family. He needs prayers, good thoughts, anything you got, Z.*

I nearly dropped my phone but held it tight. Julien was hurt? No, no, no. I'd just seen him two nights ago. Vibrant, healthy, alive. How could he be in a coma?

Me: *Where is he? I'm coming.*

Marco: *No, you can't come. Amir's barely hanging on. He's yelled at two nurses already. I don't think seeing you will help anything. Julien needs your prayers, baby girl.*

Me: *Of course. I won't stop. But I'd really like to see him too.*

Marco: *I'll keep you updated. If there's a time I think is good for you to stop by, I'll text. For now, pray, healing thoughts, vibes, all that.*

Me: *Please. I won't stop thinking about him.*

I fell back on the bed, all cried out. This was surreal. Two weeks ago, I'd had breakfast with Julien in his kitchen. Two weeks that might as well have been another lifetime. He was so far removed from me, I couldn't even go see him at the hospital.

If I let myself think about Amir, about how much he must've been hurting, I would have buckled. I couldn't even allow my mind to go there.

More sleep wasn't coming, so I got up and went through the motions of my day—busywork to keep me breathing and sane while I waited for an update from Marco.

It was for the best he hadn't told me where Julien was. I didn't think I would have been able to stop myself from going there. This waiting game was torture. But I didn't text him or bother him. I wanted Marco to give all his concentration to Julien...and Amir.

At seven that evening, I finally received the text I'd been waiting for.

Marco: *If you want to come down, I'm taking overnight duty while Amir gets some sleep at home.*

Me: *I'm coming. Tell me where.*

The hour-long Uber ride cost...a lot...but I didn't care. I didn't even blink at the number. I had to stop myself from running through the halls to get to the room Marco had texted.

And when I was outside the door, I paused, getting my breathing under control and preparing for what I might see. Marco hadn't told me the extent of Julien's injuries, only that it was serious.

As quietly as I could, I pushed open the door and stepped into the private room. Marco stood right away, tipping his chin to me. I clasped my hands together at my waist, squeezing my fingers tight.

"Hi," I whispered.

The corner of his mouth hitched. "You don't have to whisper." He beckoned me closer. "Come in. Come talk to him."

I finally let myself look at Julien as I drew near. One of his legs was casted and elevated in a sling. There were bandages around his head, a tube down his throat, and most of the right side of his face was covered in gauze. Very little of his face and arms were without bruising or scrapes. If I hadn't known this was Julien, I wouldn't have believed it.

"Oh," I choked out. "Oh, Julien."

At his bedside, I stroked the back of his hand as tears pricked my eyes.

"They're keeping him asleep to try to heal his brain. There was a bleed and swelling, but it hasn't even been forty-eight hours and they're seeing improvement."

I lifted my eyes to Marco. He was watching me closely. The last thing either of them needed was for me to fall apart, so I sucked it up and reminded myself I was here for Julien.

"Of course he's improving." I curled my fingers around Julien's, wishing like hell he could squeeze me back. "He probably heard the nurses talking about the patient down the hall who took four days for his brain swelling to decrease and Julien decided to one-up that guy. So competitive."

Marco huffed a short laugh. "No doubt." He sat back down and nodded to the seat right behind me. "Sit, baby girl. Stay a while."

I did. I pulled the chair right up to Julien's bed, held his hand, and stared at him. I counted every bruise and scrape I could see. Watched his chest rise and fall. Checked his eyelids for fluttering.

"Do you think he's dreaming?" I asked softly.

"I hope so," Marco replied. "Hope it's a good one."

"What should I talk to him about?"

"Anything. It's probably nice for him to hear your voice. Been a lot of anger surrounding him since this went down."

I bit my bottom lip to stop myself from asking about Amir. I wasn't here for him or myself. This was about Julien.

I thought he would like to hear about what had gone on at Pi Sig, so I launched into the story, leaving out no details. Marco was rapt, leaning forward in his chair to hear my quiet storytelling. He cracked up at Elena chopping up the Harvard scarf.

I grinned at him. "She's a menace."

"Sounds like it." He cocked his head. "Can I ask you something?"

I hesitated, then nodded. "Okay."

"What were you doing there? At the fight?"

"Oh." I pressed my fingers to my lips. "Vanessa told me he was fighting, and I guess I needed to see for myself he wasn't changing. I thought it would help me move on."

"Did it?"

I shook my head. "The only thing that's going to help is time."

He seemed contemplative, but he didn't speak to me anymore. We sat there together for two hours before I had to leave. It went like that the next couple nights. Marco friendly enough, but distant, Julien sleeping between us.

· · • • • • • · · ·

On the fifth night, I walked into the hospital room and Marco wasn't there. A doctor was by Julien's bed, peeking under the bandages on his face.

"Oh, hi. Should I come back?"

She raised her eyes to me, and I was struck by midnight. "No. Have a seat. I'll be done checking my patient momentarily." She didn't move back to Julien, giving me a long once-over first.

"Are you a friend of Julien's?" Her accent was so light, it was barely there, but it gave her no-nonsense tone a lyrical lilt I bet she hated.

"Yes, I am. Are you...the plastic surgeon?"

Her gaze grew shrewd. "I am." She peeled off her gloves, kicked open the trash can, and tossed them inside. "Are you a friend of my son as well?"

"Which one?" Even without looking at her nametag, I'd had little doubt who this woman was. Amir's resemblance to his mother was incredibly strong. From his long, straight nose, thick brows, bow-shaped lips, and fathomless eyes, he shared many features with her.

She sniffed. "Rahim doesn't have many friends, and those he does have wouldn't spend their evenings sitting vigil by a hospital bed."

"Rahim? I...um, don't know who that is. I'm sorry."

Her gaze settled on the tablet in her hands where she tapped away with elegant fingers, another feature she had passed on to Amir.

"My son goes by Reno. I refuse to refer to him as that."
She glanced at me again. She really was elegant all over, her
dark hair tucked neatly at the base of her head, artfully applied
makeup, small, tasteful diamond studs in her ears. "You must
be Amir's friend."

"Yes." I couldn't explain who I was to this woman when I
hadn't wrapped my head around it myself. "I am."

"I'm surprised. You seem like a nice young woman. My sons
aren't known to keep the best company. I'd advise you to be
wary and not get involved too deeply with Amir. His brother
has corrupted him to an irredeemable level. He'll only drag you
down with him."

I jerked back at her harsh assessment. This was her son and
she was speaking about him this way to a person she'd barely
exchanged words with? Amir had devastated me, yet my loyalty
was unshakable.

"Don't worry about me. I don't think you know your son
very well if you believe, even for a minute, he would drag
me anywhere. Amir is one of the smartest, most hardworking
people I know. Above that, he's protective of those he cares
about." I folded my arms over my chest. "You don't know
Amir, Dr. Abadir, and I feel sorry for you. Because you're
missing out."

The muscle in her cheek twitched. "I know both of my sons.
Do you wonder why I'm checking on my patient while Amir
and Rahim are absent? It's because my sons forced me from
his room this afternoon."

I took a step closer. "Do *you* wonder why they wouldn't
want you anywhere near them? Could it be that you and
their father neglected them for so much of their lives, all they
had was each other? Is it possible you're the one who is irredeemable?"

She scoffed. "I won't dignify your remarks with a response. You're a child. One day, when you mature, you'll understand my point of view. I don't owe my sons anything just because I gave birth to them. They are adults and capable of making their own way in the world."

As she brushed by me to the door, I whispered, "They were children once." Her footsteps stuttered, but she continued, practically leaping out the door and slamming it behind her.

I whipped around at the slow clap coming from Julien's bed.

"You're awake!" I'd been so distracted by meeting Amir's mother, it hadn't even registered that Julien's breathing tube had been removed. He was still covered in wires and tubes, but he was breathing on his own.

"Yeah." He sounded raspy and tired, but beautiful nevertheless.

I stood by his bed, taking his hand in mine. He squeezed me back, and I choked on a sob. Nothing had ever been more wonderful than Julien squeezing me back.

His mouth curved at the corners, giving me a lazy smile.

"You told her off," he said.

My nose scrunched. Heat bloomed in my cheeks. "I probably shouldn't have done that. It's not my place. She just made me so mad."

"You definitely *should* have done it. I'm just glad you did it *after* she worked her magic on my face."

I sank into the chair beside his bed, looking him over. "I can't believe you're awake and I'm talking to you. How do you feel?"

"Like I got hit by a fucking truck."

I sputtered a laugh. "That makes sense."

"For real, they're pumping me with drugs. I dread the day they cut me off. But, hey, I'm alive. Didn't think that was going to happen." His words were slurred and lethargic, but he'd never sounded more perfect to me.

"Because you were too busy being a hero to save yourself," I said softly.

Marco had explained what had happened after the fight. Julien saw the truck coming, and instead of running, he pushed the injured, slower Amir out of the way and took the hit intended for him. César had come gunning for Amir as payback for the beating he'd been given. And somehow, miraculously, César's neck had been broken when he'd crashed into a light pole after hitting Julien. It was strongly hinted that Reno had taken care of him, but Marco couldn't confirm or deny that.

"I'm no hero, Princess Z. Amir would have done the same for me."

"I believe that." I lifted his hand and pressed it to my cheek. "God, I'm happy you're awake. Did...everyone see you wake up?"

"Yeah. Amir and Marco were here. I got front-row seats to Amir evicting his uptight mama from my room too. I just pretended to nap so everyone felt free to be on their worst behavior."

I snorted a laugh. "My grandma used to do that too. Then she'd yell at us later."

"Smart grandma."

"Yeah." I couldn't stop smiling at him. He looked terrible. Really, really bad, and I was right beside him in his worries about how he'd feel once they lowered his pain meds. But for now, I had to focus on the good. The beautiful eyes I was scared I'd never see again. The way he could make any situation lighthearted. His warm presence. The simple, vital fact that every breath he took was under his own will.

His gaze traveled over my features. "You got serious."

"I'm really relieved you're alive."

He gave me the barest of nods. "Me too."

"Where's Marco, by the way?"

"He's home. He told me you were coming. I told him to get his ass home to his bed. He looked like dog shit."

"He's been by your side every second."

He stared at me for a heavy beat. "Marco and Amir. Never doubted they would be."

"They're good friends to you."

His nostrils twitched. "Are you going to ask me about him?"

I brought his hand up to my forehead and exhaled. "No. I'm here for you."

"He almost died. You know that, right?"

A tear tracked down my cheek. "Of course I know that."

"You and him need to talk."

I lifted my eyes to Julien's. "I don't know if we need to. I can't—" my voice cracked as another fissure streaked down my broken heart. "I can't go through this again, Julien. And this is...this is what it means to love Amir. It's knowing being hurt is inevitable."

He clucked his tongue. "You've got it all wrong, Princess Z. You need to talk to him. Let him explain."

Sucking in a breath, I nodded once. "If he wants to talk to me, I'll listen."

"Good. Now stop talking to me so I can take a nap, woman. These bones won't heal themselves."

Despite all the sadness, violence, pain, and turmoil, I laughed. I held Julien's hand, smiled at my beautiful, broken friend, and laughed.

CHAPTER THIRTY-TWO

Amir

I PLAYED THE MESSAGE once again through the speaker in my car.

"Amir, this is your mother. If you would like Julien to continue under my care, I can't stress enough that I will not tolerate any more scenes. As if Rahim accosting me while I attempted to care for my patient wasn't insulting enough, Julien's little loudmouthed girlfriend seemed to think her opinion of me was something I needed to know. Keep Rahim and the brunette out of my sight and I'll continue acting as Julien's physician. If I see either of them again, he'll have to find a new doctor."

I was fucking seething. First, because getting bitched out by my mother via voicemail, when the only reason she even had my number was because I was Julien's emergency contact, was not how I'd wanted to start my day. Second, and maybe the bigger reason I careened into the hospital parking lot, parked my truck between two spaces, and stormed up to Julien's room, was because of the troublemaking brunette. Vanessa was the only person it could possibly be. I was *not* on board with her being the cause of my mother bitching me out, and she shouldn't have been visiting Julien without supervision. Even then, I didn't want her skeevy ass close to him.

The ride up the elevator gave me a minute to cool off. Julien didn't need me exploding and losing my visiting privileges. And my mother, as much as I despised her, was one of the best plastic surgeons in California. There was no way I would chance her walking away from Julien's case. Not when it was my fault he was in that bed in the first place.

It was early. His room was quiet and dim when I pushed in. He was fast asleep in his bed, his chest rising and falling at a steady rhythm.

He wasn't alone in his room. Beside his bed, a woman was sleeping. She was sitting in one of the hospital chairs, her head slumped forward, resting on his mattress. Long, dark hair spilled around her onto the white sheets.

Their hands were joined.

How sweet.

I rounded the bed, pried her hand off his, gripped her bicep, and yanked her out of the chair.

"Get the fuck out of here," I seethed.

She stumbled into my chest, and out of pure instinct, I caught her to stop her from going down. Once I had her in my arms, my mistake blared. It had been three weeks since I'd touched Zadie, but the feel of her was ingrained so deeply in my mind, there was no erasing it.

"Amir." She steadied herself on my chest. "I'm...oh no, I fell asleep."

"What the fuck are you doing here?" It came out harsher than intended, but I was losing my mind looking at her sleepy eyes, the crease on her cheek from where it had been pressed on

Julien's sheet, her plump lips pursed into an *O*, and just about everything that was Zadie Night.

"I'm going." She shoved against me, wiggling her arms in my grip.

Shock had me dropping my hold on her when she pushed away. She stumbled backward, shoving her curls out of her face, then bent down, grabbed her bag, and ran out of the room. I would have run after her, but I didn't know what to say. My anger was overriding my ability to think.

Knees giving out, I sank down in the seat Zadie had just vacated. It was still warm from her, and I leaned into it, soaking it up like it was a part of her—that was how desperate I had become.

Julien turned toward me, glaring. "What did you do?" he croaked.

I poured him a cup of water from the jug on the nightstand. He drank from the straw until the cup was empty.

"What did you do to Zadie?" he repeated.

"What was she doing here?"

He reared back as much as he could while lying down. "She's always here. Every night I've been here, Zadie's been here."

That couldn't be right. I'd know if Zadie had been here. I knew Marco had texted her. Watched him do it over his shoulder. But she never showed. She hadn't been here. The disappointment stacked in my belly like logs on a fire had been the thing that had kept me going. If I could be disappointed and pissed off at her, I didn't have to remember the look of agony she'd given me at the fight.

"How would you even know? You've been in a coma." I rapped my knuckles on his bed rails. "You've been dreaming about her?"

"I've been listening to her talk to me and keep Marco company night after night. So yeah, she's been here."

"She's been coming...at night?" When I wasn't here. When it was only Marco. Fuck, that hurt worse than my shattered rib.

"Yeah." He gave me a sorry attempt of a grin. Thank Christ he was on heavy pain meds. His face had been half torn off, his leg crushed. If he hadn't been doped up, there was no way he'd be smiling. "She couldn't stay away from me. My Princess Z."

It was pretty obvious I wasn't going to get a straight answer out of him. I took out my phone to text Marco but Julien stopped me in my tracks.

"I got to witness the most epic takedown. Zadie told off Doctor Abadir when she tried to warn Zadie away from you. Dude, I wish I'd had a phone to record it, but they don't even let me have underwear up in this place."

"Zadie? My sweet little Zadie told off my mom?" There was no way. The drugs they had him on were obviously good shit.

"Yep. She did it in that soft voice that makes you act crazy. Told your mom she feels sorry for her for missing out on knowing you. Zadie also called her out on neglecting you and said if anyone is irredeemable, it's your mom."

"Fuck," I breathed.

I was in love with this girl. There was no doubt in my mind——and no going back now that I knew.

"Yeah. You messed up, my boy." If a guy with hundreds of stitches in his face could look smug, Julien achieved it.

"I just threw her out of your room." I rammed my head into my hands. "*Fuuuck!*"

"Go. I'm fine here." He closed his eyes. "I'm gonna take a nap."

Julien drifted off, but I didn't go. I stayed. Mostly because he'd very nearly died a week ago, and I wasn't comfortable leaving him alone yet. But part of the reason I couldn't seem to raise my ass out of my seat was because if I went to her and she turned me away after every-fucking-thing, it might be over.

I knew myself well enough to know I wouldn't accept that answer. If I had to chain her up in my bedroom, I'd make her mine. That wasn't what I wanted, but that was where my head was, which was exactly why I stayed where I was.

I was going to give her clean, and I wasn't there yet. But three weeks of silence was over. She had to know I was coming.

Me: *I thought you were Vanessa. I would have never thrown you out. Come back to see Julien as often as you want.*

Zadie: *Hi. It's fine. I didn't mean to fall asleep. I'll keep my visits to nighttime. Don't worry.*

Me: *Night is good, but I'm not worried. It was good to see your face, even if you were looking at me like I was an axe murderer.*

Zadie: *You startled me, that's all. I don't think you're an axe murderer.*

Me: *That's a relief.*

Zadie: *I'm really glad you're alive, btw. I'm sorry Julien got hurt, but I can't be sorry he saved you. Anyway, thanks for texting. I'll be back to see Julien soon.*

I brought my phone up, slapping it against my forehead. Fuck, this girl. She said these things, these sweet, sincere words, and they came so easily, but they were daggers that lodged in my heart.

Me: *We need to talk, Zadie. I don't know where your head's at, but I know where mine is, and I have some things to say. I'm caught up with Julien right now, but soon, mama, we're going to talk.*

Zadie: *If you'd like to talk, we can. I don't think there's anything left to say, but I'll listen.*

Nothing left to say? I had a lifetime of words to say to her.

It was about time we got started.

· · · ●·●·●· · ·

Marco and I swapped shifts. That was after I punched him in the gut for not telling me Zadie had been coming to the hospital. He thought he'd been doing me a favor. He knew better now.

When she arrived for her nightly visit, I was camped out by Julien's bed, watching a movie with him on my iPad. She stopped at the door, her eyes wide.

"Oh. Hi." Her eyes shifted to the door. She was seconds from bolting.

Julien stretched out his hand to her. She didn't hesitate to cross the linoleum floor and slip her hand into his.

"Hi, Julien." She brought his hand up and kissed his knuckles. "Still on the good stuff?"

His grin was sloppy. "I'm high as a kite, Princess Z. Amir's making me watch *No Country for Old Men* for the tenth time, and I don't even care."

"Hi, Zadie." I patted the chair next to mine. "Come. Sit down."

"Hello." She shuffled her feet, peering down at Julien before flashing her gaze to me. "Are you sure? I can come back another time. I don't want to overwhelm you with visitors."

Julien tried to wave her off. "Oh, please. You think you've ever overwhelmed anyone? You're the exact right amount of whelm."

I drew the chair close to me and patted it again. "Sit, mama."

Her nose crinkled, but she skirted the end of the bed and gingerly lowered herself into the chair. "I'm not a dog," she mumbled.

"I know you're not."

She turned her head, our eyes clashing. The apples of her cheeks were glowing pink. If I had my rights to her, I'd have reached out and rubbed my thumbs over the flames to see if I could stoke them higher.

Julien closed the iPad with a thump. "Zadie, tell Amir the Pi Sig story. He really wants to hear it."

Her fingers were clasped so tight in her lap, they were turning white. "Oh, I don't think he wants to hear that. I'm interrupting your movie."

"Did you not hear the part about it being my tenth time watching it?" he asked.

I stared at her intently. "What Pi Sig story? Did they do something?"

Unclasping her fingers, she spread them on her thighs. "It's long and—"

"Tell me. Julien and I have nowhere to be, and if he thinks I should hear it, I want to." *I want to hear every fucking thing you've been doing for the past three weeks, down to what you had for breakfast and what time you fell asleep every night. Fuck, I miss you, mama.*

"Well, okay. Elena heard about this Dogfight party the Pi Sig boys were throwing. It was absolutely disgusting. The object was to invite the least desirable girl as a date, and the winner would receive the best room in the house next year. Which is definitely worth destroying an innocent girl, right?" She scoffed, and her cheeks became even more heated. "I found out this guy, Deacon, had thought of inviting me, but changed his mind because I was 'too cute' and—"

"What the fuck?" I was up, out of my seat, ready to destroy. "There is absolutely nothing undesirable about you. Why the fuck would anyone insinuate otherwise?"

She peered up at me, her lips twisting to the side. "Do you want me to continue?"

"Sit your ass down," Julien barked. "Listen to the part where your girl was a badass."

I sat, but I was plotting this Deacon asshole's murder in my head.

Zadie sucked in a deep breath. "This isn't really about the party, but I think you should know Deacon was the one who had been sending me notes all along. It was him at the library too. He had a thing for me, and I guess he thought the notes were the way to my heart. I don't know. But once I found out the details of the party and Deacon's involvement, I made a plan to stop him. I couldn't let him or the other guys hurt the poor girls they'd invited as dates."

A rope knotted around my heart. "What did you do?" I growled.

Julien giggled like a hyena. "This is the best part."

Zadie bit back a grin. "Helen, Elena, and I went down to Pi Sig to visit Deacon."

I hissed. "You went into the frat house? Three girls?"

She nodded. "We had bats."

We had bats. We had bats. We had bats.

She'd said it so casually, like they'd gone for a Sunday stroll. With bats.

I blinked at her. "You had bats."

"Mmhmm. So, we went to Deacon's room, the girls scared him while I sweet-talked him into a confession. He named names, spilled the details, all of it, and I recorded it. I sent it all to President Whitlock and a few department heads. As of last week, Pi Sig lost its charter, Deacon and three other guys have been expelled, and all the campus frats have received an official warning that if they throw a similar party in the future, it will mean immediate expulsion for all attendees."

She was smiling by the end, sitting up straight, head high, proud of herself. I was trying to get there, trying like hell, but I couldn't get past her going to that frat house unprotected.

"Tell me the part about you having a bat."

She blinked her big blue eyes at me, and some of the pride in her spine deflated. "We were being careful. I wasn't scared. We had it handled. And by the time we got outside, Theo and Lock had shown up."

"Theo and Lock showed up."

"Yes," she replied. "One of the frat guys texted Theo that his girlfriend was getting out of hand again. Those were his exact words too."

I didn't know how not to be pissed. She should have called me. I would have handled it. She never should have been there alone. Jesus, my sweet Zadie, in a frat house, carrying a bat. The image of her like that got me hard and made me want to explode in helpless rage.

When I didn't say anything, because I was putting all my energy into not shaking her and telling her she was not allowed to take chances like that ever again, Zadie sighed and slumped in her chair.

"Well, it's over now, so that's good," she said softly.

Julien's eyes were on me, but mine were on Zadie's feet. Her ankles were crossed. She wore red Chucks she made look girly and dainty. That only served to push me further into my head where the rage and terror mixed.

Zadie rose from her chair abruptly. "You know what? I just remembered something I have to do. Study for a test, I mean. I'll see you soon. Be well." She patted Julien's hand, then rushed out of the room without a backward glance.

Like that, she had disappeared. An apparition that would forever haunt me if I didn't act. I just stared at the door, not moving. Because my head—my fucking head—wouldn't let me. It was throbbing, but for once, not in pain. I couldn't find the center of my thoughts or even ascertain how to feel. There was too much whipping me left and right. Zadie in danger, not leaning on me, her bravery, her pride. Zadie barely looking at me. Not touching me. Not being mine. Fuck, she wasn't mine, as much as I declared she was.

"Dude, go after her. Tell her you're proud." Julien yawned, then he winced, bringing his hand up to touch his face, only to be thwarted by full bandages covering it.

He was right. I couldn't let her walk out of the hospital again without saying something. I bolted from the room, spotting her near the end of the corridor, almost to the elevator. I caught her right as her hand was reaching for the button.

"Zadie."

She whipped around, pressing her hand to her chest. "Amir."

I stopped a foot away from her. She swallowed hard, fluttering her lashes before peering up at me.

"You should have called me."

She frowned. "I had Helen and Elena. I didn't need help."

"It's not about need. I would have taken care of it for you."

Her teeth sank into her bottom lip. Her eyes drifted to the side. "How?"

"How?"

"How would you have taken care of it? Violence?"

I didn't have an answer. Well, I did have one, one we both knew, but I wasn't going to say it.

"Amir." She took a step closer, leaving half a foot between us. "I don't mind leaning on my friends or family when I need it. But the truth is, I've hidden behind them when I should have been fighting my own demons. That habit led me to you, and I don't regret that, but I can't keep doing it. So, I'm relieved I couldn't call you to take care of this for me. I'm proud I handled it myself, and I did it in a way where no one else will be hurt."

I nodded, hating everything she said, but admiring it all the same. "I didn't say it in there because I was too stunned, but I am proud as hell. I wish I'd been there to see it, but you're right, I would have pushed you behind me to fight your demons for you."

"Thank you." She tucked her hair behind her ear. "I think...well, I have a ways to go, but I think I'll trust myself to recognize the battles I can fight for myself and those I truly need help with. Hopefully I won't have too many of those, but if I do, I'll know."

I crossed my arms to stop from touching her. It physically pained me to restrain myself when we were this close, but I was going to do this right.

"I'll be there. Either way, I'll be there."

The breath she released was high and sharp. "Amir...I don't know."

"You miss me?"

Her gaze snapped to mine. "Of course I do."

Her ready admission settled deep into my soul. "There's not been a day...a minute, where I haven't missed you. I'm done with Reno. I'm out."

She nodded, her lips pressed into a straight line. "Good. That's good. I'm relieved."

Giving in to the pull, I reached out and cupped her cheek. She shook under my light touch.

"Give me a time, when we're not standing in a hospital hallway, that we can talk. I have some things I need to explain, and I'm hoping like hell you'll listen."

She covered my hand with hers. "I told you I would."

I let her walk away this time, but only because I'd gotten her to agree to meet. I had a time, a date, a location, and still, the need to tie her down in my bed until she promised she was still mine pulled at my insides like heavy chains. The only thing assuaging my near insanity was knowing this would be the last time Zadie walked away from me.

CHAPTER THIRTY-THREE

Zadie

YOUR MOM HAD AN accident.

The words kept repeating in my head.

Eli said she was okay. She wasn't even in the hospital. But I couldn't stop the panic and knew it would only recede when I saw her in person—when I touched her, felt her heart beating under my ear, assured myself she was alive.

I was alone in my suite, Helen and Elena off doing something far more exciting than hanging out with their sad, freaked-out roommate, trying to figure out how I was going to get to my mom. She lived an hour away. I could take an Uber. It would cost a fortune, but I'd already racked up quite the bill from visiting Julien, and there was no question she was worth the price too.

As I scrolled through the app, there was a knock on my door. When I didn't get up to answer right away, another knock followed. Frustrated at the interruption, I tucked my phone into my hoodie pocket and threw open the door.

Even out of my mind with worry, Amir Vasquez possessed the ability to take my breath away. With his hands braced on either side of the doorjamb, he peered at me from under his thick, sooty lashes, sweeping a gaze over me that was two parts longing and a whole lot of desire.

"Amir." I sighed his name like he was a daydream.

"Zadie." He stated *my* name like it meant more than just 'princess.' It was his mission statement. *I* was his mission. "Are you ready?"

My mouth fell open, then I realized why he was here.

I'd forgotten he was coming. I'd been anticipating and dreading this day since that night in the hospital. And now that he was here, I couldn't stay.

He stepped into my room, taking my face in his hands. "What's wrong?"

"My mom...I have to go. I need to order an Uber so I can go—"

"Stop." His thumb stroked my jaw. "You need to get to your mom?"

"Yes. Eli texted. My mom had an accident. She's home, but I need to see her with my own eyes. I'm a little bit freaking out right now." I pushed my hair off my forehead. "I'm sorry, I just need to—"

"I'll drive you."

My nose twitched as my eyes burned with tears I refused to shed. "Okay. But it's an hour away, so I could just take an Uber—"

His fingers threaded in my hair, tugging hard enough to capture my attention. "You're not taking an Uber. I'll drive you, Zadie. Grab whatever you need and we'll go."

"Okay." I stared at him, into the brightness of his beautiful midnight eyes. I loved him. I ached from the hugeness of loving him. "Can you...will you hug me for a minute? I'm afraid I might fall apart and I just need you to hold me together."

He had me in his arms before I could finish asking. He held me tight against his chest, shoring up my crumbling walls until I was reasonably sure I wouldn't fall apart when he let go. And I clung to him for just a little bit longer than I strictly needed because I'd been starving to feel Amir's arms around me.

I did let go, though. By the time I had thrown a few things into my overnight bag and grabbed my messenger bag, Amir was by the front door, waiting for me. He took my things from me wordlessly and directed me to his SUV. He handled me with the utmost care, and it both rattled and soothed me.

Once we were on the road, directions in his GPS, I turned to him. "I'm sorry. If you want to have our talk on the drive down—"

"No, mama. Concentrate on what you need to. Our stuff will wait." He glanced over at me, then down at my messenger bag by my feet. "You're staying overnight?"

"I don't know. Maybe? I thought I might stay for the weekend, to see how I can help." I pressed my hands into my thighs. "Eli said she fainted at the grocery store and tipped her cart over on her way down. She's got a goose egg and some bruises, but she's okay. He thinks she ran herself ragged, which is on brand for my mom."

He glanced at me again. "Runs in the family, right? Taking care of everyone before yourself."

I dug my fingertips deeper into my thighs. "I don't know, maybe. But I'm not my mom. She never stops. She's always, always been supermom."

"There's nothing wrong with stopping and taking a break." His head canted toward my legs. "You're going to bruise yourself."

I shook my hands out, but I needed something to do with them or I'd go crazy.

Amir offered me his hand. "Use it. Abuse it. I don't break easily."

My mouth quirked. "Like my own personal fidget toy?"

"Mmhmm. Whatever you need."

I wanted badly to believe he'd be what I needed outside of this moment, but that was too big for me to even fathom right now, so I rested my hand on his and let that be enough. As the miles ticked by, I rubbed my fingertips on his palm, curled my fingers around his, and traced every line on his hand. Having my skin on Amir's eased my stress like nothing else. My focus narrowed down to the feel of his calluses, his fluttering pulse, the heat building every time I ran the pad of my finger up and down the length of his middle one.

"Fuck," he muttered, shifting in his seat.

My gaze flicked to him. "Is this okay?"

His exhale was ragged. His answer was clipped. "I told you it was."

I was bothering him. Crap. That was the last thing I wanted to do when he'd gone out of his way to comfort me and drop everything to drive me down here. I started to withdraw my hand, but he grabbed it, curling his fingers around mine.

"Don't," he uttered lowly.

"Don't?"

We stopped at a traffic light, and Amir faced me fully. "Do you have any idea how much I've missed you? You're touching my hand and I feel like I'm going to come in my pants like a kid. That's what you do to me, Zadie."

I covered my mouth with my other hand. "Then I should stop."

His blazing gaze held mine. "Don't you dare. I haven't felt your skin in three weeks. If this is all I ever get, I am taking every second of it."

"Okay," I whispered.

Amir held my hand the rest of the way to my mom and Max's house, only he was the one doing the rubbing. It started with his index finger grazing my knuckles, then his thumb stroked the soft pad of my palm. He pressed in places I'd never known about, and caressed other places he'd discovered while we were together. Those places had me trembling as we pulled into the driveway of a home that still didn't feel like mine.

"You're good, Zadie. I'm here. I've got your back." He touched his lips to my wrist then my palm before letting me go. He hopped out of the truck, circling the front to open my door and help me out. Standing in front of him, it was as natural as breathing to fall into his chest for a long, desperately needed embrace. Then he walked me to the house with his palm between my shoulder blades.

Eli opened the door for us before we even knocked, and I surged into his arms. He curled around me, shoving his face in my shoulder.

"You came," he mumbled.

"Of course I did. I'm here. Don't worry."

I'd been crumbling on my way here, but once I saw Eli's worried face and tired eyes, that was done. I'd be his pillar to lean on. I was his big sister, after all, even if the title was relatively new.

He let go of me and shook Amir's hand, then guided us into the living room to see my mom and his dad.

They were snuggled together in an oversized armchair, covered in a furry throw. Max was bald now, but he wore a knitted cap on his head to keep in the warmth. His cheekbones knifed at his skin, so sharp, they seemed like they were threatening to poke through. My mom's skin was sallow, and the rings around her eyes rivaled Saturn's. But when she spotted me, her smile was nothing but pure delight.

"My daughter's come to see her old, ailing mother." She held out her arms to me, and I went, collecting another fortifying hug. Then she spotted Amir, lingering by the door, and held her arms out to him too. "Come here, my love. I'm sorry you have to see me this way, but at least you have the memory of me looking well rested."

Amir crossed the room and was given the Felicity treatment of being hugged and fawned over. Then he met Max, who also promised he didn't normally look so much like "dog shit."

I knelt in front of my mom's chair, holding her hands. "What happened?"

She wrinkled her nose. "You know me, I'm go, go, go, then I crash. Well, the thing is, I haven't really been able to crash lately."

Max raised his hand. "My fault. My girl can't stop worrying, and I've been having some bad nights. She won't leave me alone for it—"

Mom rolled her eyes. "As if I would. Don't even bring that up again."

His eyes roamed over her like she was his beginning and end, his every-damn-thing. And this was why I was able to love Max, despite the way their relationship had started. He always looked at her like that.

"But you need to rest during the day if you're going to do that, babe. I can't have you fainting at the grocery store," he admonished gently, but firmly, exactly what she needed.

"I'm here for the weekend, so whatever you need, I'll do. I'm here to be at your service while you rest. And I'll come back as much as you need," I promised.

Amir gripped my shoulder. "Put me to work too. I have wheels. I can do whatever needs doing."

It turned out, what they needed was someone to drive Eli to his baseball game then a friend's house to sleep over. Amir jumped at the chance, kissing my temple before he led my brother out the door.

My mom and Max napped while I cleaned their house from top to bottom. Not that it was dirty, but it gave me something to do and made me feel useful when I was utterly useless. I couldn't take Max's leukemia away or make my mom rest *before* she made herself sick or drive Eli to practices and cheer him on in place of his father who simply couldn't be there. This was all I could do, so I made their house sparkle.

Later, Mom, Max, and I had dinner together. Amir had stayed to watch Eli's baseball game and texted us pictures and updates. Max cleared his throat a few times and swiped at his eyes when Amir told us Eli had hit a home run. My mom took him upstairs soon after that.

I was scrubbing the clean kitchen counters when Amir knocked on the side door. He was watching me through the glass, and I couldn't take my eyes off his heavy lids and the way he licked his bottom lip as he gave me a long once-over. I opened the door, stepping back to let him inside. He closed it, locked it, and took the towel from my hand, tossing it on the counter. Then he had me, pulling me close, cupping the back of my head, and just holding me.

That was all it took. All day, I hadn't stopped moving. I'd kept my feelings locked down tight because I wasn't here for that. This wasn't about me. If my mother saw me falling apart, she'd never forgive herself.

But I knew, despite our distance, despite how angry he'd been with me, despite it all, Amir was my safe place. I'd thought I'd needed to hear my mom's heartbeat to find my footing, but it turned out, it was his steady thumping that put me back on level ground. With him here, I could fall, and he'd be there to catch me. If I fell apart, he'd put me together. I couldn't make sense of that in my head. How could he be my safe place when he used these same hands to hurt?

I stopped trying to work it out, though. It didn't have to make sense, it just was.

Amir took me into the living room, made me sit down, and held me through it. My body trembled as the adrenaline that had kept me going all day seeped away and his arms tightened. He didn't ask for anything back. He was simply there. Even when I stopped shaking and my tears ebbed, he held me close.

I sat up, wiping my face with my palms. "I'm okay. Thank you."

"Yeah, you are." He took my face in his hands. "And if you ever thank me for holding you when you need it, I'll spank your pretty ass until you remember that's my job."

I swallowed hard. Amir wasn't treating me like an ex-girlfriend, but that was what I was. We weren't back together, even if *I* was letting him act like my boyfriend. More than letting him, reveling in his presence.

The last thing I wanted was space, but we needed it. I scooted to the edge of the cushion and twisted to the side to face Amir.

"How was Eli?"

He stared at me long and hard, his eyes narrowing on me. He knew what I was doing, but he didn't push it.

"Eli is cool as shit. He's fucking phenomenal at baseball. He's also worried as hell about his dad, and now he's got your mom on his worry list too. He'll be okay, though. Maybe he could use some extra visits from his sister—who he worships, by the way—but he's got a good head. He'll get to the other side no matter what."

I sniffled at the way he spoke about Eli, like he really cared. "I know I'm not allowed to thank you for taking care of me, but thank you for taking care of Eli. It means more than I can put into words."

He shrugged. "Don't worry about it. Like I said, he's cool, and the game was highly entertaining. I wouldn't mind coming down for more of his games. I wouldn't mind it at all."

"Amir..." I didn't know what to say. This was all too much, and the energy I was exerting to stop myself from crashing into him was exhausting me.

"Yeah." He grazed my cheek with his fingertips, then climbed to his feet. "I should probably go. Text me when you're ready to head back and I'll drive down to get you."

My heart lurched. He was leaving? I jumped up, grabbing his hand. "I know you're probably anxious to get back to Julien but—"

"He's fine. He's covered."

"Okay. Good. Then you should stay. It's already getting late and—"

"You don't have to convince me. I'm staying."

That easily, my heart settled again, even as my stomach swirled. "Okay." I released his hand even though I didn't want to. I'd let him go, and it wasn't fair for me to act like I hadn't. "Let me show you the guest room."

With a sigh, he followed me upstairs. The bed was made up, so I just had to point out the adjoining bathroom and where extra blankets were in case he needed one. He stared at me as I nervously pointed out the obvious, and he was still staring at me as I beat a hasty retreat.

We were supposed to talk, but I didn't want to. My chest felt battered from the upheaval of emotion I'd gone through over the past few weeks, and I'd cried myself dry. I was tapped out and had nothing else to give.

All that was true, but the biggest truth was I was making excuses out of fear. I wasn't sure I was ready to listen to what Amir had to say, even if I had said I was.

I went through the motions of getting ready for bed, and though I was tired once I was under the covers, sleep was well beyond my grasp. I lay in the center of my bed for what felt like hours. Thinking, always thinking. Picturing Max's face, the softness with which he watched my mother. How he loved her. How she loved him back, so deeply, she'd made herself sick over it.

Of course Amir was part of my thoughts. I couldn't stop thinking about his texts from Eli's game. God, that was sweet, and so very thoughtful. I didn't know what any of this meant, but I couldn't lie here in this bed any longer.

I crept across the hall, slowly pushing open the guest bedroom door. The room was pitched in darkness, so quiet, all I heard was my rapidly beating heart. I found the bed from memory, but once I was there, I stood beside it, unsure why I'd come.

"Get in." Amir's lacquered voice cut through the darkness. The covers rustled as he pushed them back for me. I lay down beside him before I could talk myself out of it, and he covered us both.

"Did I wake you up?" I whispered.

"No." He pulled me over to his side so we were chest to chest and almost nose to nose. "I was lying here, wondering how I was supposed to sleep when you were in another bed across the hall. Last thing I expected was for you to creep in here."

"I was having similar thoughts. You've been holding me all day, and it's really greedy of me to ask for more, but—"

"Take it, Zadie. The only reason I'm here is for you. You need my arms, my strength, anything I have, it's yours."

Exhaling, I reached up and touched his lips in the dark. "We shouldn't be doing this."

"Maybe not. But I'm not in a place where I'm thinking about tomorrow. You're here, you're touching me, letting me touch you, I'm not going to stop it."

He leaned forward, running his nose along mine, then his lips ghosted over the corner of my mouth. My fingers trailed down his jaw to the sides of his neck, pulling his face closer. Our lips met again, fitting together like lock to key. We stayed like that, connected and breathing each other in until one of us moved. It was hard to say which of us it was, but it didn't matter.

He twisted, and I unlocked. Barriers dropped, we took from each other what we both needed and had gone too long without. We were nothing but hands and lips, touching, hugging, kissing, tasting.

My worries fell away with each discarded piece of clothing. Amir's mouth traveling down my body brought me to a different place where it was only the two of us. He buried his face between my legs, and we were back in his bedroom when what we had was blossoming into the beauty it became.

Fingers sank into my flesh as he held me to his mouth, licking me and sucking my lips the way he'd discovered drove me to the brink. Pressure built in my core until I had to curve the pillow around my face to muffle my cries. Amir didn't pause. He groaned as he lapped at me, both of us soaked. I stroked my fingers through his hair as he stroked me with his tongue. He brought me over so lovingly, with absolute adoration, I choked back a sob as I cried his name.

That brought him up, nestling his hips between my thighs, his face as close to mine as he could get it. His wide head teased my entrance as he peered down at me. Even in the dark, his midnight eyes gleamed so I could see them studying me. I held his face in my hands, rubbing my palms on his scruff. He leaned into my touch, another groan spilling out of him.

"I need you," I whispered.

"I require you," he answered back.

I wrapped my legs around his waist as he sank into me. It was a slow slide, my body opening to him willingly, his seeking the end of me. When he was buried to the root, he stopped. My legs tightened, keeping him so deep inside me, I felt him in my belly. Eventually, he'd have to move, but we were as joined as two people could get, and through the silence, we communicated that neither of us was in a hurry to rush it.

"Zadie." He caressed my face, kissed my eyelids, the corners of my mouth. "I require you."

I nodded, letting that huge statement sink into me as deep as he was. I didn't know how to reply with words, so I lifted my head and kissed every inch of his skin I could reach. He shuddered, finally moving his hips back and surging into me again.

We made slow love, because there was no denying that was what we were doing. I didn't think either of us knew whether this was hello or goodbye. I knew for certain it was necessary. I had to hold him, feel him, touch him, taste him as surely as I had to breathe.

Amir brought me over again and again, with his fingers and his cock, kissing me through each time I shattered under him. I was wrung out, limp, boneless, yet I still ached for him. My lips sought his with frantic need. What exactly I needed, I couldn't say, just that his lips were where I found my answer.

Eventually, in the middle of the night, Amir let go. Like he'd held my trembling body, I embraced his. He quietly roared my name into my neck, his hips jerking against mine as he spilled liquid heat deep inside me.

We stayed like that, panting, joined together everywhere we could be joined. And then, even though I thought it would be impossible, I fell asleep while the man I loved—but might have just said my last goodbye to—kissed my face and tucked me against his thrumming heart.

Chapter Thirty-Four

Zadie

MY MOM LOOKED A hell of a lot better in the morning. We both woke up before the rest of the house, meeting in the kitchen like we'd done my whole life. She made a batch of pancakes just for us, another for the sleeping men. We sat together, eating and talking, while it drizzled outside.

"So"—she raised her eyebrows—"are we ever going to discuss the fact that your ex-boyfriend drove you down here, and if I'm not mistaken, shared a bed with you last night?"

I sighed, scraping my fork through my syrup. "It might be better if we didn't. I don't know what to say."

She crossed her arms. "Since I don't know exactly why you broke up, I can't really offer advice. But from a mother's perspective, I can't help wondering if maybe he deserves a second chance. He obviously loves you, Zadie."

That was the thing, wasn't it? The thing that kept breaking my heart. "I love him too. We just...had a difference we couldn't get around, and I don't know if anything's changed."

"And have you spoken about this difference?"

"No." I pressed my lips together, knowing what was coming.

"Why not?"

"Because..." I shook my hands out, "I still have this tiny seed of hope. What if what he has to say kills it? I don't know if I'm ready to face that."

She tucked my hair behind my ear and grazed my cheek with the back of her hand. "That doesn't sound like my Zadie. You don't hide. And from the way Amir is with you, I really doubt you have anything to worry about. He adores you, baby."

"I know he does. But sometimes that's not enough."

"And sometimes it is." She leveled me with her mom stare. "Take it from me. I messed up a lot with your dad and Max out of wanting to do the right thing. But when it came down to it, I couldn't live a life that wasn't mine anymore when the alternative was to be loved and love out loud. I think you're making a similar choice now, baby. I want you to experience love that is so aggressive, you never once question it. That might not be with Amir, but if it is, don't walk away unless that's truly the only choice you can make. Fight for it."

"You're right." I sucked in a deep breath, taking in everything she'd said. "God, you're right. I'll talk to him."

"I'm glad you're going to give him at least that chance." She kissed my temple. "Thank you for coming down here. I think a visit from my girl was exactly what I needed to reset."

I rested my head on her shoulder. "You can't kill yourself taking care of Max."

"I know. Max and I talked. We're going to come up with a plan to ease some of my load. The last thing he needs is to worry about his wife."

A throat cleared. Amir stood at the doorway of the kitchen, glancing back and forth between us. "Good morning. Felicity. Zadie."

Mom pushed back from her seat. "Good morning, love. There are pancakes keeping warm in the oven and coffee in the pot. I'm going to run upstairs and shower and check on my hubby." She dropped her plate in the sink, squeezing Amir's arm as she hurried out of the room.

I giggled. "That wasn't obvious."

He dropped into the seat beside me, gripping my legs to spin me sideways so my knees were between his. Then he held my face and crushed his mouth to mine, kissing me like we'd never stopped last night. My fingers curled around his T-shirt, holding on as he devoured my mouth.

He pulled back, but only enough so he could speak, and even then, his lips were touching mine. "It's raining, mama."

"Yeah, it is." More than a drizzle now.

"I'm never gonna experience the rain the same again."

"Neither am I."

"Are you ready to talk now?"

"I'm ready."

He took my hand in his, leading me outside to the covered veranda. The rain patted the ground gently, tinking off the part of the tile patio that was exposed, making indents in the otherwise still surface of the pool. He pulled a padded lounger to the edge of the covered area, pausing to stick his hand out into the rain. Then he traced my lips with raindrops and licked them away with a slow caress of his tongue. My knees had already been weak from nerves, but he knocked them out from under me then.

He fell down beside me on the lounger, tucking me under his arm. He didn't seem to be in a hurry to speak so we watched the rain together.

"I love you, Zadie. I'm angry as hell you walked away from me, but I love the hell out of you too."

Heart caught in my throat, I twisted my head to peer up at him as he stared down at me. His words were harsh, but his eyes were nothing but soft.

"I love you too, Amir. I'm not mad at you, but I'm really sad we couldn't work this out so we could be together."

He clicked his tongue on his teeth. "Don't like that attitude, mama. This isn't us ending. You know that, right?"

"No, I don't know that. I know what I want, but I also know what I won't accept. I really, really thought I could live with it, but I just can't. And after seeing you at the fight—"

"You don't have to give me up."

"I don't?"

"I'm not *letting* you give me up. Let me tell you what I've been doing the last three weeks." He took my hand in his, waiting until I nodded for him to continue. "I'm not gonna lie and say I saw your side right away. It took me a few days of wallowing and getting drunk off my ass to come around. It was finally your words that did it. Cognitive dissonance."

I sucked in a sharp breath, remembering exactly what he was talking about. "Marco and Julien."

"Marco pointed out the truth I'd been convincing myself was a lie because it fit my narrative. No matter how many times I said that life was separate, it wasn't true. Everything I did for Reno bled onto the people around me. Dr. Krasinski warned me about the shadow that followed my name. He almost didn't give me a recommendation but—"

I gasped. "Did he give it to you?"

Amir's mouth quirked into a slight grin. "He did."

I was so happy for him, I lost my mind, brought our joined hands to my mouth, and bit down on his index finger. When I realized what I'd done, I kissed it better as Amir quietly chuckled.

"I'm really, really proud of you," I said.

"I could tell." The way he looked at me reminded me of how Max had looked at my mom. I'd just bitten this man, and he was looking at me like I was his entire world.

My face was on fire, but I let him see it. I was done hiding from him. "Please keep talking."

"I didn't have a choice, Zadie. Not just for you, but for Marco and Julien, and fuck, for myself, my future. I got out. It took time and careful planning. Reno wasn't at all happy with me and made it as hard as possible for me to unravel all my ties. He's still pissed, but he can't come down too hard on me with Julien almost dying because of that life." Amir shuddered, squeezing his eyes closed.

"You got out?"

"I'm finished. That fight? It was the last money I'll ever earn for Reno. Like I said, he was pissed at me and wanted more than cash for me to sever ties to the business. It couldn't be easy on me, but I knew it wouldn't be. I knew it, and I ran straight for it because I wanted it so badly. I threw the fight so Reno could bet against me, allowed Ishkov to beat me to hell and back, all so I could have a clean break. And I'm clean now, Zadie. No ties. That life is history."

I couldn't get the image of him pounding his fists into that man out of my head. Nor his bloody knuckles and clothing from the night of the break-in. He might have severed those ties, but what he'd done before...how did I get past that?

"I was at the fight."

"I saw you. Fucked with my head that you were there. I was gonna come for you after, tell you everything, but you were horrified by me. I never thought I'd see you again. Never thought you'd let me hold you."

"I didn't think I would either."

He gritted his jaw. His chest rose and fell as he swept me with his gaze. "I've done things you'll never be okay with. I wouldn't want you to be okay with any of it. You wouldn't be the Zadie I've fallen in love with if you were." He patted his chest and cleared his throat, but every word he said came out choked. "But here I am anyway, asking you to look past it like you once told me you could. If it were one of your flaws, then I would revel in it because it gets me you. You've seen the worst of me, and I'm asking for you to love me anyway."

Fear enveloped me like a fog, surrounding me so thickly, until it was hard to breathe. This was a moment that would change my life. If I said yes, if I took him back with my eyes wide open to exactly who he was, this was it. He was my beginning, but he'd be my end too. I couldn't see myself ever loving anyone after him if we went any deeper. I would be ruined and made whole again, into the Zadie Night who could only love Amir Vasquez. It might have already been too late. The weeks apart certainly hadn't lessened my love for him.

At my continued silence, Amir slumped, dropping my hand to cup his head. "Fuck, mama." He looked at me, stricken, the light dimming behind his eyes. "Really?"

My mouth opened. "I don't know."

His exhale was jagged, like splintered air being forced from his lungs. "Fuck." He got up, pacing in front of the lounger. "Fuck, fuck, *fuck*!"

He strode into the rain, dropping his head back so the drops pummeled his face. I sat there, watching the love of my life awash in agony, and wondered what the hell I was doing. How could I think for even a second I didn't want Amir to be my ending?

Leaping from my seat, I ran to him. At the last second, he brought his face down, seeing me approach. I collided with his chest, his arms circling me automatically.

"Yes," I yelled over the rain. "Yes, I'll love you anyway. If you'll love me for letting you walk into the rain."

He barked a laugh, pulling me even more flush with him. "Just now?"

I nodded. "I was scared to say yes."

"But you did it, mama. You were brave and you came to me."

He dipped down, covering my mouth with his. I rose on my toes and grasped the collar of his T-shirt to bring him closer. Rivulets of rain ran down our faces, joining our kiss.

A thought occurred to me, and I pulled away, my eyes wide. "I have to tell you something."

"What?" He tried for my mouth again, but I reared back. His eyes narrowed to slits. "Don't keep those lips from me. Not after you said yes."

I covered his mouth with my fingers. "I have to talk to you, baby. I need to tell you something."

He nipped at my hand. "Like when you call me baby."

"I know you do. But I have to tell you I met your mom...and I kind of told her off."

Amir went still for a moment, then he threw his head back and laughed. The sound was so riotous and filled with joy, I smiled hard at him, even as tears joined the rain dripping down my cheeks.

His eyes finally met mine, and they were as bright as the rest of him. Bright, like midnight in the desert, when the sky's so full of stars, it's almost unreal. That was Amir. Dark on the surface, but so filled with light, it burst from him when it was least expected.

"I know, mama. I got the full report from Julien." His grip slid to my ass. "Let me tell you, if I hadn't already fallen for you, I would have then. That's when I knew I could get you back. If you didn't care, if you thought I was nothing more than a violent villain, you wouldn't have stood up for me."

"I'll always stand up for you."

He slowly shook his head. "Do you have any idea how good that feels?"

"I do, because I know you'll do the same for me."

"Hell yes I will. Never doubt that I'm gonna slay every one of your dragons."

Just like that, I was brought back to our first night together, where he promised the same thing. We barely knew each other then, and I'd been his hostage, but he promised me anyway, and he'd meant it.

That was when my fear joined the rain, rolling off me and dripping to the ground. Why would I be afraid when this man had kept every single one of his promises to me?

"Thank you for the offer, Captor, but I'd rather we slay our dragons together."

He grinned down at me. "I'm still Captor? After you've locked up my heart and soul?"

"Maybe we've captured each other."

"Hell yes we have, mama."

He hugged me close, running his beautiful hands over my ass, my face, my hair, and kissing me for a long, long time on the space just below my ear. Rising on my toes, I found the same place on him and kissed him there even longer.

"Heart and soul," he whispered in his rough, lacquered voice.

We didn't have a *Go* moment. What we had was so beyond a movie ending, because this was real. We wouldn't walk off into the sunset. Not us.

No, we were going to walk off, hand in hand, captor and hostage, into the brightness of midnight.

Epilogue

Amir

Five Years Later

Zadie was a terrible driver. It was a fact I'd learned to find endearing about her while it drove me out of my mind. It wasn't that she was reckless. My baby would never be reckless. She was on the other end of the spectrum, overly cautious, verging on grandma behavior. The only way she ever exceeded the speed limit would be for a medical emergency or rescuing an injured raccoon.

"I can drive," I told her.

"Pfft." She waved me off. "This is *my* car. Do you think I want you speeding in my precious?"

"It's not speeding if you keep up with traffic, mama."

Her smile was serene as she focused on the road. "Haven't we had this conversation before?"

"A hundred times."

"And?"

"And my baby still drives like a turtle."

She giggled, and something in my chest went *pop*. Never in my first twenty-one years would I have believed I'd end up with a sweet, giggling, slow-driving accountant, but here I was, at twenty-six, fucking mad for this woman. There was a lot about me she probably never considered as someone she would want in her life, but I was lucky as hell she continued to look past all of it to love me like *no one* ever had.

"I'm keeping you safe," she claimed.

"Appreciated. I'd like to get there before tomorrow, though."

Her eyes slid to the side then right back to the road. "Why are you in such a rush? Hmmm? I thought I get you all day today."

"You do. I just want to be there so I can get my hands on you."

Her cheeks lit up like stoplights. Yeah, she liked that answer. It wasn't a lie, since she was no nonsense while she drove and I wasn't allowed to feel her up, but it wasn't the whole truth either. I had tricks up my sleeve she wasn't going to know about until it was time.

Leaning back in my seat, I accepted my slow ride and took in the scenery. We'd lived outside of Portland, Oregon for the last three years, and the lushness of the landscape still hadn't gotten old. There were mountains, waterfalls, forests, fresh air, and blue skies. I'd never wanted to leave California, had never even considered it, but when Zadie had brought me home to meet her dad, I started considering. I saw my girl in her element and kind of thought it could be my element too. It didn't hurt her dad was cool as hell and had welcomed me just as readily as Felicity and Max had.

When Reno was arrested on manslaughter and a slew of other drug-related charges a year after I left the business, my considerations turned into a decision. My brother was going to prison for a long, long time, so there wasn't any reason for us to stay in California. Julien and Marco had practically pushed us out of the state.

Once Zadie graduated, we'd settled in a little rental house, and I got a job with a shipping company, thanks to my internship with Sparta. Every day was different. I never spent much time at a desk, since I managed operations at a large port. It was exactly what I'd envisioned doing, and every time I thought about how I'd played fast and loose with my future in my college days, I wanted to travel back in time and slap myself upside the head. But hindsight was twenty-twenty and all that, and I knew a hell of a lot more now.

I rubbed my forehead, but only out of habit. There were still days when my head would throb hard enough to send me to a dark room, but since leaving Reno's business and moving out of state, those were few and far between. I hadn't even realized the level of stress I'd been living under until I'd ridden myself of it.

Zadie pulled into the parking lot at the beginning of the trail we were hiking. This was one of our favorite places to explore, and most of the time, there weren't too many other people around.

"Wow, it looks like other people had the same idea as us," she remarked at the other cars in the parking lot.

"Maybe. But no one knows about our path." I steered her attention away from the cars, grabbing my backpack out of the trunk.

Zadie had turned me outdoorsy. I regularly hiked with her or a couple guys from work. I biked, mostly on my own, occasionally with my baby or friends. I'd ridden a horse since we'd moved here, though I wasn't too interested in repeating that. I'd even been foraging for morels more than once with Zadie's dad, Keith. That was the kind of life I was leading. A far cry from the vicious kid I'd once been. I'd never known life could be like this, though. Peaceful but never, ever dull.

As we walked the narrow trail we'd discovered during our first year living here, my stomach clenched. My girl was in front of me, a place where I always put her when we couldn't be side by side. It was mostly for protection, but the view of her peachy ass bouncing as she climbed over rocks and stumps did not hurt one bit.

God, I loved this woman. I questioned sometimes if people experienced different types of love. There was no way everyone had it as good as Zadie and me. If they did, there would be no more wars. Global warming would be under control. Politics wouldn't get dirty. People wouldn't have time for hating each other. They'd be too consumed with getting back home to love their partners.

Whatever the truth was, I knew without a doubt I was a lucky man.

"Zadie."

She turned around, a questioning smile tilting her lips. "Yeah, baby?"

So fucking lucky.

"Do you love me?"

She pressed her hands to my chest. "Have I not been showing you enough?"

Exhaling, I closed my eyes and thanked the rain for giving me this girl. "You have, mama. Just jonesing for you to say it."

She lifted on her toes, biting my chin, then kissing it. "I love you so, so much, Amir Vasquez. Like the moon loves the tides. Like the stars love midnight. Like Michael Meyers loves slashing horny teenagers."

With a laugh, I took her in my arms and kissed her hard on the lips. "I wasn't convinced until that last part. Michael Meyers *really* loves murdering horny teenagers."

And Zadie, my sweet, pacifist girlfriend, it turned out, loved more than cult-classic nineties movies. She was a slasher film fan too, the cheesier, the better. The first *Halloween* was her ultimate favorite. We traded off on who picked movies when we Netflixed and chilled. Hers were always bloody in the most unrealistic way. My choices usually veered more toward crime dramas.

"Are you gonna ask if I love you?"

She shook her head. "I don't need to. I already know."

I touched my lips to her temple. "Yeah, you do." She'd *really* know in a few minutes.

As we neared the clearing overlooking the falls no one but us ever seemed to find, voices rose above the rushing water.

Zadie's nose crinkled. "Damn. It sounds like our luck has run out. Someone else found our spot."

I squeezed her hand. "Let's check. Maybe you're hearing things."

A surprised laugh burst out of her. "Are you saying you don't hear anyone?"

I shrugged, needing her to stop questioning me and just trust me. "Come on, crazy girl."

We rounded a copse of trees, and it became clear we weren't alone at our secret spot. Zadie stopped in her tracks, taking in all the people staring back at us.

Eli, who had grown even more than when I'd met him at sixteen. He was playing ball in college in San Francisco. Zadie and I went to his games as often as we could. Now, he was grinning at his sister like the Cheshire cat.

Felicity and Max were beside him. Felicity was ready to burst. She'd been holding back this secret for almost a month, and it'd been killing her. Max, healthy and in remission after a long, scary battle with leukemia, held on to his excited wife so she wouldn't lunge at us.

Elena and Lock had shown up too. Helen and Theo hadn't been able to fly in since she'd just given birth a few weeks ago, but Elena had her on FaceTime so she could watch.

Julien and Marco pulled through for us. With Julien's leg, I hadn't been positive he could make the hike, but he'd flipped me off when I'd expressed my doubts. And here he was, not the same as he'd been before the accident, but alive and living.

Keith was on the other side of them with his partner, Sarah. They weren't married but lived together. She was an Oregon hippie who shared his love of weed, foraging, and Zadie...and by extension, me.

This was my family. They didn't all live nearby, but when push came to shove, they showed up. They got excited for us, loved us, supported us. I'd never had anything like this growing up, but I had it in spades now. I knew, without a single doubt, I was a better man for it, which meant I was a better man for Zadie.

She pressed her hands to her mouth. "What...what are you guys doing here?"

I took her hand, leading her to the rock overlooking the waterfalls we always sat on when we came here. Instead of sitting, I knelt in front of her. She gasped. My sweet, beautiful girl, who'd stuck by me for nearly five and a half years, actually gasped at me getting down on one knee. I should have done this years ago. My intention for forever had always been solid, but life had gotten in the way. First, Reno's trial and Max's illness. Then school, jobs, moving.

We talked about it. Knew we were on the same page with what we wanted for the future, but we were happy. Zadie had never once mentioned a rush to get engaged. It was me who was ready to make what we already had legal.

"Zadie."

"Hi," she choked out through a laugh. "Are you proposing?"

I couldn't stop the laugh. "I'm trying to, mama. You're kind of stealing my thunder."

"Nooo." She caressed my cheek. "Thunder is all yours, baby. I'll be quiet. I'm just really excited."

Damn, I was too. Excited to propose, to give her my ring, to marry her, to spend my life with the woman who continually blew me away on every level.

"Here we go." I rubbed my thumb on her empty ring finger. "From the minute we met, I knew you were something I'd never experienced. You were the greatest kind of surprise. A nuclear blast of sweet in a world that had gone bitter. Ever since then, you have been the bright in both my light and dark...and there has been some dark. You've been there, loving me, giving me all of you willingly, selflessly, forgiving me, embracing me, never doubting me. Zadie, once, I asked you to love me despite my flaws, and you accepted. Today, in front of everyone we love, I have another question."

She nodded. "Yes."

I laughed again, but this time, it was through a thickly coated throat. There was no fucking way I was getting through this without crying. That was what this woman did to me.

"Let me ask before you answer."

"Okay, but just so you know, it's a sure thing."

My head dipped, forehead to her arm. Her other arm came around me, lending me strength, giving me support, loving me like she always did. God*damn* was I lucky.

"Zadie." I tipped my head back to meet her shining blue eyes. "I want you to know, you still hold my heart and soul, and they are yours to keep. You've taken such good care of them, you're the rightful owner anyway. I don't want to walk this earth without you ever. I want to take care of you, support you, love you, make babies with you, get old and dusty with you, and follow you into the dark. Before all that happens, I have to know, will you marry me?"

Reaching into my pocket, I took out the small black box I'd tucked there and flipped it open. Zadie barely looked at it. Tears streamed down her cheeks as she nodded again and again.

"Yes, yes. I will," she whispered to me.

I slipped the ring onto her left hand and pressed my lips to it. Then I wrapped both arms around her middle, pulling her close. I rubbed my face against her stomach, wiping away the tears I couldn't keep at bay. After all these years, she still smelled like berries and rain. The scent I'd take with me to my grave.

Climbing to my feet, I took her in my arms again, kissing her hard and deep. Our friends were cheering, clapping, celebrating, but they were lost in the background. For those minutes, it was only Zadie and me, our very own moment.

She finally looked at her ring and sighed. "Oh, Amir. This is perfect. I love it so much."

It was antique, classic like her, with a sapphire stone set in platinum. I knew it was for her the second I saw it.

"You never even hinted at what you liked," I said.

Her teeth dug into her bottom lip as she gazed at the ring. Yeah, she liked it.

"Obviously, I've thought about marrying you. But the details never mattered to me." Her mouth turned up in a grin. "Thank you for giving me this. I would have said yes at home on our couch and I know you knew that, but you did this for me anyway—for us... I love you, Amir Vasquez. I really did an exceptional job choosing you."

"Damn right you did."

After that, we were passed around from friend to family to friend. Our own moment was over, but a new moment had started, celebrating with the people we loved.

I'd write to my brother to tell him the news, and I'd most likely send a wedding invitation to my parents. I already knew I wouldn't hear back, but it didn't matter. My good far outweighed my bad.

One day, when we had kids, they'd probably ask how Mommy and Daddy had met. I'd tell them the truth. Or my version of it.

Long ago, I captured the beautiful princess, holding her for ransom. She captured me back, revealing I didn't have to be the villain. There was a prince underneath it all, if only I tried. For her, I tried like hell until I got it right. Together, we faced the dark and slayed each other's dragons until there was nothing but clear skies.

Yeah, I thought they'd buy that.

Especially the happily ever after part. I was pretty sure they'd like that part the most. I knew I did.

Playlist

"Bloody valentine" MGK, Travis Barker
"Beautiful Undone" Laura Doggett
"Sad Happy" Circa Waves
"Cupid's Chokehold" Gym Class Heroes
"Lady in the Wall" Danny Knutelsky
"Training Wheels" Melanie Martinez
"One Day" Tate McRae
"Animal" Sir Chloe
"I Need My Girl" The National
"Brooklyn Baby" Lana Del Ray
"Gangsta" Kehlani
"Gods & Monsters" Lana Del Ray
"I'm Not Angry Anymore" Paramore
"Bad Things" MGK, Camila Cabello
"Wolves" Selena Gomez
"Ruin My Life" Zara Larsson
"Back To You" Selena Gomez
"The Heart Wants What It Wants" Selena Gomez
"Infinity" Jaymes Young

https://spoti.fi/3ifGj60

Stay in Touch

Join my reader group to learn the latest book news and see exclusive teasers and snippets from my books.

https://www.facebook.com/groups/2086152844974595

Follow me on TikTok:

http://www.tiktok.com/@authorjuliawolf

Acknowledgements

IDEAS FOR MY BOOKS come from the strangest places. Sometimes they're from movies I watched in my formative years (like *Go*). Others pop into my head randomly, or I'll hear one sentence and it will inspire an entire storyline.

I wasn't sure exactly what I wanted to do with Zadie and Amir, so I asked my 10-year-old son to brainstorm with me. He loves to write, and I thought it might be a great exercise for him. Some of his ideas were over the top—mobsters, lots of death, a few aliens—but he also had some excellent suggestions that I wrote down and eventually made part of the story. Julien wouldn't exist without our conversation, which is crazy since he might be my new favorite.

Thank you, P, for being my writer buddy. You can't read this book for several more years, but I'll let you read this part. Keep writing! Your creativity is something to treasure.

Thank you to Alley Ciz for being my other brainstorming buddy and explaining fraternity business to me. Thanks to Laura Lee for beta reading even though Amir drove you crazy!

Thanks to Jenny and Jenn for your awesome beta reading skills.

I wouldn't survive without my girl, my PA, Jen.

Thank you Kate Farlow for being ultra-patient with me when I changed cover photos on you last minute. I love what we ended up with so much.

As always, thank you to my readers. Your love for Helen gave me the warm fuzzies. I hope you're happy you got to be a fly on the wall and finally find out what happened between Zadie and Amir in the dorm room!

About the Author

Julia Wolf is a bestselling contemporary romance author. She writes bad boys with big hearts and strong, independent heroines. Julia enjoys reading romance just as much as she loves writing it. Whether reading or writing, she likes the emotions to run high and the heat to be scorching.

Julia lives in Maryland with her three crazy, beautiful kids and her patient husband who she's slowly converting to a romance reader, one book at a time.

Visit my website:

http://www.juliawolfwrites.com

Printed in Great Britain
by Amazon